Secret
ROMANCES

A Forbidden Thirst for Love

DR. MELISSA CAUDLE

Absolute Author
Publishing House

Publisher: Absolute Author Publishing House
Publishing Editor: Dr. Carol Michaels
Developmental Content Editor: Jamie Dwyer
Associate Editor: Kathy Rabb Kittok
Copy Line Editor: Phoebe Zimmerer
Additional Line Editors: Janine Francois, Maddy D
Copy Editors: Isabel Pettibone, Janine Francois
Proofreaders: Robby Cook Stroud, Igra Bashir
Cover: Germancreative @Fiverr
Author Photographer: Tina Rubin
Rose Icon: IllustAC.png used with permission with full commercial rights

---

Library of Congress Cataloging-in-Publication Data
Caudle, Melissa.

Secret Romances / Dr. Melissa Caudle
p. cm.

Hardback ISBN: 978-1-64953-624-2
Paperback ISBN: 978-1-64953-625-9
eBook ISBN: 978-1-64953-626-6
Audiobook ISBN: 978-1-64953-627-3

1.   Romance   2. Comedy

0 1 2 3 4 5 6 7 8 9

Printed in the United States of America

Dedication

To all hopeless romantics. May you find your true love, laugh every day, and find your happily ever after.

Acknowledgment

Many individuals inspired me to write this book, and I wish to acknowledge. In the beginning of 2022, my computer crashed, and I lost over one terabyte of documents, including this manuscript, on *iCloud*. After learning this valuable and heartbreaking lesson to save not only your manuscripts to the cloud but also to an external hard drive, I started over. Trust me, I wanted to give up as I was in the final editing stages when I lost the manuscript. Faced with either forgetting about this project or starting over, my family and friends encouraged me to write it again. As frustrated as I was because I had to start over, luckily, I had the screenplay and the beat sheet to follow. It took me eight months to rewrite this book to get it into the hands of my beta readers and my team of editors. I persevered, and I hope you love the results.

Foremost, my daughter **Jamie Alyson**, who helped me to create the characters and the original plot. The inspiration for this novel came in 2005 when she and I lived in Orange Beach, Alabama, after Hurricane Katrina. We were two girls, all alone, while my husband remained in New Orleans to rebuild our home. During this time, we came up with the characters, the plot, and subplots. Thank you, Jamie, for your creativity and inspiration. Don't ask me what took me so long, please.

Second, my husband **Mike**, an endless romantic at heart and the backbone of my life, who keeps our home in order, the pool ready for a swim, the gourmet meals, the fresh flowers you always send to me for no reason other than your pure love for me, and of course our fun "elopement" times into the French Quarter for our "staycays" to see New Orleans Saints games, Christmas in the Oaks, Broadway plays, and Friday night date nights to our famous local restaurants, which some are featured in this book. After almost forty years of marriage, I don't regret marrying you forty years ago on our third date. On that note, a bit of backstory that inspired this story is that we eloped and got married at 1012 Royal Street, in the French Quarter, and we found our happily ever after. I love you, and I finally did it. I wrote a romance novel.

Third, to my family, who always encourages me to pursue my writing and supported me through all my early endeavors. This includes my other two daughters, **Erin** and **Kelly**, and my two sisters, **Caylen** and **Robby**, whom I bounced many things off of to create engaging characters and the plot.

Fourth, to **Tina Rubin**, my best friend. Thank you for the wine, and the time you spent reviewing this novel's first, second, and final edition while we were on our girl's cruise. After I lost this draft, if it weren't for your encouragement, I might have not rewritten it. Your endless support does not go unrecognized by me.

Fifth, to my editing team **Kathy Rabb Kittok, Robby Cook Stroud,** and **Dr. Carol Michaels** from Absolute Author Publishing House. I always welcome your edits, feedback, and comments. Each brought something different to this novel in the writing and editing stages, making it what it is today. To the copy editors, line editors, and proofreaders, thank you for your eagle eyes, diligence, and insights, who include **Isabel Pettibone, Janine Francois**, and **Iqra Bashir.**

Sixth, I'd like to thank **Garmaine** for her beautiful design of this book's front and back jacket. You always create amazing covers for me and did not disappoint me this time.

Finally, to my focus group, I value their opinions, and I'm grateful for your time and support. In no particular order, the focus group members include **Tina Rubin, Anne Shepard, Sally Mayfield, Haley Wells, Maria Gomez, Molly Perry-Ortega, Loretta Pines, Tammy Boudreaux, Sandra Belington, Sasha Standford-Smith, Jonathan Hayes, Larry Samuels, Helen Mumphrey, Fiona Edwards, Tabitha Andrews, Michael Ratzinger, Jessica Sanders, Robin Andrews, Carrie Lacey, Jennifer Aniston,** and **Diane Lang.**

Other Novels by Dr. Melissa Caudle

www.drmelcaudle.com/

The Keystroke Killer: Transcendence Part I
A.D.A.M. The Beginning of Life
Never Stop Running
MK-ULTRA
The Creek Dweller in the Bayou

Table Of Contents

CHAPTER ONE

Fate

The downtown district of New Orleans, Louisiana, bubbled with the morning's excitement along Canal Street. The brisk fall air swept through Angela Abadie's long blonde hair as she threaded through the morning commuters. Everything about her said wealthy socialite. She clutched her black leather messenger bag in one hand and her cell phone to her ear in the other. "I take that as a compliment, Dad. Your faith in me is what I've always wanted. Take note; the magazine still hasn't fallen apart, and it's been four days since you turned it over to me."

She exuded confidence from the way she strode toward a high-rise building entrance to her prestigious royal blue Armani suit she wore. Heads turned as she passed. Although forty years old, she didn't look a day over thirty. "Thank you, Dad. You don't have to worry. You and Mom enjoy your world cruise. For the last time, I can handle the magazine. You've groomed me for this position since I could first read."

Angela stopped on the corner of Royal Street and pompously gazed toward the sky-rise building. A vast, confident panther-on-the-prowl grin graced her lips. "Of course, Dad. If anything goes wrong, I'll notify you immediately." She took a deep breath and pressed the end call button on her cell phone. *It won't. It can't.*

The heavy morning traffic always provided a challenge to cross the street. Those who did were wary of the pugnacious drivers who didn't watch for those making their way to work. In the distance, streetcar 941 approached, ringing its iconic bell as it neared intersections, clickety-clacking along.

I've always loved our streetcars. Angela patiently stood amid the crowd as they tightly squeezed in around her, entering her personal space at the crosswalk, waiting for the walking signal to flash white. She scarpered into the crosswalk lane when it did, closing the distance toward her destination. The crowd seemed like one as they crossed.

A man in a gray, dingy, baggy, Blue Bayou cleaning jumpsuit accidentally collided with Angela, knocking her possessions out of her hands. His blue eyes, black hair, and masculine jawline with a faint beard made him exceptionally handsome. "Lady, I'm sorry. Let me help you." He flashed a rueful grin.

Unapologetically, she drilled into the man with her penetrating stare. "I think you've already helped enough." Her glare gave way to a brief smile at the corner of her lips when her mesmerizing blue eyes met his, instantly being attracted to him. It was as if, for the moment, time stood still. The sheer magnetism of his expression melted the ice-cold blood running through her veins.

He quickly gathered her belongings and handed them to her. "Again, lady, I'm very sorry."

Several horns blew as the red light changed to green. An elderly, bald Caucasian driver with trucker tan lines on his upper arm and a lit cigarette in his mouth stuck his head out the car window with a glare of pure fury. "Hey, move out of the way!"

Angela's ruby lips contorted into an expression of stunned surprise. "I guess we're blocking traffic."

The handsome stranger nodded, shooting one of his patented winks in her direction. "Have a good day, ma'am."

Honk! Honk! "Move it, lady!" He swooshed his arm for her to move, revealing his trucker tan line.

The man in the Blue Bayou jumpsuit strode quickly to the opposite side of the street. Angela clutched her belongings and dashed toward the high-rise building. Hurriedly, she glanced at her crystal sapphire-faced diamond Rolex watch. *I can't be late. There's too much riding on this.* She increased her pace, sprinting through the rotating glass doors and into the building, the marble floors and golden brass trim glistening from the morning sun.

The Hispanic muscular jovial security guard in his thirties smiled. "Good morning Ms. Abadie."

"*Buenos dias*, Miguel."

With her heels clicking against the polished gray marble floor, she briskly strode to the elevator, and repeatedly pressed the up-arrow button. "Come on! I don't have all day."

Other businesspeople gathered and waited too. Everyone seemed in a hurry for their workday to begin.

Finally, the elevator door slid open, and several people hurriedly exited as she waited for it to empty, then entered. She pressed the button for floor twenty-three as several others entered, crowding the elevator like packed sardines. Angela quickly scooted to the back and leaned against the mirrored wall. *Could this thing get any slower?*

The elevator doors shut, and it smoothly ascended, stopping on the fifth floor. Six people exited. Angela stepped forward and snippily pressed the smooth close button several times. The elevator door, slow to shut, agitated Angela. She repeatedly pushed the close button.

A lawyer-type man grasping a briefcase next to her frowned. "You know that doesn't speed things up."

"It might not, but it makes me feel better."

"Enough said." His eyes cemented straight ahead at the door.

So did she, her knuckles turning white as she gripped her phone.

The elevator stopped on the eleventh floor. The man exited. "Have a great day. Go ahead and press that button, since it makes you feel better." His tone, full of sarcasm, grated Angela's nerves.

Angela smirked. "What a jerk." The remaining people's eyes accusingly darted her way. "Sorry, but he's a jerk."

After several more stops, the elevator finally reached the twenty-third floor. Angela immediately exited when the door opened, stepping into a lavish foyer; in the center was a forty-two-inch mahogany table that displayed a massive, fresh floral orchid arrangement showcasing the elegance of the office. She smugly gazed at the impressive silver and royal blue inlaid 3D signage for *Elite Magazine* behind the reception desk as an I'm-the-boss-now-smile pursed her lips. The floor-to-ceiling windows provided a perfect view of the city's skyline.

She passed Monique, age twenty-four, a blue-eyed, beautiful red-haired receptionist wearing a Michael Kors navy blue cap sleeve stud trim Ponte dress and bright green glasses with blue dots representing her quirkiness. "Good morning, Ms. Abadie. You have several messages that I gave to your secretary."

"Thank you, Monique."

"My pleasure." She adjusted her glasses, pushing them to the brim of her nose.

Angela advanced through the industrious cubicle journalist area, which buzzed as if the stock market exchange bell had just rung. The area was all abuzz with clacking keyboards and cellphones ringing. By the size of the workspace and the number of cubicles, at least thirty people had started their fast-paced workday with publishing deadlines to meet.

Katie Summers, a self-confident thirty-four-year-old senior journalist, stood as Angela passed. "Excuse me, Ms. Abadie. I completed the article on the Smyth and Smyth Architect firm; I look forward to your feedback." The tone in her voice was more than reminiscent of brown-nosing the boss, which never settled well with Angela.

"I'll get to it as soon as possible." She barged past her steadfast to get to her office without further delay.

Dejected from not getting the recognition from her boss she thought she deserved, Katie shrugged in disappointment, sighed, and then sat briefly, slumping her shoulders. Finally, she grabbed a bag of chips and ripped into them.

As if on a rescue mission, Angela continued her relentless pace toward her office. Several employees who stood to the side engaged in conversation greeted her or froze in place as if they had done something wrong when she passed.

Francis Murphy, a beautiful brunette, age thirty-three, dressed in a Kasper sleek black dress; its hemline demurely bisecting her knees, and black pumps with opaque stockings, met Angela as she approached her corner office, which overlooked the Mississippi River. The plaque on the door read, "Angela Abadie – Senior Vice President."

As her brow furrowed, Angela stopped short of entering. "When is my nameplate going to be updated? I'm the CEO now. Not the Senior Vice President." Her words were stated with absolute conviction and impatience, which annoyed Francis.

"Hopefully today, ma'am." She huffed, hoping Angela wouldn't notice, trying to appease her boss' agitation.

"It better be. Please follow up on that. Immediately!" She struggled to rip the nameplate from the door; however, it wouldn't budge. To add insult to injury, she broke her index fingernail. "Just what I needed. Now, call in a manicurist to fix this. Immediately!"

"Ma'am, I'll make both my top priorities."

The women scurried into Angela's private office, decorated exquisitely in teal and white as if on Fifth Avenue in a posh New York building. The office exuded wealth and stature, from the elegant glass desk to the sumptuous leather, teal chairs. When she sat, the Mississippi River Bridge loomed behind her.

"Ms. Abadie, a quick update. Your ten o'clock meeting with Mr. Morgan was rescheduled because of a family emergency. I took the liberty of scheduling another meeting with a new client."

"You did this without checking with me? You know I vet all our potential advertisers. We have prestigious clientele. Not anyone who walks in from the street can purchase ads in our magazine."

"I must confess, I did. However, it is for Mr. John Legions of Legions Airlines. Does he need to be vetted?"

Angela sighed, easing into her chair. "I guess not, but don't make that a habit. I know you're new here, but decisions like that are mine. Understood?" An old impulse led her to tap her nails on her desk for emphasis.

"Yes, ma'am. Are you ready for your interview with KWNC this morning?"

Frustrated, she hid her broken nail from view. "I forgot about that. Of all days, why today? We have a publishing deadline, and I need my nail fixed."

"I believe it has something to do with you making the top list of the most influential businesswomen in Louisiana. Now that you're CEO of one of the nation's top magazines, everyone wants to know everything about you besides being a socialite."

"I get it, but I don't have time for this. I don't need to be marketed. If I wanted that, I'd just put an ad in my magazine."

"Like you always say, there's no such thing as bad press."

"Fine, just give me a heads up before they prance into my office." Her commanding, dismissive tone seemed harsh. "No, wait. I'll do the interview in the journalist area. I don't want them in here. Arrange that."

"Consider it done."

George Sidwell Preparatory Senior High school's gymnasium filled quickly with students sporting red and black school colors as they made their way to the hard wooden bleachers. The walls were plastered with championship football banners honoring previous years' wins and posters for the game. Preston Alcott Billiford III, blonde hair and hazel eyes, considered a teen heartthrob, sat in the front row sporting his number nine quarterback jersey. At the end of the basketball court, there were four rows of chairs filled by the football team, who waited patiently for the pep rally to begin.

The band played the school's fight song at the opposite end of the court as the majorettes and flag team performed.

In one section of the bleachers sat the nominees for Homecoming Queen, each wearing a magnificent mum with red and black ribbons glittered in silver with the words -- "Homecoming Court."

Mr. Hayes, the sixty-year-old plump silver-haired principal, high-fived several students as they entered. "Good morning!"

Lance Billiot, an eighteen-year-old senior with raven shoulder-length hair and blue eyes, a striking contrast to Preston, looked more like a gothic-punk rock star in a school uniform than someone who attended an exclusive private school. He was inclined toward the slightly offbeat and impulsive. He sat midway in the bleacher section next to his best friend, Conrad Pierce, who similarly identified with the gothic-punk style. Conrad elbowed Lance. "Can we talk about Jamie? I don't know what you see in her. Besides, don't you think she's out of our social class?"

Lance's brows creased. "Just because she's not rich doesn't mean I can't date her."

"I still don't see what you see in her." At his sharp inhale, smugness crept over Conrad's face. "You're from old-school money; her family is dirt-bottom broke; you know, from a no-money family. The only reason she's here is because of the scholarship she received. I think they call that integration."

"Conrad, you sound like a snob."

"That's because I am. Like my daddy always says, it's just as easy to fall in love with someone rich as it is with someone poor."

"You're a definitely a snob. You'll understand what I see in her when you get to know Jamie."

"I'm just saying, save yourself. You'll find a girl more suited to your ranking at Harvard next year. You at least owe yourself that much. You don't need a tag-along. Oh, wait. Jamie won't be there because she can't afford it."

The band's song ended as the flag team and majorettes took their seats in the bleachers.

Conrad exhaled. "Please pray that the Glee Club doesn't perform."

"Since when do you pray?"

"At the thought of the Glee Club. I'll take classic rock and roll any day of the week."

"Here they come." Lance pointed to the girl's locker room exit.

The perky cheerleading squad sprinted into the gym, screaming, "Go, Spartans!" as they shook their pom-poms. In contrast, the crowd screamed back with equal energy vibrating the bleachers as they stomped their feet and clapped their hands. Three male cheerleaders and the team's Spartan mascot dashed from the boy's locker room. Several cheerleaders performed backflips until they lined up in formation across center court. As his red cape flowed, the mascot strutted his way in front of the bleachers; his fake-gold, plastic Spartan helmet almost fell off as he clutched it.

Conrad elbowed Lance again and then pointed at the mascot. "I wouldn't dress like that even if they gave me a million dollars. Oh, wait. I already do. Trust fund baby."

"Now I know you're a snob."

"A rich snob, absolutely. But what male in their right mind wears a gladiator dress exposing his hairy ass legs? He looks ridiculous."

"You're one to talk. Have you noticed we don't exactly fit in either?"

"It's not because we can't. It's because we don't want to. Big difference!"

Conrad raised a rocker fist pump. "Rock on!"

Lance smiled and gestured a thumbs-up at Jamie Seamore, a seventeen-year-old senior with long curly brunette hair and green eyes, who held the head cheerleader position. She stopped at center court several feet in front of the squad.

Jamie took her position as she quickly glanced from left to right at the other squad members. "Ready? Okay!"

The squad performed a cheer, which included Jamie as the flyer at the end of the stunt. She flipped backward, landing in a male cheerleader's arms.

Lance never took his eyes off her as the squad cheered and danced in formation.

"Is she still pressuring you about the homecoming dance tonight?"

"I've got it handled."

"I'm just saying, if you give in now, you'll always have to give in. Set your precedents early in a relationship."

"This explains a lot. Like why you don't have a girlfriend."

"I don't want one. I'm waiting for the finer women to come my way. College women. The more, the merrier."

Lance cupped his hands over his mouth. "Go, Jamie!"

Jamie nodded and smiled, having heard Lance's encouragement.

Conrad elbowed him again. "Please don't embarrass yourself. Let's get out of here."

Lance offered him an annoyed look as he rose to his feet. The pair exited the gym as the squad performed their dance routine.

Jamie's animated cheerleader demeanor momentarily faded as her eyes followed Lance.

Self-assured in her stance, Angela stood in front of the floor-to-ceiling window in the journalist cubicle area. A few feet away, Francis observed as she wrote every question Houston Meadows, a handsome KWNC reporter, asked of her boss as his camera operator continued filming.

"Ms. Abadie, one last question. How do you intend to keep the magazine's reputation as number one now that your father has retired?"

Angela bumptiously pursed her lips, pulled back her shoulders, tilted her chin, and flashed a fierce smize. "My father would not have put me in this position if I wasn't ready. Since I was sixteen, I have worked for this magazine. The first thing I did was scrub the toilets. I delivered the mail. I served as a receptionist. I sold advertisements. I copy-edited. I wrote articles. My father made sure I understood every aspect of this company. There isn't a job at this magazine that I haven't done myself or willing to do again. As the nation's top magazine, our reputation at *Elite* will maintain." She glared at the reporter. "Any more questions, Mr. Meadows?"

"That just about does it. It's a wrap."

The camera operator switched off his camera.

Houston forced a fake smile, ready to finish the interview. "Thank you, Ms. Abadie. This story should air tonight on the evening news."

"I'm looking forward to it. Enjoy the rest of your day."

He nodded, and then he and the camera operator departed.

Angela rolled her eyes, lifting her brows. "Francis, that was one of the worst interviews I have ever had. The guy is a complete jerk."

Monique approached Angela and Francis with a message in her hand. "I hate to tell you I told you so, but I told you so."

Angela rubbed the back of her neck. "How did you know?"

"I dated him in college. He was a jerk then, too, and he clearly hasn't changed."

"Well, at least you got out of that relationship before it was too late."

Monique handed her the note. Angela glanced at it. "Great, simply great." She huffed, knowing how important each client was to her company's success. "Another appointment canceled." *I need clients; I don't need them to cancel. Dad will be furious.*

Francis smiled. "Look at the bright side; this allows you to vet other potential clients."

"I suppose you're right."

Behind Angela, on the outside of the window, a portable davit carriage dropped with the man in the Blue Bayou cleaning uniform in it whom Angela had collided with on her way to work. His tanned skin glistened from the sweat, enhancing his jawline. He grabbed his squeegee and cleaned the windows, smiling and waving at everyone.

Several female journalists stood as they stared googled-eyed at the window washer.

Angela's brows furrowed. "What is everyone staring at?"

Monique grinned and pointed toward the window washer. "Him."

Angela turned around; her eyes widened. "You've got to be kidding me."

Enamored, Francis swallowed and exhaled. "I love the way he washes windows." Sighing, she batted her long, thick, black lashes.

Dreamy-eyed, Monique nodded in agreement with a full-fantasy smile. "He can wash my windows anytime."

"I agree." Francis' heart fluttered as she waved at the window washer again. "I wish he could come right through that window and get closer to me. I want to smell him."

One rope that held the platform suddenly loosened, tilting it, and dropping the window washer several inches.

Monique's heart raced. "Oh, my God!"

Everyone in the room now focused on the window washer. The ropes which held the platform loosened again, jolting him once more.

"He's going to die! We have to save him!" Monique's eyes widened with fear. "Somebody, do something! Anything!"

Angela clenched her jaw as she studied the situation, her heart pounding as her skin prickled with alarm. *This is getting more dangerous by the second. I've got to do something.*

The window washer knocked on the window with the squeegee and yelled, but they couldn't hear him. He tapped on the window again as the platform swayed, pressing the carriage's remote to send it back to the roof, to no avail. "Please help me! Help!" Only his mouth moved as the glass prevented anyone from hearing him.

Angela took a deep breath. "He's asking for our help. We have to get him inside before that thingamajig drops. Somebody, call for help!" She attempted to open the window, but it didn't budge. "It won't open." Her heart skipped a beat as terror encapsulated her. *Dear God, please don't let him fall to his death.*

"For the record, they don't open. Try something else." Kate furiously typed on her keyboard, searching *Google* for a solution. "Hey, try slamming something heaving into the corner. It should break according to this."

Monique frantically dialed 911.

Francis bolted to the far side of the room toward the fire safety alarm system, franticly pulling it. The alarm blared, sending most scurrying toward the stairwells.

Angela threw her hands up into the air. "Why in the hell did you do that? He's not on fire. We have to get him in here before he falls." She continued trying to open the window as the window washer's panic-stricken face turned pale.

An overweight African American journalist, Richard Hastings, grabbed a trashcan and ran toward the window. "Move out of my way; we have to break the window." He hurled the trashcan in a missile-style formation toward the glass. The trashcan launched into it but bounced right back, knocking the journalist onto his butt, and hitting his head on the corner of a desk.

Monique hightailed it toward Richard. "That's not what I had in mind for men falling at my feet."

John Legions, the dapper owner of Legions Airlines, stepped through the door during the commotion. His curious eyes widened, staring at the scene in fascination. He confidently crossed his arms, and casually leaned against the wall, taking it all in. No one noticed him.

Angela took control. "All right, people, Plan B." She raised the left side of her skirt, exposing a black lacy garter belt, thigh-high black stocking, and a leather holster with a semi-automatic gun, and quickly retrieved it.

John's brows lifted as he grinned and stared admirably at Angela. *She's got guts. Impressive.*

A bead of sweat formed across Francis' upper lip as her heart raced. "So, you're going to shoot him? Seriously!"

Angela aimed her weapon toward the glass pane.

The platform dropped another couple of inches as the window washer's eyes widened. He put his hands in the air, waving a frantic no, and almost fell.

The platform jolted a couple more inches downward and swayed more, almost sending the window washer off of it. He tousled, grasping the carriage's railing just in time, preventing his fall.

Angela frantically waved her hands, gesturing for him to slide to the right. "Move! I'm going to shoot the glass."

John, who remained across the room observing, raised his left index finger. "He can't hear you."

The window washer obeyed her pantomimed command as he grasped the platform and kneeled.

"You're going to kill him." Monique put her hand over her eyes. "I can't watch." She peeked through her fingers as if watching a thriller movie.

Katie bolted toward Angela. "Shoot at the corner! It should shatter the glass."

Angela darted her eyes at Katie. "Are you serious?"

"Extremely. I just researched it."

A crowd gathered outside on Canal Street as they gazed at the platform, which dangled and swayed. As sirens blared, people chaotically bolted from the building as though it were on fire.

Houston and his camera operator immediately acted by broadcasting a live remote in front of the building. "I'm Houston Meadows, and I'm live in front of Abadie Towers on Canal Street. Moments ago, a window washer almost fell to his death. Stay with us here at KWNC as this story develops."

Several fire trucks pulled up and stopped in front of the skyscraper. The firefighters exited their vehicles, bolting into the building.

A news helicopter flew over and maintained its position. Several local news trucks pulled to the side of the skyscraper.

"It's now or never." Angela aimed her weapon at the corner of the window and fired three times. The glass splintered and cracked, shattering with a loud cascading sound. "Good thing I'm a marksman." Angela handed her gun to Francis as Richard and several journalists pushed the rest of the glass away as much as possible.

Richard hurled the trashcan toward the window again, making an escape path for the window washer.

Angela and Richard pulled him into the office just in the nick of time. The people below scattered in chaos, screaming as the platform hurled toward the ground splattering onto the sidewalk in a cloud of dust.

The window washer landed face down in extreme pain.

Monique's hands trembled as she returned the gun to Angela. "I don't like guns. They kill people."

Eight firefighters and four police officers led by Sergeant Danielson bolted into the area. The Sergeant eyed the gun in Angela's hand. "Put down your weapon."

Angela stepped forward. "Officer."

"I said put down your weapon, now!"

Angela obeyed the order against her better judgment, having fired the weapon moments before. Then, bang! A bullet ricocheted throughout the area, sending everyone to take cover. Monique fell to the floor and rolled, as she'd once learned during a shooting drill in high school. A pool of blood puddled around the window washer's left leg having been hit by the stray bullet.

The police officer cautiously approached Angela as several more paramedics darted into the room.

Richard grabbed his chest. "I'm having a heart attack."

Now under a desk, Monique fainted, and the rest of the office personnel remained gobsmacked.

Two paramedics rushed toward Richard and immediately performed CPR, the others dashing toward the window washer as a police officer handcuffed Angela.

"You have the right to remain silent…"

"...But, Officer, I shot the window. I didn't shoot to kill."

"Tell that to the judge, lady." He forced Angela's hands behind her back clamping the handcuffs around her wrists.

John, still unnoticed by all, smugly dialed his cell phone.

Angela's face flushed. "I saved that man's life. People! Tell him I saved his life."

The window washer blinked several times before opening his eyes. The room spun; his vision went in and out of focus. "Excuse me, officer. She saved my life. She's my guardian angel."

Francis, grinning like a Cheshire cat, sauntered toward the officer batting her lashes. "Now, Officer, that man would be dead if Ms. Abadie didn't shoot the window. She's a hero, not a villain." She glanced at the officer's name tag on his uniform. "Now wouldn't he, Sergeant Danielson?"

"Even if that were true, she illegally discharged a firearm. I'll have to take her in. Now, everyone needs to evacuate the building."

"I pulled the fire alarm to get help. The building isn't on fire." Francis nervously bit her lower lip.

Angela pursed her lips trying to adjust the metal cuffs crimping the skin at her wrists, which sent pain shooting up to her shoulders. "Francis, call my attorney." *This is the worst thing that could have happened during my first-week flying solo.*

"I'm on it." Francis bolted to Angela's office.

Sergeant Danielson escorted Angela toward the door, passing John. "Ms. Abadie?" His golden-brown eyes caught her attention as he swept his fingers through his thick, raven hair.

"Sir, you need to evacuate with everyone else." The officer pointed to the door. "Use the stairs."

"Mr. Legions, this isn't what it looks like." *My dad is going to kill me.*

"Everyone out of the building until we clear it! Now move!" Sergeant Danielson nodded toward several officers to clear the building.

The prep school student parking contained sports cars, sport utility vehicles, and luxury cars, showing the type of family wealth possessed by the students who attended the exclusive private school.

Most of the vehicles were decorated with streamers, balloons, and white shoe polish on the rear windows for the upcoming homecoming game. Several older vehicles stood out like a sore thumb, such as an old beat-up van and a blue ten-year-old Chrysler convertible Sebring decorated with streamers with the windows written on with white shoe polish, "Senior Homecoming Court."

Smoke escaped from the windows of the old van. Inside, Lance, Conrad, and Jeremy each smoked cigarettes as heavy metal music blasted from the console.

Conrad nudged Lance. "Dude, if I have to go to another pep rally, I'll…"

"…You'll do what?" Lance took a puff and coughed. "It beats a Glee Club performance."

The boys chuckled.

Conrad's eyes darted out of the window. "Mr. Hayes is heading our way. Put it out, man."

Flustered, Mr. Hayes briskly approached the van.

The boys lay on the floor, extremely still. Smoke drifted from Conrad's mouth.

Mr. Hayes' left fist pounded the side door as he leaned in to peer into the blackout window, blocking the sun with the other hand. "Boys, open up. I know you're in there and exactly what you're doing." He peered through the driver's window and then strode to the front of the van. He shook the van's bumper. "Boys!"

After moving to the passenger side, Mr. Hayes banged on the window. "Boys, last chance." His posture stiffened as he clenched his jaw as an I-got-you grin crossed his face.

He shuffled to the other side of the van, bent down, and then released the air out of the back driver's side tire. "That'll fix them." He swiped his hands together as he walked away, grinning, heading back toward the gym.

The bell rang as the students emptied the gymnasium and headed for their first-morning class. Several ran right into Mr. Hayes. *I must get another job*; he thought as the students scurried toward their classes.

One of the last students to leave, Jamie, took her time exiting the gym. Several of the cheerleaders ran past her. Some patted her on the back.

Her best friend Melissa, junior captain of the cheerleading squad, stopped. She took a deep, exasperated breath. "Are you coming or not?

"Give me a minute. I have to talk to someone."

Melissa glanced over her shoulder and gazed toward Preston. "You're waiting for him, aren't you?"

"What makes you think that?"

"You two were an item since freshman year."

"The key to this, Melissa, is that we are no longer together. I broke it off. Remember? I couldn't stand his uppity parents and sister anymore. I reached my breaking point."

"You mean to say his parents didn't like your family's status, right?" Melissa flipped her hair.

"Exactly! I wasn't good enough and never will be in their eyes. Not everyone can be born with a silver spoon in their mouth."

"I hear ya. My family is new lottery money. They don't like me either if it makes you feel any better. So, we're trash in their eyes too.

Jamie felt butterflies in her stomach. "At least you have the last name of Sidwell; that helps."

"I'm not related to the school's namesake, but people think I am, so that helps a little, but not much. My parents aren't even related to that family.

"At least you have a mom and a dad." A sadness prevailed over Jamie's mannerism and expression as she reflected on her mom's death.

"I didn't mean to bring up bad memories. I know it's been difficult for you since your mom died."

"That's an understatement." For a moment, Jamie indulged in her reflection.

"How's our plan to get your dad dating going?"

"I haven't started it, but I will soon."

"You better. In a couple of months, you're free to go to college. You said it yourself; you won't leave unless your dad finds someone to love."

"I know. I just haven't had the time to talk to him about joining a dating website."

"Then don't. Just do it."

Jamie rolled her eyes.

"Don't look now, but he's coming our way." Melissa nudged Jamie's shoulder.

Preston approached with an overlarge grin. "Melissa, can you give us some privacy? I need to speak to Jamie."

"Whatever!" Melissa flicked her hand and walked away. "Later gator."

"Jamie, our feud has to end. I'm going to ask you one more time. Will you please go to the homecoming dance with me?"

"I told you I'm not going with you, period!" She furrowed her brow, annoyed as her flesh crawled with dread. "Besides, my new boyfriend doesn't want to go, so I'm not going either."

"The homecoming queen is expected to attend the dance and show off her crown."

"I'm just in the homecoming court. The winner won't be announced until halftime in tonight's game. Seriously, what chance do I have, anyway?"

"A good one. Just about everyone I know voted for you."

"It's better this way. Besides, at least he accepts my widowed father and me, unlike your snobbish family."

"So, this means you'll be with that mysterious boyfriend of yours we never see and only hear about. And he won't take you to the dance? He sounds like a fantastic guy."

"He doesn't care that we live on the wrong side of the tracks." A sadness prevailed over Jamie's face as she twirled her hair around her index finger.

Lance, Conrad, and Jeremy approached.

"Look, Preston; I've got to get to class." She walked away.

"This isn't over, Jamie; I'll get you back. I still love you and always will."

Over her shoulder, her death stare penetrated Preston. "Try telling that to your parents and see what you get." She picked up her pace.

Lance eyed Jamie and dashed toward her. "Jamie, wait!"

She kept her pace.

He caught up and walked backward to talk to her. "See ya at our meeting place tonight?"

"I guess. Why did you leave the pep rally?" Her nose wrinkled as she sniffed the foul odor embedded in his clothing. "Never mind, I know. If you plan on being with me, you can't smoke. I refuse to kiss an ashtray mouth. How many times do I have to keep telling you this? We've been dating for six months now. If you keep smoking, we won't make seven. *Comprendo?*"

"You know I'm trying." He touched her shoulder to calm her.

Jamie jerked away from his touch. "Obviously, not hard enough. Look, I have to cheer at the game tonight. I'm going to be homecoming queen, I think. I have to go. Are you going to be there?" She popped her hip, challenging.

"To the game or the dance?"

"Both."

"I've had about all the formal dances I ever care to attend in my life. Besides, if I can't be with you, I won't go."

"What if I'm not over formal dances? That means no winter formal or prom for me. I won't go alone."

"Then we have a problem."

"You think?" She pushed him away.

Preston ran up behind them, eyeing Lance suspiciously. "Jamie, this creep giving you a hard time?"

"You know, Preston. I've changed my mind." She leered at Lance to let him know she was in charge. "I will go to the homecoming dance with you. We're both in the homecoming court. We belong there, together." She immediately regretted her words once she realized she'd be with Preston, not Lance.

"Yes! I knew you'd change your mind." Preston grabbed her hand, kissed it prince-style, and then escorted her to class.

Lance bit his lower lip. *If I don't do something, I'll lose her to Mr. Arrogance.*

"See you around, creep." Jamie flipped her ponytail as she strode toward the door. To get under Lance's skin, she flaunted her relationship by continuing to hold hands with Preston.

Lance clenched his jaw, slamming his fist into the brick wall.

CHAPTER TWO

Let the Games Begin

The ambulance, with sirens blaring, pulled through the emergency room entrance at East Jefferson Mercy Hospital before coming to an abrupt stop; brakes squealing. The back door flung open, and two paramedics slid the gurney with the window washer from the vehicle. Two hospital emergency room personnel rushed toward them and took over, rushing into the entrance. The window washer grimaced. "Call my daughter." He tilted his head back and screamed in excruciating pain.

"Sir, can you tell me your name?"

"James. James Seamore."

"James, help is on the way. Stay with us."

His eyes rolled toward the back of his head.

"Here you go." The husky, wrestler-type, five-foot, thirty-something Black female processing officer and Angela stood in a ten by twelve-foot room lit by fluorescent tubes from a low ceiling, casting unfavorable lighting. The room was small and barren, with only a nondescript lab table similar to those in a high school biology lab. It was covered with fingerprint forms, ink pads, and a single container of baby wipes. The officer stood beside Angela. "Let me have your left hand." The intake officer pressed Angela's thumb onto the ink pad. "Roll your thumb onto the paper."

"I know the drill. You just finished my right hand." She gave the intake officer a closed-mouth smile, although she felt like vomiting.

"Just do it and cut the chitchat."

Angela pressed her thumb onto the fingerprint booking paper; the intake officer rolled the digit, huffing as she did.

"It's a good print."

Angela sighed. *I'm a goner if Dad gets wind of this overseas.*

"See, that didn't hurt a bit." The intake officer handed her a wet wipe. "Clean yourself up and stand behind the red line against the wall."

Bewildered, Angela glanced at her ink-tipped fingers. "Is this necessary? There's been a mistake." Angela tossed the wipe into the rusty trashcan that looked like it had seen better days before stepping toward the red line.

"You're innocent, right?"

"As a matter of fact, I am. Do you know who I am?"

"According to the arrest documentation, you're Angelica Elizabeth Humphrey Billiot Abadie. Face the front."

Angela grudgingly faced the front. "Yes, my attorney will be here any minute and stop this nonsense. There's been a grave misunderstanding."

The intake officer snapped the picture. "Face to the left."

She turned accordingly, feeling a fluttering of nerves in the pit of her stomach. "My family alone donates millions of dollars to support the police, and this is how you repay me?"

"When you break the law, you get arrested. Face right."

"I was trying to save a man's life."

"Face to the right, Ms. Abadie."

After shaking her head, Angela slowly faced to the right.

Flash! Even though it was a mugshot, Angela looked like a supermodel.

James, dressed in a hospital gown and attached to medical equipment and an I.V., lay lethargic in bed in the darkened room. The pale beige walls, plug-ins for equipment, florescent lighting, a whiteboard with his specific patient information written on it, looked larger than life to him. His heart pounded, recognizing the last time he was in such a room was with his deceased wife. He could hardly move as he winced in pain in his attempt to roll over to his side, finally closing his eyes.

The door creaked open without a knock. Sally, a pompous, gorgeous, thirty-eight-year-old, well-dressed blonde as if competing with Alexis Carrington, entered carrying a fall bouquet. She prowled around the bed. "Wake up, Sleeping Beauty." She placed the flowers onto the tray and gently shook the window washer's shoulder. "Rise and shine."

He barely opened one eye as they seemed to weigh five pounds. "It's you. The devil incarnate."

She flicked on the lights. "Now, James, is that any way to treat the sister of your daughter's mother?"

"I told you before; you're not going to come into our lives. You lost that right when you tried to gain custody of Jamie after her mother died. What are you doing here?" He narrowed his blue eyes in a stare of sheer incredulity.

"I'm still listed as your emergency contact, sweet cake. After that dreadful wreck, when you were unconscious, the courts appointed me. You never had it changed, and poof, I'm here."

"Just like the Wicked Witch of the West. What do you want?"

"Now that you're hospitalized, I want Jamie to come back with me to Georgia. You can't take care of her like this. She's a child."

"Who turns eighteen in March. She's not a child. Please, just leave and don't come back."

"I've traveled all this way to ensure my niece will be taken care of during this horrid time, and you treat me like this. How are you going to work? They just pulled a bullet out of your leg after you played Tarzan. I'm only trying to help you and Jamie."

"You call this help? You want to take away the only thing I have left in my life. That is not help. Help is paying my mortgage when I can't work. Help is buying us food. Help is you leaving us alone."

"I distinctly remember you didn't want any handouts. Although we spend that nightly on a fine bottle of wine and dinner, paying your mortgage is still a handout. What happened to your pride, brother-in-law?" Her condescension was evident of her intolerance of him.

"Maybe it's because a woman shot me, and I'm on pain meds. Like I said, please leave. Jamie and I will be fine. I've always been able to figure something out."

"A woman shot you? Since when are you seeing another woman?"

"How many times have I told you I'm not ready to date? Listen to me. I'm not interested in dating women."

"So, you prefer men?"

"No, I don't! I simply am not ready to date."

"Then you must have done something terrible to make that woman shoot you. That totally makes sense."

"No need for sarcasm. She was trying to save my life."

"Right, that's why you're in the hospital with a bullet hole in your leg. She was trying to save you. I think I've heard it all, now."

He grabbed the remote control and pressed the nurse's call button.

"Yes, Mr. Seamore, how may I help?"

"I need more pain meds and for you to get this woman out of my room."

"I'll be right in."

Sally glared at James. "Fine, if you don't want my help, I'll leave. May I at least take Jamie to dinner tonight?"

"Oh, crap." A sudden realization hit James, and he tipped his head back with a grown. "It's homecoming night. She's up for homecoming queen. I'm supposed to escort her. Where's my phone?"

"I don't see it. Try the old-fashioned push-button phone. Since it's obvious, you don't need my help, I'll leave. Toodledo." And with that, she strutted from the room with her nose tilted arrogantly toward the ceiling.

A very overweight nurse soon came into the room and shot a syringe full of medication into the I.V. port. "That should do you for at least eight hours."

James instantly felt drowsy. "What... did... you... give... me?" His eyes closed.

"The good stuff. Nighty-night."

Jamie entered the small two-bedroom house, threw her pink solid with green trim Mackenzie book bag onto the couch, and flipped on the floor lamp illuminating the room; her gaze quickly went toward the old, brown leather recliner with a tear on the seat where her dad watched television. In front of the window, which was covered with sheer lace cream curtains, was a tattered floral loveseat with two beige throw pillows and a small mahogany coffee table with a box with a half-eaten day-old pepperoni pizza. The wooden floor, dusty, was half-covered with a large worn oriental rug featuring reds, black, and browns. On the left wall was a small old wooden desk with a computer, and the swivel black office chair was tucked nicely by it. The sage green, faded painted walls didn't offer much. As for the decorations, a bare minimum featuring pictures of Jamie and her father, Mardi Gras masks, a couple of manly items such as a football helmet, black and white photographs of French Quarter scenes taken by James, and a coat rack by the front door. "Dad?" Her brows furrowed as she let out a pent-up breath sawing out of her puckered lips. *That's weird. He's always home before me.*

She searched the house, first glancing into her dad's bedroom, hoping she'd find him there. She flipped on the light. "Dad?" The full-size unmade bed was vacant. The navy-blue comforter was rolled into a ball in the middle of the bed, and a basket full of dirty laundry was in the corner, including several Blue Bayou uniforms. On his nightstand, a picture of his late wife, and on the wall above the bed, a black and white photograph of a rustic camp on the bayou taken by James. His signature and the date scribbled on the lower right-hand corner, which was barely visible.

Next, she searched the kitchen, which was extremely small, with only one counter. In the corner was a 1950s-style aluminum table with four red, gold-flaked leatherette chairs. A stack of dirty dishes filled the sink, and a trashcan filled to the brim. She scooped out the trash bag, tied the top in a knot, carried it to the backdoor, placed it on the back porch, and then shut the door. Her lips twisted as she replaced a new trash bag into the canister. She fixed a peanut butter and jelly sandwich, poured a glass of milk, and grabbed a bag of chips, taking them to the small computer desk in the living room.

She sat down and booted the computer, devouring half of her sandwich as she waited. Her cell phone rang. She glanced at the caller's I.D. and pressed the green button to answer before turning on the speakerphone. "Hey, Melissa, what's cookin' chicken?"

"I'm just excited about tonight. I voted for you to be homecoming queen."

"Finally, this is the twenty-first century." She took a bite of her sandwich.

"What do you mean by that?" A crease parted Melissa's forehead in confusion.

"Not about you voting. My computer. You'd think computers would boot at a faster rate. I'm taking advantage of the time. My Dad isn't home, and I'm going to enroll him on *Singlematch*. If he finds out, I'll be dead." Jamie typed in the answers to enroll him on the website, continuing to talk over the clack of the keys.

"If he finds out, who else would have done it?"

"I'm going to blame you." She gulped her milk.

"Some friend you are."

"You're the one who suggested it." Jamie bit her lower lip.

"That's a valid point. However, since I'll get blamed, I want to at least help you write his profile."

"He's an official member now. Let's see, upload a picture. What picture should I use?"

"I like the one you took of him at the father-daughter dance last year."

"Great idea. The women ought to love that." Jamie uploaded the picture of her dad, feeling satisfied she chose the best one.

"I'll say. Your dad's hot."

"Ew. That's my dad you're talking about."

"He's still hot."

"Okay, picture loaded. Time for his profile. You write, I'll type."

"Let me think." A long silence ensued.

"You still there?" Jamie twirled her hair around her finger.

"I'm thinking. Got it."

"Wait, this is ridiculous. I have to answer all these questions. How tall? What do you like to do? Hold on. Let me do it." Jamie started clicking on the check boxes she felt her dad would like. "Do you like sports? Check. Do you like to watch movies? Check. Do you like… Oh, good grief. Check. Check. Check. And, Check, check. Last one… Check! Okay, I'm ready for his profile."

"Great. While you played check the box, I wrote one. You ready?"

"Yep!"

"I have a great sense of humor and am adventurous."

"Slow down. I'm typing as fast as I can."

"Sorry. I… love…"

"…Just copy and paste it and email it to me."

"Fine."

Jamie received the email within a minute and read it aloud. "I love to go to fine restaurants and enjoy the arts. I love all sorts of music, old AMC movies, especially musicals with Doris Day, and those with Fred Astaire and Ginger Rogers, and I love Broadway shows. One of my ideal vacations would be to go to Napa Valley on a wine-tasting tour with my soul mate. I also love to attend Saints games and after eating at many of the fine restaurants here in our fabulous city."

"You know we're talking about my dad, right?"

"Yes, but to snag a refined woman, you gotta be a refined man."

"Oh, brother, we're going to get into a lot of trouble for this if he finds out."

"Then don't let him."

Jamie copied the description from the email and entered her dad's profile. "That should do it. Here's to dating, Dad!"

Bing!

"That was fast." Jamie's eyes widened. "He's already been matched."

"See who it is."

Jamie opened the attachment and a picture of a forty-year-old woman with greasy long red hair and missing two front teeth. "Yikes! Boy, oh boy. Nope! I wouldn't let her near me, much less my dad."

"Why? What does she look like?"

"Let's say, a female wrestler who resembles Dog the Bounty Hunter and probably hadn't washed her hair in months."

"Ouch! This isn't going to be easy, is it?"

"Nope, not at all."

Bing! Bing! Bing! The matches poured in quicker than Jamie could open them.

"Oh, boy, what have I done? Who are these women?"

Angela, twiddling her thumbs, sat in the police interrogation room with a single-window twelve inches from the ceiling, allowing only the slightest hint of what the outside weather was like when John Legions entered. "Good afternoon, Ms. Abadie."

Yanked out of contemplation, Angela adjusted her posture. "Please don't tell me you bailed me out." Out of habit, she looked at her watch, which wasn't there.

"Then, I won't."

"I don't understand. I've been waiting for my attorney all day. I haven't heard a word. It's very rude of him if you ask me." She tried with might to conceal her bitterness. "I might just have to replace him."

"May I sit?"

"By all means. This is a public place."

"After you were arrested, your secretary was kind enough to fill me in on why you shot the window washer. Although I did witness most of it."

"I didn't shoot him; I shot the window to break it. He was about to fall to his death if we didn't get him inside."

"That story matches. But, in your defense, I saw the whole thing."

"Why didn't you leave?"

He smugly grinned. "And miss all of this? I haven't seen this much excitement in my lifetime since… never. Corporate Aviation isn't the most exciting job in the world."

"I'd have to disagree. You have private jets at your disposal. You can travel anywhere and anytime you want. That's what I call exciting."

"I indeed use a jet like most people use their cars, but like cars, it is a means of transportation. A means of transportation that I want to expand; thus, our appointment this morning."

"I'm sorry about that. As you can see, I've been entertained by the fine New Orleans men in blue. But, as I said, I've been waiting for my attorney all day."

"Not for long. I called my on-call attorney and flew him in from California. That's why it's taken me all day. However, I signed an advertisement contract with *Elite Magazine*. There's a particularly quirky young woman who was very persuasive, Monique. I like her." His eyes sparkled when he mentioned Monique's name. A wry grin crossed his plump lips.

Angela studied John's expression after he mentioned Monique. "She's not an ad associate. She's the receptionist." It was almost as if she was jealous.

"I think you're underutilizing her knowledge and skills. Do you know who her father is?"

"I don't make it a point to get into the personal business of my employees, so no, I don't."

"I'll put it to you this way. He has more money than Rockefeller and maybe Elon Musk, and he made it all in public relations and marketing. Interested in knowing now?"

"I'm game. Who's her father?"

"Gordan B. Stiller."

"Gordan Stiller of Stiller Worldwide Enterprises?"

"The one and only."

"How did you find that out?"

"I met her at a gala in New York City last year. Her father and I are good friends. It's a private jet thing."

"What is she doing working for me?"

"I didn't ask. I just signed on the dotted line for a five-million-dollar campaign. She guaranteed me she'd handle it."

"I don't know whether to fire her or hug her."

"I think a promotion is in order, don't you? She graduated from Yale with top honors in business marketing."

"She never said a word about any of this. Not even on her resume. Her last name isn't Stiller."

"She uses her mother's maiden name so she can make her way up the corporate ladder. You can identify with that, can't you?"

A double tap on the door sent Angela's eyes darting toward it.

From the outside, Abraham Bilcher, fifty-four, five feet four inches wearing a Yarmulke, opened the door and entered.

John rose and shook his hand. "Abe, it's good to see you. Thank you for coming to Ms. Abadie's rescue."

Angela stood to great the lawyer as well. "Yes, thank you."

Abraham placed his briefcase on the table and sat. "Please, everyone, sit."

The pair sat; John leaned back.

Angela leaned forward, crossing her hands on top of it, ready to intensively listen. "How much do I owe you?"

"Mr. Legions has already taken care of that since I am on call."

"No, I insist. You flew him here, and he bailed me out. I owe you something."

"How's dinner sound, and we'll call it even? You must be hungry. The food in here can't be to your liking."

A hefty female police officer entered the room and handed Angela a brown envelope. "You're free to go, Ms. Abadie. Sign here that I returned your belongings."

Angela quickly signed the paper. "The best news I've heard all day. I can leave, right? I mean, there isn't anything else stopping me, correct?"

"Yes, ma'am." The officer handed her a slip of paper. "Here is your court date, don't miss it, or the judge will put a warrant out for your arrest."

"That's a day I won't be looking forward to." She shivered at the thought of having to go in front of the Judge who probably knows her and her father. *I have to keep this from my dad.* She felt queasy as her heart raced.

John glanced at his attorney.

Abraham nodded and winked at Angela. "Don't worry, Miss Abadie. I'll have the charges dropped in a blink of an eye."

CHAPTER THREE

Homecoming

The football game between the Dolphins and Spartans was in progress. A sea of crimson on the Spartans' home team side and a sea of blue on the visitors reflected each school's team spirit. The bleachers, full of fans, some with foam fingers, shook from pounding their feet as the gladiator mascot raced up and down the sideline in front of Jamie, Melissa, and the other cheerleaders.

Preston broke the huddle with a clap. "Let's do this." He led the Spartan football players to the thirty-yard line. They lined up in a shotgun offensive formation.

Cheerleaders waved their pom-poms in the air. "We want a touchdown!"

Lance and Conrad slowly entered the stadium, making their way to the top of the bleachers. Lance stared at Jamie from a distance. Christine, Preston's sister, and Rae, both female freshman students, noticed.

Christine swatted her hair away from her face. "What a couple of freaks. They're both so weird. They never say anything to anybody but to each other."

Rae grabbed Christine's leg. "You don't think they're Columbine freaky, do you?"

"I really don't want to find out."

Preston threw a fifty-yard pass only to be intercepted and ran back for a touchdown. Within seconds, the kicker nailed the extra point, further sinking the jubilation of the home-team crowd. The Dolphin side erupted in pandemonium as they were now six points ahead of the Spartans.

The cheerleaders, along with the rest of the Spartans, were stunned.

Jamie glanced at Preston and then back to Melissa. "He's very upset about this."

"I'd be too if I just threw an interception. Maybe he's not all that great as they make him out to be."

"Give him a break. He has his future riding on this. He wants to play in the NFL."

"Since when do you care about Preston?"

"Wait, don't get me wrong. I don't. But I don't want him to fail either."

Jamie looked up into the stadium. "My dad is still not here. How could he forget about homecoming? I need him to escort me."

"Don't worry. You mean everything to your dad. He wouldn't miss it for the world."

"Right. That's why he's not here."

"He'll be here."

"This isn't like my dad. I'm getting worried. He better have a great excuse for being late. Something bad better have happened to him."

"Again, he'll be here."

"What happens if he doesn't show? I'll still need an escort."

Melissa pointed to Preston, who had just thrown a twenty-yard pass. "Him."

"You've got to be kidding me."

"What other choice do you have?"

"Drop it. We better cheer. Girls, you ready?"

The cheerleaders got into formation.

"Ready, okay! V. I. C. T. O. R. Y. Victory, victory is our cry. Go Spartans!"

Preston threw a Hail Mary pass with only four seconds remaining to the end of the first half. The receiver caught it in the end zone, tying up the game as the Spartan fans exploded into cheers.

The buzzer ended the second half, and both teams ran to the locker rooms. The cheerleaders, all but Jamie and Melissa, ran from the field, while Jamie, one more time, scanned the stands for her father. "He isn't here. How could he do this to me? Now what?"

"Don't look now, but I think I have your answer."

"What are you talking about?"

"Does the name Preston Billiford ring any bells?"

"You've got to be kidding me."

"Nope, he's heading your way."

"Great, just freakin' great."

Preston rushed toward Jamie. "Where's your escort?"

"That's what I've been trying to figure out."

"No problem." Preston extended his left arm. "Shall we? I'd be honored to escort you."

"Well…" Melissa tapped Jamie's shoulder.

"…Well, what?"

"What other choice do you have?"

Jamie takes a long-exasperated breath. "I guess none. What's a homecoming queen with no escort? Let's do it."

Angela, still disheveled from being in jail, and John, sipping a cucumber martini, sat in a private booth at the Bombay Club. The elegant and ambient club reflected an upscale English Pub with its dark hunter-green walls and massive cherry-wood bookcases. Over in the far corner, a jazz singer with a three-piece band played.

"Thank you again, John, for helping me out today. I still don't know what happened to my attorney. He's fired once I find him." The broken nail on her right index finger looked out of place, although she caught herself trying to hide it.

"My pleasure. I'm glad I could be of assistance. You come here often?" He sipped his martini.

"I love the English pub vibe of the place."

"Have you ever been to a real English pub?"

"As a matter of fact, yes. I studied in London for my master's degree and frequently visited them. I play a pretty mean game of darts, especially if I'm full from eating shepherd's pie." She grinned, having reminisced about the past.

"I took you as a Beef Wellington lady." John nodded attentively, maintaining eye contact with her.

"You've heard the saying when in Rome, do as the Romans do."

"London is a far cry from Rome."

"It's the meaning of the saying. What can I say? I simply love pub food?" Angela sipped her cocktail, and then wiped her lips with the starched cloth napkin.

"You're full of surprises, now, aren't you?"

"Indeed. I like to keep people guessing. Just when you think you know me, you don't. It's a woman's prerogative."

"Meaning?"

"We can change the rules at any time. And, when you think you know them, that's when we change them." She teasingly lifted one brow.

"That explains a lot about my mother. She always changed the rules to suit her."

"Are you close to your parents?"

"Used to be. You see, Angela, after my father died, my mother changed. She became overbearing, demanding, and righteous. She tried to control everything I did, including where I went to college, who I could date, what time to be home from soccer practice, and what to eat. The list was endless. Then one afternoon, I was five minutes late from school. Actually, the bus was late, but that didn't matter to her. She grounded me for six weeks."

"Wow, John, I find that hard to believe. That doesn't even seem fair. Did you try to talk to her?" She shivered at the thought if she ever couldn't find her son.

"When I confronted her about it, she said I could leave if I didn't like the rules. That was my last straw. So, I packed my things into a duffle bag and left on a bus headed to God knows where, and never returned."

"How old were you?" Angela sighed, feeling John's discomfort with the conversation. "You don't have to talk about this if you don't want to.

"I'm fine. I was seventeen. I didn't even graduate from high school." A hint of remorse captured his expression.

"Wait. You're a very prominent business executive. So, you didn't finish high school?"

John shook his head. "I earned my GED and joined the Air Force when I was eighteen. That's where I learned to fly, earning my degree. After my stint in the military, I walked into a private airline company and asked for a pilot's job. Before I knew it, I was running the company, which was employee stock owned." He sipped his martini. "I lived in my van for three years to save overhead expenses, showered in the employee's gym locker room, ate Ramen noodles heated in the lounge microwave, and purchased as much stock as possible in the company. I also admittedly got lucky dabbling in stock investments, including Amazon. The rest is history."

"That's some rags to riches story. I always assumed you were born into a wealthy family." She sipped her cocktail.

John took a deep breath. "Not at all. My dad was a lawyer who worked for free defending those who couldn't afford it, and my mom was a housekeeper to make ends meet. After his death, we barely had food; thus, my taste for Ramen noodles. So, I took a job flipping burgers. All the money went to help with the bills."

"Where's your mother now?"

"Not sure. Honestly, I really don't care. I've never looked back."

"Ouch! That seems harsh." She shivered at the thought of never seeing or hearing from her son.

"She's the one who asked me to leave. I guess I should thank her for that. I might not have joined the Air Force or become a pilot if she hadn't. For that matter, I wouldn't have become the man I am today."

"Then maybe it's time to tell her. Do you ever wish you could find your mother?"

"Maybe one day, when the timing is right. But, for now, I'm not interested. She doesn't even know my name." John briefly looked away, hiding his true feelings.

"She has to know her son's name. That doesn't make sense."

"I legally changed my name to John Legions when I was eighteen. It sounded better than the name my parents gave me."

"Now, curiosity has set in. I have to know. What's your real name? Where were you born and raised?"

"That, Angela, will never leave my lips. If I told you, I'd have to kill you."

"I'll keep that in mind. Are you ready to order?"

James, lay helpless, propped up the hospital bed in excruciating pain, pressed the nurse's call button. The sterile odor was finally getting to him, as was the beeping heart and blood pressure monitor. He pressed the nurse's call button.

The speaker crackled back at him in response. "Sir, how may I be of assistance?"

"I'm in terrible pain."

"Sir, the nurse will be right there."

Grimacing, he adjusted his position.

The night nurse entered his room carrying a syringe. "How are you feeling, Mr. Seamore? Can I see your wristband, please?"

He lifted his arm with the wristband to show her; she quickly scanned it. "Can you please help me find my phone? I need to call my daughter. Ouch. Ouch. Do you know where my phone is?"

She placed the needle into the I.V. portal and emptied the syringe.

"I... need... to..." Discombobulated, he dozed off.

"Sleep tight, don't let the bedbugs bite."

The homecoming court promenaded onto the field as the band played *Gotta Feeling* by the Black Eyed Peas -- each girl escorted by their father except Jamie. The announcer continued introducing the court and was on the second to last name with Jamie and Preston last. "Next, we have Shanna Livia Du Pont. Shanna is a junior and president of the student council..."

"Thanks for the escort." Jamie's eyes darted to the top of the stand, and she discreetly waved at Lance.

"No problem. I'm every guy's envy right now."

"Shanna is escorted by her father, Desmond Franklin Du Pont…"

"Not my father's, or he would've been here."

"His loss, my gain. You'll do fine."

"We'll do fine."

"Feels like old times, doesn't it?"

"If you mean at last year's homecoming, not at all. That was a nightmare I don't care to remember."

"Not then, when we were boyfriend and girlfriend. I miss you."

"Just stop, Preston. Your parents disapprove of me, and you know it. They're the reason we broke it off. Honestly, if they were in the stands, would you be escorting me now, or would you coward at your father's hatred of me?"

"Last but not least, we have Jamie Katherine Seamore. Jamie is a senior and the captain of the varsity cheerleading squad. She is also a member of the Glee Club, drama team, and serves as the student council treasurer. Jamie is escorted by Preston Charles Billiford the Third and plans on attending LSU and studying veterinary medicine."

Preston frowned. "I didn't know that. What happened to you becoming a nurse?"

"I'd rather work with animals, like you."

"Ha, ha. Very funny, Jamie." She released a controlled laugh, quickly pursing her lips.

"Glad I made you laugh. But you never answered my question."

"Which question?"

"Would you be escorting me if your father was in the stands watching?" She threw one last glare before crossing her arms and stiffening her stance.

The homecoming court formed a single line across the field in front of the spectators, and the band stopped playing.

"Now Spartan fans, it is time to announce our homecoming queen."

All eyes in the stadium and on the field looked at Jamie.

"This year's homecoming queen is… Drum roll, please."

The drum line displayed remarkable talent as they performed their award-winning drum roll.

Up high in the stands, Lance smiled. "Here we go."

Preston squeezed Jamie's hand. "Here we go."

"Miss Jamie Seamore. Congratulations, Jamie."

The band played the school's fight song as the previous year's homecoming queen placed the crown on Jamie's head. Mr. Hayes handed her two dozen red roses.

"Congratulations, Jamie. I told you, you had this." Preston leaned over and kissed Jamie on the cheek, which sent Lance bolting out of the stadium with Conrad on his coattail. "And, yes, I'd escort you even if my father was in the stands."

The rest of the homecoming court closed in on Jamie to congratulate her, while Jamie's eyes searched for Lance. "Where is he?"

"Your dad?" Preston squeezed her hand.

"Sure, my dad." She heaved a sarcastic sigh. "He'd better be close to dying for missing this, or I'll kill him for sure."

"I'm sure there's a logical explanation. Now, I've got to get ready for the second half, then off to the dance with the most beautiful girl in the world. I mean, Your Majesty."

As the chauffeur held the passenger door open, John and Angela stepped into a black limousine outside the Bombay Club, and slid down the wrap-around black leather seats to the middle. John followed and sat close to her. The door gently closed behind them. To the right was a stocked mini bar and above a dropdown television. The light lavender ring track lighting on the ceiling cascaded a soft glow casting a hint of color onto the couple.

"What shall be your pleasure?" He sank back into his seat, crossing his legs.

"I'm good right now. But thank you, anyway." She placed her purse on her lap and crossed her hands. "It's been a wonderful evening, and I hate to cut it short, but I have an early meeting in the morning, and frankly, I need a long, hot bubble bath to get this jail stench off me. Oh, let me see. I have a five-million-dollar campaign to begin, too, have to see my manicurist, and…"

"…I'm sure you have a qualified staff to handle this."

"But, of course. However, Legions Airlines deserves my individual attention."

"Trust me, you're doing that now." He flashed her a flirtatious grin.

"And my son has an early morning competition I promised to attend."

"Very well. Home it will be."

"Maybe a bottle of water."

"A bottle of water, it is."

He handed her a water bottle with the label "Legions Airlines."

The Spartan's gymnasium decorated to the hilt with red, black, and white streamers, and balloons for the homecoming dance filled quickly. Jamie and Melissa stood at the punchbowl and refreshment area while Preston and his entourage stood center court, eying the ladies.

"I've got to get out of here." Jamie shifted her weight to her left leg. "Preston is driving me crazy. I don't want to give him the idea we're back together because we're not!"

"There could be worse things in life than a rich boyfriend with the last name Billiford." Melissa placed her hand over her heart as if saying the Pledge of Allegiance.

"It won't happen! Never, ever in a million years. Besides, I have my eyes on someone else."

"You keep saying that, but I've yet to meet this mystery man of yours."

"When the time is right. And, trust me, the time isn't right. You wouldn't understand."

Principal Hayes hobbled onto the stage, and grabbed the microphone. "And, now Spartans, it's time for our king and queen to dance. We all know who our queen is. Congratulations again, Jamie. And without further ado, your homecoming king is… Preston Billiford the Third."

Jamie rolled her eyes. "Just great. Of course he is. Now I have to slow dance with him. Melissa, I'm telling you. Once this is over, I'm outta here. Me and my Sebring are heading home."

Preston approached Jamie, extending his hand. "Shall we dance, My Queen?"

CHAPTER FOUR

Where Are You, Daddy?

T he Abadie Mansion, in the Garden District on St. Charles Avenue, radiated pristine old-family New Orleans' wealth as the black limousine arrived, coming to a slow, gentle stop. The lit three-story mansion with eight massive columns and wrap-around veranda looked something out of a fairy tale. The iron fence which guarded the property was as elegant as the house and gently gave a glimpse to the manicured lawn and flower gardens, which shone as the solar lighting lit it up as if viewing the Magic Castle. John exited, extending his hand toward Angela and helped her ease from the car.

"Angela, I had a wonderful evening with you. For a jailbird, that is."

"Don't make a joke about that!" Her spine stiffened as she momentarily leered at him. "That was never my intention. I was trying to save a man's life."

"Sorry, I didn't mean to offend you. The evening was most enjoyable. I would be honored if you accompanied me again tomorrow night for dinner. Are you free?"

"I'll have to check my calendar." She softly smiled.

"Oh, the calendar blow-off. "

"Not at all. I think I have a charity benefit tomorrow night. I don't have a date; it would be my honor if you'd like to attend it with me.

But, again, I have to check my calendar as I don't remember whether it's tomorrow night or next Friday."

"I'll clear both dates. Just let me know."

"Perfect, I'll have Francis call you tomorrow to confirm."

From the third story, Lance slid open his bedroom curtain and peered out the window at his mother before quickly closing it, contorting his expression to one of disdain.

The Seamore's porch light flickered, barely illuminating the house in the Marigny District. The blue Sebring car pulled up into the driveway, parked, and Jamie, wearing her homecoming crown, exited the vehicle, grabbed her roses, and made her way to the front porch steps.

She fumbled with the keys to unlock the front door and entered, flipping on the lights scanning the room. Once again, the brown leather recliner was vacant.

"Dad? You home? Where are you?" Her stomach somersaulted as her heart pounded. "Daddy, where are you? I'm too old for you to be playing this game." *Something's wrong.* She gulped as a frown of despair marred her brow. *If he's not dead, I'm going to kill him.*

Jamie tossed her crown across the room, threw the roses onto the couch, and flipped off her high-heeled shoes. Burning tears cascaded her cheeks as she plopped down onto the couch, propping her feet onto the coffee table, almost knocking off the aromatic gardenia candle. After reaching for the lighter, she lit it, and the sweet fragrant smell filtered through the room as the corner of her lip twitched. *Dad, where are you?*

Lance's bedroom, decorated elegantly black and accented with red, perfectly fit his style and taste. The walls lined with famous skateboarders' posters added to the vibe, and the South wall displayed eight mounted autographed skateboards. After the eighth, one space held a piece of typing paper taped to the wall with "Reserved for Tony Lark's Skateboard," written on it.

Sitting on the edge of his bed, Lance wore a black T-shirt and gray and black plaid boxers playing his cranberry apple with gold flakes Fender electric guitar. He continued to pluck the strings to a languid-blues melody when a knuckle-tap on Lance's door interrupted his jam. "Come on in, Mom; it's open."

She peeped her head in. "I'm home."

"Glad to see you're alive. I haven't heard from you all day, which is highly unusual for a helicopter mom. Wait! You look like hell. Where have you been?" He continued playing an improvised lick on his guitar.

"Tomorrow, son. I'm tired and need to sleep. You get some sleep too."

"You know, if I came in looking like that, I'd have some answering to do."

"That's why I'm the mom. I don't have to provide any explanations. Now, get your rest. Your big competition is tomorrow. Sleep tight."

"I'm just saying your behavior is out of character. I don't think I like it. I don't care what you're doing, but I care who you're with. And, by your looks, I don't like who you were with. Somehow, he leaves a bad taste in my mouth."

"You don't even know him." A worried scowl emerged across her brow, sending Lance a strong message to back off.

"I recognize fake when I see it."

"Do you, now?"

"He's a fake hiding something. Don't trust him. Mom, I didn't like the way he…"

"…He what?"

"The way he looked at you and kissed you." He strummed a bad chord on the guitar as if nails were scratching down a chalkboard. "It isn't appropriate for a first date and unbecoming of an Abadie. You need to practice what you preach. We Abadie's have a reputation to maintain. Besides, he's a creep. I don't like him."

"Don't be ridiculous. John is extremely nice, funny, and intelligent. It's not as if we're getting married or eloped. Good grief."

"Mom, you shouldn't be dating at all."

"I'm just going to pretend I didn't hear that. Now go to sleep." Angela blew him a kiss and gently shut the door as Lance continued to play the guitar.

Jamie's tiny bedroom was charmingly bubblegum pink and filled with cheerleading trophies, pop star posters, and a wish board filled with her life goals and dreams, including a photograph of her dream wedding dress. About twenty inches from the ceiling, across three walls, were shelves filled with myriad piggy banks, seventeen in all for each birthday celebrated. There were small ones, big ones, animal ones, princess ones, colorful ones, one marked college fund, one marked car fund, one marked shoe fund, and several with Jamie's name. Jamie plonked onto her twin bed, tossing her cell phone to the side, her legs dangling off it. If there was ever an Edith Ann moment for her, this was it. *This is the worst night of my life.* She grabbed the picture of her from when she was two and her mother strolling along the beach, holding hands from the nightstand. She put two fingers to her mouth, kissing them before gently tapping them on the picture. *No, make that the second worse night.* "Mom, if I ever needed you, it's now." She slammed her fists into the mattress. "I hate this. Where are you, Dad?" She lay back, hugging the picture.

She felt the phone vibrant, so she returned the photo to the nightstand and quickly answered her phone without looking at the caller's I.D. "Daddy!"

"Nope, it's me. I took a chance you'd answer. I can't stand fighting with you, especially when you throw Preston back into the picture."

"Forget Preston! Lance, I'm really worried. My dad's not home. He never even made it to the game, and he's not answering his phone."

"I'm sure he's out with the guys or has a logical explanation." His words to comfort her failed.

Jamie removed her dress, tossed it to the corner onto her overstuffed, pink, fluffy camping-style chair, put on a T-shirt, and then crawled into bed. "He's known he had to escort me for homecoming for a solid month or more. It's not that he didn't have a fair warning. He broke his promise and the long-standing tradition. What's a queen with no dad for an escort? Preston ended up having to do it."

"I saw, and I saw him kiss you." His fists tightened.

"He didn't kiss me. He gave me a peck on the cheek to congratulate me."

"Not from my point of view."

"Well, in European cultures, a peck on the cheek is a simple way of saying hello. A handshake, if you will."

"We're not in Europe. He kissed you!"

"I looked for you. You left."

"Yes, I did, right after he kissed you."

"It sounds like you're a tad bit jealous."

"I should've been your escort."

"You know we can't do that. The timing isn't right."

"I know. It would ruin your good-girl reputation. Blah, blah, blah."

"You knew what you were getting into when we decided to date."

"I didn't know it would be so difficult having to stay away from you all the time."

"Well, I'm sorry, but that still doesn't tell me where my dad is."

"Grow up. He can take care of himself. He's a big man."

"That doesn't stop me from worrying. This isn't like him." She fought to hold back her tears.

"I get it. By the way, a quick reminder about my competition tomorrow. Are you still planning on coming, or did you make plans with Preston?"

"Come on. Nothing is going on between Preston and me."

"You're leading him on or using him to get to me."

"Wait a minute. Yes, I used Preston to escort me. That's all. Again, nothing is going on between us."

Lance puffed his cheeks, holding his anger. "Maybe you should tell him that."

"Trust me; I have."

"You didn't answer me before."

"About what?"

"Are you coming to my competition in the morning?"

"Absolutely. I'll see you there."

Jamie placed the phone under her pillow, grabbed her hot pink plush throw blanket, and snuggled with it. "Dad, where are you?" She flipped to her stomach, to her left side, to her right side, and back to her stomach, but she couldn't sleep. So, instead, she buried her face into her pillow and sobbed, worried sick about her father's whereabouts. She tried one more time calling her father; it went straight to voicemail. "Dad, where are you? Please call me back. I'm worried something terrible has happened."

CHAPTER FIVE

The Morning After

James lay in the hospital bed. He moaned in excruciating pain, falling back onto the bed's pillow. Gritting his teeth to keep his scream in, he pressed the call button for the nurse's station.

"How may we help you?"

"I can't get up and need to go to the bathroom. Can you help me, please?" He gritted his teeth, feeling the throbbing in his leg.

"I'll send the assistant in."

James struggled to sit. Once he did, he scooched until he reached the side drawer. He slid it open. There it was -- his phone. A faint smile fluctuated. He quickly grabbed it, wincing in pain, and dialed. "Finally."

Jamie fumbled to find her phone. When she did, she immediately recognized it was from her father. "Daddy, where are you? You didn't come home last night? I've been worried sick. You better have a good explanation, or I may never speak to you again. So, spill the freakin' beans! What was so important? You missed me being crowned homecoming queen, and I may never forgive you."

"I'm in the hospital. I had a minor accident."

"An accident!" She gasped. "How bad? Are you hurt? Are you okay? What happened? Where are you?" Her heart thrummed against her ribcage, beating faster than it ever had.

"Slow the questions down. One at a time, please."

"I've been really, really worried. How bad are you hurt?"

"Mostly my ego and reputation. Other than that, just a small gunshot wound."

"Gunshot wound! Aunt Sally was right. The city is getting too dangerous to live in."

"It's not what you're thinking. It was an accident."

"Where are you? I'm coming to see you."

"First, go to school. After school, you can visit me."

"You're so silly. I don't have school today. It's Saturday. Let me get dressed, and I'll be on my way."

"I'm really sorry about missing homecoming. I wish I could've been there."

"When you didn't show up, I wished something terrible would happen to you, and it did. This is all my fault." Her voice quivered. "Mom always said to be careful what you wish for because it might come true."

"Nonsense, this happened way before homecoming. Every time I tried to call you, they knocked me out with pain meds. I'm so sorry, sweetie, I let you down." He inched his butt closer to the curve of the bed, hoping to ease his leg pain, but that plan backfired. "Ouch!" Grimacing, he held his breath.

"Dad, you okay? I'm on my way."

"Wait, don't you need to know the name of the hospital first?"

At the breakfast table, Lance ate the breakfast of champions -- cereal. Angela stood at the bar island as she ate a blueberry muffin with cream cheese and drank a cup of coffee. Their housekeeper, Miriam, packed a picnic basket with cheese, crackers, assorted fruit, and several Moon pies. "How much fruit do you want, Master Lance?"

"Enough for two large hungry boys after a winning skate."

"Anything else special you want packed?"

"Great question, Miriam. How about some of your famous crab dip? And please don't forget Tabasco this time; the garlic-flavored one."

"Anything else, Master Lance?"

"Just whatever, thanks."

47

Angela smiled and handed Miriam several paper napkins. "You're so good to my son."

"I treat him as if he's my own." Miriam placed the napkins beside the basket and then busied herself gathering items for the picnic, including retrieving a blue and white checkered tablecloth and folding it into a perfect rectangle before placing it in the basket.

"Mom, now that you have had your coffee, tell me what happened last night."

"Have you watched the news?"

"Do I ever watch the news?"

"Great point. You'd probably won't believe me if I told you."

"Try me. You've raised me well. I'm listening."

"You and Dr. Frasier."

"Dr. Frasier? I don't get it."

"He's a television character. Never mind. I don't know where to start."

"Try starting with the man who brought you home last night?" Lance flashed a frustrated, are-you-serious glance as he gave her the evil eye.

"That was John Legions, a new client. We went to dinner. That's all."

"You went to dinner and came home looking like that! That's some dinner, Mom."

"That's the ending. The beginning starts at the magazine."

"I'm all ears. This has to be good."

"A window washer was about to fall to his death, so I shot at the window to break it to save him. Then, I got arrested."

"Arrested! On what grounds?"

She raised her hand, signaling to stop. "Hold on. It's not what you think. When the police and paramedics arrived, they saw my gun and told me to drop it. So, I did. It fired, sending a bullet right into the man's leg. Then the next thing I knew, they put me in a jail cell with perverts. Dreadfully awful, perverted criminals."

"Well, Mom, I told you that gun would get you into trouble one day."

"I saved a man's life." Her argument seemed futile, as Lance wasn't buying into the story. "If it weren't for me, he'd be dead."

"Where is he now?"

Angela took a sip of her steaming coffee. "That's precisely what I plan on finding out. After that, the least I can do is go see him and bring him flowers."

"I don't know if you should do that. You know what Grandpa always says, 'Let sleeping dogs sleep.'"

"That's sleeping dogs lie."

"Dogs don't lie. Does Grandpa know you went to jail for shooting a man?" He tilted his head, waiting for her response.

"I hope not. And I don't want him ever to find out. Please, keep this little secret between us."

"Little secret? I'd say a huge one. Mom, that'll cost you." He pursed his lips.

"I guess the bargaining chip is in your hands. You can't tell a soul. What do you want?"

Lance rose and hugged his mom. He strode quickly toward the door. "Let me think about it, but it'll cost you plenty." He smirked, knowing he had the upper hand.

Miriam raised the picnic basket. "Don't forget your lunch. There's enough for you and Conrad, as you requested, Master Lance."

"Thanks, Miriam, you're the best. And, for the umpteenth time, it's just Lance." He grabbed the picnic basket. "I'm outta here. Mom, don't forget about my competition today."

"I wouldn't miss it for the world. I have a manicure scheduled, and then I'm headed for the lakefront. I'm so proud of you, son."

Lance slammed the door. Angela grabbed her cell phone. "Siri, what is the number for Blue Bayou Cleaning?"

"I have found one listing for Blue Bayou Cleaning. Would you like for me to call the number for you?"

"Yes."

"…This is Ms. Abadie; you had an employee injured yesterday at *Elite Magazine*… That's correct… Do you know where they took him?… I own *Elite Magazine*. Please put me through to the President of the Company… I don't care if you're just the answering service. Have the President call me immediately… Wait, don't you need my number? …I see, caller I.D. Please repeat it to me so that I am certain you have it… Yes, that's correct. Thank you." Angela slammed the phone down. She grabbed the remote and turned on the news.

Miriam shook her head. "Never a dull moment with you and this family."

"Don't remind me. Sometimes I wish I had a simpler life."

"Breaking news update. I'm Houston Meadows reporting live in front of East Jefferson Mercy Hospital. The window washer who almost fell to his death will make a complete recovery after being shot in the leg by socialite and CEO of *Elite Magazine*, Angela Abadie, when she allegedly discharged her firearm to break the window. Witnesses on the scene say Abadie attempted to rescue the man dangling from the platform. The name of the window washer is being withheld until family members can be located. He is resting comfortably. Stay tuned for more details as we continue to follow this developing story."

"Finally, I've found you. I just need his name."

The phone rang, and Angela picked it up. "Yes, yes! That is great. Thank you for letting me know."

A faint glimmer of a smile touched Angela's lips. "So, window washer, your name is James Seamore. Miriam, I don't think I'll be home for dinner tonight. Can you make sure Lance eats?"

"Of course, Ms. Abadie. I'll make his favorite."

"Oh, don't let his friends come over. I'm not sure if I trust them."

"Of course, Ms. Abadie. No house guests, pool parties, binge parties, pajama parties, pot parties. I get it. Enforce the rules. The no fun house for Master Lance."

"Very funny, Miriam."

"I aim to please."

Jamie glanced at the time on her cell phone and tossed it back onto the bed. After putting on a T-shirt, she shimmied into her jeans, pulling and tugging them. The jeans were a little tight, so she reclined on the bed, flattened her stomach by sucking it in, and holding her breath, she struggled to zip them up. "Okay, I need to exercise. This is getting ridiculous."

She brushed her hair, threw it into a ponytail, and put on tinted moisturizer, blush, and clear gloss. The perfume bottle caught her eyes. She quickly snatched it and sprayed her wrists. The aroma of spring flowers filtered the air as she sniffed, smiling. Bolting for the door, she soon came to a halt, and after glancing at her feet, she realized she hadn't put on her tennis shoes. "Fuzzy socks won't cut it today!"

She searched her closet until she retrieved her favorite pair of tennis shoes. She laced them as quickly as possible and then raced out the bedroom door to the kitchen, grabbed an apple and a cupcake, and bolted out the front door.

Skaters and observers packed the skate park as the metallic bee-hive sound of skaters ripping down the bowls and obstacles built for this tournament filled the air. Several food trucks and assorted merchandise vendors under their shaded canopies created the parameters, as did a row of Porta-potties with long lines. The Thirtieth Annual Lakefront Skateboard State Tournament was in full swing.

Lance, Jeremy, and Conrad, who sat beneath a shade tree, watched skater after skater attempt to set the best record for their run. Lance sat Indian style with his board braced upside-down across his knees. Behind them, four teenagers engaged in competitive, but fun-loving dishing.

Lance took a deep breath as he glanced around the park. "She's not here."

Conrad's brow furrowed as he lit a cigarette. "Who's not here? Your mom?" Sarcasm radiated through his words.

"You know how I hate that stinky smell." Gagging, he fanned the smoke away from his face. "No, a girl from school. She's interested in skating, so I invited her."

"You want a hit." Conrad handed his cigarette to Lance.

"You know I quit." *I quit for Jamie.* "It's too much on my lungs. I'd rather live longer and not smell like an ashtray all day."

"Who are you looking for? I could help you find her."

"Nobody in particular. Just a girl." His eyes darted about, searching for her.

Jeremy pursed his lips. "You're kidding. We both know you're waiting on Jamie."

"Busted! But, come to think of it, my mom isn't here either. Now, that's completely weird. I just spoke to her about this. Our division is up next. I have a title to uphold."

Lance adjusted his knee pads and then strapped on his helmet. In a quick release, he flipped the skateboard into his hand. "Wish me luck; I'm up seventh, and you both know I'd rather go last."

Conrad nodded. "You've got this. You'll nail it on your first run."

"I'm confident; I just don't know where Jamie or my mom is."

"You better go get in line." Jeremy shoved Lance on the shoulder. "We'll watch out for Jamie and your mom. Now go!"

"I will defend my title. Why? Because I'm the best, there is."

Conrad and Jeremy high-fived each other. "He's got this."

"Yes, I do. I'm going to remain the State Champion and then off to Nationals. But, first, I've got to win this. It's all or nothing."

On the wall across from James' hospital bed, the television, although muted, played the news recap of yesterday's tragic event. James lay propped up in bed, blankly staring at the tile ceiling. Because of boredom, he counted the individual tiles. "Thirty-four, thirty-five, thirty-six." A knock on the door sent his eyes toward it. "Enter; I'm decent."

Angela, carrying a spring bouquet and a colorful get-well balloon, entered. "Mr. Seamore, may I come in?"

James looked up bewildered and smiled at Angela. "It's you, the woman with the gun."

"Sorry about that. I didn't mean for any of the bullets to hit you."

"How can I be mad? I would've fallen if you didn't shoot me."

"Correction. I shot at the window." Angela handed him the flowers. "These are for you. I thought maybe they would brighten your day."

"Thank you. I've never been given flowers by a woman before. Please, have a seat."

Angela furrowed her brow, confused as she glanced at the flowers his sister had brought him, still sitting nearby. "I'm not staying long. Work calls. I just wanted to make sure you were alive and not too badly injured from my firing mishap."

"Alive indeed. We haven't formally met. I'm James Seamore."

"Sorry about that. I should've introduced myself when I entered. I'm Angela Abadie, the CEO of *Elite Magazine*. The window you were washing was mine. Well, my family's."

"You saved my life. Ms. Abadie."

"Please, call me Angela. I went to jail because of that."

"I've been watching the news." He grabbed the remote and shut off the television. "That shouldn't have happened. I guess we'll see each other in court."

"I was hoping to avoid that. I can pay all of your medical bills. That's the least I can do for you. My building, your bad luck."

"Angela, I'm kidding. We'll get this dropped. I know you saved my life. You're my guardian angel. And I have insurance, and workman's comp will fill in the rest, so you don't need to cover my bills."

"I really must be going. I have a son who's competing today in a skateboard competition. I promised him I wouldn't miss it for the world."

"Trust me; you don't want to do that. I missed escorting my daughter to homecoming last night. She was crowned queen. I don't think she'll ever forgive me."

"She must be crushed. Being the homecoming queen is the ultimate when you're in high school. How I remember those days." Her lashes fluttered as she reflected on her crowning moment.

"Crushed, but she understands I wasn't out drinking with the guys or bringing home women. Just breaking through windows and getting shot."

"Bringing women home? A playboy?"

"Not at all. Ever since her mother died, she's resented any woman in my life. I'm all she has, so I don't date. And, since we're getting personal, what about Mr. Abadie?"

Angela strolled to the door. "Mr. Abadie is my father. My husband no longer exists in my life, anymore. Don't get me wrong; he's alive but lives in another part of the world with a younger version of me. You know how that goes. His mid-life crisis led to him looking for an alternative way to feel young again. Look, I better be going. The only significant man in my life competes this morning. Take care, James. I'm glad you're alive."

"Come back and see me, okay?"

"I can't make any promises, but I'll keep in touch to stay up to date on your progress. And, James, please call my office if you need anything, and I mean anything at all." She dug through her purse and retrieved her business card. "Here, this is my number. I should be easy to reach."

"I look forward to it."

"Until next time." Angela left, making sure not to let the door slam behind her. *Things are looking up. Thank God he's going to live.*

Angela impatiently stood at the hospital elevator, pressing the down key multiple times. "Come on; I don't have all day."

The elevator door opened, and Jamie bolted from it as Angela entered, the two bumping into each other, without making eye contact.

"Excuse me. I'm so sorry, miss." Angela pressed the first-floor key multiple times.

Jamie ignored Angela and scarpered down the hall.

With butterfly nerves in the pit of his stomach, Lance, seventh in line to skate, tied his shoelaces and double-checked his skateboard's wheels by spinning them. The deafening crowd cheered for Anthony McVay, the winner two years ago, hoping for a comeback run of a lifetime from him. Jeremey stood two people behind Lance. "Give it a rest; you've got this."

Lance glanced around. "That's not it. My mom, she's not here."

"Your mom never misses a competition. She'll be here."

"First, Jamie's dad, now my mom. What's going on?"

"My question exactly. What is going on?"

"I'd have to kill you if I told you."

"Don't pull your CIA crap on me. You're not CIA, and neither is your father. So, give it a rest. She'll be here."

"Guess you're right, but sooner would be better than later."

"Have you tried calling her?"

"Seriously? What do you think?"

"Maybe her phone is dead. Maybe she's caught up at the office. Maybe…"

"… Maybe she just doesn't want to come."

"You know you're talking about your mom, not mine, right? She'll be here. Now, concentrate on your next run. You nail this; it's over for everyone, champ."

While stuck in traffic on the interstate, Angela drew in a long, exasperated breath. Feeling lightheaded, she pressed the recirculate button on the dash to prevent further exhaust fumes from entering her car. A honk fest ensued from several impatient drivers nearby, as if that would ease the traffic jam. "Of all the days. I don't need this." The wreck ahead caused rubberneck traffic to back up for miles, and frustration filled her haughty expression. She glanced at her watch, then at the car's clock. *I have fifteen minutes, or I'll miss it.* "Come on, people, move! I don't have all day." She pressed the speaker call button. "Call Lance."

The phone went directly to voice mail, "I'm skating; you know what to do. If you don't, stop calling me."

"Lance, you need to answer me. What is going on with this traffic?" She impatiently tapped her fingers against the steering wheel.

Angela switched on the radio. "That's right, folks; another wreck on such a beautiful Saturday morning. You know, they make traffic laws for a reason. Don't ride someone's bumper; it causes wrecks, and in today's accident, an eighteen-wheeler toppled, spilling chemicals all over the interstate. Talk about backing up traffic to create a nightmare for the weekend travelers; this was it. Stay your distance, or we all get backed up even more. Off-duty police, the National Guard, and State Troopers have been called in to help. If you can, avoid taking the interstate and try the back roads. It's going to be a while before this chemical spill is cleared."

"Damn!" *He's going to be mad at me. This is all I needed today.*

Angela's cell phone rang. She glanced at the caller's I.D. *Oh, no! He knows.* She pressed the accept button on the console. "Hello, Dad."

"Good morning to you. How's everything going?"

"Oh, office as usual. Nothing out of the ordinary. I'm headed for Lance's skateboard competition."

"I'm hearing rumors there's trouble at the magazine."

"That's the rumor mill for you. Everything is perfect. I even landed a new client this week."

"Tell me more."

"Dad, you left the magazine to retire and enjoy traveling with Mom, so quit worrying about it. I have it all under control."

"Once it's in your blood, it's hard to let go."

"Just let go. Have fun. I have a call coming in. Got to go. Tell Mom I love her."

What else can go wrong? She grabbed a water bottle and chugged its contents.

Jamie sat on a chair beside her dad's hospital bed, holding his hand. Tears filled her eyes. "So, how bad does it hurt?" She used the bed sheet to wipe her tears. "Geez! These sheets are rough."

"Bad enough to say you don't ever want to get shot."

"That bad? I still feel guilty about wanting you to get hurt, you know? I should've never wished that."

"No need to feel guilty, baby girl. I stood you up for an important date. A date we can never get back. Your mom would be so proud of you. She always dreamed of seeing you go to homecoming, graduating, go off to college, get married, and give us seven grandbabies."

"Wait a minute. Hold your horses. Seven grandbabies? I don't think so." She wrinkled her nose.

"All of that in due time; first, we have to get you graduated and enrolled in college. How're the entrance essays coming along?"

"Dad, not now. How long before you can come home?"

Dr. Jennings, carrying a chart, entered the room with several eager interns. "Good morning, Mr. Seamore. How are you feeling today?"

"See, Jamie, you can ask the good doctor yourself?"

"When does my dad get to go home?"

"Well, young lady, that depends on your dad's recovery. It'll be at least a couple more days. We want to ensure he doesn't develop complications or get an infection. There's nothing to worry about. Your dad was lucky; the bullet didn't cause any nerve or bone damage. He'll make a full recovery in time and will need physical therapy."

"See, Jamie. I'll be just fine, just like I said. There's nothing to worry about."

"Other than infection or complications." Dr. Jennings wrote on his tablet.

"Wait, what complications are we talking about?" Jamie's eyes widened in fear. "How long will it take for him to heal and go back to work?"

"Not now, Jamie. There won't be any complications. Will there be, Dr. Jennings? I'll return to work when I can."

Dr. Jennings cleared his throat. "I certainly hope there aren't any complications. The bullet barely grazed your thigh. It looked worse than it was. The goal is to keep the wound clean and let it heal. I say you'll be back to normal within four to six weeks. You'll have to be careful not to aggravate it and not attempt to use your leg too quickly. That's when complications set in."

"Got it! No complications. Four to six weeks of recovery with no work. All of that is doable."

"Dad, you're not the best patient, so you better behave, or I'll call Aunt Sally."

"You'll do no such thing."

"Well, Dad. You better be on your best behavior and follow all the doctor's instructions. Or else! Speaking of instructions, Dr. Jennings, what are your orders for my dad?"

"Mr. Seamore, we'll keep you on antibiotics and pain meds for the next seven days and keep a close eye on things for the next two before we assess whether I can discharge you without complications. Once discharged, you'll begin physical therapy, and in due course, make a complete recovery. I'm certain of that. I don't think you'll even have a limp, since there is no bone or muscle damage. Just a few centimeters more, the outcome would have been devastating. Again, you're one lucky man."

"That is for a gunshot victim."

"Dad, that's not fair. You said it was an accident."

"Sweetie, I was kidding. I have to keep my sense of humor in this, or I'll lose my mind."

"Do you see me laughing? Dad, I'm worried sick about this."

"I assure you, your dad will make a full recovery. He'll need lots of help once released, though. The best thing you can do during this time is to be there for him. Mr. Seamore, I'll arrange home health care for you before you're discharged."

"I'm a gunshot patient, not a geriatric one. I don't need home health care."

"Dad, you'll do exactly what Dr. Jennings says. Nothing more, and nothing less. Got it?"

"You are your mother's daughter."

"I'll take that as a compliment." She tilted her nose upward, taking pride that she was like her mother, sweet music to her ears.

The skateboard park was filled with enthusiastic cheering spectators, expecting the next run. "And next to skate is our defending state champion, who scored the highest score ever in our tournament last year." The announcer's voice boomed over the speakers. "Are you ready? Lance Garrett Billiot will certainly put on a show for us on this glorious Saturday morning, but he needs the run of a lifetime to overcome McVay's last run. He has his work cut out for him."

Lance proudly stood at the top of the pipe. He glanced around for his mother and Jamie, but saw neither. He briefly closed his eyes, took a deep breath, and then put on his game face and rolled fast down the first slope to a cheering crowd as Conrad and Jeremy watched. His first trick, a caballerial, a 360-degree turn while riding backward, was flawlessly performed. *One down, five to go.* A kickflip ensued, followed by a McTwist, a 540-degree turn on the ramp with a perfect landing.

"Look at this run. This kid is amazing. Wait, wait for it. Yes, a switch stance. Wow! Incredible, the centripetal force this kid has. I would have to place this kid up there with Rodney Tullen, Eric Rodriguez, Bucky Masek, and Tony Lark. We'll surely see this kid in the Olympics if he keeps this up. And now an ollie! I can't believe my eyes. That has to be at least forty feet in the air. The world record is forty-five, held by Adrian Garcia. If it is measured at forty feet, that will be a new world record in this divisional group. He must be going at least ninety miles per hour. Folks, you don't see this kind of skate every day at the high school level. Lance just made the run of a lifetime. I don't think anyone in this field of skaters can beat this run. Maybe not even Lance could do this perfect run again. Now, that's how it is done."

Once Lance completed his run, he stood at the landing and gazed at the crowd, pursing his lips. *It's lonely at the top when the ones you love aren't here.*

Frustration abounded as Angela blew her car horn. "Please, please, move." She slammed her fist against the steering wheel and broke another nail. *Just great! What else can go wrong?*

"It looks like the traffic jam on the interstate won't clear for hours because of a chemical spill. If you're stuck in that mess, I hope you brought your lunch with you and water. It will be a very long wait to clear the roads."

She rolled her eyes as she turned off the radio. The phone rang, and she quickly answered using the speaker.

"This is Angela Abadie."

"Good morning, Angela. It's John."

Her heart skipped a beat, hearing his welcomed voice. "Good morning. Well, not really; I'm stuck in traffic."

"You mean that nasty spill on the interstate?"

"The very one. This is when flying would've been better than driving."

"I can send a chopper for you if you'd like."

"A chopper? I don't think they'll allow a helicopter to land on the interstate to pick me up. But thanks for the offer."

"Speaking of offers, have you checked your calendar for our date tonight?"

"Not yet. I haven't even made it to the office today. I went and paid a hospital visit to the window washer."

"You went to see him?" John's face turned crimson as he clenched his jaw. "Interesting, he didn't shoot you back, did he?" Although his statement sounded like a joke, it was filled with anger.

"Not at all. He was kind and grateful that I saved his life."

"He should be. He'd be dead without you."

"At least he'll make a full recovery. I'm thankful for that."

"Look, even if you don't have the charity event tonight, how about dinner? I have reservations at Commander's Palace in the Garden Room."

"Consider it a date if we don't attend the charity event. I'll let you know after I confirm things with Francis."

"Perfect. By the way, how did your son do in his competition?"

"Your guess is as good as mine, I'm stuck here, and according to the time, he's already made his run. I've tried calling him, but it keeps going straight to his voicemail."

"Look, where's he competing? I'll drive by and check things out for you."

"That's not necessary. He'll call me, eventually. I just hope he maintained his title."

"Title, as in royalty?"

"Don't be silly; he's the Defending State Champion headed for the Olympics someday."

"He's that good?"

"Better than good."

"A friend of mine is a professional skateboarder. Maybe your son has heard of him. Does Tony Lark ring any bells?"

"That's my son's idol. He worships him. His room is filled with his posters."

"I'll set an appointment up so they can meet."

"You don't have to do that."

"I never said I had to. This is something I want to do for him. Lance, right? I'll set it up."

Jamie glanced up at the wall clock above the television – 11:16 a.m. and then handed her dad a cherry Jell-O cup. "Anything else? Are you sure you don't want to finish your lunch?" She waited patiently for his answer.

"Nope, all's good. And thank you for showing me your homecoming pictures. You look so beautiful. I wish I could've been there for you."

"Me too. I'm just glad you're alive."

"Better than alive."

Jamie glanced at her watch. "I've got to go to the library for my semester research project." She felt the tinge of guilt deep in her stomach from the lie she had just told.

"Since when is the school library open on a Saturday?"

"Not that library. The public library down the street from the school."

"Whatever happened to researching on the Internet? Not fast enough for you?"

"Very funny, Dad. Teacher's guidelines. We have to use at least two resources besides the internet. One of them can be an interview of someone famous or making a name for themselves."

"Sounds intriguing. What's your project?"

"Don't know yet. That's what I'm trying to figure out. I'm thinking of doing it about one of Louisiana's most successful businesswomen. Maybe Ms. Abadie, who runs *Elite Magazine*."

"You can't do that!" His heart raced.

"Why not?"

"Not a good idea. Maybe focus on the Saints owner. She's made quite a name for herself."

"I'll consider her. Anyway, gotta go, Dad."

Jamie's cell phone rang, and she looked at the caller's I.D. before answering it. "I'm on my way. I had to see my dad. He's in the hospital. I'll explain later."

James, questionably, gawked at Jamie.

She twisted her ponytail around her index finger, trying to come up with a good lie. "Study group with Melissa. I'm late. Gotta go." Jamie fled the room. "Yes, I'm on my way now. I promise."

The hospital door closed, and James confusingly shook his head. "Not even a kiss goodbye."

Jamie quickly reentered and planted a kiss on her dad's forehead. "Oh, I love you. Stay in bed."

"Like I have a choice."

"No choice. Stay in bed." She held her phone several inches from her ear.

"After your study group, go straight home. I don't want to have to worry about you."

"Dad, I'm almost eighteen. I got this. I'll take care of the house. We have plenty of groceries and peanut butter and jelly sandwiches." She kissed him again. "Love you, now rest."

"Love you too, girl. Just let me know when you get home, please."

"Sure thing." She bolted from the room pressing her phone against her ear. "Yeah, I'm on my way now. Where do you want to meet?"

Jamie waited patiently under the tree at the park. She saw Lance approach, carrying the picnic basket in one hand and his skateboard in the other.

Waving enthusiastically, Jamie grinned as her heart fluttered. "About time you got here."

"As if I'm even late." He gently kissed her on the cheek.

She sniffed his shirt and smiled.

"What are you doing?"

"Checking for cigarette smoke. You know I hate that awful trashcan smell."

"I quit for you. I told you that."

She sniffed him again. "Good job, keep it up. Here, let me take the basket."

"If you insist." He handed it over.

They strolled hand in hand.

"How's your dad?"

"He's doing great."

"What happened, if you don't mind me asking?"

"He had a small accident at work and will be out of work for about six weeks."

"Yikes! Give me the details, please."

"It's kinda embarrassing, and he would rather I didn't talk about it, so I won't. Please don't think I'm hiding anything from you; I just promised my dad I wouldn't say anything."

"I completely understand. Weird. Something happened with my mom yesterday at work, and she doesn't want me to talk about it either. Parentals, they're as crazy as they come."

They stopped, stared at each other, and Lance leaned over to kiss Jamie.

Jamie beamed from ear to ear. "Congratulations on winning again. I'm really, really sorry I wasn't there."

"No apology necessary. Things happen. If it were my mom in the hospital, you better believe I would've seen her first. You did the right thing."

"I still feel bad about it. I promised you I'd come and watch. Now, that moment is gone forever,"

"Not so; I just won State, so, now on to Nationals and the X-games. So, be there or be square."

"Where is Nationals? Not sure if my dad would let me go out of state without him, and I'm not asking him to take me. He can't know we're dating until after I graduate."

"Don't worry; the tournament this year is in Biloxi."

"That makes me feel better. Only an hour and a half drive. Now, that's doable, for sure."

"You hungry?"

"I thought you'd never ask. This basket is getting heavy."

He placed the skateboard down and then grabbed the basket, stationing it at his feet. He opened the lid, retrieved the blue and white checkered tablecloth from the top, and spread it out beneath one of the oak trees. "I think you'll like what I packed. That is, if you like cheese, fruit, and crackers." He extended his hand.

"Sounds delish."

"Here, My Queen, take a load off your feet." Reaching for her hand, he helped her to sit on the tablecloth. Once she settled, he sat next to her and unpacked the food, presenting a nice spread for their lunch.

"Man, you went all out."

"I can't take all the credit. I had help packing this."

"Your mom did this for us?"

"Not exactly; our housekeeper, Miriam, put this all together. She loves doing this for me. Even when Conrad and I were in kindergarten, she made us a picnic basket for the backyard. Granted, mostly cookies, chips, and candy back then, but now that I have a refined taste, the picnic items have changed. The only thing I don't like is caviar."

"Man, my family picnics are peanut butter and grape jelly sandwiches and a bag of chips. On a lucky day, maybe a cookie or two."

"That still sounds amazing."

"Only if you're into peanut butter and jelly. My friend Melissa ate one, not knowing she was allergic to peanuts. She broke out in hives and had to go to the hospital. It wasn't pretty. She almost died."

"That sounds a bit scary."

"Scary, yea. Especially when you're only seven."

"Shall we eat? I'm starving. I worked up a major appetite."

"You don't have to ask me but once. I'm hangry."

Lance opened the crab dip, carefully put it on a cracker, and handed it to Jamie. "This is the best crab dip ever. Miriam is famous for it at our parties."

She sniffed it. "Smells wonderful. I've never eaten crab dip before."

"You've got to be kidding me. You live in Louisiana and never had crab dip?"

"We can't afford things like this. So, it's a real treat."

"Take a bite; tell me what you think."

She took a small bite, savoring the taste. "Amazing." She engulfed the rest. "This is truly the best thing I've ever eaten."

He quickly prepared several more crackers with the dip. "We have plenty, so no need to be shy."

Her eyes widened, taking another bite. "This is so good." Crackers spewed from her mouth as she talked.

Lance grabbed a napkin and gently wiped the crumbs from her lips. "I'm glad you like it." He smiled.

"I don't like it; I love it. I'm hooked on crab dip. My lips are even tingling because this is so good."

The wind blew Jamie's hair into her face, and Lance gently brushed it away, securing it behind her ear. He leaned in and kissed her.

Jamie sneezed, spewing even more crackers and dip.

Lance chuckled wiping the crumbs from his face and shirt. "That certainly wasn't the most romantic kiss I have ever had."

"Ah-chew!" She covered her mouth and nose with her hands. She squirmed, scratching her arms, neck, and legs. "Ah-chew. Ah-chew!" The intensity of her sneezes increased, including the automatic jerking of her entire body.

"You okay?"

"I think I'm allergic to something." Jamie's eyes swelled, and she broke out into more hives.

"As long as it's not me, we'll be okay."

"No, really, take me home. I need Benadryl or something. I can't stand this itching." Jamie rigorously continued to scratch her arms and legs. "I'm not feeling too good."

"Define not feeling good."

She clutched her stomach. "Cramps! Itching! Sneezing!" She gagged. "And, nausea. Ah-chew!"

"Jamie, I don't want to be the bearer of bad news, but…"

"…But what?" She scratched her neck as it reddened, and more hives developed. "I can't take this. What is going on? I don't have time for this. The homecoming committee has to meet up at the gym later today to clean up from the dance."

"Are you sure you want to go looking like that?"

"Like what?" The hives glowed redder as her complexion turned pale.

"You don't want to know."

Within seconds, Jamie vomited, barely missing the blanket. "I'm not feeling so well. Please, take me home." Jamie gasped for air as she furiously scratched her arms and legs.

"Maybe I should take you to the emergency room. Your hives are getting worse, and you're sweating bullets. I'm no doctor, but I think you might be going into anaphylactic shock. You don't think you're allergic to crab, do you?"

"How am I supposed to know if I've never eaten it before?" Jamie's eyes swelled almost shut as her lips engorged, making her look like a puffer fish. "This isn't good. Is it?"

"Not in the least. I'm taking you to the emergency room. And don't even try to talk me out of it. Never mind, maybe I should call for an ambulance." He searched for his phone. "Oh crap, I didn't get my phone back from Conrad. The emergency room it is."

"I have my cell."

He grabbed it and dialed 911.

Angela, still stuck in traffic, talked on her phone to Francis. "Listen, I know, just check my calendar. When is the charity event?"

"It's next Saturday, Ms. Abadie."

"Are you certain?"

"Yes, of course, I am. Your calendar is clear for this evening."

"Perfect, please call John Legions and tell him I am free for dinner tonight, and the charity event is next Saturday."

"You want me to call Mr. Legions for you?"

"Didn't I just tell you to?"

"Absolutely. Anything else, Ms. Abadie?"

"Yes, call Nancy at the salon and tell her I need her to come to my office this afternoon to do my nails. I don't know when I'm getting out of this gridlock."

"Yes, ma'am. Oh, Ms. Abadie. You have a secret admirer. I forgot to tell you a dozen yellow roses were delivered to your office about thirty minutes ago."

"Who are they from?"

"It doesn't say, it only says, 'Waiting to hear from you. Have a pleasant day.' Do you have any idea who they are from?"

"I have my suspicions."

In the East Jefferson Mercy Hospital's emergency triage unit bed, Jamie slept to the rhythm of the heart monitor. When she opened her eyes, she was at first dazed and confused, continuing to scratch her arms and legs.

A nurse entered carrying a syringe and inserted it into the I.V. "You've got to stop scratching. It'll only make things worse."

"What hospital is this?"

"You don't know?"

"I don't remember."

"You're at East Jefferson Mercy Hospital."

"I just remember eating crab dip and getting sick."

"That's what the young man who brought you in said. He hasn't been here in a while, though."

"I vaguely remember sending him home."

"We've called each number on your emergency card on file. We didn't reach your dad, but your Aunt Sally is on her way."

"My dad will kill me."

"Are you in danger at home?"

"No, it's nothing like that. My aunt and dad don't get along, that's all."

"Toodledo!" Aunt Sally pulled back the curtain and entered. "How's my sweet baby girl? You look dreadful. Simply dreadful!"

"Thanks, Aunt Sally. Like I needed to hear that."

"Well, dreadful doesn't describe whatever this is." She waved as if to dismiss the incident. "Has your father been here to see you?"

"No, he's here in this hospital, too. Will you take me to see him?"

The nurse scolded Jamie with her gaze. "I don't think you're going anywhere until the doctor sees you. You'll just have to stay put."

"You can't make me. If you don't find me a wheelchair right now, I'll get up and walk out. I mean it. I do. I want to see my dad."

The nurse recorded Jamie's blood pressure. "It's a little high, but understandable with the stress your body is experiencing. I gave you epinephrine, and the steroid shots from earlier should be kicking in soon. You'll be back to normal in a day or two."

"A day or two. I don't have a day or two."

Aunt Sally kissed Jamie's forehead. "Honey, let's see what the doctor has to say first. She's only the nurse."

"Now! I want to go see my dad."

"As soon as the doctor comes in to check on you, I'll promise to take you to see your dad."

"Aunt Sally, you pinky swear?" She held up her hand and curled her pinky.

"Have I ever lied to you? Don't answer that. Pinky swear!" They twisted their pinkies together as if they were best friends in middle school. "Now, how did you get into this dreadful situation?"

"A friend of mine brought crab dip for our study break. Apparently, I'm allergic to it."

"I'd say by the looks of you. So was your mother."

"I didn't know that."

"There's a lot you don't know about your mother."

"Like what?"

"Like her being allergic to crab and all shellfish, for one."

"No way."

"Afraid so. She had the same reaction you're having if she even touched a crab. It was dreadful."

"Nobody thought to tell me this. Are you serious?" She gently brushed her right cheek, grimacing.

"I guess I always thought you knew."

"Any more family secrets I should know about? Like, what else could kill me?"

"Your mother was allergic to bees, too. So, I'd stay away from them at all costs. And poison ivy, and snakes."

"Snakes? You can be allergic to snakes?"

"No, silly, they bite and are poisonous, which equates to possibly killing you."

"Snakes. Got it. Stay away from snakes."

"And grasshoppers. Especially the chocolate-covered ones."

"Are you kidding me?"

"You're probably not allergic, but they taste crunchy gross."

"You don't have to worry about that, Aunt Sally. Chocolate-covered grasshoppers won't be on my diet anytime soon. And neither will crab dip."

The small curtain pulled open. "Good afternoon, I'm Dr. Jennings. Wait, don't I know you from somewhere?"

"I'm Jamie Seamore. We met earlier today. My dad, James Seamore… the gunshot to the leg by a crazy lady."

"Oh, yes. It didn't take you long to get into trouble, young lady. What happened?"

"Come on, can't you read the chart? I'm having an allergic reaction to crab. Now, can I go see my father?"

"Allergic to crab. Well, you certainly can't afford to have another episode like this. Let's run other tests to see what else you're allergic to. Another exposure could kill you."

"Seriously! Kill me for eating something." Tears flushed as horror swept up her spine. "Wait, like my friend Melissa, who can't eat peanuts?"

"I don't know about your friend, but you were lucky this time. You'll have to spend the night for observation, and we'll start with a skin prick test this afternoon. With each exposure, the potential to do more harm or even kill you increases. By early morning, you should be able to go home."

"What about this itching? When will it stop?"

"I've ordered you cortisone cream with lidocaine and another dose of Benadryl on top of the epinephrine. Those will help with the itch. I'll also prescribed you prednisone to take home. And I strongly advise you to stop scratching the hives before leaving scars on your pretty face. A long soak in a tub with oatmeal will help, too."

"An oatmeal bath? What the heck is that?" Her lips twisted as her brow creased, resembling a Pekingese dog.

"Exactly how it sounds." Dr. Jennings observed Jamie's reaction. "Oats contain avenanthramides, polyphenols that soothe irritated and itchy skin. So, you'll get relief from the itching."

"Sounds dreadful. Now, Aunt Sally, can you take me to see my dad? There isn't anything wrong with me that oatmeal can't fix."

Aunt Sally glanced at Dr. Jennings. "What do you think about her going to see her dad?"

"I'll order a wheelchair and an orderly. You'll only be able to see him for fifteen minutes, though, for both of your sake, then right back here. Are we clear on that, young lady? Fifteen minutes, and that's it."

"Yes, sir. Fifteen minutes."

Angela rested her head on the steering wheel, listening to the traffic updates on the radio. "Word is in; traffic has started to clear after the chemical spill. For some, it has been a long seven hours."

Her cell phone rang, and she quickly picked it up. "Angela Abadie."

"Mom, I defended my title. I won the State Championship!"

"That's great, honey. I'm sorry I wasn't there; I've been stuck on the interstate. There was a chemical spill, and it was deadlocked."

"I wondered why you didn't make it. Everything okay?"

"Traffic is starting to move a little. I still have to go to the office, and tonight I have another business dinner."

"With who?"

"It's with whom and none of your business."

"Mom, you know I don't like you dating. What would my dad think?"

"Honey, he lost that right when he divorced me. So, I'm not concerned about your father, and nor should you be."

"You're going out with Mr. Legions, aren't you?"

"Why would you say that?"

"After last night, you looked very friendly with him. Too friendly, if I may say so."

"Who's the parent here?"

"You are, Mom, but sometimes, I think I am. After all, I am the man of the house now."

"What are your plans for this evening?"

"The skateboarders and I are going to celebrate by getting burgers. The owner of Skater's Paradise invited me. He says he has a surprise for me as one of my sponsors since winning back-to-back titles. Then, I'll come home. I'm exhausted. It's been a long day."

"Long day indeed. Just be careful and have fun. Please text me when you get home."

"I always do. I'm the responsible one. You come home in one piece and try not to shoot anyone."

"Enough, Lance. You're never going to let me forget about this, are you?"

"For a price, which I haven't decided on just yet. Just kidding. I love you, Mom. Don't stay out too late, and don't do anything foolish. I don't need a baby brother or sister taking over my inheritance."

"Very funny, Lance. But I assure you, if any hanky-panky goes on, we'll use protection."

"Mom, don't go there. That's just too much information and grosses me out."

"Then stop butting into my dating life."

"That's the point. You shouldn't have a dating life! You're in your forties and not twenty anymore."

"You know what they say, the forties are the new twenties."

"Not by the way I count. Mom, seriously, be careful, and don't do anything stupid."

CHAPTER SIX

All's Fair in Love and War

L ance, proudly carrying his three-foot brass trophy in the shape of a skateboard and engraved with "Louisiana State National Skateboard Championship," Conrad, and Jeremy entered the small burger joint near Skater's Paradise skatepark decked out with corrugated metal walls, red leather booths, red lacquered shelves full of collector skateboards and first-place trophies, various plaques, and a black-and-white checkered stained concrete floor. The chalkboard menu behind the counter listed drinks and food items named after famous skateboarders. Over in the corner sat Preston and several of his jock friends.

"Look who crashed our party." Lance nodded toward Preston. "I guess winning last night's football game wasn't enough."

"They aren't worth the time of day. Ignore them." Conrad gently shoved Lance toward a booth. "Let's sit as far away from them as possible."

"Agreed." Lance plopped down and sat his trophy next to him, ensuring Preston could see it in full view.

Jeremy scooted into the corner of the booth, and Conrad quickly followed.

"You certainly made a statement today. Winning State two years in a row." Conrad hurled a sugar packet at Lance. "Hey, you in there? You seem lost?"

"Sorry, I was daydreaming."

"Since when do you daydream?"

"When I have a beautiful girl in my life."

Jeremy's brow creased with disgust at the saccharine sentiment. "Where is she?"

"In the hospital."

"What? Wait! Why?" Conrad's eyes lit as he pushed his hair away from his face.

"I blame myself. I didn't know she was allergic to crab. Lunch didn't turn out well."

"Crab! You mean Miriam's famous crab dip? Wow, sorry to hear that."

Rae, a high school server, stopped at the table. "You guys ready to order?"

"Your name is Rae, right?" Smiling, Lanced glanced up at her.

"Yes, how'd you know that?"

"Besides your nametag, we have physics together. Third period."

"Oh, didn't notice. Sorry. What would you like to order?"

Lance held up his trophy. "I'll go first." He quickly sat it back down. "I'll have a burger with extra sharp cheddar cheese, extra crispy fries, and a chocolate milkshake."

Conrad crossed his arms leaning back. "The same. And I'm dying of thirst. A glass of water too."

"Me too!" Jeremy nodded.

Rae held up her finger. "Wait, you're Lance, the skateboarder. I saw you on the news. Congratulations. I should've known by the trophy. Duh! I thought you were just a creepy kid, but I guess you have ambition and goals. I've always wanted to skate."

The manager approached Lance and his friends. "Congratulations on your big win, Lance! After today, I named a burger after you, and your order is on the house." The manager strolled back to behind the counter and pointed to the chalkboard. He picked up the chalk and scribbled, "Lance Burger Combo."

Rae smiled as her cheeks blushed crimson. "One Lance Burger Combo coming your way."

"See, guys, not everyone is stuck up around here." Lance's celebration was quickly cut short. "Oh, boy, don't look now, but guess who's heading our way."

Jeremy rolled his eyes. "Mr. Arrogant Quarterback."

"You got that right."

Preston strode right up to Lance, stepping into his personal space as if he had a reserved invitation. "Nice trophy for a punk." He leaned against the table.

"If that's your way of congratulating me, you missed your mark. Move on; there's nothing to see here."

"I was only trying to be friendly. Just remember, it's all fair in love and war."

"What do you mean by that?"

"My girl, Jamie. I see the way you look at her. Keep your hands off, or else."

"If you're looking for a fight, don't! I wouldn't want to have to smash your pretty boy face."

Lance stood as the manager quickly emerged from behind the counter. "Boys, not here, not now! Or you both can leave and never come back."

After clenching his fists to knuckle-white, Lance slowly sat back down. "You're not worth it."

Preston slammed his fist onto the table. "You're right; you're not worth it. You're a weasel!"

"I don't care if you think I'm a serial-killing cannibal related to Jeffrey Dahmer, I know I'm better than you."

"Boys, I said enough." The manager threw his hands up in the air. "It's over. Move on!"

Preston gestured for his entourage to meet him at the exit. They all obeyed as if in a cult and left.

"You know, guys, if either of you were creeps like him, you wouldn't be my friends." Lance held up his trophy. "To the sweet victory of success."

"To the Lance burger!"

The orderly pushed Jamie into her dad's hospital room. "Dad, Dad, wake up. It's me, Jamie."

"Miss, Dr. Jennings has allowed you fifteen minutes to visit your father, then I'll have to return you to the E.R."

"Yes, sir. I'll be ready."

The orderly left.

"Jamie, sweetheart, I wasn't expecting you." Bemused, he slowly rolled over and opened his eyes. "What the hell happened to you?" His eyes widened.

"Toodledo."

"Please don't tell me Aunt Sally's here."

"Then I won't. Dad, how are you feeling?"

"Better question, how are you feeling, and what is going on?"

Sally held up her finger. "Well, James, if you insist on knowing, Jamie is just like her mother."

"Meaning?"

"Dad, I ate crab dip."

"Wow, I didn't know you were allergic."

"Me either. But, I am."

"Like mother, like daughter. And why did you call Aunt Sally?"

"She didn't. I'm on the emergency call list, remember? Just like yours."

"We've got to immediately fix that."

"Wait a minute. I think it is imperative now that she's ill and you're still in the hospital she live with me. I'll make the arrangements to take Jamie back to Georgia."

"Absolutely not!" James winced in pain.

"I agree with my dad. I'm staying here to take care of him."

"Both of you are making a serious mistake. My sister is probably rolling over in her grave."

James struggled with the pain, wincing with every move. "That's on account of you, Sally. Don't you think it's time for you to return to Georgia?"

"Aunt Sally, do you mind stepping out of the room for a minute? I need to speak with my dad in private."

"I know when I'm not welcome. Seeing how you both have everything under control, I'm leaving."

James smiled at his sister-in-law. "Is that a threat or a promise?"

"You haven't heard the last from me, James Seamore. And Jamie, the offer always stands for you to come live with me in Georgia. I know that's what your mother would want."

Jamie placed her hands on her hips. "You have no idea what my mom would want. You weren't there when she spoke her last words to us. I remember them as if it were yesterday. You know what she said?"

"I haven't a clue."

"Exactly! Because you're clueless. She told us to always take care of each other, no matter what. And that's what we've been doing."

"Don't you think it's time to keep your promise?" James pointed at the door. "Toodledo, Sally."

"Fine, but you haven't seen the last of me. Just remember, all's fair in love and war." She bee-lined for the door just as the orderly returned.

"Miss, it's time for me to take you back."

"Just one more minute, please."

"Jamie, do as he says. You need to be taken care of, too."

"But Dad. I don't want to leave you. Why can't I just stay here?" She pouted and batted her lashes at the orderly, hoping he'd change his mind and let her stay.

James smiled. "I think it is called because you're in the hospital."

"Miss, I have to take you back."

"Jamie, you need to listen to the orderly, and your doctor."

"Yes, sir. Dad, I'll be back as soon as I can. I love you."

"I love you too. Now, go back to your room and do what your doctor says."

The limo pulled up in front of the iconic teal and white striped awning of Commander's Palace, nestled in the Garden District of Uptown, New Orleans. The driver exited and opened the door for Angela and John. "Have a good evening, sir. I'll be here when you're finished."

"Thank you, Robby. It's always a pleasure for you to drive me when I'm in town."

"My pleasure, sir."

John extended his arm. "Shall we?"

Angela hooked her arm in his. "Absolutely, I'm starving. I haven't eaten all day." She sniffed the air, taking in the aroma coming from the kitchen. "It smells heavenly."

"That's not good on your system."

"I didn't exactly have food in my car while stuck on the interstate for seven hours. Then, the rush to publish the latest edition, had to get my nails done, check on Lance, hire a new wardrobe specialist, fire a reporter, and the list goes on forever."

"Forget all of that. Let's enjoy dinner and each other's company."

"Agreed."

He opened the door to the restaurant, and they stepped in. The hostess immediately approached. "Good evening, Mr. Legions. It's a pleasure having you dine with us again."

"Thank you, Rachael, the pleasure is all mine, I assure you."

"This way."

Rachael led John and Angela through the main dining room, up the stairs, and into the green garden room. She sat them at the best table in the corner. One server immediately approached Angela and pulled her chair out for her. She sat, and he gently placed the crisp white linen napkin across her lap and left.

"This is one of my favorite places in all of New Orleans. Every time I fly in, I make reservations."

"You have great taste, John. I've been coming here with my family for forty years or more. It's our go-to for special events."

"Lucky family. People come from around the world to eat here, and it is literally right up the street from your house. It doesn't get better than that."

"What about you, Mr. Lucky? I'm sure you've eaten at your fair share of famous places worldwide."

"This I can't deny. That's one perk of owning a corporate jet liner company." He nodded extremely arrogantly.

The server, an old Black man with salt and pepper balding hair, dressed in the restaurant's signature black tuxedo with a crisp white shirt and black tie, approached. "Good evening, Mr. Legions." He placed a menu in front of both. "Welcome back. Do you want your usual cocktail?"

"It's good to see you again, too, Reginald. First, Angela, what would you like?"

"I'll start with my favorite cranberry cosmopolitan."

"One cranberry cosmopolitan, and for you, Mr. Legions?"

"A dirty martini, extra dry, shaken."

"I'll be back with your menus and cocktails."

Angela smiled at John. "The staff seems to know you."

"As I said, I frequently come here. I love everything about the Haute Creole cuisine they serve."

She opened the menu. "Don't forget about the bread pudding souffle." Angela's eyes glistened.

"How can I? It's the best in the world."

"Maybe we should bypass dinner and start with the dessert."

"I'm looking forward to the Wild Louisiana White Shrimp."

"You haven't even opened your menu."

" I can only get it here. My mouth waters just thinking about it. And you?"

Angela glanced up from her menu. "I'm leaning toward the Chimichurri Marinated Veal Tender. I can never go wrong with that."

"Excellent choice. How did Lance do in the tournament?" John sipped his water.

"Wow, this conversation took a three-sixty. I'm the proud mother of a two-repeat State Champion. He goes to Nationals next spring and hopes to qualify for the X-games. He hasn't been old enough until now."

"That's quite the ambition. Does he get that from you or his father?"

"Neither. My dad dabbled in high-octane sports, racing cars mostly. Corvettes. But he did his fair share of mogul racing and snowboarding. Living in the South, the closest thing to that was a skateboard. So, he gave Lance his first skateboard and then gave him lessons. I never approved, thinking it was rather dangerous, but they overruled me. And now, I have a future Olympic Champion on my hands."

"So, is he going to compete and not go to college?"

"He'd better not. He's destined to take over the magazine one day. He'll need that college education."

"I've done a little research." He scratched his chin. "Did you know that skateboarding improves a person's mental health, fosters community, and encourages diversity and resilience?"

"Whose side are you on?"

"No side, just stating the facts. I would be a lawyer now if I had listened to my mother, which sounds dreadful. And besides, my dad wanted me to follow in his footsteps, too. I think it's important for everyone to find a career they love."

"So, you're one of those. Find a job you love and never work a day in your life."

"Exactly! Are you happy running *Elite*?"

"Absolutely! It's my life. I've always wanted to own it. I love it. So, I guess this means I don't work."

"Great point."

Reginald returned with their cocktails, gently placed them in front of them, and left the table.

John held up his glass. "To loving what we do and never working a day in our lives."

"I'll cheer to that."

Staring into each other's eyes, they sipped their cocktails.

"Oh, I forgot to thank you for the beautiful roses you sent. They were such a pleasant treat to see after my hectic day."

"Roses? I didn't send you flowers, but now I think I should have." A pinch of jealousy shot through him.

"If you didn't send them, then who?"

"Now, that's the mystery question of the evening." He clenched his jaw.

The hospital room was dark, with only the streetlamps illuminating the room through the blinds. Curled up in the peach recliner with a pillow and blanket in the corner, Lance dozed on and off. Jamie slept even though she scratched herself in her sleep, tossing and turning. "Mom? No!" Inundated with a nightmare, her sleep created a restless slumber; she whimpered in her sleep as flashes of her mom's last breath surfaced.

Lance sat up and went to Jamie.

"No! Mom! Come back!" Her mumbles had a painful and remorseful tone.

He rose and tip-toed to the bed. "Jamie, wake up! You're having a nightmare." Lance gently shook Jamie's arm. "Wake up."

Jamie slowly opened her eyes. "Lance, what time is it?"

"It's one in the morning. My mom is out late tonight, so I thought I'd sneak out and see you. I felt like a spy sneaking in here to be with you. How are you feeling?"

"Still itchy, but the vomiting and cramps are gone. It could be worse. I'll never eat crab dip again."

"I would think not."

"How long have you been here?"

"About an hour. I didn't want to wake you. You needed your rest."

"How thoughtful. Thanks for being here."

"I couldn't leave you here all alone, especially since it's kinda my fault you're here in the first place."

"I should've known I was allergic, but no one bothered to tell me."

"Shhh. Get some rest." He gently stroked her hair, trying to comfort her.

The night nurse entered the room. "Excuse me, sir, visiting hours were over hours ago. You're not allowed to spend the night unless you're family."

"We're engaged; does that count?"

Puzzlement filled Jamie's expression. "We're engaged?"

"Afraid not, it's time for you to leave." The nurse stared fiercely at Lance. "Sir, now!"

"I'm sorry, Jamie. I have to go. I'll come to see you in the morning."

"No, you can't do that. I'm being discharged. My aunt will be here in the morning. She can't know about you."

"Here we go again. When will we be able to tell our families we're going to get married?"

"After we're married, when they can't do anything about it."

"That's not for months and after graduation. I'm not sure if I can wait that long."

"Sir, it's time for you to go home."

Lance gently kissed Jamie on the forehead. "Will you marry me?"

"Are you asking me?"

"Yes, Jamie; let's get married."

"Sir!"

"Okay, okay! I'm leaving." He kissed Jamie on the top of her head. "I'll propose properly one day, but consider us engaged." The rest of the night, Jamie tossed and turned.

Bright and early at 7:00 a.m., Dr. Jennings entered Jamie's room with his interns. He flipped on the lights, waking her from her restless sleep.

"Good morning. How's my patient feeling?"

"A lot better. The medication is working. I'm going to live."

"That's great to hear. Are you ready to be discharged?"

"When? I'm ready."

"I'll start the paperwork and should have you released within the next couple of hours."

"What about my dad? Can he go home too?"

"There's a good possibility. After I complete my rounds, I'll be able to assess that. I suppose you want him home."

"Without a shadow of a doubt."

"Toodledo!" In pranced Aunt Sally. "How's my baby girl?"

Dr. Jennings stepped forward. "Ma'am, she's being discharged this morning."

"That's the best news I've heard in days."

"Dr. Jennings, when will I know when my father gets to go home? Right, you said after you see him."

"That's correct. If neither of you has additional questions, I'll start the discharge process and go check on your father."

"Sounds great." Jamie beamed from ear to ear. "I know we're both going home today."

CHAPTER SEVEN

Home, Sweet Home, or Not!

Six Weeks Later

James lay in his recliner with his injured leg propped up, his crutches resting to the side, and a stack of mail lay in his lap. He opened one past-due bill after another. *How am I going to keep the lights on? Insurance, mortgage. Something has to give.*

In her cheerleading uniform carrying her bookbag, Jamie entered the front door. "I'm home!"

"I would've never known without your announcement."

"Dad, don't be ridiculous."

"I'm just trying to lighten the mood."

"Why, what's wrong?" Jamie eye-balled the stack of bills. "We're short on money, aren't we?"

"Nothing I can't handle."

"Dad, I told you I'd quit cheerleading and get a job. They're hiring at Skater's Paradise."

"You'll do no such thing. We'll be fine. I have clearance to return to work Monday. I promise."

"You're not going back to window washing, are you?"

"Jamie, we discussed this. That's my job. It comes with risks every time. That's what I signed up for; to keep food on our table and a roof over our head."

"Then find another job. This one is too dangerous. You were almost killed."

"It was a freak accident. And, besides, my boss is transferring me to clean interior windows until I am completely healed. I'll be grounded, so to speak."

"Dad, we've got to talk. I don't want to leave you here by yourself. You know how you insist I apply to all those Ivy League colleges? Well, I applied to our local community college instead."

"You did what?"

"You heard me. I can't go off and leave you alone. Remember what Mom said, 'We have to take care of each other.' And that is what I plan to do."

"Listen to me. I'll be fine. Going off and living in a dorm is a rite of passage."

"Nope! I've made up my mind. As long as you're alone, I'm not leaving."

"What do you mean by that?"

"Dad, it's time for you to date. It's been eight years since Mom died."

"Dating? I can't even afford the electricity right now. How do you suppose I pay for a date?"

"Let me see. I get a job."

"No way, and that's final. I'll get a second job."

"Doing what?"

"I was only two courses shy of my graphic design degree when your mom passed. I was pretty good at it. Maybe *Elite Magazine* will give me an internship while I finish my degree. I also bartend. I could do that in the evenings."

"You mean you would work for the lady who shot you?"

"She said she wanted to make things up to me. So, the answer is no until you ask. Isn't that what your mom always said?"

"I suppose so. But I don't like that woman. I tried to interview her for my research project, and her assistant was so rude to me. I never even got an appointment, and she never returned my calls when I called. She's rude and arrogant. Rude! Rude! Rude!"

"Why don't you tell me how you really feel?"

"I don't like her! How's that?"

"So, you would rather see me bartend than complete my degree?"

"No, I suppose not. Just keep your distance from that woman. She's been nothing but trouble for you. You hungry, Dad? I can make you a mean peanut butter and jelly sandwich."

"I have a better plan. Let's order pizza and have a movie night."

"Can't, Dad. Tonight's the Halloween party at Melissa's. We're going as zombie cheerleaders."

"I guess I'll do pizza on my own and hand out candy."

"Dad, we don't have candy and can't afford to buy any. So, keep the porch light off, go to bed, and watch the movie, resting. Besides, you shouldn't be getting up and down on your leg."

"That's not so. I have clearance to only to use my crutches when I have to, and I can start working on it."

"Still, no giving out any candy. We need more peanut butter, jelly, and bread."

"You're so grown up. I'm very proud of the woman you're becoming."

"That's because I have such a good father and my mother's genes."

"Honey, can you do me a favor?"

"What is it?"

"I'll make you a deal. You keep submitting your essays to Ivy League colleges, and I'll think about dating again. How does that sound?"

She nodded and smiled. "Sounds like a plan. Besides, I already enrolled you onto *Singlematch*."

"You did what?"

"Yes, I said it. I signed you up on a dating site. Women are lining up to date you. You just have to find one you like."

"I don't know whether to be mad or happy about this."

"Don't worry, be happy. We'll look at your matches over the weekend. Now, I need to start my zombie process and head off to Melissa's party. I'm so excited."

"Don't get too excited. You still have a curfew."

"Can we talk about that? I am almost eighteen. Don't you think I've outgrown a curfew?"

"We'll talk about this when you're eighteen and not seventeen going on thirty."

"Very funny!"

Jamie's cell phone rang, and she glanced at the caller's I.D. "It's Melissa. She's probably wondering what time I'll be at her house." She strolled to her bedroom, talking on her phone. "Hey, you ready for Zombie Skate Night?"

Lance, carrying his skateboard, stumbled into the kitchen. He strolled to the pantry, opened it, and closed it. He opened the refrigerator and quickly closed it, too.

Miriam, stirring a pot of spaghetti sauce, observed. "Looking for something?"

"Yea, I need electrolytes in my system before tonight's skateboard event."

"Skateboard event? Nationals isn't for another month or so."

"Tonight's the Halloween bash at the park. It's going to be an open trunk skate trick or treat party. Of course, as the State Champion, I'm expected to make a run or two."

"You'll find what you're looking for in the garage refrigerator."

"Thanks, Miriam."

Angela eased into the kitchen, dressed to the nines. "Good afternoon. Wow, it smells so good in here. I can't believe I won't be home to enjoy it."

"No worries, ma'am. I'm making this for tomorrow's lasagna."

Lance returned, chugging a bottle of blue Gatorade. "Mom, where are you going looking like that?"

"John and I have the Vampire Masquerade Ball tonight. You know, the one started by Anne Rice."

"I think that requires fangs and a mask, and I don't see either."

"Don't you worry about that. John and I have everything planned. We even have matching outfits, masks, and fangs. He's having them flown in from Transylvania."

"I don't like the way this sounds. And, Mom, I'm not sure if I even like you dating this guy. Doesn't Grandpa always say never to mix business with pleasure?"

"He did, but I don't handle his account; Monique does. So, dating him isn't out of the question for me."

"Doesn't mean I have to like it."

"Would it make a difference to you if I told you he has a huge surprise in store for you tonight?"

"Now I am more confused than ever."

"Before our ball, we're coming to see you at the Skater's Bash when you receive the key to the city. He's arranged for a very special person to be there to hand it to you."

"If you're talking about the mayor, she's not so special."

"Not at all. Think more in terms of your skating idol."

"Tony Lark!"

"Now, you're getting the picture. He's friends with Tony and asked him as a favor to come in for the ball and to hand you the keys."

"You've got to be kidding me? This means you're going to be there?"

"You don't sound pleased about this."

"I... I... I am." He gulped. "I'm just shocked, I guess." His heart sank realizing that if his mother attended, Jamie wouldn't. *Jamie is going to kill me.*

CHAPTER EIGHT

Zombies, Vampires, Lions, and Tigers

Had the zombie apocalypse started? Zombies, creatures, pirates, Marvel Characters, and so many more packed the Lakefront Skatepark for the Halloween bash. The atmosphere resembled a small country fair with bean bag toss, corn hole, face painting, bobbing for apples, darts, cotton candy, snowballs, bake sale, musical chairs, etc., all manned by costumed parents. A local band played on the stage at the front as the crowd gathered. Kids of all ages dressed in costumes took part in the Trunk and Treat activities.

Lance pulled up in his BMW, backed into a parking spot, exited wearing a zombie leather outfit, and opened the trunk filled with bags of Halloween goodies. He retrieved two camping chairs from the back seat and carefully placed them near the car's trunk before looking at his watch. *It's now or never.* He dialed Jamie's number.

Jamie's expression turned to pure joy when she saw the caller's I.D. on her cell phone. "Hello. I'm running a little late. I need about thirty more minutes. Zombie make-up isn't the easiest to apply."

"Wait! I have bad news."

"Please don't tell me you had a skating accident and are in the hospital."

"No, nothing like that. I found out that my mom and her boyfriend are coming to see me receive the city's key. So, do you know what that means?"

"I can't come. So, now what?" She huffed in disappointment.

"Go to Melissa's party. And, as soon as my mom leaves, I'll call you. Unless you're ready to announce our relationship to the world."

"Lance, we've been over this a dozen times. I've been down that road before. No one can know! I mean it. The last parents I met broke us up. I can't let that happen again."

"I hear ya. My lips are sealed. Besides, we both graduate soon, so it's only a couple of months away, not an eternity."

"Actually, we don't graduate until May. We still need to talk about that. I can't marry you until I know my dad will be all right. I can't leave him alone. He's at least agreed to start dating again."

"He'll bounce back and find love."

"I know, but since my mom…"

"…Since nothing. You worry too much about him."

"He's the only dad I have. We'll talk about this later. Call me when the coast is clear."

"I see my mom and her boyfriend now."

Angela in her black Elvira ball gown, and John in his tuxedo strolled hand in hand, taking in the activities. She saw Lance and waved, hugging and kissing him when she reached him. She glanced at the two chairs. "Expecting company?"

"Just you two."

"Then why not three chairs?"

"I plan on standing. I'm full of nervous energy."

"Lance, I want to introduce you to Mr. John Legions."

John extended his hand to solidify their introduction with a shake. "Nice to finally meet you, son. I've heard many great things about you."

I'm not your son. Lance rolled his eyes, holding back what he wanted to say. "You too. Mom, you know, you didn't have to come to this."

"I know; it was our choice. Besides, you're meeting Tony Lark. I wouldn't want to miss that for the world."

"I'm excited about that. Thank you, Mr. Legions, for arranging this." For the first time, his tone was sincere.

"Call me, John. And it was nothing at all. Tony has always wanted to attend the Vampire Ball, which gave him the extra incentive to come to New Orleans."

A group of trick-or-treaters walked up to Lance's car. "Trick or Treat!"

Lance grabbed a handful of goodies from his trunk. "I'll say, treat! You all look great." He pointed to a young boy dressed as a gothic skateboarder with Lance's portrait on his T-shirt. "Especially you."

The little boy handed Lance a black Sharpie pen. "Will you autograph my shirt? You're my hero."

"Absolutely, by the way, this is the first autograph I've been asked for." He signed the shirt as the boy beamed with pride. Then he dumped the goodies in each of the kid's pumpkins.

As that group left, another quickly arrived. One ten-year-old girl, dressed as a zombie skateboarder, stood in awe of Lance. "You're Lance, the State Champion."

"Yes, I am. I see you're a skater too."

"I'm trying to be, but I'm not so good at it."

"I wasn't either when I started. I fell so many times. I even broke my arm once and my ankle."

"But you're the best."

"Sometimes, even the best fall. I'll tell you my secret. Actually, my grandpa's." He bent eye-level to her. "It's not how you fall; it's how you get up. I'll tell you what, kid, come to the skatepark next Saturday morning. I'll show you a thing or two."

The little girl jumped with glee. "Mom, did you hear that? Can we, please?"

His mom nodded. "Next Saturday. That's very nice of you."

"I love helping kids, especially those who want to skate."

The group left to go to the next car.

"Lance, I'm proud of you. As moms, we dream of our kids being helpful and nice."

"That's how Dad raised me." His quipped response was meant for John.

"I'm impressed too." John's brow lifted in approval. "You'll make a great father someday."

"Well, that someday better be later than sooner. He has Harvard to attend. I have plans for him to become a lawyer and handle all the legal things for the magazine." Angela patted her son on the back. "I'm proud of you, son."

Dismayed, Lance huffed as another group of costumers approached.

The neighborhood partook in the Halloween festivities block-party style by the look of things. The yard, filled with other zombies and costumed partygoers, was decorated to the hilt, including an old-fashioned carriage drawn by skeleton horses, tombstones, and ghosts dangling from the tree. A black and white silent horror film was projected onto the garage door, and just in front of it two clowns popped popcorn. Jamie, dressed as a zombie cheerleader, sat alone with her chin resting in her hands on Melissa's front porch.

Melissa, in her matching costume, opened the front door. "There you are. You disappeared on me."

"I just needed some air. Preston was all over me with his vampire teeth. It grossed me out."

"There's more to this story than you're telling me. Spill the beans." Melissa plopped down beside her.

"Why didn't you tell me you invited Preston?"

"I didn't see a reason to. Besides, I didn't. He and his jocks just showed up. What was I supposed to do? Call the police?"

"I guess not."

"You seem down and out. What's going on with you?"

"Nothing."

"I've known you since we were five. When you say nothing, you mean everything. So, I'm not buying it. Tell me what's really going on."

"Okay, besides my dad not being able to pay our bills, not having money even to purchase a winter formal dress, and him wanting me to leave for college, I've had it."

"That may be true, but I've got a feeling there's more to this than meets the eye."

"Fine, it's my boyfriend. We had plans tonight after this party, and now he had to cancel because of his mother."

"Please don't tell me he's a momma's boy."

"Not in the least. She's dating this rich hot shot, and they're showing up to where we were going."

"How is that a problem?"

"She doesn't know about me, and we plan on keeping it that way until the time is right."

"Time is right for what?"

"To announce we're getting married."

"Wait! What? You can't do that. I haven't even met this guy. How do you know I'll approve?"

"I don't need your approval. We're in love. It's almost like a forbidden thirst for love."

"I don't get it. If you're in so much love to consider getting married, why not tell his mother?"

"Think Preston. The way I understand things, his mom is best friends with the Billifords. I think they might be cousins. Heck, Billiot and Billiford are so close; I think one of them changed their last name. And, once I met his parents, everything went downhill from there. I don't ever want to face that kind of scrutiny again. Does that tell you anything?"

"So, he's a rich dude?"

"Honestly, I don't know. He doesn't act or dress that way. But he insists his mom is a socialite snob born with a golden spoon in her mouth. I tried to look up Mrs. Garrett Billiot and can't find her anywhere. It's like she doesn't exist."

"What about his dad?"

"He's nowhere in the picture from what I gather from our conversations."

"So, what are you going to do?"

Before Jamie could answer, the front door opened and out stumbled Preston. "My Queen, there you are." His breath smelled like a distillery, slurring his words.

"I'm leaving. I've had enough. I'll see you at school on Monday. Thanks for listening, Melissa." Jamie hopped up to leave.

"Wait! Jamie, I love you."

"Get over me, Preston!"

He stumbled toward her, falling flat on his face. "Never, never, ever! I'll win you back." He rolled over onto his back as the sky seemed to spin.

Jamie glanced over her shoulder. "Never, never, ever!" She got into her Sebring and sped off feeling cheerless.

The mayor, dressed as Medusa, climbed the stairs to step onto the stage as the band finished their version of the song, *Monster Mash*. She grabbed the squealing microphone. "Welcome to all trick and treaters, zombies, vampires, lions, and tigers, oh my. Are you having fun? As the mayor of this fine city, it is my pleasure to announce a special guest. But this doesn't come without the fanfare of this city. Drum roll, please."

The band's drummer performed a solo drum roll.

"First, I want to invite our State Skateboard Champion, Lance Garrett Billiot, to the stage. Lance, get on up here!"

The crowd erupted into cheers. Lance! Lance! Lance!"

Angela beamed with pride, grinning from ear to ear. "I'm so proud of you, son."

"Thanks, Mom."

"Now, get up there. It's your time to shine."

Lance snaked his way through the crowd, fist-bumping along the way.

John squeezed Angela's hand. "You have a reason to be proud."

"I am. But not as proud as I'll be when he graduates from Harvard and becomes our magazine's attorney."

"Angela, is that what your son wants?"

"I don't know. But he knows my expectations."

Lance finally made it onto the stage, where the mayor immediately shook his hand.

"Lance, I want to congratulate you on winning the State Skateboarding Championship, not one year, but two years in a row. Here's looking forward to a three-peat. We, as a city, are proud to have you represent us, and now, the City Council and I want to applaud you and give you a key to the city."

"Thank you, Madam Mayor. I'm honored."

The mayor pointed upward. "Please, everyone, look up into the sky."

Everyone did. Most of the onlookers pointed toward the sky.

Puzzlement took over Lance's face as he gazed upward. "Madam Mayor, what are we looking at?"

"There!" She pointed to a tiny figure floating downward. "This is your surprise."

"I'm confused."

Within seconds, the figure in the sky became recognizable -- a man parachuting toward them. On the parachute was a picture of a skateboard with the name Tony Lark.

Lance could barely contain himself, smiling. "Madam Mayor, now that's an entrance."

The crowd applauded as Tony descended and landed in the open field. Several security guards ran toward him, assisted with removing the parachute, and escorted Tony to the stage, where he shook Lance's hand and then the other dignitary.

Jamie pushed through the crowd to the front of the stage, hoping Lance would see her.

"It is my pleasure to introduce the one and only Tony Lark. He doesn't need an introduction to this skating family. Welcome, to New Orleans, Tony."

"Thank you, Madam Mayor. I can't begin to tell you how excited I am to be here in your wonderful city and meet Lance. He's a very talented skateboarder and will make this city and America proud in the next Olympics. I'm just glad I don't have to compete against him. The benefit of retirement."

The crowd laughed and applauded, while the mayor handed Tony a sizeable golden key to the city. "Now, without further ado, it is my pleasure to have Tony give Lance the key to our fine city. We have officially declared today as Lance Garrett Billiot Day."

Tony gifted the golden key to Lance. "You're very deserving."

"Thank you, Mr. Lark."

"Please call me Tony."

To her dismay, Jamie waved to Lance, but he didn't see her. "Go, Lance!"

Finally, he noticed her and grinned as the band started playing. Several security guards entered from stage left and escorted Tony, the mayor, and Lance backstage and out of sight from Jamie.

She tried to fight the crowd to get to the back, but the security personnel abruptly stopped her. *This is hopeless.* She retrieved her cell phone and dialed it.

"You've reached Melissa; leave a message at the beep."

She dialed Lance. "You know what to do. If you don't, stop calling."

"Lance, please call me back. I can't find you. I know you know I'm here."

With tears in her zombie-red eyes, she returned to her car. Finally, her phone rang.

"Lance, has your mom left? Where can we meet?"

"Jamie, I don't know how to tell you this, but my mom insists I go to the Vampire Ball with her and her boyfriend. Tony Lark is coming with us too."

"So, you're ditching me for your mother and Tony Lark?" Disappointed, she felt her stomach plummet.

"No, just postponing our date. This is a once-in-a-lifetime opportunity for me. That is, unless you want to join us and meet my mother."

"No, thank you. I guess I can't get mad at you for that. Our rules are our rules."

"I'll tell you what. I'll make it up to you sooner than later. Are you going to go to Melissa's party?"

"Been there, done that. I left because Preston was there. I didn't want to be near him."

"So, now what? It's Halloween."

"Home to my dad to keep him company and watch a movie. I'm so bummed, I don't want to do anything else."

"Pep up! In six months, we get married."

"It'll be the longest six months of my life."

"That goes for me, too. Gotta go. I love you."

"Love you back." Click!

Jamie shuffled her way back to her car, uncertain if her feelings were hurt or if she was angry. *This is my fault. I'm the one who wants to keep this a secret. I have nobody to blame but myself.* She huffed. Frustration abounded, as nothing had gone her way this evening.

Jamie pulled up to her dark house, passing many costumed trick or treaters along the way. Every costume imaginable – goblins, zombies, vampires, Darth Vader, Aquaman, pirates, animals, robots, princesses; you name it; they were on the streets carrying lighted pumpkins. *Oh, to be that young again.* She exited the vehicle and entered the dark house. "Dad, it's me!" Her voice drifted through the house as her eyes darted toward the empty brown leather recliner.

"I'm in my bedroom."

Jamie made her way in the dark through the living room to his bedroom. "Dad, can I come in?"

"Of course. Is everything okay?"

"Yes, and no."

"Okay, have a seat. Start with the yes."

Jamie crawled up into the bed next to her father. She grabbed a pillow and hugged it. "Yes, I'm fine. Unfortunately, the night didn't go as I planned. Preston showed up at Melissa's party and got on my last nerve, so I left."

"I'm so sorry, sweetheart. I know he broke your heart. Trust me, you'll get over him as soon as you've been married twice."

"Don't be ridiculous. I'm only getting married once. I'm a true and blue kind of girl."

"I'm happy you're concentrating on getting your diploma and not dating anyone. One of the biggest mistakes you could've made was to fall in love your senior year and then move off to college and start all over again."

"How is that a mistake? Isn't that what you and mom did?"

"We fell in love in the sixth grade, and were married by the time we were in college. After that, it was hard to keep food on the table and a roof over our heads."

"I don't get it. You said that was one of the happiest times of your lives."

"That it was, but times were also different. Today, you have to get a college education to make a living. Back then, you didn't."

"Is that why you quit college?"

"I quit to keep a roof over our heads and to feed you and your mother. You were the best thing that happened to us."

"You regret dropping out of college?"

"I didn't until…"

"…Until what?"

He patted his thigh. "This. Now, I'm struggling to make ends meet. Maybe if I had finished college like your mother wanted me to, I'd be a better provider for you."

"Dad, you're perfect. We've always managed. You know you can always go back to college and finish that degree. We can go together."

"Me going back to college is one thing, but we won't be going together. You'll earn your scholarship and go to an Ivy League college. I'll make ends meet one way or another. Just don't go falling in love and ruin your future. Promise me; your studies will always come first."

Jamie drew in a long, exasperated breath. "I, Jamie, promise to concentrate on my studies." Jamie crossed her fingers behind her back. *Just after I marry Lance.*

"That's my girl. How about some popcorn and a movie just like old times?"

"Movie and popcorn it is. Thanks, Dad, for the pep talk."

CHAPTER NINE

Working Nine to Five

A t 6:30 a.m., the alarm clock blared in James' room. He swatted at it, only to miss it. "Not now, too early." He swatted at it again, still missing. "Turn off, already!" Losing patience, he lobbed a pillow toward the clock.

Jamie, dressed for school, entered her dad's room, turned off the alarm, and handed him a cup of coffee. "Good morning, Dad! It's your first day back at work. Rise and shine. Are you excited?"

"That's not what I'd call it. It's back to the grind after six weeks of being laid up."

"Don't you think it went by fast?"

"For you, maybe. It seemed to drag out forever, if you ask me."

"Drink your coffee. I made breakfast too."

"With what? I don't recall having breakfast food in the house."

"We didn't. I went to the store yesterday and bought bacon, eggs, and biscuits to surprise you."

"With what money?"

"From one of my piggy banks. I've been saving all these years for something special. This is special."

"You shouldn't have spent that. You'll need it when you go to college."

"Dad, not another word. One breakfast isn't going to break my piggy bank savings. I bet I have a couple of thousand dollars. Get dressed and come eat." Jamie skipped out of the room.

James slowly got out of bed, and looked at himself in the dresser mirror. "I look rough."

"Dad, you coming? Eggs are getting cold!"

"Yes, just dressing."

"I ironed your uniform. It's hanging in your closet."

He made his way to the closet, grabbed his uniform, and dressed.

When he turned around, he jittered because, surprisingly, Jamie stood in the doorway. "You scared me."

"Sorry, Dad. Wanted to make sure you're up. You have twenty minutes before I load you up into my car and drive you to work."

"Sweetie, I can drive myself."

"Are you sure?"

"Absolutely, now let's go eat. My nine-to-five job is calling me."

Lance and Angela sat at the breakfast table as Miriam prepared an apple pie. The mixture of apples and cinnamon simmering on the stove filled the air with a sweet aroma.

"Mom, you know Thanksgiving is just around the corner."

"And your point is?"

"A group of skaters want to take a trip to Colorado and check out the pipes."

"Out of the question. Next subject."

"Why is it out of the question? I'm eighteen and considered an adult."

"Because you know we always go see your grandparents for Thanksgiving. This year, we're going to Rome."

"I've been to Rome. I don't want to go."

"Again, next subject."

"Mom, you go. I'll go to Colorado with my friends."

"Lance Garrett Billiot." She shot him a warning smile. "This is not up for debate, so get it out of your head. You're going to Rome, and that's it. Enough said. Am I clear?"

"When I go away to college, are you still going to insist I go with you?"

"We'll cross that bridge when we get to it. Now, I need to talk to you about something very important."

"Can it wait?"

"Not really. It's about John."

"I can't wait for this."

"You know we've been dating for three months."

"Three long months."

"Things are moving along, and he asked me to marry him?"

"Mom, you can't!" He slammed his fist against the table, rattling the dishes from its force. "It's too soon. You've only known him three months."

"I didn't say tomorrow. But that's only one reason for going to Rome. John's coming with us and plans to ask Grandpa for my hand in marriage."

"This has to be a joke. You're still in love with Dad."

"Son, things were over with him a long time ago. You can't expect me to stay single and grow old alone."

"No! But I don't expect you to marry the first guy who sweeps you off your feet, either. Are you trying to ruin my life?"

"That's the furthest thing from my mind. It's only a matter of months before you head off to Harvard, and I'll be alone."

"Mom, I'm thinking of going pro."

"Pro what?"

"A professional skateboarder. College isn't in my future."

"You can do that as soon as you finish Harvard and not the other way around."

"That's why my father left. You were trying to control him like you're trying to control me."

"Watch your tongue. I never asked him to divorce me. He's the one who decided to leave us and take up with that hussy."

"Enough, Mom." Lance stormed out of the house.

Miriam grabbed the coffeepot. "More coffee, Ms. Abadie?"

"Sure." Angela paused for a moment. "Do you have this problem with your son?"

"Ms. Abadie, my son hasn't spoken to me in twenty-five years."

"I'm sorry. I didn't know that. I shouldn't have brought up bad memories, but now that I have, do you mind sharing what happened?"

"We had a falling out. He wouldn't follow the house rules, so he left. I never heard from him again."

"Do you know where he is?"

"Sadly, no. It's like he disappeared from the face of the Earth. As his mother, I know he's okay and will come back to me one day. That's why I never moved from my house. Take it from me, some fights aren't worth fighting because you'll surely lose and possibly lose your son."

"Are you suggesting I let him bypass Harvard and be a skateboarder? If so, that's insane."

"That's something you'll have to deal with, but the way I see it, don't push him out of your life. Listen to his dreams and what he wants, because it's his life, just as your life is yours to live."

"Do you have an opinion about me marrying John?"

Miriam pursed her lips, wiping her hands on her apron. "I haven't met him, remember? He's a fine catch, and by the way you talk about him, you could do a lot worse. But do you love him? Does he make you happy? Does he take your breath away?" She placed the apple pie in the oven.

"I don't have to answer, do I?"

"Only to yourself, ma'am. I just know the entire time I was married before Harold's death, I couldn't imagine my life without him. He was my soul mate. I was in a constant state of happiness."

"How do you feel now?"

"He's still the love of my life. That's why I'm not in another relationship. No one could ever replace my Harold. A love like that only comes once in a lifetime. And, as for sons, once you lose them, you may never get them back."

"Miriam, I had no idea."

"I'll let you in on a little secret on this marrying topic. When love bites you in the ass, you'll know it. Nothing will stop you, and you won't have to ask anybody else whether you're in love. It's the simplest but most complicated human emotion. It's a forbidden thirst that needs quenching." A tear formed in the corner of Miriam's eye. "Anyway, you'll cherish every moment of being with him when you're in love."

The hallway bristled with students during the exchange of classes. With her arms crossed over her chest, Jamie leaned against her locker. Melissa removed several items from her bookbag and placed them in her locker and then retrieved a book for her next class. Several students from the Honor Society took down the Halloween decorations from the halls. "Can you believe it?" Jamie huffed. "My boyfriend dumped me Saturday night for his mother."

"You have to watch out for those momma's boys." Melissa retrieved a folder from her locker. "I've told you that before."

"He's not a momma's boy." She unlinked her arms and walked away, leaving Melissa, who quickly chased after her. "He just had a family obligation to meet. Don't get me wrong. He invited me."

"Why didn't you go?"

"I've been over this. I won't meet his mother until after... you know."

"Don't mention it. I think you're being ridiculous, though. If you can't get along with your future mother-in-law before you get married, what makes you think you will after you are?"

"Cause she won't have a say so, that's how."

"Do you even know who she is?"

"Don't care too. He doesn't talk much about his mom at all. He freezes up every time I mention her. It's like he's ashamed of her or something. Not sure why. All I know is Lance's last name is Billiot. His parents are divorced, his dad is part of Billiot Bakery, and he was named after him."

"You mean those awesome king cakes?"

"Yep!"

"Lucky you."

"How, so?"

"If you marry this mysterious guy, you'll get to eat all of those cakes and goodies free for the rest of your life."

Preston strode up to Jamie, stopping her in her tracks. "Missed you at the party the other night. Where did you go?"

She stepped into him, pushing him out of her way. "I'm not answering that, Preston. Can't you just leave me alone?"

"Better idea. Let me walk you to class."

"Nope, nope, and never." Jamie stomped to the classroom across the hall, bumping right into Lance. "I'm sorry, excuse me." She pulled back, her knit sweater latched onto his jacket's zipper. "Oh, no, we're stuck." She struggled to act like she didn't like him.

Lance puckered his lips and gave her an air kiss. "No problem." He fiddled with her sweater until it was released, creating a snag. "After you."

Preston shoved Lance's shoulder. "Jamie, this creep bothering you?"

"Both of you leave me alone." She pulled the string, snapping it loose, storming into the classroom, then sat in the third row, the fourth seat, in front of Rae, the server from Skater's Paradise. "Jeez, boys!"

"Boys indeed. I see you and Preston are getting along better." Rae giggled. She lifted one shoulder, matching the way the corner of her smile rose.

"Shut up, Rae. Nothing is going on between us. Besides, I have my eyes on someone else, so you can have him."

"Funny thing. I don't want Preston. I have my eyes on someone else, too."

"Well, good for you." A skeptical smile haunted Jamie's lip.

Preston plopped into his chair, which was across from Jamie's. "Can I borrow a pencil and some paper?"

Jamie scolded Preston with her eyes. "No! Why don't you have your rich dad's butler bring you one?"

"That's a bit harsh."

Lance made his way down between rows three and four and sat across from Rae, who immediately smiled at him.

"Hello, Lance. How's skateboarding coming?"

Confused, Lance glanced at Rae. "Wow, we've been in class all semester, and this is the first time you've spoken to me."

"Sorry about that, but after seeing you Saturday, I realized you're a stand-up guy." She giggled and batted her eyelashes just as Jamie looked over her shoulder to see the interaction. "Again, congratulations on your championship and having a burger named after you."

Jamie's face turned crimson. "Preston, I've changed my mind. Yes, you can borrow a pencil and paper."

Lance slammed his fist on the desktop. "Rae, can I borrow a pen, please?"

Rae quickly retrieved a pen and handed it to Lance. He smiled at her.

The tardy bell rang as Mrs. Frederick entered. "Class, please open your books to chapter six and pass your homework to the front."

Lance handed his homework to Rae, gently brushing his hand on hers. "Here's mine. Pass it to the front, please."

Rae gladly took the papers and passed hers and Lance's to Jamie, who jerked them from her hand.

The sun glistened against the dew dropped windows behind Angela, who sat at her desk in the corner office, proofing an article. "No, you can't have a split infinitive." Concentrated on her task, she marked the document with a red pen. "This is simple editing. How can a journalist not know not to end a sentence with a preposition?" She furiously continued to copy edit. This time, the red ink wouldn't come out of the pen. She slammed it five times against the paper, but it still didn't work. She pressed the intercom button. "Francis, get in here! Bring me a dozen red pens that work and a fresh cup of coffee."

Within seconds, Francis bolted into the office with a fist full of red pens and a cup of coffee with the *Elite* logo. "Here you go, Ms. Abadie."

Angela spun her chair to gaze out the window. "Unbelievable. I don't think these windows have been cleaned since… forget it." She spun back, facing Francis. "Any update on the window washer? Once he left the hospital, I haven't been able to find out anything about him."

"No, ma'am. I didn't know I was to follow up on that. My apologies."

103

"You weren't. I was just curious. Speaking of window washing, please call Blue Bayou and tell them I need my interior windows cleaned."

"You asked me that on Friday, and I notified them and scheduled them for today."

"Great news. Stay on top of that."

Tina Powell, the thirty-something new raven-haired temporary receptionist who replaced Monique, popped her head into the office. "Excuse me, Ms. Abadie. Mr. Legions is here to see you."

"Tina, I haven't thanked you for filling in. You're everything the temp agency said you were. Please send him in."

"Yes, ma'am. It's a pleasure to work with you." She promptly left.

"Francis. Send in Monique and tell her to bring in the files for Legions Airlines. Stat!"

Just as Angela spat the words, Monique entered, carrying a display board with an easel. "I think you'll love the design for the new ad campaign for Legions Airlines."

"I certainly hope so, since he's on his way in here. Speaking of the devil."

Dressed to impress and carrying a spring bouquet, John made his grand entrance into Angela's office. "It's a wonderful morning, don't you lovely ladies agree?"

From behind her desk, Angela stood, extending her hand to shake his.

He gave her a conspiratorial wink, shaking her hand. "Mighty formal this morning, Ms. Abadie."

"You know my motto, business is business, and pleasure is pleasure."

John glanced at the bouquet in his hands. "First, these are for Monique." He handed the flowers to her. "For your promotion and taking great care of my campaign."

Abruptly, Angela stepped from behind her desk. "Francis, take Monique's flowers and put them in a vase for her."

"Of course, anything else, Ms. Abadie?"

"Bring us coffee, please. You're dismissed."

Francis left the office, flirtatiously batting her lashes at John.

Angela's smile quickly turned to a smirk. "Shall we get down to business?"

"That's what I'm here for. Proceed."

Angela pursed her lips. "John, Monique and I have your new display ad ready to share. I know you'll love it. So, Monique, set it up and let's begin."

James, in his Blue Bayou uniform, pushed the cleaning cart out of the service elevator, entering the grand foyer of *Elite Magazine*. Tina glanced up. "Good morning, sir. The office in question is in the far corner to the right. Please knock before you enter."

"That's protocol." He made his way through the journalists' cubicles. *It looks so much different on the inside than from the outside.* When he saw Connie, he smiled and waved. "Good morning!"

"Good morning. Wait! You're the window washer. Glad to see you. I wasn't sure if you were going to make it."

"I did, and here I am in the flesh."

Francis hurriedly approached James. "Great. You're the Blue Bayou guy. I never forget a face. Ms. Abadie is finishing up with a client. I'll let you know when she's finished."

"Thank you. Where do you suggest I wait?" He looked down the way to the corner office where Monique presented Legions Airlines' new campaign as Angela and John watched.

"Down by her office. You can wait over there in the corner cubicle. It's empty today."

"Very well." He winked at Connie. "Have a good day."

Connie swooned inwardly. "You too."

He pushed his cart to the corner and stared at the floor-to-ceiling window. He shivered as he touched it, reflecting on that fateful day Angela had rescued him. *What a nightmare.*

Angela's office door opened, and Monique glanced back at John with a wide-toothed grin. "Thank you, Mr. Legions. I'll immediately make those minor changes."

John strode to the door, followed by Angela. "Ms. Abadie, such a pleasure seeing you again." He kissed her cheek.

"See you for dinner?" Angela caught of glimpse of James in the corner of her eye, and suddenly her cheeks blushed.

James nodded and smiled.

John took a particular interest in the way Angela gazed at James. "Yes, I've made reservations for seven at Mr. B's at our special corner table. Until then." In a princely manner, John kissed her hand, only for her to quickly jerk it away, eyeing James.

"Have the limo pick me up at six. We'll have cocktails at the bar first."

"I look forward to it." John made his way to the front of the journalist pit.

Francis approached James. "You may enter Ms. Abadie's office. She's expecting you."

"Thank you."

Monique escorted James to Angela's office. "Ms. Abadie, the window washer is here. This might be a good time for you to hold the editorial meeting with the new journalists."

"Not now, Monique. I have to finish editing Connie's article. He can clean them as I work."

"I'll have him come in. Sir, you may enter."

James pushed his cart to Angela's office door. "Good morning."

"Good morning. It's Mr. Sea... Sea..."

"Seamore. But please call me James."

"How have you been?"

"I'm healing nicely. Today's my first day back at work since you shot me."

"I still feel bad about that. If there's anything I can do for you, just let me know."

"Do you mean that, or are those just words to appease me?"

"I mean every word."

"I do have a favor to ask."

"I'm all ears."

The school's lunchroom bristled with chatter. Posters promoting the next football home game against the Panthers were plastered on the walls alongside those reminding students to eat healthy meals. Many students stood in line waiting their turn to be served by the six white-uniformed cafeteria ladies wearing plastic gloves and hairnets. Jamie sat with Melissa and the rest of the cheerleaders, Preston with his jocks, and Lance, Conrad, and Jeremy sat at a table in the East corner. Rae sat two tables away from Lance and stared at him. An otherwise normal day.

Jamie stood, grabbing her tray. "I'm outta here. I have one more article to find for my paper. The library calls."

"I thought you interviewed that magazine lady."

"I tried. She never returned my call. She's arrogant, rude, stuck on herself, and has lost all my respect. I don't want to have anything to do with her. Ever! So, I had to find me another. I'm sticking to a famous woman who invented something. Ever heard of Hedy Lamarr?"

"Nope!"

"She was a Hollywood actress who invented a radio guidance system for Allied torpedoes at the beginning of World War Two. That's who I chose for my research project."

"You're such a geek, Jamie." Melissa stood. "I'll come with you."

"Not necessary. I got this. My pass is only good for one."

"Have it your way."

"Don't I always?"

The girls giggled.

Jamie proceeded to the trashcan. Before reaching it, Lance stood and headed that way, carrying his tray. As Jamie cleared hers, Lance bumped into her and passed her a note.

"Excuse me. Watch where you're going!"

"Sure thing." He winked at her, and she abruptly left.

She made her way to the library, and before she entered, she read the note Lance had passed her. "Meet me at the skatepark after school. We've got to talk."

James finished cleaning the last section of the window. "There you have it, all clean."

Angela spun her desk chair and looked through the crystal-clear window. "It's never looked better. Thank you, it was driving me crazy."

"That's what I'm here for. I'll be on my way if there isn't anything else."

"Nothing I can think of."

"Thank you. And please let me know your findings on what we discussed."

"I certainly will. That's the least I can do for you."

"Have a great day. And now that I'm back on my feet, your windows are scheduled to be routinely cleaned."

Angela, smiling, stared stubbornly at James. "You know what? Why don't I buy you lunch? We can talk more about that graphic design internship you asked me about."

"I'll have to take a raincheck on that. More windows need cleaning before lunch."

"Raincheck, it is. I'll hold you to it."

"Sounds great. Have a wonderful rest of your day, Ms. Abadie."

"Please, it's Angela."

"Angela, have a great day." He strode to the door.

Angela watched him, unable to take her eyes off his backside. A certain enamored gaze filled her eyes, causing them to sparkle. "Have a great day."

Francis entered as James made it to the door. "Excuse me, let me get out of your way."

"Have a good day, ma'am." James left, retrieved his cart, and headed for the exit.

A smirk filled Francis' lips. "You like him."

"Mr. Legions and I are strictly business."

"I meant the window washer."

"What! No, nothing is going on. I have a magazine to run. I don't have time to date."

"Sure, keep telling yourself that. Deny, deny, deny. I saw the way you looked at him."

Jamie and Lance sat on the blue checkered picnic blanket under a tree near the skateboard ramps as his skateboard rested to the side.

"So, Jamie, did your dad go back to work today?"

"Yep."

"Doing what?"

"He's working, well, I'd rather not say."

"Why not?"

"I'll put it to you this way. He took a job at this place, but the boss lady is awful. When I say awful, she's rude, and arrogant, and I think she's using my dad."

"Ouch! That doesn't sound good."

"Nope, but let's not talk about it anymore. I'm ready for my skating lesson."

He held up his skateboard.

"Lesson one. Learn the parts of your skateboard."

"Okay, I know those are the wheels, and you stand on the back."

Lance tilted his head back, bellowing into laughter. "So, we start at square one. First, you stand on the deck, not the back. That's the technical name." He ran her hand down the deck. "Do you feel that concave?"

"Oh, yeah. I actually do."

"They designed it that way. The nose and tail are concave, allowing a rider to have a functional kicktail."

"A what?"

"Kicktail. The front of the board, or nose, is slightly larger than the tail. The grip tape on the deck feels like sandpaper, which gives riders more control and traction." He flipped over the skateboard and spun the wheels. "The wheels are very important."

"Duh, without them, you can't roll."

"More than that. Each wheel is attached to the skateboard by axel nuts, bearings, and bushings, also called the truck. A skater must take care of these parts and keep them clean and greased. We'll go over that later."

"Do I need to know all of this? I just want to learn how to skate."

"Baby steps. First, you need a helmet, knee pads, and a skateboard."

"Can't I use yours?"

"You can't borrow Lucille."

"Lucille?"

"My skateboard. I named her that because of B. B. King."

"Now I'm more confused. Why isn't your skateboard's name B.B. or King?"

"He named his guitar Lucille, and you know how much I love the blues and B.B. King."

Jamie laughed. "I have a wonderful idea."

"Can't wait; what is it?"

"Let's get married during the Thanksgiving holidays. We can run off to Vegas."

"As much as I want to, we can't. My mother is forcing me to go to Rome to see my grandparents."

"That sounds exciting."

"Not in the least. I've been so many times, I'm over it. And her boyfriend is asking my grandfather if he can marry her."

"Sounds serious."

"I don't like the guy at all. I'm not sure why, but there's just something about him I don't like."

"Please tell me it doesn't have to do with him being on the wrong side of the income chart."

"Not in the least. He's extremely rich. He's just a snob or something sleazy. I can't really put my finger on it, but he's got something to hide. I can feel it."

"Don't judge him too harshly. You have something to hide, too. We all do."

"What am I hiding?"

"Seriously, you don't know?"

Lance shrugged, waiting on the answer. "Are you going to tell me or not?"

"Me! Us! The fact we're engaged."

"That's not because I want to. It's because you insist. So, you have something to hide."

"At least your mom is dating. I can't get my dad to budge. I told him about the dating site, and he's not interested. I don't know what I'm going to do. I can't go off and get married and leave him alone."

"Here we go again. He's a grown man. He can take care of himself."

"I promised my mother we would always take care of each other."

"And, you will." He leaned over and kissed her.

110

Angela rushed toward a small café on Canal Street, her stomach growling. Through the doors, the wooden stools butted up against the brass rail of the high granite counter were prominent. Out front inside a makeshift barricade, an outside seating area was occupied, except for the corner table. Each table was covered in a red and white checkered plastic tablecloth with a mason jar holding several white and pink carnations in the middle. The condiment tray included the typical ones, along with the added specialty Louisiana hot sauces, and a jar of small pickled peppers with garlic. As she approached, she bumped into James. "Oh, we meet again."

"Angela, we have to stop bumping into each other like this."

"Agreed. But now that you're here, and I'm here, how about cashing in on that raincheck?"

James hesitated. *I can't afford to buy her lunch.* "Not sure if I have time. Duty calls."

"I insist. My treat. It's the least I can do."

He took a deep breath. Everything in him wanted to eat lunch with her, but everything else told him he shouldn't. "Are you sure? I mean, I can buy my lunch."

"Nonsense. Call it an appreciation luncheon or a welcome back to work after being shot by me luncheon. I insist."

"Okay, you win." A grin crisped his lips.

A bubbling waitress approached. "Sit anywhere you like."

The two sat at the outside corner table.

"So, James, how long have you worked for Blue Bayou?"

"Going on twenty years. I had to quit college to support my family, and it was the first company that hired me."

"If you're serious about returning to school and interning at the magazine, I would love to help you out. We offer scholarships."

"I'm not looking for any handouts. I'll figure out a way to pay for the tuition. I need a second job to cover the expenses."

"Instead of interning, why not apply for a job with us? I have connections."

"I bet you do. You know someone in human resources?"

"Don't be silly. Of course, I do. I'll set you up for an appointment to review all available openings. I'm sure there will be one you're qualified for."

"You don't have to do that."

"I know. I want to. So, what can you do besides wash windows?"

"I dabble in photography. Maybe I can work as a photographer's assistant in the advertising department during night shoots or on weekends."

"You have a portfolio?"

"Are you kidding? I'm an amateur. I've never had one, but I can put something together, I'm sure."

The server approached. "Good afternoon, Ms. Abadie. What will you have today?"

"The house special for me. James, what do you want?"

"Make it two house specials."

The server nodded. "That comes with a drink of your choice."

Simultaneously, they smiled and then answered. "Unsweet iced tea."

"Two unsweet teas coming your way. I'll be back in a jiffy." The server pranced off toward the kitchen.

Angela leaned in closer to James and patted his arm. "We seem to like the same things."

"It seems that way."

"How's your daughter?"

"Driving me crazy. Since the injury, my bills have been piling up. She's all worked up about wanting to quit cheerleading to get a job and help me with the bills."

"Why didn't you say something?" Angela retrieved her checkbook, wrote one for five thousand dollars, and handed it to him.

James quickly tore it up. "I'm not after handouts, but thank you, anyway. I'd rather work for my money. I'm old-fashioned that way."

"I didn't mean to offend you. I want to help. After all, I'm the one who shot you."

"No offense taken, but if you're serious, I will take that appointment with your human resource director."

"Consider it done."

The server placed their teas in front of them. "It'll only be a couple more minutes before your order is ready."

"We're in no rush." Angela sipped her tea. "Now, back to your daughter. She's a senior, right?"

"Set to graduate in May and then off to veterinary school."

"Sounds like she's a smart girl."

"Too smart. She has ambition, that's for sure. I'm glad she's focusing on her studies rather than boys."

"My son, he's not into dating either. I was worried at first. You know, never introducing me to a girl, never going out on dates. I thought he was gay or something."

"So, is he?"

"No, just into skateboarding. That skateboard of his is his girlfriend."

"Doesn't sound like you approve."

"Approve? I didn't when he started, but he finds happiness in it. It beats doing drugs and getting into trouble. That's all a mother can hope for, right? Next year, he's going to Harvard."

"He's already been accepted?"

"Not yet, but he's an Abadie. All male Abadie's attend Harvard."

"Us Seamore's go to the local junior college. My daughter is applying for scholarships. She's smart. It's only a matter of time before a school accepts her."

"You're a proud father. I admire that."

"Very proud of her."

The server set down their blue-plate special consisting of fried shrimp and catfish, potato salad, and cole slaw in front of them. The aroma filtered the air. "I'll be back to check on you in a few minutes to see if you need anything else."

"Thank you." Angela took the first bite. "This is so good."

"Indeed. There's no better place to get this kind of seafood." James ate a shrimp after dipping it into the tartar sauce.

Their eyes locked, forming an instant connection as Angela embraced the warm-tingling electricity pelting throughout her spine.

The evening sun radiated from the sky, turning it into several hues of orange, pink, and yellow. James sat on his front porch, admiring it when Jamie pulled up in her Sebring and exited.

"Hi, Dad. Why are you out here?"

He pointed toward the sky. "Look at the majestic beauty." He seemed starry-eyed.

"You okay, Dad? What gives? You're acting strange."

"I have an interview with the human resource department at *Elite Magazine*."

"What! Why?"

"The lady who shot me set it up. We had lunch today."

"Lunch! Dad, I told you to stay away from her. She's nothing but trouble."

"Actually, she's very nice. She's probably swamped running a magazine. I'm sure of it."

"I don't like her. Watch your back. You know how rich people can be."

"Honey, she's not like that."

"Please, don't tell me you like her. This has trouble written all over it. You're setting yourself up for a heartbreak."

"It was a small lunch with my future boss, that's all. Besides, a woman like that doesn't take an interest in a man like me."

"Why not? You're a great guy."

"A great broke guy. Hell, I couldn't even afford to take her to dinner, much less keep her in the lifestyle she's used to. So, you don't have to worry about her. She's out of my league."

"So, what woman do I need to worry about?"

"None, remember, I'm not dating anyone."

"Exactly, but maybe it's time. Don't forget, there are tons of ladies hitting you up on that dating site."

"Jamie, I said forget it. I'm not interested in dating."

"It wouldn't hurt to look, now, would it? One date wouldn't hurt you."

"Why is it so important I start dating?"

"So, you won't be alone when I go off to college, or I'm not going."

"You're going to college has nothing to do with me not dating."

"Oh, yes, it does."

"We'll discuss this later. Get cleaned up. I have a surprise for dinner."

"Peanut butter and jelly."

"Nope! I made red beans and rice. The only thing missing is the salad."

"We're not finished with this conversation. After dinner, you're looking at that dating site, and that's final."

"We'll cross that bridge when we come to it."

"We've come to it, Dad."

"Let's eat. And, after dinner, you can help me choose the photographs to include in my portfolio."

"Dad, after dinner, you and me have a date looking at the ladies on *Singlematch*. I've already uploaded your picture."

Several uneventful days passed. In a suit and tie, James anxiously sat in the reception area of *Elite Magazine*, along with several other would-be employees, waiting patiently. A young woman flipped through her portfolio as James observed.

James adjusted his tie. "Beautiful work? You took those?"

"Yes, sir. Nature photography is something I enjoy. I'm hoping to get a job here when I graduate next month."

"I didn't know *Elite Magazine* needed a nature photographer."

"They don't. I'm hoping they like my work and give me a chance. I've wanted to work at this magazine since I started college."

"I wish you luck on that."

"What are you interviewing for?"

"Don't really know. I'm here to see what job they have available, and then I'll take it from there."

"They list all job openings on their website. Maybe you should've started there."

"I thought about it, but Ms. Abadie set this up for me."

"You know Ms. Abadie? Can you introduce me? Can you put in a good word for me? I admire her so much."

"Wait, this isn't what it seems. A freak accident had our paths crossed. I barely know the woman."

"Oh, I recognize you now. You're that window washer she shot."

"Afraid so."

Tina strolled to James. "Mr. Seamore, Mr. Eagleton will see you now. This way, please."

James rose, grabbed his portfolio, and followed Tina through the doorway, down a long haul, and into a small office to the right marked "Human Resource Department." Tina softly knuckle-knocked on the door.

"Enter!" Mr. Eagleton, a grumpy bald man in his sixties, glanced up over the top of his tortoise-shell reading glasses. "Please take a seat."

"Thank you for taking the time to see me."

"Please know, this isn't how I run my office. You're only here because of Ms. Abadie. Frankly, I don't think you're *Elite Magazine* material, but she does. So, what do you bring to the table besides being able to wash windows?"

James handed him his half-page resume. Mr. Eagleton skimmed over it. "As I said, not *Elite Magazine* material, but I'm sure I can find you something in the janitorial department."

"I know I don't have much on my resume, but I am an excellent photographer and know a little about graphic design. I'd love to work in any capacity in those departments, even if it is holding the camera or bounce cards. I plan on finishing my degree online in graphic design. I started it twenty years ago."

"Things have progressed since then. Let me see your portfolio, please." He huffed, not expecting much of a presentation.

James handed him the portfolio, and Mr. Eagleton flipped through its contents page by page. The first photograph was of Jamie, age three, with her mother in front of a large teacup at an amusement park. The wind perfectly caught their hair and dresses, creating a fantastic vision. The second photograph of an elderly gentleman feeding the pigeons caught Mr. Eagleton's eye. "When was this one taken? This is a piece of art, not a photograph."

"I took it about seven years ago in the French Quarter. I don't know the man in the picture, but his presence spoke to me. It was his expression that captured my attention. It was as if he spoke telepathically to birds."

"Nice work." He flipped through the portfolio and stopped on a photograph of a bride holding her bouquet, looking out over Jackson Square from the Pontalba Apartment Building on a second-floor balcony. "This is interesting. So, you photograph weddings?"

"Not really. I was invited to a friend's sister's wedding. The photographer got food poisoning, and they needed one extremely fast. Again, I was in the right place at the right time and stepped in. Have camera will travel is my motto."

"These are amazing. You captured something extraordinary. It's pictures like these we want in our magazine. You may be a fit, after all."

"Thank you, Mr. Eagleton. I'm a hard worker, and I won't let you down. I know I can't start in a photographer's position. Still, I'm willing to be an assistant, the gopher, the fetcher. Whatever it takes."

"We have one opening in that department. It's not glamorous and is only part time for now, so no benefits. The good news is the pay is decent. Are you still interested?"

"What does the job entail?"

"You'll be the photographer's assistant. Whatever he needs, you'll do it. I must warn you; Javier is a bit different and can be demanding. Many others before you quit after the first hour."

"Sounds like a challenge, but I love a challenge. When can I start?"

"First, your paperwork, and you'll need to pass the drug screening test. So, if all goes well, you can start Monday. I'll have Tina set everything up for you. She'll contact you with the details."

"Thank you so much, Mr. Eagleton. I won't let you down."

"It's not me you'd be letting down; that would be Ms. Abadie. I'll inform her of your hiring. I'm sure she'll be pleased."

"I want to make one thing clear. I want to be treated like everyone else here at *Elite Magazine*. Just because Ms. Abadie set this up doesn't mean I need to be treated any differently."

"Mr. Seamore, I assure you no one knows your connection with Ms. Abadie, other than what has been on the news. So, if the cat gets out of the bag, that's on you. Just to make myself clear."

"Yes, sir. Are we finished?"

Mr. Eagleton swished James away. "By all means."

James left the office, fist-pumping. "Yes!"

Located in a junkyard along with several stray cats and dogs meandering about, James entered the office of Blue Bayou inside a small rusty white trailer with one window unit about to fall off. The 1970s paneling, warped from the years and covered with yellowed OSHA safety posters, and the chipped unwaxed olive green tile floor didn't leave much of an impression. His boss, puffing a cigarette, leaned back in his torn, fake leather desk chair with his feet propped up on his tan, rusty metal desk. Behind him were several years' worth of pin-up calendars. Of significance was this year's which featured puppies with large red Xs marking a countdown to a Hawaiian vacation coming up in two weeks. He took a long drag and then blew smoke rings into the air that slowly drifted toward the ceiling.

James cleared his throat. "Excuse me, Oliver. You have a minute?"

Oliver, a pleasantly plump guy around fifty, looked up. "Of course, is there a problem?"

"No, sir. I'm here to put in my two weeks' notice."

"You're quitting? If you don't want to clean the outside windows, I'll leave you in the interior. Just say the word."

"That isn't it. I've accepted another job. The times you need me will conflict with it and I'm going to take online classes to finish up my degree. So, I need time."

"How so?"

"I need to work during the day. I can't be in two places at once."

"You won't have to. Listen, James. How about you stay on with us? You set the hours you want to clean interior windows. It doesn't matter if you decide to clean them at midnight. Whatever time works best for you, as long as the work gets done."

"You'd let me do that?"

"To keep you on the payroll, yes. You're hard to replace. I found that out when you were recuperating. It wasn't the same without you. I'll even give you three dollars per-hour raise. So, what do you say?"

"I'll give it a go. God knows I could use the extra income. And if it doesn't work out, we'll discuss my resignation again."

"Glad to hear. So, where is this job? If you don't mind me asking?"

"*Elite Magazine.* It's been a long time coming. I will be the photographer's assistant. I should've done this years ago."

"I may not like it, but I understand."

Jamie paced in front of her couch while talking on the phone with Lance, who sat playing his guitar in his bedroom.

"My dad is up to something. I know it." She twisted her lips.

"What makes you think that?"

"He's all giddy and acting like a teenager."

"That bothers you, how?"

"Lance, you don't get it. This isn't like him. He's up to something."

"Have you thought of asking him?"

"I can't do that."

"Why not? If you're worried, you have the right to ask."

"Maybe I don't want to know the answer."

"What is the question?"

"Let me see. Hey, Dad, what are you up to? You're acting weird."

"How about, Dad, can we talk? There's something on my mind."

"Just drop it." Jamie heard a car door slam. "Speaking of… my dad just pulled up."

"Fine, but talk with your dad, okay?"

"No promises." Through the window, Jamie watched James exit the truck. "Got to go. Love you." She quickly hung up the phone and pretended to complete her homework.

James entered the house with a white-toothed grin. "Glad you're here. I have something to talk to you about."

"Me too. You go first." Jamie put down her pencil. "Homework can wait."

"I got a part-time job today. I start Monday. Now you can quit worrying about our bills."

"That's great, Dad. Where? Doing what?"

"I'm going to be a photographer's assistant at *Elite Magazine.*"

Jamie's eyes bulged. "You've got to be kidding me, right?"

"No, Ms. Abadie is a woman of her word. She said she'd help me out, and now she has. She set this up for me."

"You can't work for her. She's an awful person. She's rude and, well, rich. She'll use you just like she uses everyone else."

"Jamie. People might say I'm using her. She's the one who gave me the job. It's a blessing and not a curse. Now, I can pay our bills. Although it's part-time, I'll earn more in a week there than I do cleaning windows all day. Also, as great karma goes, Oliver gave me a raise and I get to set my hours to continue washing the interior windows, so I'll be making twice as much as I've been making."

"If you say so. Is that what you wanted to talk to me about?"

"Yes, now your turn. What's on your mind?"

"Thanksgiving."

"Glad you brought that up. There's going to be some sort of family reunion. Aunt Sally wants us to go to Georgia."

"Unbelievable. I wanted to go with Melissa and her family on a cruise." She shrugged to hide her hurt feelings and disappointment.

"Not this time. First, we can't afford it. Second, we can't afford it. Third, we can't afford it. You get that? We can't afford it. You'll have years for that once you're out of college and making a living."

"But Dad, the cruise is free. They have to have someone in the room with Melissa. The cabin is the same price for one person or two. That's why they invited me."

"No, not this year."

"Do I have to go to Aunt Sally's?"

"I think you know that answer."

"Just great. Really great."

"I'm glad you see it that way."

"Dad, that was sarcasm at its best."

Angela sat at her desk, deeply involved in her work. Stacks of folders covered her workspace. Classical piano instrumental music created the ambiance as the sun filtered through the windows. Francis entered, carrying a bouquet of spring flowers and a marked-up draft article. "Special delivery."

"Who are they from?"

Francis placed the flowers on the corner of Angela's desk and read the card out loud. "Looking forward to our next adventure."

"That's it? No name?"

"That's it, but they are from the same florist as those yellow roses you received several weeks ago."

"You know this how?"

"I tried to find out who sent those to you. I didn't have any luck, but I remember the florist."

"It seems late for flowers to be delivered. It's after seven."

"Oh, they came earlier this afternoon. I've been so busy I hadn't had time to bring them to you."

Angela looked up. "Anything else you were too busy to inform me about?"

"Mr. Eagleton called to tell you he hired Mr. Seamore. He starts Monday morning."

An enormous smile crossed Angela's lips as her cheeks blushed. "Perfect."

"I don't mean to butt into your business, but is hiring the window washer the best thing to do?"

"Don't go there. It's none of your business. Now, bring me the Earhart file. I want to review it before our meeting in the morning."

"Ms. Abadie, you have dinner in thirty minutes with Mr. Legions."

Angela exhaled. "I completely forgot." Her cellphone vibrated, and she glanced at the caller's I.D. before picking it up. "Can you hold for a second... Perfect." She looked at Francis, "I'll take this in private."

"Do you need anything else?"

"No. Have a great evening, Francis."

Francis nodded her head and left, closing the door behind her.

"John, sorry I had to put you on hold. Business is business."

"I have to cancel our dinner tonight. I have an unavoidable change in plans. My sincere apologies, but I have to leave for London in the morning."

"I hope everything is all right?"

"Just business. A certain Royal is requesting my private jet."

121

"Sounds intriguing. So, why do you have to go? You have pilots that can handle this."

"They don't trust anyone, and their pilot has COVID. They want me to be the pilot."

"That's serious. Please be careful."

"I'm calling to see if you want to go with me. We can take in a couple of shows and be tourists. And, maybe with any luck, introduce you to my client. Can you?"

"As great as meeting a Royal sounds, I have a magazine to run. Who's the Royal?"

"I'm sworn to secrecy, but I think you two would become great friends. She's a lot like you."

"A female Royal? Should I be jealous?"

"Not in the least. She's taken."

"How long will you be gone?"

"I'll be back in time to fly you and Lance to Rome."

Jamie and James sat at the computer in the living room.

"So, Dad, you ready to see all the lovely ladies interested in dating you?"

"Not really, but if it makes you happy, it'll make me happy."

Jamie logged onto *Singlematch.com*. "Your login is your email address. And your password is handsomeguy. No spaces and all lowercase."

"Handsomeguy? What kind of password is that?"

"One I knew you would remember. You can change it if you want to. It's your account."

"I'm good for now."

"Look, you have over six hundred women interested in a first date with you. Pick one out."

"Oh boy, I'm regretting this." He rolled his eyes.

"Get use to it."

James leaned in close to the screen to read the first message, and a picture of a woman appeared.

Jamie frowned, pursing her lips. "Nope, I don't like her."

"Why not?"

"Seems arrogant and unsure of herself."

"What makes you think that?"

"Geez, Dad. She wrote I am extremely good-looking; every man wants to date me. But, I don't know if I can find the right guy for me."

"I see what you mean. Next one."

Jamie clicked the next message. "Nope." Then she opened another. "Nope."

"Wait, aren't you even going to let me see?"

"Nope."

"This is going to be an all-nighter, isn't it?"

"Nope."

"Dad, look at her. She has potential."

James reviewed the file. "Interesting. A dentist."

"Let's set up a date." Jamie furiously typed in a response.

"Wait, what are you doing?"

"Setting you up on a blind date."

"How do you expect me to pay for it?"

"You just took a second job. Besides, it's only a meet-and-drink coffee date to see if you two are a match."

CHAPTER TEN

Dust in the Wind

Café Joe's, the corner coffee shop, provided the perfect spot for James to meet his first *Singlematch.com* date. The long granite counter stacked with chrome espresso machines, coffee bean grinders, coffee carafes, bottles of coffee flavors, high-end coffee mugs, and stacks of to-go cups created the coffeehouse ambiance. Several college-aged couples leaned over their cappuccinos at chic bistro tables, while others engaged on their computers worked diligently. As the barista called out filled takeout orders, James secured a corner table as agreed upon in their earlier messages. He used a paper napkin to sweep the crumbs away left by the previous occupant. To identify his blind date, he carefully looked for a woman wearing blue carrying an orange file folder.

His stomach turned as he fidgeted in his chair, glancing at his watch, thinking fifteen minutes had passed, but in reality, it had only been five. *This anticipation is killing me.*

Several minutes later, in walked an attractive brunette in her early forties wearing a solid blue dress and carrying an orange folder. James stood and waved at her as she slowly approached the table. "Hi, you must be James."

"And that would make you Carmen Sanchez. It's a pleasure to meet you. Please, take a seat."

Carmen flashed a grin as she sat. "I'm a little nervous. This is my first date from *Singlematch*." Her Spanish thick accent made it difficult for James to understand her. She bit her lower lip.

"That makes two of us."

They shared a nervous laugh.

The server approached and placed two menus on the table. "Excuse me; I'll be right back to take your order."

"Carmen, are you hungry?"

"No, I ate before I left home. I didn't know if I'd stay once I met you."

"I take it I'm safe because you haven't left yet."

"For the time being." Again, she bit her lower lip.

"What would you like to drink?"

"Just black coffee."

"We at least have one thing in common, I drink my coffee black too."

Carmen took a deep breath. "Tell me about yourself."

"Okay, I'm a widower and have a teenage daughter who will graduate next spring. And you?"

Tears flooded Carmen's eyes. "I'm sorry, I can't do this." She scooted the chair against the tile as she rose and bolted out of the café.

"Was it something I said? You flew out of here like dust in the wind." *So much for a first date.*

Angela sat at the kitchen bar, watching Miriam prepare dinner.

"Miriam, you're such a sweetheart cooking dinner for us tonight."

"My pleasure. Besides, I finally get to meet Mr. Legions. I've heard so much about him."

"Just remember, let's keep things simple."

"I wouldn't say that Cornish game hens and wild rice is a simple dinner, but I understand what you mean. I won't overdo it."

"Perfect, he should be here any minute."

Lance bolted into the kitchen. "I'm outta here. Off to the skateboard park."

Angela looked up. "Are you sure you won't change your mind and eat dinner with us? I'm sure he wants to get to know you better before our trip to Rome."

"That's the problem, Mom. He tries too hard and seems fake. So, please don't jam him down my throat."

"I get the hint. But, honey, he's not trying to replace your father. He'd never do that."

"I never thought he was. I just don't like the guy, and all of his money and connections won't make me change that. I should be home around midnight. Please have him gone by then."

"Lance, I can't promise you that, but I'll try."

"Call me when he leaves, and I'll come home." Lance kissed his mom on the cheek, waved at Miriam, and left.

"Miriam, I guess boys will be boys."

"That's one way of putting it. When is Mr. Legions expected to arrive?"

"Any minute. He's usually very punctual. I love that about him."

As if on cue, the doorbell rang.

"And, just like that, here he is now." Angela walked to the front of the house and answered the door.

John held a bouquet of white lilies. "These are for you."

"Thank you; they're beautiful. Please come in. Follow me to the kitchen so I can put them in a vase."

The two made their way to the kitchen, and when they entered, Miriam grabbed her heart. "Opie, is that really you?" She couldn't believe her eyes.

John stopped in his tracks. "Mom?"

"It is you." Tears flowed from Miriam's eyes.

Angela's brow furrowed. "Can someone explain to me what's going on?"

"Ms. Abadie, this is my son, Opie."

"Opie? You're kidding, right? This is John Legions."

John scratched his forehead. "Angela, it appears your housekeeper is my long-lost mother. Now you know why I changed my name."

Angela shivered from the tension in the room. "I'm speechless. I don't know what to say."

"Opie, I have waited over twenty years for you to return to me. Can I give you a hug?"

Indignant, he froze in place before slowly sitting at the kitchen bar. "Not right now. I'm processing all of this."

"John, she's your mother."

He stared at her in righteous outrage. "Angela, she stopped being my mother when she kicked me out of the house."

"Opie, that was never what I wanted to happen. I lost your father; I wasn't thinking clearly. I'm so sorry." She wiped her tears with her apron. "Ms. Abadie, maybe it's best if I left for the day."

"Nonsense. You'll stay and eat with us."

John taciturnly glared at his mother. "That's not what I signed up for. Maybe it's best I left."

"Stop it! Both of you. It's time to mend the fence. She's your mother." Disgusted, she shook her head at them both with her hands on her hips.

"It's okay, Ms. Abadie. I get it. He doesn't want to have anything to do with me. May I be dismissed for the day?" Miriam dried her hands on her apron and then wiped her tears again before John interjected.

"Mom, wait. Angela's right; it's time to end this feud." He rose and hugged his mother.

"Opie? That's a far reach from John." Angela winked at him.

"Please keep that name to yourself and never call me that again."

"Miriam, I had no idea I was dating your son."

"That makes two of us."

The skateboard park was unusually crowded for this time of day. Several families enjoyed picnics with their children. Of note, one family with a little girl with long braided pigtails in a pink frilly dress chasing bubbles blown by her mother caught Jamie's eye, bringing back a bittersweet memory. *I would give anything to do that with my mom and dad, again.*

"Lance, go, Lance!" Jamie watched Lance maneuver the pipe at the skateboard park, unable to take her eyes off him. Conrad came up behind her and poked her in the ribs, causing her to jerk.

"Conrad, stop that. You know how that annoys me."

"If it didn't, I'd stop."

"Just grow up for a change. That kind of prank belongs in middle school. No wonder you don't have a girlfriend."

"I can have any girl I want."

"Right, that's why they're lining up at your locker to date you."

"I'm saving myself for a college woman."

"Lucky girl." Her tone dripped with sarcasm.

Lance popped up on the last pipe and stopped at the top, waving at Jamie and Conrad.

"Look, your boyfriend is waving at you." Conrad snickered, abruptly.

"So is yours." Jamie waved back.

Lance exploded down the pipe and stopped in front of Jamie.

"Great run, Lance. When will it be my turn?"

"As soon as you get a skateboard."

"Let's make a date to buy me one. That way, during the Thanksgiving holidays, you can teach me."

"Deal. I can do it Monday, but then I leave for Rome Tuesday. We'll have to wait until after the weekend. So, when I return, I can teach you how to ride it."

"It's a date." She hugged Lance, who returned her energetic hug.

Conrad blew air through his nose. "Aren't y'all the cutest couple ever? Not!"

Monday morning brought a new enthusiasm for James. He rose early, fixed breakfast for Jamie, did his physical therapy exercise routine, then showered and dressed. "Finally, I'm not cleaning windows."

"What was that, Dad?" Jamie came flying into James' room at the sound of his voice.

"Just talking to myself."

"You know, that's a sign of being crazy." She twisted her lips.

"Not if you're venting."

"Vent away. I'm all ears."

"I'm excited. I'm starting my new job today."

"Promise me you'll stay away from that lady."

"Honey, she's my boss. I'm sure our paths will cross."

"Then, keep it professional. I don't like her."

"You don't even know her."

"I know enough. She's rude, a snob, and a wealthy socialite. I'm sure she hired you to save her own skin."

"What do you mean by that?"

"She's playing nice, so you won't sue her. She's all about the money and nothing else, and don't forget extremely rude."

"That's not the answer. Besides, she's been more than accommodating, and I don't find her rude at all."

"If you say so."

"Why aren't you dressed for school? You have to leave in fifteen minutes."

"Seriously, Dad. It's the Thanksgiving holidays. I don't have to be back in school for another week."

"I guess you told me that. What are your plans for today? May I suggest you send off another essay and apply for college?"

"That is on my to-do list a bit later today. But first, I'm meeting up with Melissa and a couple of other friends. We're getting skateboards."

"Skateboards! Are you crazy? Those are dangerous. I forbid it. Make a better plan. And where do you even plan on getting that kind of money?"

"Dad. Don't be silly. I won't be doing any flips or crazy stuff. I just want to learn. It beats doing drugs."

"Drugs? Is that meant to appease me? If it is, it isn't working."

"Dad, I really want to skateboard. I have money in my piggy banks. It's about time I spend it. Besides, I can ride it around on campus next year."

"Only punks ride skateboards, and you're not one. Stick to cheerleading. It's less dangerous, so save your money. You're going to need it when you go to college. No skateboard. Period! Have I made myself clear?"

Jamie stormed from his room. "Dad, you're being overbearing. I'm getting a skateboard. You don't have to approve or even like it!"

"Not until you're eighteen!"

The large production set for *Elite's* upcoming Christmas cover bustled with people -- hairdressers, make-up artists, models, production assistants, three assistant cameramen, Javier, the main cameraman who James must answer to, and James. The set design resembled a Hallmark movie postcard filled with fake snow, snowflakes, trim, an overflowing Santa sleigh, Christmas lights, and so much more.

Javier stomped his foot. "Get those models ready! Time is money, and I don't have money to waste. We have a campaign to shoot."

Everyone scurried into action, all except James, who scrutinized the others. His perplexed eyes darted from one person to the other as his brows furrowed and his lips twisted.

"New Guy, what are you waiting on, a personal invitation?"

James' eyes bulged. "No, sir, I'm needing some direction. Not sure what you want me to do. First-day jitters."

Javier's stone-cold glare of annoyance quickly turned to eyes rolling. "Keep busy is what I want you to do. You're not paid to watch. Don't stand around. Make yourself useful. Do something, even if it is picking up trash or delivering a piece of wardrobe to a model. Do you know how to do that?"

"Yes, sir." James picked up the empty water bottle at Javier's feet and stared at several candy wrappers. "Excuse me, it looks like you dropped something." He hurled an accusatory evil-eye toward him.

"Pick them up, shoo, shoo..." Javier dismissively flicked his wrist.

James took three steps backward, holding his sharp tongue.

"Clearly, you're deaf. Shoo, that's for you." He flicked his wrist, again waving for James to scram. "Make yourself useful." He scooted the candy wrappers with the tip of his shoe toward James. "Useful is, as useful does." Then, he pranced off toward a white-haired, bearded model dressed like Santa Claus and two of his elves.

I guess he doesn't know where the trashcan is.

From across the room, the slim, almost anorexic-looking model holding up a white princess wedding gown with sequins and pearls yelled, "If you think I'm wearing this piece of crap, you're mistaken.

Bring me something that fits. I refuse to look like freaking Cinderella!"

Javier snapped his fingers as he popped his hip. "You, new guy. Go to wardrobe and tell them Princess Daniella is requesting something that fits her size zero body. This time, make it a mermaid tail dress."

"I'm on it." James glanced around the room, but the wardrobe personnel were nowhere to be seen.

"Now, new guy! Wardrobe is across the hall."

James briskly strode out of the room and into the wardrobe area, where chaos prevailed. Expensive designer wedding dresses filled the racks, seamstresses stitched away, altering runway masterpieces, and Posey, resembling Rue Paul in drag, strutted across the floor wearing a flowing designer tunic.

Boy, what have I gotten myself into? James took a long, deep breath. "Javier says to bring Daniella a new outfit that fits her. Size zero. Oh, he requested it to be a mermaid tail. Whatever that means." He waited, but nobody responded. "Who's in charge here?" Again, everyone ignored him.

Angela entered the wardrobe area unnoticed to check on the progress.

"Okay, I know I'm the new guy, but I need to bring Daniella a new outfit that fits, and nobody seems to care. Anybody?"

Angela huffed as her brow furrowed. "Posey, are you the head of wardrobe?" Sarcasm filled her tone. "Did you hear Mr. Seamore? Get a new outfit for Daniella, pronto. Don't make me or Mr. Seamore ask you again."

Posey flicked his hand in the air. "You heard Ms. Abadie. Quickly, chop, chop, people. Find a size zero mermaid tail wedding gown. Pronto!"

James' cheeks blushed. "I'm not making a great first impression, am I?"

"It's not you. This team gets a bit cocky. They're the best in the business, and they know it. Any outsider is quickly frowned upon until they prove their worth. Don't let them bother you."

"Here, new guy. Take this to Daniella!" Posey tossed the dress to James, hitting him in the face.

"Posey, that's no way to treat a colleague." Angela glared at him. "Treat Mr. Seamore with the same respect you give me. Have I made myself clear?"

"Crystal clear. I'm sorry, new guy; please take that to Daniella and see if she likes this better."

Angela drew in a long-exasperated breath. "His name is James, not New Guy, unless you prefer to address him as Mr. Seamore."

James held up his hand. "That's unnecessary, Angela. I'm the new guy and need to earn their respect."

"Nonsense, not here at *Elite Magazine*. I see I need to issue a memorandum on how to treat colleagues. James, let's take a walk."

"Angela, I honestly appreciate what you're trying to do, but I think I need to get this dress to Daniella before Javier calls out for an all-points bulletin on me."

"I'll handle Javier. Let's go."

Together, they walked into the large production set. James immediately found Daniella and handed her the dress. "If this isn't to your liking, I'll be glad to get another; just let me know. I aim to please."

Daniella jerked the dress from his hands and immediately looked at the size. "This might not work. I insist you fetch another one to be on the safe side."

James inhaled, pursing his lips.

"A new dress, now!" Daniella put her hands on her hips. "Are you deaf?"

James turned, but Angela grasped his shoulder, holding him in place. "Wait!" Angela clapped her hands. "Attention everyone, I have an announcement." The room became silent. "By now, you have met James Seamore. He's working here at my request. Period. Treat him with respect. I have large plans for him here at *Elite*, so don't burn your bridges. I've promoted him to Campaign Ad Liaison. From here on out, he will be my eyes and ears during these photoshoots. If anyone has a problem with that, then leave. I won't tolerate this toxic culture any further."

Everyone glanced around, but no one budged toward the door.

"Good. As a reminder, we'll be closed Wednesday through Friday for the Thanksgiving holidays. So, use your time wisely to regenerate. And, Saturday, bright and early, we start the Legions Airlines' photoshoot. We must be on our top game with this one. Nothing can go wrong with that campaign. Any questions?" She surveyed the room to ensure everyone understood her directives, and since no one spoke, she felt confident. "Carry on."

Javier clapped his hands. "You heard Ms. Abadie. Play nice and get back to work."

Angela smiled at James. "I expect you in my office immediately after today's shoot for updates."

"Yes, ma'am."

Angela's cell phone rang. She scurried from the room, answering the phone. "This is highly unusual for you to call this time of day."

On the other end of the line, John relaxed in a white leather chair on his lavish private jet. "I have bad news. I have to break our date for tonight. A company emergency came up, and I'm flying to Spain."

"I wasn't expecting this. Be sure to eat some chips and salsa for me."

"That's not exactly why I'm going."

"Then guacamole."

"Seriously, Angela. I won't be back in time to fly you and Lance to Rome."

"Just great. Now, I have to scramble for last-minute plane fares." Her response seemed hostile for a moment as frustration filled her.

"Not at all; I'm still sending a private jet for you. The only thing that'll change is that I'll meet you in Rome."

"Well, this isn't exactly how I planned it, but I completely understand. Business always comes first."

In his BMW, with blues drifting from the speakers, Lance pulled up to Jamie's house and honked the horn. She bolted from the front door and quickly entered the vehicle, flashing a smile. "I'm so excited. I get my skateboard today."

"Just when I thought you wanted to be with me. I guess I now know how you feel about me." He leaned over and planted a kiss on her blushing cheek, and then drove off.

"I'll update your status as soon as I get Dusty." She rubbed her palms together in anticipation.

"Dusty?" He raised his left eyebrow.

"Yep, Dusty. That's what I'm going to name her."

"Her?"

"Yes, my new skateboard."

"What kind of name is that?"

"As in dust in the wind. Once I learn how to ride her, I'll fly by everyone, leaving them in the dust."

"I like your ambition, but that'll take lots of practice. I've been at this since I was at least three."

"If there's a will, there's a way. Besides, I have the best teacher in the world, unless you're not really a champion."

"Let's just take this one step at a time."

"Don't you mean one skateboard at a time?"

"You can be a real dork, you know?"

"So, now I'm a dork. I guess that beats preppy cheerleader."

"That was an attempt at sarcasm. I wouldn't want you any other way."

The car turned the corner, and a short block ahead was Ezrider Skateboard Shop. The 1950s Texaco gas station, transformed into a skate shop, held the era of its time, and was considered an icon of sorts in the area's architecture. In the corner of the parking lot was a snow cone shop built from pallets and painted in bright colors with skateboards attached to the side. Three families stood in line.

Jamie leaned forward to take a closer look. "This looks like a time warp. You should've told me, and I could've worn my pink poodle skirt."

"Hilarious. You want a world-famous snow cone? They have the best right here. It's shaved ice."

"I never took you for a snow cone kind of guy."

"Oh, with these snow cones, I am. I've traveled the world and never had one like this."

"Sounds like a plan, but after we buy Dusty."

"Let's do it." Lance exited the car, walked to the passenger's side, and opened the door for Jamie. "My Lady, shall we?" He extended his arm toward her, and she quickly used it to exit the car.

"I thought you'd never ask."

They strolled toward the front door; the handle was a miniature skateboard about five inches long.

Jamie rubbed the skateboard handle as if it were a magic lamp. "How cute! It's a bity." Jamie smiled. "Now, I'm excited."

Lance opened the door for her. Once inside, Jamie's eyes widened as she glanced at the hundreds of skateboards in every color and design imaginable. She felt her heart pound with excitement.

"There must be thousands in this place. This explains why you have so many. How do you choose?"

A man in his late sixties, with a silver ponytail midway down his back, wearing jeans and a Tony Lark T-shirt, approached. "Welcome to Ezrider. You have something special in mind?"

"Do I!" Jamie beamed from ear to ear. "I'm looking for my very first skateboard. She's got to be special."

"And, for you?" He stared at Lance. "Wait, I know who you are. Congratulations on a great win. That was some run."

"Thank you. It felt pretty good."

"You ready for nationals?"

"Ready is my middle name." Lance glanced up at a poster behind the counter featuring the man standing in front of him. "Wait, aren't you Billy Ray Lark?"

"The one and only brother of Tony Lark."

"Sorry, man, for your accident. You were just as good, if not better, than your brother back in the day."

"That's all in the past. I do alright with the skate shop. But, life has a way of opening doors when one slams you in the ass, or in my case, takes out both your knees."

Jamie cleared her throat. "Can we find me a skateboard, or will we stand around reminiscing what could've been?"

A soft smile graced Billy Ray's lips. "How long have you been skating?"

Lance put his arm around Jamie. "She hasn't yet. This will be her first skateboard, and I'll be showing her the ropes."

"A newbie. Welcome to the family. You're one lucky young lady. Not everyone has Lance for a teacher."

"Imagine that." Jamie pointed to five skateboards one at a time. "I love that hot pink flamed one. And that purple one. The blue one, that green one, and wait… that could be her. That's Dusty."

Puzzlement filled the silver-haired man's face.

"Don't ask." Lance pulled Jamie closer to him. "We need to purchase her a skateboard she can handle."

"Wait here; I think I have something special in the back that'll be perfect." Billy Ray exited through the 1960s wooden-beaded curtains.

"This is so exciting." Jamie shivered with anticipation. "What do you think he's going to bring out?"

"Well, duh, a skateboard."

Jamie playfully slapped him on the shoulder. "I know that; it's a skateboard shop. I didn't think he was going to bring out roller skates."

"You can be so silly."

"What do you think he's going to show me?"

"I don't have any clue, but I'm sure he'll know the perfect one for you."

Soon, Billy Ray returned carrying a purple-metallic, holographic-looking skateboard. "I've been waiting for the perfect girl to come into the shop for this beauty. It's one of the best beginner boards on the market." He handed Jamie the board. "It's hand-painted by Newman Michaels."

"Wait! You mean the artist and not the saxophone player?" Jamie tilted her head toward Lance.

"The one and only. He custom-painted ten boards for my shop. This is the last one, and it's an original."

"Sounds way too expensive for my taste. I don't have much of a budget." Jamie's smile twisted into a frown.

Lance took the board out of Jamie's hands and examined it. "Hmm, made by Birdcage. Seven-ply, for sure, with large wheels for a smoother ride and one heck of a paint job. How much?"

"If this were your run-of-the-mill board, it would lay you back about one-fifty, but this one is a special edition and hand-painted, so it runs closer to three-fifty, not including safety gear."

Jamie's eyes bulged. "I don't have that. You'd better show me something under a hundred, including safety gear."

"Not so fast. I'm willing to give you a deal on this."

"Whatever deal it is, I can't afford it unless it's under one hundred, including tax, title, and safety gear."

Lance observed Jamie and his heart went out to her. "Look, Jamie, I'll buy it for you. Consider it your early Christmas present."

"I can't let you do that. I'll have to wait and save up for it."

"Hold on, you two. I told you I have a deal to make."

"What kind of deal?" Jamie put her hands on her hips.

"It involves your boyfriend."

"I'm listening." Jamie grinned from cheek to cheek, and a scowl enveloped Lance's brow as his eyes darted between the others.

James stood at Jamie's bedroom doorway, watching her haphazardly pack. "Dad, do I have to go?" She tossed a pair of sleeping boxers, followed by a T-shirt, into her cheerleading duffle bag.

"Unfortunately, I promised Aunt Sally we'd come for Thanksgiving. She says she has some things to give you that belonged to your mother, and besides, it's a family reunion."

"I was looking forward to doing nothing." She grabbed a dress from her closet, held it up to her body, and then quickly tossed it into the basket in the closet.

"Then do nothing at Aunt Sally's."

"Why did you agree to go? You don't even like her." After digging in her top drawer, she removed five pairs of panties, three bras, and a nightgown, then chucked them into the bag.

"I agreed for you."

"Next time, don't do me any favors. You've ruined my Thanksgiving. I should be on that cruise with Melissa."

"Jamie, this trip will be the last one I make you take. After you graduate and go to college, you can make your own decisions, just as long as you promise to come home for Father's Day and Christmas."

"I'm holding you to that. Do you know what Aunt Sally wants to give to me?" She tossed a pair of jeans, followed by a pullover sweatshirt, into her luggage.

"Not at all. The only thing I know is that it belonged to your mother. Doesn't that intrigue you?"

"Not in the least. Don't I already have everything that was Mom's?"

"Apparently not."

"She could've brought them or mailed them to me a long time ago. This is her way of being manipulative. You know that, don't you?"

"We leave in the morning around six. You finished packing?"

"Does it look like it? I haven't even started." She tossed two more pairs of jeans into her suitcase.

"Remember, this is only a four-day trip, and we'll be in the car for two days. You don't need much."

"Obviously, you forgot how much stuff a girl needs. I'd rather have it and not need it than need it and not have it."

"Your mother always said the same thing."

"Then I come by it honestly."

CHAPTER ELEVEN

When in Rome or Peach Country

The morning came early, too early for Jamie, as her father's voice drifted from down the hall. "Jamie, rise, and shine. We leave in fifteen minutes."

Her eyelids slowly fluttered opened. After glancing at the nightstand clock, she drew in an elongated, deep breath. *Why does it have to be five in the morning?*

James popped his head into the door. "Sweetie, we leave in fifteen minutes."

"I heard you the first time."

"That means it's time to get up."

Jamie rolled over, sheltering her face with her pink fleece blanket.

"Oh, no, you don't." He promptly approached the bed and jerked the covers away, singing a jingle he'd learned as a child from his grandmother. "Good morning, good morning, good morning, it's time to rise and shine. Good morning, good morning, good morning; I hope you're feeling fine. Just wiggle your toes, get out of bed; there's lots of fun to do ahead; good morning, good morning, good morning!"

"Wow, you're pulling out all the stops."

"I thought we'd stop for breakfast around eight or so."

"Sounds great, Dad. I'll get dressed and load up my stuff." She drizzled herself out of bed.

139

"We leave in ten minutes." He scurried from her room.

As the sun ascended over Pontchartrain Lake, creating an orange, yellow, and violet sunrise, the extended black limousine pulled up to John Legions' private hangar at the Lakefront Airport. The pearl white Gulfstream G650 jet with the sapphire blue Legions Airlines' logo sat about a hundred yards away. Once stopped, Lance and Angela exited the vehicle with the help of the chauffeur. "Ma'am, please watch your step."

A roar from another jet overtook them on takeoff. Lance watched as it ascended and slowly vanished.

"Thank you, Raymond."

"I'll get your luggage. Have a safe flight. If you need anything, the flight attendant will happily accommodate you." Raymond lifted a four-piece, bright orange Valextra luggage set from the trunk and plunged them into a luggage carrier.

"I'll take my own. I want it on board with me." Lance grabbed his black leather Maxwell-Scott duffle bag from the trunk as he ogled the jet. "Nice ride, Mom. Mr. Legions might not be so bad, after all."

"He does own the company. I wouldn't expect anything less from him."

They strolled toward the jet with Raymond on their heels, pulling the luggage cart.

"Why four pieces of luggage, Mom? We're only going to be gone five days. It's a bit overkill, don't you think?"

"That's questionable. I never know what I'll need, what parties I'll attend, or what events might surface that call for my attendance. So, I plan for everything. Unlike you, I wear more than black on black."

The handsome uniformed pilot exited the cabin along with a tall, blonde flight attendant and swiftly bolted down the stairs to greet his passengers. "Good morning, Ms. Abadie, and you, Lance. I'm Captain Freeman. This way, please."

"Nice. Does this thing come with a remote control?" Lance hurried to catch up with the others.

The pilot frowned as the group neared the steps. "If you mean autopilot, then yes. Please watch your step and take a seat of your choosing. We'll get airborne as soon as your luggage is onboard, and everyone takes their seat."

Angela smiled at the pilot. "He's gorgeous. Things are looking up."

As they entered the luxurious cabin, the first things that caught Lance's eye were the six overstuffed, white, ostrich leather recliners, the elongated couch that could seat at least ten people, the granite table tops, and the area midway that looked like a fancy game room equipped with a big-screen television.

He strolled down the aisle, absorbing it all. "I'll take this one." Lance, grinning, dropped his duffle bag and sat. "This beats first class by a mile."

"I'd say so. John has refined taste; it shows by the amenities on this plane."

"Welcome aboard, ma'am. I'm Terri, and I'll be taking care of you and your son during this flight. Please take your seat and buckle in." The flight attendant gracefully pointed to one recliner.

"Do you mind if I move back a bit?" Lance winked at her.

"Not at all. Please make yourself comfortable. Once we take off and the safety belt restriction is lifted, you're free to explore the rest of the jet. Aft is the master bedroom where you can rest if you like, the kitchen is forward, and there are two restrooms, one in the master bedroom and one before you get to it."

"Wow, only one bedroom. How disappointing." Lance settled back in his recliner.

"Sir, for your comfort, this jet is equipped with four smaller sleeping areas, more like bunk beds, but I've been told they are extremely comfortable and equipped with a private television as well. I don't think you'll be disappointed."

Lance buckled in and grabbed his cell phone. "I was kidding, but good to know." He held up his phone. "Will this thing work once we're airborne?"

"Absolutely, Legions Airlines equips all their jets with the best satellite service provided by Elon Musk. So, you'll be able to communicate with whomever you want for the duration of the flight once we're airborne."

"This definitely beats first class."

"Would either of you like a pre-flight drink?"

Angela nodded and smiled. "I'd love a spicy Bloody Mary with extra olives and celery, please."

"And for you, sir?"

"I'd like a dirty martini, shaken, not stirred."

"Lance! Behave yourself. You're not old enough to drink."

"I was just kidding, Mom."

A wry grin crossed the flight attendant's lips. "Sir, how about orange juice on the rocks?"

"Sounds boring, but I'll take it. Orange juice on the rocks will be fine."

"Very good choice. Now settle in and enjoy your flight."

"I hate to be a pest, but does this jet come with pillows and blankets?" Lance flashed a wanting grin.

"Of course, sir. I'll bring them once we take off."

"What about peanuts? I'm starving."

"I'm sure we have those. However, I'll serve you breakfast after we take off and the pilot turns off the seatbelt sign."

"So, you cook, too?"

"Lance, leave the flight attendant alone. Let her do her job."

"Come on, Mom, I'm trying to go with the flow. Since you made me come with you, I might as well take advantage of the situation. Free food and free drinks. I might survive the flight after all."

Angela glanced up at the flight attendant. "Boys will be boys. Sorry about that."

"No problem, Ms. Abadie. I'll bring your drinks right away." The flight attendant headed for the kitchen area in the front cabin.

Lance reclined his chair.

Ding, dong! "This is Captain Freeman, welcome aboard. My co-pilot is Captain Amanda Sterling, and you've already met Terri. Once the flight tower has cleared us for takeoff, we'll depart for Rome. The flight duration is eleven hours and twenty-five minutes, and I expect no delay in our arrival. It should be a smooth flight as weather conditions are premium, and I don't anticipate any turbulence. Please fasten your seatbelts and remain seated until I give the all-clear sign. Once in flight, you will be free to roam the cabin and make yourselves at home. Should you need anything, please alert Terri, and she'll be happy to assist you."

Terri soon returned with a tray and two drinks. She delicately placed a crisp white napkin on the side table next to Angela and her Bloody Mary, then repeated her action with Lance's orange juice. "I must prepare for takeoff. Once we reach our designated altitude, I'll promptly serve breakfast. So, please sit back and enjoy your flight."

James' truck, which had a cracked windshield, sped down Interstate 65 toward Atlanta. Jamie leaned against her pillow, which rested against the passenger door, and snuggled with her fluffy pink throw blanket, barely able to keep her eyes open. She yawned and stretched, watching the scenery pass as if from a film reel, and listened to the road noise.

"The long and winding road…" James sang along to the tune.

"Dad, do we have to listen to this?" She leaned over and snippily turned off the radio.

"If you asked, I would've changed the station."

"No, thank you, Dad. I want peace and quiet."

"You have no taste in music."

"Look who's talking. At least I'm not stuck in the sixties, seventies, or eighties."

"Meaning?"

"Your taste in music."

"I could say the same thing about yours."

"Forget I said anything. I'm starving, and I have to go to the bathroom. Can we stop soon?"

"Of course, it's time for breakfast. What's your choice? That is anything that doesn't involve a drive-thru. I need to stretch my legs."

"Perfect. Look, just our luck. Our favorite breakfast spot. My mouth is already watering."

The truck exited and made its way to the restaurant.

"Dad, can we even afford this?"

"Honey, we have money now."

"I don't get it; you've only had your second job for two days. You couldn't have made any money that soon."

"Actually, I did. It's a paid holiday. Since it's Thanksgiving week, I got paid for the entire week yesterday. So, we're fine. See, my boss isn't that bad after all."

"I still don't like her, no matter what you say."

Angela sat at a small table with a starched white linen tablecloth near the aft of the jet. A small vase with three red roses graced the tabletop, and a gold-embossed envelope was attached. Rachel served Angela her eggs Benedict, three strips of crisp bacon, a blueberry muffin with cream cheese, and another Bloody Mary while Lance slept soundly reclined in the luxurious leather chair.

"Should I wake him, Ms. Abadie?"

"No, let him sleep. He doesn't eat this early, anyway. He's more of a lunch kind of guy."

"Yes, ma'am. Do you need anything else?"

"No, Terri, I'm good."

"Very well; I'll be back to check on you soon."

Angela sipped her Bloody Mary and took one bite of her eggs. The gold embossed envelope caught her attention again, so she gently placed her fork on the plate and opened the note. A smile graced her lips as she opened it and read it. "Angela, I hope you're enjoying your flight. I'll be waiting to take you and Lance to your hotel. I miss you like crazy. Love always, John."

James and Jamie pulled up to a massive iron gate with an ornate initial 'C' on it. The plantation-style, three-story home surrounded by peach trees made its presence known through the arches. Jamie took a deep, relaxing breath as she stretched. "We've made it here in record time."

"That's your opinion. It always goes fast when you sleep the entire way."

"I didn't sleep the entire way; I woke up to eat, didn't I?"

"Let me put it to you this way. You weren't much company." James leaned over and pressed the intercom button.

It buzzed in response. "Sir, the service entrance is around the back."

"Excuse me, whoever you are. We're invited guests of Sally Collier. Actually, we're related." A lump formed in his throat.

"Names please."

"James and Jamie Seamore."

"Please wait while I verify your arrival."

James, tapping his fingers against the steering wheel, shrugged as if it wasn't any big deal and calmly smiled at Jamie.

"How embarrassing, Dad. He thinks we're the hired help."

"Not for long."

Static came through the intercom. "Mr. Seamore, I apologize for the misunderstanding; you may proceed through the gate."

The massive iron gate slowly opened, scraping a small area. Once opened, James pressed the gas pedal and proceeded down the long driveway, stopping in the front. Before he could shut off the engine, Aunt Sally opened the front door.

Jamie, holding her pillow and duffle bag, eagerly leaped down from the truck and stood in awe, gobsmacked at the mansion that seemed so incredibly detached from her everyday life. "I don't remember it being this big." Her words were casual, but held enough excitement to show she was glad to be there.

Aunt Sally hugged Jamie. "Sweetheart, this isn't the house you remember. Your uncle and I moved here about ten years ago."

"No wonder I don't remember it. Speaking of, where is Uncle Brad?"

"He sends his best, but he couldn't make it home from Singapore in time. His flight has been delayed."

"Well, I'll miss him."

Aunt Sally flashed a condescending grin at James. "It's good to see you arrived in one piece. How's the leg?"

"Just fine." He snatched his tattered, blue duffle bag from the truck's back bed.

"You two must be tired after that long drive." Her southern charm dripped of organic honey.

"Not really; I slept all the way."

"Shall we go in?"

"Can't wait." James rolled his eyes.

When they arrived at the front door, the English butler, dressed in his black tuxedo uniform with a crisp white shirt and a black tie, greeted them. "Welcome to Collier Mansion. I'm Edmund Wadsworth. This way, please."

They entered the exquisite marble foyer with a chandelier hanging above, and Jamie immediately noticed the two winding staircases on either side.

Jamie glanced at her father and then at Edmund. "Are you a real butler? I mean, I know you're a real person, but are you a real butler?"

Edmund nodded. "Indeed, and who do I have the pleasure of greeting?"

"I'm Jamie Seamore, and this is my father, James." She dropped her pillow and cheerleading duffle bag and then curtsied. "Nice to meet you."

A glimmer of laughter came into Aunt Sally's eyes. "Jamie, there's no need to curtsy. Why don't both of you get settled into your rooms? Dinner will be served in the formal dining room promptly at seven. Dress for the occasion. Edmund, please show them to their quarters."

Jamie puckered her lips. "What do you mean to dress for the occasion? I only brought jeans and tennis shoes."

"I anticipated that. No worries. Aunt Sally to the rescue. I shopped for you both. You'll find appropriate attire in the wardrobe in your bedrooms."

James huffed. "You shouldn't have. I'll wear my jeans and T-shirt; thank you very much."

"Embarrass yourself if you like. I have special guests coming over for dinner who will be dressed for this special occasion."

"Now, I'm confused." Jamie stepped forward. "Who's coming to dinner?"

"If I told you, it would ruin the surprise. Now, Edmund, please show them to their rooms. At this rate, you'll barely have time to bathe and dress before company arrives."

After picking up Jamie's duffle bag and pillow, Edmund smiled. "This way, Mr. Seamore, and Ms. Jamie."

Edmund headed up the long, winding staircase to the left while Jamie bolted to the stairs on the right. "I'll meet you at the top!"

"Jamie Seamore, stop!" Embarrassed, James' face turned crimson.

Aunt Sally touched James' shoulder. "It's quite fine, James. Let her have fun. Besides, I've waited a long time to have her in my house."

James followed Edmund up the stairs. When they both reached the top, Jamie stood waiting for them.

"This way, Ms. Jamie." Edmund led her down a long hall with multiple closed doors, stopping at one midway, and opened it. "Your quarters, Ms. Jamie. Shall I place your luggage in the wardrobe?"

"That won't be necessary." She took her duffle bag and pillow from Edmund and entered her room. "This is amazing. I feel like I'm in a palace. Whoa! This room is bigger than our entire house, Dad, and it's pink."

"Ms. Collier had it decorated for you when she moved in. She thought it would become yours."

James cleared his throat. "Don't get used to it, Jamie; we're going home as soon as Thanksgiving is over."

"That doesn't mean I can't pretend to be a princess, does it?"

"You'll always be my princess."

"Ms. Jamie, if you need anything, just press this intercom button."

"Thank you, Edmund. I'll be just fine."

"Mr. Seamore, if you'll please follow me to your quarters. You're only two doors down from your daughter."

"Thank you, Edmund. Jamie, I'll knock on your door at seven; we'll go downstairs to dinner together."

"Great plan, Dad."

Edmund exited the room and led James two doors down. "Your room, Mr. Seamore."

James reached for the doorknob, but Edmund beat him to it. "I'll get that for you, sir." The butler opened the door. "I hope you find this room satisfactory."

With wide eyes, James stepped into the emerald-green suite. "Wow, I've only seen something like this in the movies." Glancing around, he dropped his bag on the long bench at the foot of the massive canopy king-size bed covered in a gold and emerald-green bedspread and matching pillows.

"Will there be anything else, sir?"

"Does this room come with a bathroom?"

Edmund sauntered across the room and opened a door, exposing an elegant bathroom. "This is your private ensuite. I hope it's to your liking?"

"I'll survive. I've been known to rough it a time or two."

"Excellent, sir. If you need anything…"

"…I know; press the intercom button."

"Indeed, sir. As a reminder, there is a tuxedo in the wardrobe for you to wear to dinner, if you choose."

"I'm good. I'll wear my jeans. I'm not much of a tuxedo frills kind of guy. Well, unless I'm getting married, which I won't be doing anytime soon. No, make that never."

"I bid you a good evening and take my leave." Edmond closed the door behind him.

What have I gotten us into? James shuffled to the wardrobe and opened it. Like Aunt Sally said, a tuxedo, a white shirt, and a red bow tie hung on the rack. A pair of black patton shoes rested on the bottom shelf. "You've got to be kidding?" He glanced at his watch -- 6:38 p.m. His sigh was laced with bitter frustration, but he wasn't about to be defeated. He stood his ground, deciding to wear what he had on.

The Learjet landed smoothly; three beeps interrupted the silence. "This is your Captain. Please remain seated until we have come to a complete stop. It has been our pleasure serving you today. Welcome to Rome."

"About time." Lance stretched.

Angela smiled at him. "Please be on your best behavior this week."

"I'm always on my best behavior."

"That's what I mean. Be better than that. John is going to be with us."

"So, let me get this straight. Because Mr. Legions is our third wheel, I have to pretend to be perfect to impress him. Is that what you're saying?"

"Not at all. I don't want any complications. I'm more worried about what Grandpa is going to say."

"I wouldn't worry about that. Mr. Legions is a wealthy man, and Grandpa Warbucks loves rich people."

"Don't disrespect your grandfather like that."

"How is that disrespectful?"

"You called him a name."

"Mom, I was referring to the show, *Annie*. You know, Daddy Warbucks?"

"I didn't find it amusing."

Terri approached them. "The captain has given the clear sign, and you are free to disembark. It has been a pleasure serving you today."

Angela smiled. "Where may we retrieve our luggage?"

"The agent will place them in your limousine once Mr. Legions arrives. We received a message that he's running about fifteen minutes late. You may wait in the private waiting area in the terminal."

Angela's brow furrowed. "How many waiting areas are there?"

"Once you enter the terminal, you'll see the private entrance marked with the Legions Airlines' logo. You'll find all the comforts of home until Mr. Legions arrives."

"It shouldn't be that difficult to find, Mom. Can we go already?"

They departed the plane and made their way to the terminal. Like Terri had explained, the gold embossed logo for Legions Airlines was prominent. As Angela and Lance entered, Angela's cell phone rang. She combed through her purse and retrieved it. "John, we're here."

"I know. The pilot called and told me. Sorry, I'm running late, but the good news is I'll be there in fifteen minutes. Make yourselves comfortable, and if you're hungry, help yourself to the snacks. There should be plenty, or somebody's going to get fired."

"Sounds like a plan. I can't wait to see you."

James, dressed in jeans, a black T-shirt, and tennis shoes, gazed at himself in the floor-to-ceiling mirror in his Collier mansion quarters. *Spiffy enough.* After fiddling with the door latch, he escaped his quarters and headed for Jamie's room, tapping gently on her door. "Sweetie, you ready?"

Jamie cracked the door open and peeked out, barely showing her face. "Not yet, Dad. I'm still getting dressed. I'll meet you downstairs."

"Okay, don't be too long. You don't want to make Aunt Sally mad."

"Since when do you care?"

"Just hurry. Honestly, I don't want to be alone with her. I need my sidekick."

"Now that sounds like the Dad I know." She closed the door.

Jamie, in her T-shirt and boxer shorts, briefly leaned against the door, taking her magnificent princess room into view. She hurried to the wardrobe closet, opened it, and admired several formal evening gowns; one pleated tulle floral applique designed by Rickie Freeman, one purple Zac Posen two-tone tulle bustier, one Oscar de la Renta sapphire blue strapless, and one red Marchesa draped rose falille. Several pairs of stilettos matching each ballgown rested on the bottom shelf. A knock on the door interrupted her. *I could get used to this.* "Dad, I'm dressing. Go away!"

"It's Aunt Sally. May I come in?"

Bouncing to the door with a huge smile, Jamie opened it. "Sorry about that, Aunt Sally."

"No need to apologize. I have something of your mother's I want to give you."

"Oh, the reason you insisted we come here."

"Among other things." She handed Jamie a small gift wrapped in pink foil paper with a beautiful handmade glittered bow. "I know your mother would want you to have this. She bought it for you the day she found out she was having a girl. She wanted to give it to you when she felt you were old enough. I'm not sure what that meant, but I think you're old enough now."

Jamie gracefully unwrapped the gift and opened the black velvet box containing a pearl necklace and matching bracelet. "Whoa, these are beautiful."

"As beautiful as you are, wear them tonight with one of the dresses I selected for you, along with these." Aunt Sally handed Jamie another small, gift-wrapped box that matched the first. "Open it."

Jamie enthusiastically ripped into the gift, which contained pearl earrings. "These from my mom, too?"

"These are from me. I wanted you to have the complete set."

"They're beautiful. Thank you, Aunt Sally."

"My pleasure. Let me help you put on the necklace. The clasp can be a bit tricky."

After Jamie handed her aunt the necklace, she carefully clasped them around her neck. "You look like a princess, fit to meet your prince." Aunt Sally beamed with pride. "I hope you like the ballgowns."

"They're beautiful. It'll be hard to decide."

"You'll know the right one once you've tried them on. Now, finish dressing sugar pie; you don't have much time." She walked to the door.

"Thank you again, Aunt Sally. I feel very special."

"You are special and deserve nothing but the best, like this room and the gowns. There's a lot more to come. You know you can stay here as long as you want."

"I know, but I can't leave my dad."

Aunt Sally closed the door behind her.

Jamie retrieved the red dress, held it up, and stared at herself in the mirror before glancing at the price tag -- $3,799. Her eyes bulged. She quickly put it back and grabbed the purple one. She put it on, but something was not quite right about how it fit, so she undressed and grabbed the pink one. *This should work.*

The doorbell gonged several times, catching her off guard and sending her into a frenzy to get dressed.

Downstairs, Edmund sauntered to the front door, adjusting his coat jacket before opening it. Upon opening, he abruptly bowed to three Royals dressed as if ready for a coronation. King Egbert

Salmondi of Maldovichia, Queen Helena Salmondi, and the Reigning Prince, Karl Salmondi, a handsome man, age twenty-two, with a strong jawline and matching dimples on each side, green eyes, and chestnut hair, nodded in response. "Your Majesties, Prince Karl, welcome once again to Collier Mansion. Please enter."

Queen Helena entered first, followed by the King and then Prince Karl.

Before Edmund could close the door, Aunt Sally entered. "Your Majesties, welcome." She curtsied. "It is my honor to have you in my home. Shall we go to the parlor?"

Prince Karl's eyes widened as he gazed at the top of the stairs. "May I inquire who this beauty is that my eyes behold?"

Everyone turned around, their jaws dropped, as they gawked at Jamie standing at the top of the stairs looking like a fairytale princess in the pink ballgown, pearl necklace, earrings, and bracelet. The prince couldn't take his eyes off her.

"That's my niece. She and her father are visiting for the holidays." Aunt Sally gestured to Jamie. "Come on down; I want to introduce you to our distinguished guests."

Jamie gracefully grasped the handrail and slowly made her way down the stairs. Before she reached halfway, James entered from the parlor. Tears filled his eyes, gazing at how beautiful his daughter looked, reminding him of her mother.

Prince Karl proceeded to the stairs and extended his hand to assist her with the final step, placing his other behind his back as he bowed. "I'm the Reigning Prince of Maldovichia, Prince Karl, and who do I have the pleasure of feasting my eyes upon?" His charm and signature flirtatious smile melted her.

"I'm Jamie Seamore, the reigning head cheerleader from New Orleans. The closest I've ever come to being royalty was in school when I was crowned homecoming queen or in a play when I played the Queen of Hearts in *Alice in Wonderland*. That man over there is my father, James." Uncomfortable being around royalty, Jamie wasn't sure how to act or what to say. It showed by her biting her upper lip.

"The Queen of Hearts is my favorite."

Edmund rang a small handbell. "Dinner is to be served in the formal dining hall. Please make your way."

Prince Karl extended his left arm. "May I have the honor of escorting you to dinner?"

"Why not?" Jamie hooked her arm at the elbow into his.

James stormed toward Aunt Sally and leaned in close to her ear. "What kind of game are you playing?"

"Simply showing my favorite niece how the other side of the family lives. Buckle up, sweet peach. I'm going to win her over. She'll never want to leave here. I'll see to it."

Furious and feeling threatened by Sally's banter, James whipped his head around, doubling his fist until his knuckles whitened. "Jamie, go change. We're leaving immediately."

Jamie winced in evident embarrassment at her father's demand, her eyes full of protest. "But Dad, Aunt Sally has gone through a lot of trouble to host us." Her gaze roamed over the crowd as she realized all eyes were on her. She froze for a split second before tears filtered through her scowling eyes.

"Now, Jamie!" James' veins throbbed in his neck. Without realizing it, he made the situation even more embarrassing than it was or needed to be.

Queen Helena stepped forward, regally inclining her head toward him. "I know it's not my place to intervene, but our family would be honored if you both stayed and had dinner. Rarely do we meet commoners."

"That's it! Jamie, get your things. Now! And get out of that ridiculous dress. We're leaving." His eyes narrowed toward Aunt Sally.

The room fell silent as Jamie, visibly upset and in tears, bolted up the stairs, losing one of her shoes. When she reached the top, in defiance, she threw the other toward her father, barely missing Prince Karl. Not the Cinderella moment she had envisioned.

The black limousine journeyed through Rome's streets, passing many famous landmarks, including the Vatican and the Colosseum. In the back convened John, Angela, and Lance. John gently grasped Angela's manicured hand, causing Lance to roll his eyes. Angela noticed his reaction and quickly put both hands on her lap. John handed Lance a bottle of water. "You must be thirsty after that long trip."

"Not really. Your jet had everything. No thanks." His words were sharp and impetuous.

Angela extended her hand. "I'll take it; I'm dry as a bone."

John opened the water and handed it to her. "Lance, you sure you don't want anything?"

"I said I'm fine." He turned toward the window and ignored them with an irritated glower.

"Magnificent view, don't you think? Have you ever been to the Sistine Chapel?" John's attempt at small talk quickly backfired.

"Mr. Legions, I'm not happy I had to come to Rome, and I don't need a tour guide. I've been here hundreds of times. Yes, I've seen it all. So, if you excuse me, I'd like to be left alone."

"Lance, show some respect. There's no need to be rude." Angela brought her fingers to her mouth like she was zipping her lips shut, then leered at him.

"It's all right, Angela. I can't say I blame him. When I was his age, I didn't want to be with my mother either, much less with my mother and another man."

"It's not okay. I raised him better than that. Manners are important, and it seems he's forgotten his."

"I'm right here." Lance defiantly rolled his eyes. "How long until we get to the hotel?"

"It's just around the corner. I've made arrangements for a special dinner tonight to celebrate. Hope everyone is ready."

"I'll pass. I just want to crash. You two lovebirds enjoy the evening. Besides, we'll have to be together all day tomorrow with my grandparents."

The limousine pulled up to Hotel Palazzo Manfredi, a small luxury hotel in the heart of Rome.

Angela beamed with delight. "How did you know this was my favorite hotel in Rome?"

"I did my research for my future bride."

Lance stuck his finger in his mouth, pretending to vomit. "I think I'm going to be sick."

"Well, the good news, son, is you have your own room, but it connects to mine."

The silence inside the Seamore truck was thicker than ever; you couldn't cut it with a butter knife if you tried. Seething, Jamie, dressed in her pajama pants and a T-shirt, puckered her lips, glaring out the window, her eyes puffy.

"Jamie, I'm sorry. I really am." Remorse flooded James' face.

She quickly put her index fingers inside her ears. *I wish I could talk to Lance.*

"Please, say something." He darted his eyes toward her with an expression of pained reproach.

His plea was met with an abrupt huff from her. To make an impact, she slanted him a fault-finding scowl.

"Jamie, Aunt Sally shouldn't have done what she did. She's trying to bribe you away from me."

"Dad, there's nothing she can do to drive me away from you. You're doing that all on your own. Seriously, you freaking embarrassed me. And, to top it off, in front of royalty. What were you thinking? No, you weren't thinking. You never do. Blah, blah, blah! You were being self-centered, unforgiving, overbearing…"

"…Enough! I said I was sorry." James, unnerved by her blustering speech, tightly gripped the wheel, turning his knuckles white.

"Your apology is not accepted." Judging by how her glare of furious contempt intensified, she wasn't having it. She jerked her shoulders toward the door, tightly squeezing her pillow, and screwing her face into a pout reminiscent of a pug.

"Sweetie, I did what I thought was best for you."

"No, you did what you did because you hate Aunt Sally. You're full of baloney, as usual. Your best would have been to let us stay. But no! I'll make that a big fat no while I'm at it. Here we are, driving in the middle of the night to spend Thanksgiving at home when I could have been on a cruise with Melissa. Oh, but wait! You ruined that for me, too. I'm never, ever going to forgive you for this." She curled up and buried her face into her pillow, pulling her fluffy pink throw blanket over her head.

"She had no right inviting them. She misled both of us."

"Dad, I'm not talking to you. Keep your excuses to yourself. At least I got mom's pearls out of it." She hung her head, not knowing what else to say. "Just leave me alone."

James shook his head as he inhaled and exhaled, exasperated. *What a fine mess I've gotten us into.*

The next day, John, Angela, and Lance sprinted from the hotel's grand entrance and entered the limousine. Lance entered first and sat in the side seat as far away as possible from the other two. *I can't wait to get this over with and go back to the States. I miss Jamie.*

Angela flashed an energized grin toward John. "I'm excited about you meeting my parents, but I'm warning you, they're intense." A slow chuckle puffed her lips.

Lance, mimicking nervousness, wiped his brow with the back of his hand. "You've got that right. Good luck meeting the grand-parental units. They're a trip." His impatience filled him with a suppressed urge to tap his foot.

"I consider myself warned."

Angela patted John's leg. "Speaking of parents, I'm glad you finally made up with your mother."

"Me too. It was a long time coming."

"For a minute there, I thought maybe she'd quit." Angela took a deep breath.

"I don't think you have anything to worry about." John smiled, nodding toward Angela.

"Other than your parents approving me."

"Get real. What isn't there to like about you?"

"Let me count the ways." Lance eagerly held up his hand with his index finger pointed toward the sky. "One... You're not my father." A second finger shot up. "Two..."

"...Lance, that'll be enough." Angela scolded him with her unappeasable eyes. "Play nice. I won't tolerate you belittling John."

"I thought I was playing nice. I'm here with both of you. Aren't I? Never mind. I just can't wait to go back to the States. I have to practice for nationals, and I can't do it on the cobble streets of Rome, now, can I? Oh, wait, you wouldn't let me bring it."

The roar of engines permeated through the limousine's windows. Lance quickly glanced up. "Now that's a sight to behold." Several red, black, and yellow Lamborghini's zoomed past them. "Now, that's what I want. Forget a skateboard."

"Son, you know how to make that happen?" For an instant, her frigid stare thawed.

"Yep, tap into my trust fund."

"Try again. Get your Harvard law degree."

"Mom, not now, please. Especially in front of Mr. Legions."

John cleared his throat. "Why don't we all relax and enjoy the view of the streets of Rome? And, Lance, for the record, I'm not trying to replace your father; however, I love your mother very much. I suppose I should've asked you first for her hand in marriage instead of your grandfather's."

"You got that right, but the answer is no! She shouldn't be dating at all."

Angela wiped a small tear away. "Lance, you don't have to approve of my relationship with John for me to marry him, but you must know I love him, and regardless of your feelings, I will marry him."

"Just forget it! Let's get this luncheon over so I can return to the hotel and leave you two lovebirds alone." Lance glanced at his watch. "We can't get there soon enough so I can get out of this car and away from you both."

Minutes passed in silence and turned to a little over an hour on the way out of the city and into the Italian countryside. John persistently remained on his cell phone to Angela's agitation.

"Do you have to do that?" She gave a dismissive blink that made John feel like a pauper.

"Yes, that's correct, Mr. Nixon. Your jet is almost complete." John glanced at Angela. "I'm sorry. Business before pleasure."

In retaliation, Angela grabbed her cell phone and began reviewing models for Legions Airlines' upcoming shoot. She stopped on one model, extremely handsome, and smiled. John noticed as he clenched his teeth. He leaned over for a closer look.

"That's all. Yes, I'll be in contact as soon as I return to the States." John put his phone away and looked at Angela's phone again. "Who's that?"

"Just a model. I'm trying to decide which one to use for your campaign."

"Not him. I don't like the way he makes you smile."

"What? How am I looking at him?"

"Forget I ever said anything."

Bewilderment overcame Angela's expression as she tucked her phone inside her purse.

Finally, the limousine stopped in front of a glorious three-story villa with thirteen bedrooms, fifteen bathrooms, a parlor, a library, a billiard room, a terrace balcony, and so much more. The magnificent grounds were fit for a palace and immaculately manicured. A pond with a pristine, wooden bridge glistened under the sun, creating a picture-perfect moment.

Lance's eyes widened. "Grandpa considers this downsizing?"

Angela smiled and winked at John. "You know Grandpa; he doesn't know the meaning of small. Everything is grandiose, including his vacation home."

"Very charming, indeed." John gently slid his hand across Angela's leg. "Somehow, I'm not surprised. Very fitting for the man, I imagined."

"Hold that thought. You haven't met my mom and dad yet. They're going to love you. I know it."

Lance glared at his mother. "Well then, you won't need Grandpa's approval to get married." He curled his lip, gazing away.

The limousine came to a stop, and Lance bolted from the car. Before he could get to the front door, Grandpa and Nana stepped outside. Grandpa, in his mid-seventies, dressed in a gray suit, white shirt, and black tie, carried himself with dignified arrogance. His silver hair whipped in the slight breeze that crisped the air.

Nana stood all of four feet, four inches, and looked younger than her age of sixty-seven. She rushed to Lance and pinched his cheeks. "It's so good to see you; let me look at you!" She stepped back and gave him the once over. "My, my, you've grown at least three inches. What has your mother been feeding you?"

"Nana, that happens to boys. We grow up into men."

"You didn't have to do it so fast. You're only fourteen."

"I'm eighteen."

Grandpa shuffled to the limousine. As Angela exited, a huge smile crossed his face. "How's my magazine? You haven't run it into the ground, have you?"

Frustrated with her father's micro-management, Angela's cheeks flushed. "Dad, I told you everything is running smoothly. You have nothing to be concerned about."

John stepped out from the backseat, straightening his jacket as he stood next to Angela.

"Mom and Dad, there's someone I want you to meet. This is John Legions. He's a dear friend of mine."

Lance almost choked on her words, pretending to cough. "Bullsh…" Everyone glanced at him. "I'm fine."

"John, this is my father, Arthur Abadie, and my mother, Anna. "

John extended his right hand toward Angela's dad. "It's an honor to meet you, sir. I've heard so many wonderful things about you from Angela." Turning to Angela's mom, he smiled. "And you, my lovely lady, are far more beautiful than Angela described. It's a pleasure to meet you as well. Thank you both for hosting us in your beautiful villa."

Nana stepped toward John. "Get over here. A handshake won't do. I'm a hugger." She pulled him close to her and gave him a massive hug. "Now, that's better. Let's all go in. Lunch will be served shortly on the terrace."

"Mrs. Abadie, I've been looking forward to this all month."

"Please call me Anna; most do unless you prefer to call me Nana, like my grandchildren."

"I prefer Anna if that's okay with you."

"Perfectly!"

"Nana, I'm starving." Lance's stomach growled. "I can't wait to have some of your turkey and dressing."

"I hate to disappoint you, but we're having an Italian Thanksgiving meal."

"Wait! Nana, it's not Italy's Thanksgiving. I know my history."

"I realize that, but the Italians celebrate this day, too. They do it a bit differently with specialty dishes. I've learned that having antipasto, olives, roasted peppers, San Marzano cherry tomatoes, specialty cheeses, and meats is their tradition. Another favorite I've learned to love is marinated mushrooms with mini onions. Then we'll enjoy tortellini in broth."

"I wanted turkey and dressing with gravy, mashed potatoes, green bean casserole, and corn. It's not Thanksgiving without them."

"I promise you won't be disappointed. You know the saying, when in Rome, do what the Romans do."

John smiled. "It all sounds delightful. It's making my mouth water."

Lance stood with a blank stare and droopy shoulders. A wince of dread flickered over his face.

"Come, everyone, to the terrace for lunch. Lance, we'll have turkey and dressing, just not like you're used to, and for the potatoes, they're roasted with rosemary." Nana took Lance's hand.

John's phone rang. "Excuse me, I have to take this."

Angela's brow deepened. "On Thanksgiving?"

"It's not Thanksgiving to the person calling from Sweden. It's important. I won't be long. Start without me. I'll meet everyone on the terrace." John strode quickly to the side of the villa.

Grandpa placed his arm around Angela's shoulders. "What's happening with the magazine?"

"Dad, stop! We'll have plenty of time to discuss business after lunch."

"Very well. Let's eat!"

The villa's terrace, overlooking the Olympic pool with a fountain at one end, was extraordinary, spotlighting the magnificent grounds. There was plenty of seating and quiet areas for all. A cool breeze filtered from the far end, where a table was set as if in a pristine five-star restaurant. The gold plate chargers accentuated the bone heirloom China, Waterford crystal water, tea, wine glasses, and gold silverware place settings. A beautiful fall centerpiece of orange and burgundy flowers surrounding yellow sunflowers and small gourds stood as the focal point. Nothing was left to chance, including the calligraphy name cards identifying the seating arrangement. Grandpa and Nana sat at each end of the table, Angela sat to the right of her dad with an empty seat next to her for John, and Lance sat opposite to Angela.

Grandpa lifted his crystal tea glass and sipped. "Where's John? He's been on that phone for some time. He needs to put that thing away."

Lanced giggled. "That'll never happen. Get used to it. He lives on that phone. He doesn't know how to turn it off."

"Lance, that's uncalled for." Angela once again scolded him with her eyes. "He's an important man and has an international business to run."

"Now, you got my interest." Grandpa leaned forward. "What does Mr. Legions do, Angela?"

"Have you ever heard of Legions Airlines? He started at the company when he was thirty, after earning his pilot's license in the Air Force. It wasn't Legions Airlines at the time, but he bought stock, ultimately becoming the largest stockholder, and changed the name. It mushroomed into an international private jet company. It's a true rags to riches story."

Grandpa approvingly nodded. "Come to think of it, the company is popular here in Italy. We've even flown on it when we toured Greece. One of the finest jets I've ever been in."

"All of his jets are like that. He designs most of the interiors himself. He wants each jet to be unique and leaves nothing to happenstance."

"Grandpa, you'll like him. He's wealthy." Sarcasm took over Lance's words. "You two share that in common."

"You don't sound like you like him much yourself."

"Let me put it to you this way; he's full of himself."

"Who's full of themselves?" John strutted onto the terrace.

Angela immediately stood. "The chef, John. Today's chef!" Angela's eyes darted at Lance to tell him to behave.

"There's nothing wrong with that. I'm looking forward to this Italian feast." John kissed Angela's cheek, took her hand, and guided her to be seated.

Nana patted the table in front of the empty chair. "John, please sit. Lunch is about to be served."

John eased into the chair next to Angela and guided his napkin to his lap, gazing boldly at Angela's dad. "After lunch, Mr. Abadie, may I have a private conversation with you?"

"That sounds important."

"Trust me, sir; it is."

Lance rolled his eyes. "Nana, bring on the antipescho. I'm starving."

"It's called antipasto, not antipescho. And look; just like magic, Isabella is bringing it out."

Isabella, a late-fifties Italian woman with long silken raven hair tied in a ponytail, dressed in a black uniform with a white apron, and carrying a large antipasto board, approached the table and gently set it down. "Please enjoy. I'll serve you the soup soon, followed by the main course."

"Angela, please say grace." Nana took Angela's hand, and everyone else followed suit.

The Italian Thanksgiving meal ended, and the feeding frenzy slowed just as Chef Gino, age forty, dressed in a starched chef's coat with the sleeves rolled up to his elbows and traditional chef hat, approached the table. With equinox-black hair and eyebrows affixed to an aesthetic face, sensuous azure eyes that radiated like pure diamonds, and a firmly built torso like a knight waiting to rescue a damsel in distress, he looked more like a model for a romance novel cover than a chef. "I hope everything was to your liking." He watched as Grandpa devoured his last bite.

Angela's heart skipped a beat as warmth enveloped her body. "You're perfect. I mean, the meal was magnifico!"

Greener than the Wicked Witch of the West, John scowled at her slip of the tongue and glared at her with abhorrence. He leaned over to whisper in her ear. "I don't like it when you look at other men like that. You seem a little infatuated by him."

"Nonsense." Her resolved smile turned into a frown as her eyes scolded him.

"Don't let it happen again." John squeezed her thigh as if to provide a stern warning while wryly smiling at Mr. Abadie.

Angela jerked his hand away; Nana took a particular interest in the interaction.

"Everything okay, Angela?" Her brow inequitably furrowed.

"Perfectly, Mom. Nothing I can't handle."

Grandpa scooted back in his chair and rubbed his stomach. "It doesn't get better than this. Simply divine. Another fine meal from the best chef in Italy."

John nodded, placed his fork flip side down onto the plate, neatly folded his napkin, and placed it on the table. "I agree. This is the best Thanksgiving meal I have ever had. I think I'm more stuffed than a traditional turkey." Angela couldn't put her finger on it, but his response was superficial.

"I'm glad you enjoyed it. I must return to the kitchen." Chef Gino shook Grandpa's hand and left as Angela's eyes followed him, again riling John.

"Thank you again for having me, Anna." John wiped his lips with his napkin, hoping no one observed his jealousy.

"Now, John. You ready for our talk?" Grandpa's gaze turned serious as he scooted his chair back and rose. "There's no time like the present."

"Indeed, Mr. Abadie." John leaned over, kissed Angela on the cheek, and then stood. "I'll be right back."

Lance's eyes rolled. "Oh, boy! Here it comes. Thanks for lunch, Nana. Mom, may I be dismissed? I want to take a nap, since skateboarding is out of the question."

"Very well."

Lance bolted from the terrace and disappeared into the villa.

"Mom, I'll help clear the table." Angela picked up the plates; she secretly desired to go to the kitchen and speak with Gino.

"Nonsense, my child. Isabella will handle that. Let's have tea in the garden."

"Perfect plan. That way, I can keep my eye out on the men."

Grandpa laughed. "Rubbish! We're big boys."

John tilted his head toward Grandpa. "Sir, I'm ready when you are."

"Follow me!"

The two men sauntered to the stairs and headed out for their walk-and-talk chat. "Son, call me Arthur."

Angela took a deep breath. "Mom, this is it. I'm getting married."

"Nonsense! You don't even know him."

"We've been dating for a couple of months, but when love bites you, you can't stop it, and I've been bitten."

"Honey, are you sure you know what you're doing? How do you know he's not after the family money?"

"Mom, he's a billionaire. I don't think he's interested in our family money."

"That does change things a bit."

"Look at them." Angela peered across the lawn as Grandpa and John chatted on the other side of the swimming pool. "It's looking serious. My stomach is in knots."

"Whatever for? You're not the one asking your dad for your hand in marriage."

"I think Dad said yes. They're shaking hands, and both are all smiles."

"I guess congratulations are in order."

From the corner of Angela's eyes, she observed John place his cell phone to his ear and walk away from her father. She let out a huff, rolling her eyes. "Mom, we can't stay much longer. We have to get back to town, and it's a bit of a drive back. We leave early in the morning back to the states so I can prep for a big campaign shoot."

"I understand. You have your father in you. He could never take time off, either. Please, don't make the mistake of working every minute of your life. You must stop and smell the roses."

"I know, Mom. I have big shoes to fill, and I don't plan on failing Dad."

"If you're doing this for Dad, you'll only disappoint yourself. Do what you do because you love doing it and for no other reason. Then you're guaranteed not to fail."

CHAPTER TWELVE

Let the Sparks Fly

The sun shimmered over the Seamore's house, brightening the cloudless sky, while Jamie tossed and turned on her bed. Her phone rang, disturbing her already restless sleep. She searched relentlessly to secure it, and when she saw the caller's I.D., she answered. "Lance, I've missed you so much."

"Ditto! I couldn't wait to get back."

"You're home?"

"Yep! I'm all safe and sound. When can I see you? There's a skateboard lesson involved."

"You don't have to ask me twice. I can be ready in less than thirty minutes. Meet me at the skatepark in an hour."

"It's a date, but make that four hours. I have to pick up your skateboard and do that autograph promotion thing you hooked me into for the shop."

"Thanks for agreeing to that. At least I get Dusty for free."

"Dusty? Oh, that's right. That's what you named your wheels."

"Yes, indeedy, and she's a beauty. Thank you again for agreeing to do that promotion. There was no way I could've afforded her."

"No worries. I want you to be happy. See you in four hours. Don't forget to bring your safety gear."

165

"Good morning, Angela." James, dressed in khaki pants, a blue golf shirt with the *Elite* logo on the left, and sneakers, stood across from her desk as she reviewed the Legions' campaign file.

"It's a great morning. How was your holiday?" She glanced up, fixing her soft eyes on his.

"I'll put it to you this way. A disaster! We left early and never ate."

"Ouch! That sounds bad. What went wrong? Never mind, none of my business."

"How was your trip to Rome?"

"Very eventful." She held up her hand and wiggled her ring finger, flaunting her sparkling new four-carat pear-shaped diamond ring. "I got engaged."

His mouth dropped; his eyes widened. "Wow, that's some ring. Lucky man! Tell me to go away if it isn't my business, but who is the groom-to-be?"

"Glad you asked." She flashed a knowing smile. "Mr. John Legions, our client, for today's photo shoot. You must make sure everything goes smoothly. Absolutely nothing can go wrong, and I mean nothing."

"I'll try my best."

Angela's cell phone buzzed. "Hold on, James. Let me answer this."

James nodded, strode to the massive office window, and took in the view.

"Good morning, John... Yes, everything is set for the shoot. I was discussing this with Mr. Seamore, my ad liaison... Wait, you're running late... I understand. We'll proceed without you. However, please show up before noon to approve the setting." Angela picked up her coffee cup and took a sip. "Yes, yes. I'm looking forward to seeing the results too. John, remember, today is business and not pleasure, even if you're my fiancée. See you soon." She placed her phone back on the desk and glanced at James. "Now, do your best. I want updates every fifteen minutes. I want to know if the slightest thing looks weird or goes wrong. That's why I promoted you."

"Understood."

The Legions Airlines' production set featured the interior of a Learjet, complete with ostrich leather recliners and gold features. "Snap to it, girls!" Javier clapped his hands three times as he sashayed toward Posey. "Where's the stewardess? Where's the pilot? Why aren't they dressed and on set? I called final looks thirty minutes ago. We don't have all day. Time is money, and money is time."

Posey flicked his wrist. "Our stewardess is ready, but we're having problems with the pilot's uniform. It seems our male model indulged a bit too much on his Thanksgiving feast and doesn't fit into his uniform pants. We're altering them."

"Any other problems I need to be made aware of?"

James bolted over to Posey and Javier. "What problem are we having?"

"Oh, it's you again." Javier pursed his lips. "If you must know, ask Posey. It seems he has all the details."

"Posey, what problem?"

"None; he'll be ready to go soon."

Ping! James received a text from Angela.

How's everything going?

"That was Ms. Abadie. She wants to know how everything's going. What do you want me to tell her?"

"Not my job!" Javier clapped his hands. "Everyone, be ready to shoot in ten minutes. Get the models in here and make sure they're camera ready. Snap! Snap!"

James wiped a bead of sweat from his forehead. "Is anyone else hot?"

No one answered as they scurried away.

"I guess not." James went to craft services and retrieved a soda, gulping it down. Out of the corner of his eye, he saw the stewardess model enter the set, her logo embellished Legions Airline's uniform, fit to perfection. "That's one down, one to go."

Javier stomped his foot. "Someone take the initiative and get the pilot in here, now!"

James cleared his throat. "I'm on it." He bolted for the dressing room area and approached the male model. "Excuse me. We're ready to shoot. We need you on set."

The male model stepped from behind the curtain. The pilot's jacket fit tight, and the pants wouldn't zip. "Not looking like this. I gave wardrobe my size. They must be idiots not to have extra sizes available."

"Let me check on things." *I guess I need to inform Angela of this hiccup,* he thought as he blew air out of his mouth and rubbed his temples before taking a deep breath and furiously texting her.

> We have a slight delay. The pilot's uniform doesn't fit. We're trying to get another, and Posey is trying to make the alterations. So, we're delayed. Just an update.

> I'm on my way down to set!

Angela's text unnerved James. He strode over to Javier. "We need alternatives if we don't get that pilot's uniform to fit."

Javier studied James, giving him a head-to-toe scan. Then, he retrieved a seamstress measuring tape which hung around his neck and started measuring James' height, chest, and inseam.

"What are you doing, Javier?"

"Measuring. I think that uniform will fit you."

"Oh, don't even go there."

Angela barged into the room. "Where's the pilot?" Silence fell throughout the room. "I want answers. Do you people know how important this shoot is?"

John dressed to impress, entered. He brushed his hair back as if it was a mess. "Hello, everyone. I'm glad you haven't started without me. We must get everything right." He glanced around the set. "Beautiful! The production design reflects my company perfectly. Great job!" He reached his hand out and shook Angela's. "This is exciting."

James walked up to Angela. "Excuse me. I need to speak to you in private."

"Now, James? Our client is here. It needs to wait. I'm sure you remember Mr. Legions." Angela's palms became cold and clammy.

"Yes, ma'am. Nice to see you again, Mr. Legions." He shook John's hand. "I hear congratulations are in order."

"Thank you."

"Have y'all set a wedding date?"

Angela smirked. "Not yet; we're newly engaged and haven't had time to discuss it."

The male model, not fitting into the replacement uniform, stormed into the area. "This isn't going to work. I've tried on four uniforms, and nothing fits. I won't take Posey screaming at me because he thinks I overate. I quit!" He stormed off the set.

"Wait!" James bolted after him. "I'm sure we can fix this."

Angela's cheeks flushed scarlet. "John, excuse me. I need to see what's going on and, at minimum, get a new model in here stat."

"Angela. What about your assistant?"

"What do you mean?" Puzzlement overtook her expression as she inhaled.

"The guy who just left. He's handsome, well-built, and looks like he could work for my company. Let's try him."

"You've got to be kidding me."

"No, I insist."

"I'm not sure if he'll do it. He's not even a model."

"How hard can it be to stand on a set, look handsome, and smile? Here he comes now. Please ask him."

Still hesitant, Angela grabbed James' attention by following him. "James, I need to see you for a second."

"It isn't my fault he quit, and he has left the building, Elvis style."

"I know it's not your fault, but you're in a position to save the shoot."

"Tell me how; I'll do anything."

"Good to know."

James, looking dapper in the navy-blue pilot's uniform, tottered from the dressing room, not making a great impression, and revealing his lack of confidence. Nevertheless, the uniform fit as if Posey had tailored it for him. Finally, the hair and makeup team closed in to complete the final touches. "How do I look?"

Posey stood proud as a peacock. "Fabulous, my darling, just fabulous. Stand up straight, shoulders back, tuck the tummy in, and the badonkadonk out. Oh, and as the great Tyra Banks says…"

…Clap! Clap! Clap! "Everyone, take your places. It's time to get this show on the road." Javier strutted behind the camera and stood by the photographer. "Make this happen. Do your magic. Team A, take your places."

James released a nervous breath, straightened his pilot's jacket, Picard-style, and entered the makeshift jet set, the stewardess following on his heels.

"So, we meet again." She batted her long, lashes. "You look great, just like the real deal."

James shook hands with the stewardess. "I'm James. I guess I'm your counterpart for the day." He swallowed, feeling anxious.

"Relax, you look the part."

"Any advice? I've never done this before."

"Just relax, be yourself, find the light, suck in your gut, and smile. Pretend you love what you're doing."

"Got it!"

"Let's make this happen!" Javier looked over his shoulder and smiled at Angela.

The photographer rapidly shot. Click. Click. Click. "Pilot, I need a little more energy. You're happy to be flying for Legions Airlines."

James shook off his nerves and posed with the stewardess.

"Brilliant! Give me another pose." Click. Click. Click.

The photo shoot continued as Angela stared at James. Smitten, she smiled brilliantly, and a warm, fuzzy feeling enveloped her from head to toe as her heart pumped faster, unable to take her eyes off him.

John took notice of her reaction as puzzlement filled his face. "Angela, how do you think the shoot is going?"

Angela remained starry-eyed, focusing on James.

"Did you hear me? How do you think the shoot is going?"

"Perfect! I'm surprised. James is getting into it."

"What can I say? I know how to pick them."

"Yes, you do." She felt her heartbeat through her veins.

Suddenly, James tripped over the prop, a small pilot's carry-on leather bag. "Whoops!"

Angela bolted to the makeshift jet. "James, are you okay?"

"I'm fine." He slowly rose, brushing off the dirt from his pants.

"Here, let me help you." Angela patted the dirt away from his jacket, noting his muscular torso with her fingers. Her eyes fixed on his. It was as if time stood still for everyone except for John, who watched the interaction, his lips pursing as a scowl formed, as if he had morphed into a rabid dog. Watching the exchange from a distance, a pit formed in his stomach.

Angela left the set and stood next to John. "He'll be fine."

"I'm sure." He glared at James. "Is there something you're not telling me?"

"I'm not sure I understand the question. What are you implying?"

"What's going on between you two?"

His abruptness caught her off guard. "What?" She huffed at his deplorable accusation. "Nothing, absolutely nothing."

"Are you sure? I don't like the way you look at him."

"Are you really going that route?"

"Just protecting my interest from a possible threat."

"You're kidding me, right? I'm an interest, and James a threat?"

"I didn't like how you looked at him or how he looked at you."

"Now I know for certain you're the jealous type. I thought it was my imagination." She suddenly viewed him as less than perfect, and

171

his sex appeal faltered in her mind. "Just because we're engaged doesn't mean you can control my actions or limit who I can look at."

"Is that what you think I'm doing? Controlling you?"

"Yes, in fact, I do. You don't own me. Nobody owns me."

"Forget I said anything about it." His stoic expression increased in intensity.

"I'm not sure I can. You chose him, not me."

"He looked like a pilot. Besides, we had to do something. Thanks to your team, our model walked out, and I am about to if you don't get your behavior together and stop flirting with every piece of meat that gets in front of you."

"That's enough! I can't deal with your jealousy. I lived for years with a jealous husband who left me for a younger woman. I should've known and seen the writing on the wall. First, your true colors surfaced in Italy with Chef Gino, and now James. I'm not doing this again. Lance was right; something is wrong with you." Sneering nastily, Angela removed her engagement ring, thrusting it into John's hand. "I'm calling off our engagement. If this is any indication of how things will be when we're married, I don't want any part of it. Business before pleasure. I should have followed my dad's advice."

"So, do I take my campaign to your competitor?"

Disgust settled in her stomach. "Do what you want, just leave me out of your jealousy. We're finished."

"I have faith that the campaign will be taken care of, and I signed the contract. Finish the shoot. But, from here on out, I only deal with Monique." John stormed from the set. "You're making a serious mistake!"

All eyes were now on Angela, the photoshoot frozen in place at the public display. "Go back to work! We have the campaign to finish. Someone get Monique down here, stat!"

Jamie's eyes sparkled with excitement as Lance buckled her helmet beneath her chin. Behind them, the skatepark was filled with skaters. "That's not too tight, is it?"

"Nope! I'm good. Safety gear on." She scrunched her nose at him jokingly.

"You look so cute. You ready to take Dusty for a ride?"

"I've been ready. What do I need to do first?" Reality penetrated her ponytail-to-within-an-inch-fear mind.

"You're going to put your front foot over the front truck bolts on your board and push with your other foot. You'll put your back foot on the tail when you get going. Oh, make sure your front foot is sideways. And most of all, learn to balance by leaning forward and backward. It's not as easy as it looks. I'll hold you until you get the swing of things."

"Easy-peasy. I've got this. I'm a cheerleader who does stunts." She held Lance's shoulders and carefully stepped onto the skateboard, which swiftly took off from under her.

Lance caught her, preventing her fall. "Easy-peasy, you say. You ready to try again?"

"I can do this. I can do this. I can do this."

"Are you trying to convince yourself or me?"

"No, just remembering *The Little Train that Could*. My mom used to read that to me, and it kinda stuck with me."

"Get back on. Take it slow."

"It's like falling off a bike; you get back on, but I've never ridden a skateboard."

This time, Jamie remained on her skateboard, maintaining her balance as Lance gently pushed her. Soon, she rode it alone, but not fast. "I got it. I got it. I got it! Let go!"

CHAPTER THIRTEEN

The Dating Game

Angela stormed into her office, followed by Francis. "Ms. Abadie, is there anything I can get you?"

"A new boyfriend. I stayed engaged for two days. He has some nerve thinking he can control me. Nobody owns me. I've had it." She plopped into her chair. "The most hurtful thing is I let myself down. I think I was enamored with John because he was a safe bet. I don't want to grow old alone. Now, I'm stuck back in the dating game and don't even know where to start."

"I've been trying to tell you to join *Singlematch*."

"You honestly think it'll work?"

"Absolutely. I have several girlfriends who found husbands that way. I'm sure you'll be matched with your soul mate."

"What does it take to join?"

"It's simple. We create your profile, add your bio, and a picture."

"I don't want people to know it's me. Can I use a fake name and picture?"

"There's nothing to stop you from doing that. The men might get peeved expecting you to look like your picture, but who cares? You're beautiful."

"Keep my profile reflective of me, but don't tell them I own *Elite Magazine* or that I'm a socialite. I want them to like me for me and not my money."

"I can do that for you."

"Okay, let's do it. I'm at my wit's end."

"May I sit at your desk and use your computer to create your profile?"

"Absolutely. Let's get this show on the road."

"What picture do you want me to use?"

"Just go onto one of the photo stock image sites and find a woman who resembles me."

"Got it."

Angela stood over Francis' shoulders as she created her profile.

"Great job, Francis. I'm exhausted. I'm taking the rest of the day off. Let me know when you find me, my soul mate." A wisp of sarcasm hinted at her inflection.

"I'll be sure to put your dates on your social calendar."

Jamie bolted through the front door carrying Dusty. She quickly hid it underneath the floral sofa. "Dad, you home?" She proceeded to the kitchen. As she passed by the computer, it dinged. "Oh, another match for my dad." She sat at the computer and read the profile. "I'm an independent woman who doesn't need to be taken care of by a man. I'm seeking a man who knows how to treat a woman with respect, loves the finer things in life, and enjoys trips to the Wine Country and Broadway shows." She looked at the woman's picture. *Wow, she's beautiful. I think Dad's a match.*

She called Melissa. "Hey girl, what's up?"

"You're back. How was Atlanta?"

"Better question, how was the cruise?"

"OMG! It was fantastic. We went to a sloth reserve, and I got to hold one. Her name was Lola. She was so cute! I'm in love. Let's get together. I miss my B.F.F."

"I can't tonight; I have to have a serious talk with my dad. We're not exactly on speaking terms."

"What happened? Spill the beans."

"Nothing much other than my aunt invited a king, a queen, and a prince to dinner. My dad got all hot and bothered, forcing us to leave before we could eat, embarrassing the crap out of me. That's all. I was mad. The way I see it, someday my prince would come, and he did, and I left."

"Tell me more."

"Later. I need your advice."

"I'm all ears."

"My dad got pinged from *Singlematch* by a beautiful woman with an amazing profile. I like this one. Should I set him up?"

"Duh, heck yea."

"He'll get mad."

"Use that to your advantage. You want him to date, right?"

"Yep!"

"Then tell him you'll forgive him for the prince fiasco if he goes on three dates."

"That might work. He's begging for my forgiveness."

"What are you waiting for? Do it!"

"Okay." Jamie hit the response button to set up the date. "What! She can't meet until next Friday. Oh well, I'll book it."

"Yes, book her, then find two more."

"I'm on it."

James entered through the front door. "I'm home!"

"I can see that. Melissa, I got to go! If you get my drift."

"Good luck with your dad."

Jamie placed the phone next to the keyboard. "Dad, we have to talk."

"I'd say. At least you're speaking to me. Sweetie, I'm so sorry for the Thanksgiving debacle."

"Not for long if you agree to something."

"I don't like the way this sounds, but go ahead. List your demands."

Angela casually dressed in slacks, a silk blouse, and flats, read the novel *Never Stop Running*, relaxing in the overstuffed chair with her feet propped up on the ottoman in her bedroom, when a text chimed in from Francis.

"Your first date is in an hour. Tea at Winsor Court at four. Look for the gentleman with a yellow rose on the table."

She glanced at her watch, reapplied her makeup, and combed her hair before sauntering from her bedroom, heading directly to the kitchen.

While sitting on the bar stool at the kitchen island, Lance inhaled a piece of apple pie.

"Good afternoon." Angela entered the kitchen. "It looks like you're really enjoying your snack."

"Mom, what are you wearing?" Disgust filled his tone as he gave her the once over.

"What's wrong with it?"

"I didn't even know you owned pants."

"I do, and sometimes I like to dress down."

"Ms. Abadie, Lance tells me you're engaged to my son." Miriam hugged Angela. "Congratulations!"

"Was engaged. We broke up."

"Yes!" Lance fist-bumped the air. "I knew it wouldn't work. I hate to tell you I told you so, but I told you so."

"Lance, that's enough."

"I can't say I'm going to lose sleep over it. I hope you've learned your lesson, Mom. No more dating! You're too old for that."

"Lance, stay out of my dating life."

"That's the point. You shouldn't have one." Lance headed for the door. "I'm out. I'll be back in a couple of hours." He closed the door behind him.

Angela's lips hinted at a worried smile as she gazed at Miriam. "What a roller coaster ride, don't you think?"

Miriam wiped her hands on her apron. "Ms. Abadie, I'll always cherish that you brought my Opie back to me. That'll never change."

"Thank you, Miriam, for understanding. Please know this won't change anything between us here."

"Never thought it would. You and Master Lance are all the family I have had for twenty years. Nothing else matters."

"You're special to us here, Miriam. I don't know what we'd do without you." Angela grabbed her car keys from the rack beside the back door. "I'll be back later; I'm going to the gym." Her cheeks flushed at the lie.

James pulled on the glass door to Fleur di Lis Deli, a family-owned sandwich shop in a strip mall. The door chimed as James entered, dressed in a T-shirt, jeans, and tennis shoes. The smell of freshly baked bread sent his stomach into a festive flurry. An expansive glass case filled with fresh meats, including pastrami, salami, black forest ham, roast beef, chicken, and turkey, looked appetizing. A dozen customers stood shoulder-to-shoulder in a line snaking along the counter. Only two tables were occupied, one with an elderly couple and one by a businessman eating alone, his nose was planted inches away from his cell phone.

James placed a New Orleans Saints cap on the table and sat facing the entrance, anxiously glancing at it. Moments later, a shapely, petite Caucasian woman in her forties with long blonde hair, holding a teacup, black and brown apple-head chihuahua dressed wearing a doggie tuxedo entered. He waved at her with his Saints cap, and she approached his table. When she arrived, he stood to greet her. "Hello, I'm James Seamore. You must be Colette. You look exactly like your profile's picture."

"A pleasure to meet you, James."

"Please be seated. Who is your little furry friend?"

"This is Macho Man, my emotional support dog. I can't go anywhere or do anything without him." She kissed the top of Macho Man's head. "Isn't that right, baby boy?" Her tone reflected talking to an infant with baby talk.

James reached over to pet Macho Man but was met with white fangs, offensive doggy breath, and a fierce growl. He quickly jerked his hand back. "I see where he got his name."

"He doesn't like men." She cracked a mordant smile and kissed her dog. He licked her multiple times in her mouth. "You're so cute; yes you are my little macho man. Kissy, kissy poo."

"My apologies, Collette." James scratched his forehead. "This isn't going to work. Two's company, and three's a crowd." He placed a twenty-dollar bill on the table. "Please, order yourself a cup of coffee. Have a great day."

Angela pulled up to the front of Windsor Court, exited her car, and handed the valet her keys. She proceeded to the tearoom, where a harpist played classical tunes, and most of the tables were taken up by groups of women. Only one firmly built male patron with Viking blonde hair and tattoos that covered his arms sat at a table with a single yellow rose. *That must be him.* She promenaded to the table; the gentleman immediately stood as she arrived. "It's a pleasure to meet you. You don't exactly look like your picture, but you're beautiful."

"I'm Angela. You must be Thornton."

"Yes, of course. Please sit."

"You look familiar." She scrutinized his face as if trying to remember if they knew each other. "Have we ever met?"

"Honey, I'd remember a heifer like you if we had. Maybe you've seen me on television. I'm a professional football player and considered one of the best." He met her gaze with a cocky smile.

"Who do…"

"…I've played eight years in the league. I hold many, many records."

"What positi…"

"…There's nothing that can stop me. I'm invincible."

Her blood boiled as she held back her anger at his constant interruption and rambling. "But, what…"

"…I started as the number one draft pick, and now look at me. I'm all pro and bound for the Hall of Fame."

"Where do…" her spine stiffened, becoming more agitated, and her scathing gaze went unnoticed. Her jaw stiffened the more he interrupted her.

"...The thrill of game day and running through the tunnel to a roaring crowd pumps up my blood. I become a beast." His nostrils flared like a mad bull as he flashed a conceited smile.

"Where did..."

"...I know I'm the best because..."

"...Excuse me, do you think you could let me finish a sentence without interrupting me?" In righteous anger, she clenched her jaw, realizing she had made a serious mistake agreeing to this date, wanting to kick him in the shins beneath the table. Instead, she resorted to furiously tapping her foot. She felt like screaming at the top of her lungs for as long as she could, but remained dignified.

The scowling behemoth shoved his cup across the table. "Lady, I don't know who you think you are, but you're not the one for me. You obviously don't like football and hold the attention of a mouse. Keep the rose." The oaf's arms flailed awkwardly as he stormed from the table, leaving Angela stunned and alone.

Oh, boy! I have two more of these.

James placed his Saints cap down on the table. This time, the meeting place was a small sandwich shop on Magazine Street, resembling a Parisian café, including noir music. In the back was an open kitchen brimming with activity as several cooks prepared meals. The aroma of the burning grill filled the air as hamburger patties sizzled on it. He glanced at his watch. *I'm going to kill Jamie.* Before he could sit, a remarkably tall lady at the adjacent table stood and approached him, gazing down into his eyes. "I'm Billy. You must be James."

"You must be a professional basketball player."

"I get that a lot. I actually have never played the game." She nervously hiccupped.

"Too bad. Your profile said you love going to the Saints' games."

"I do." Another embarrassing flagrant hiccup. "My parents have been season ticket holders for over forty years. They didn't have a babysitter, so they always took me to the games." Hiccup! "Here's some trivia; I was named after Billy Kilmer."

"That name doesn't ring a bell."

Hiccup! Hiccup! "He was the Saints' quarterback in the late sixties."

"Impressive."

Hiccup! Hiccup! Hiccup!

"Maybe you should drink some water." Despite his best effort to hide his reaction to the obnoxious hiccups, he laughed as he covered his mouth.

"This isn't going to work, is it?"

James' blank expression gave her the answer.

Angela sighed, tightly gripping the steering wheel as she prudently drove. "Call Francis, at home."

The phone rang three times before she answered. "Sorry, Ms. Abadie, I was getting out of the shower. How was your date?"

"Horrible. This isn't going to work. I give up. Take my profile off the site."

"Wait! You have one more date scheduled. I think this one will be your soulmate."

"Fine. One last date, but then I'm finished. I didn't see it on my calendar."

"Oh, it's not until the end of next week."

Both wearing their cheerleading uniforms, Melissa and Jamie, ponytails swinging, skipped down the hall and into the cafeteria. Jamie flopped onto a bench. "It's Friday, it's Friday. You know what that means?" She lifted her brows twice with a silly grin on her face.

"Yea, no school for two days."

"Well, that too. But, it's game night, then skate night."

"Since when are you into roller skating?" Her lips twisted.

"Silly girl, it's skateboard night after the game. Be there or be square."

"You're going to get yourself hurt."

"No, I won't; I'm really getting good at it."

"I can't believe your dad is letting you do this."

Jamie jerked her head around toward Melissa. "What he doesn't know, won't kill him."

"He doesn't know?"

"Not in the least, and we're gonna keep it that way."

"Oh, boy." She shrugged. "This sounds like nothing but trouble."

"Trouble is, as trouble does. Besides, I have the best teacher in the world."

"Don't look now, but here comes Preston."

"I'm out!" Jamie bolted from the cafeteria.

Lance witnessed the small exchange and took off after her. They met up beneath the bleachers at the far end of the stadium. On the field, the band and majorettes practiced their routine, putting the finishing touches on it.

"Jamie, you took off like a bullet. Everything okay?"

"Of course, I simply didn't want to deal with Preston."

"I get it. Never mind him. You have me."

"I'm excited to skate tonight."

"Can't you skip cheering for once and join me early?"

"You shouldn't ask that. You know my answer."

"You can't blame a guy for trying."

"I guess I can't."

"You never told me how your talk went with your dad. Everything okay?"

"If you're asking if we're on speaking terms, the answer is yes. He agreed to go on three dates I found for him on *Singlematch*."

"I can't believe that. Actually, I'm not sure what to think. The women must be losers to resort to that type of dating."

"Are you calling my dad a loser?"

"No, just the women. If a woman can't find a man the old-fashioned way, they shouldn't be dating. I know I would never tolerate a girl I found on a site like that, much less approve of my mom doing it. Nothing but trouble and heartache there, for sure."

"Get over yourself. At least my dad is finally dating, and once he's found love, we can announce our engagement. Speaking of, how's your mom's fiancée? When's the wedding?"

"I was right; she was wrong. They broke up, and she's agreed to never date again."

"Sounds like a lonely life."

"I still have high hopes that she'll get back together with my father. No other man will ever compare; I don't care who he is; he'll never be worthy of my mother. The good news is I think she's finally learned her lesson. Enough about the parentals, let's focus on us." He kissed her as she melted into his arms.

James finished dressing in a long-sleeve Polo shirt, black jeans, and black tennis shoes. He splashed cologne onto his face, sniffed his underarms, and then tested his breath on the palm of his hand. He put on his jacket, and, moments later, headed out the door carrying a long-stem lavender rose. After a twenty-minute drive to New Orleans City Park, now decorated with millions of Christmas lights forming multiple festive displays, a favorite for the locals known as Christmas in the Oaks, he located a parking space. He exited the car, heading for the entrance. Once he arrived, Angela, wearing a leather coat with a fur collar and black knee-high boots, stood at the gate; her black slacks bellowed below the jacket's hemline.

"Angela, what brings you out?" Her warm breath puffed small clouds as she talked.

"Christmas in the Oaks; a family tradition."

"Is your son with you? I'd love to meet him."

"Not tonight."

"You came by yourself, then?"

"No, I'm meeting someone here."

"What a coincidence. Me too, but I don't see her anywhere."

"Yours seems like a no-show, too!"

They simultaneously glanced at their watches.

"I think I've been stood up." James shivered, pulling his coat tighter. "I can't believe how cold it is."

"Me either."

"I hope she gets here soon. Oh, no! No wonder she can't find me. I'm supposed to have a purple long-stem rose so she can identify me. I accidentally left it in the car. It's a blind date from *Singlematch*."

"You're kidding, right?" She felt a ping in her stomach.

"Is there something wrong with *Singlematch*?"

"You're not going to believe this, but I think I'm your date."

"Impossible. You look nothing like this woman's profile other than having a pretty face and blonde hair."

"You know Francis, my assistant, correct?"

"Absolutely."

"After I called off my engagement with John, she created a profile for me so I could meet my soulmate. She swears by *Singlematch*. I agreed to three dates; this is my third. I'm supposed to meet a man holding a long-stem purple rose here."

"This is a joke. Please tell me it's a joke."

"Do you see me laughing?"

"Not in the least. Shall we stroll through the park and get this date over with?"

"I don't want to force you into it since I'm not who you were expecting."

"I'm delighted and extremely relieved. I don't think I can go on another bad date."

"Amen, to that. Mine were nightmares."

He extended his arm. "Shall we?"

Time flew as James and Angela meandered through the park, taking in the sights and sounds of the Christmas display. They stopped for hot chocolate and continued their sightseeing, giggling like teenagers along the way. As they approached the end of the tour, they slowed their pace and sat on a park bench beneath the mistletoe. Two teenagers dashed in front of them, one pointing up. "Kiss her, mister. It's Christmas."

They glanced up, and before Angela knew it, James' lips touched hers as she froze, stiffening her entire body. She immediately backed away. "James, I don't think this is such a good idea. Mixing pleasure with business. You know how the last one ended for me."

He studied her eyes for a second until he realized she was serious. "Then I quit!" His fingertips trailed over her sensitive cheek as he kissed her again. Goosebumps ricocheted throughout Angela's body as if the cool air had triggered them.

They sat silently for a couple of minutes, taking in the blinking decorations. "Honestly, James, I think I've wanted you to do that since I first saw you outside my window. Then I shot you."

"That's a hell of a way to get my attention. Why didn't you say anything?"

"I didn't realize it until now. Somehow, I think John knew before I did. You're the reason I broke off our engagement."

"I don't understand. I had nothing to do with that." The utter seriousness of his hardened expression gave her pause.

"Not from John's perspective. He accused me of being infatuated with you. He didn't like the way we looked at each other."

"Wow, I don't know what to say."

"How about asking me out for another date? I'm free tomorrow. That is, if you don't have another *Singlematch* planned."

"No more dates from *Singlematch*. I'm good. I'm also free. My daughter is going to the winter formal dance tomorrow night. She won't even know I'm gone."

"James, I have a small favor to ask."

"Ask away."

"No one can know we're dating, especially people at work or my son. Can you keep this our secret? My son would be furious if he knew I was on *Singlematch*, much less dating an employee."

"Only if you can do the same. My daughter doesn't like you much."

"She doesn't even know me."

"That's the point. She tried to interview you for an English term paper a couple of months ago, and you refused. She's not exactly a fan of yours because of it. She told me she thought you were rude, arrogant, and only out to use people. She hates the fact that I work for you."

"I thought you quit."

"Can I have my job back?"

"Of course, you can." All smiles, she kissed him again.

CHAPTER FOURTEEN

Happy Holidays

A ngela flipped through the photo shoot for Legions Airlines. A smile graced her lips, feeling giddy as she admired James in the photographs. Francis entered with a Christmas bouquet of red and white roses, baby's breath, and a single long-stem purple rose and placed them on the desk. "Another secret admirer sent you flowers!"

"This time, it's no secret admirer. I have an inkling who sent them, this time."

"Do tell. I'm all ears."

"None of your business."

Monique knocked on the open door. "Excuse me, Ms. Abadie, may I come in? I want to update you on the Legions Airlines' campaign."

"I'm sure you can handle it. You have the full confidence of Mr. Legions."

"I'm aware of that, but there's something you ought to know."

"Come in. Please make it quick. We have the Christmas party to attend."

"Yes, ma'am. That's what's on my mind."

"Please tell me you're going."

"I am, but I'm bringing a guest; if you approve."

"Of course, plus ones are always welcome to our holiday parties."

"Even if it's Mr. Legions?"

Bewildered, Angela's brows lifted as a scowl enveloped her forehead. "What do you mean, Mr. Legions is coming?"

"I invited him."

"Seriously?"

"Yes, ma'am. We're dating."

Angela threw her hands up. "I forbid it! You can't mix business with pleasure. A clause in your contract explains this loud and clear."

"Ms. Abadie, I know things ended badly for you, but his intentions are sincere with me. My family has known him for years. Honestly, if you don't allow this, I'll resign. I can write my own ticket at any major marketing firm, including your biggest competition."

"I'm sure you can. You're fired!" Angela, furious at Monique's announcement, bit back her smile.

Dressed in his oversized faded terry cloth bathrobe and matching slippers he'd owned for years, James read the newspaper reclined in his chair. Jamie, dressed in the beautiful red Marchesa draped rose ballgown and stilettos Aunt Sally had given her, pranced into the living room. "Dad, how do I look?"

Tears filled his proud eyes the moment he glanced up. "As beautiful as a princess. You'll be the queen of the ball."

"I'll settle for being me."

"Who's the lucky boy escorting you tonight?"

"Nobody, just us girls. We're all going solo."

"Things have changed since I was in high school."

"You mean in the old days when you walked through three feet of snow to get to school?"

"Don't be silly. It rarely snows here. We walked through three feet of flood water."

A horn honked. "My ride's here."

"Who's driving?"

"Melissa's mom. She insisted. So, no need to worry. As soon as the dance is over, I'll be home. Probably around eleven. Then you can make hash browns, and we can watch your favorite musical with Fred Astaire and Ginger Rogers you're so fond of."

"You know your curfew isn't until midnight? Heck, stay out to one."

"I don't think so. I really don't want to go. I'm only going because Melissa is making me. Besides, once I'm away at college, we won't have these types of nights. So, it's a date. I'll be home by eleven."

The Magnolia Mansion on Prytania Street, lit with thousands of Christmas lights, created the perfect atmosphere for *Elite Magazine's* party. When Angela arrived in her limousine, a smile graced her lips as she noticed James, in a tuxedo, standing on the front porch and sipping a martini with all the charisma of James Bond. The vehicle came to a slow, rolling stop. Raymond, her chauffeur, assisted Angela from the car. Her Tadashi Shaji one-shoulder green velvet ruffle gown made quite an impression on James. Excited, James sat his martini on the banister and strode toward Angela. The closer he came to her, the harder his heart pounded, and he stopped short of kissing her. "You look radiant tonight. I want to kiss you."

"You clean up pretty good yourself. I remember you telling me you'd never wear a tuxedo unless you were getting married."

"Well then, Angela, will you marry me?"

"Slow down, lover boy. Let's give this relationship time to develop."

"Shall we go in and pretend we're colleagues?"

"Absolutely. Please try not to get too close to me. We don't want people to talk."

"I get it, business before pleasure. However, I can't stay late. I've been given a curfew."

"A what? By whom?"

"My daughter is going to the winter formal dance with her girlfriends. She told me to be back by eleven to watch movies with her. I tried to extend her curfew until one, but she wasn't buying it. I couldn't exactly tell her I had a date with you, could I?"

"I guess not. But strange you said that. My son has been on me like gravy on rice. He suspects something, and I can't tell him about you. He'd disown me."

"What a fine mess we've gotten ourselves into. Merry Christmas, Angela."

"Merry Christmas, James." She surreptitiously squeezed his hand.

"You know, this is going to be the best Christmas and the worst one simultaneously."

"Meaning?"

"We can't be together on Christmas Day because of the kids."

"I know. But next year, things will be different. We just have to be patient before we break the news to the children we're dating. Probably best after they both graduate, don't you think?"

"Agreed, Ms. Abadie."

"One more thing; I'm going to Rome until after the new year to spend the holidays with my parents. My son doesn't want to go, but I've given him no choice. I promised my dad, and the office is closed until the second week of January. Will you be going back to Atlanta?"

"Over my dead body. My daughter and I have plans to decorate our tree, drink hot chocolate, and watch old movies."

"Yours sounds about exciting as mine."

"Now enjoy your party. It's your night to shine."

The Seamore house's decorated yard with red and green lights blinked as if twinkling stars had fallen from the sky. Christmas carols filled the air as James and Jamie decorated a small tree. "Dad, I miss Mom most of all this time of year. Do you?" Jamie's heart wrenched, thinking of her mom's casket as it was lowered into the grave twelve years ago to the night.

"Of course, this was her favorite holiday. The pain still brings me to my knees." He heaved a sigh. "She used to put up three trees. I always thought she was silly for it, but I'd give anything to see those again."

Jamie dug through a box of ornaments until she found one she'd made in grammar school. The ornament featured a snowman. "Then, let's put up three trees in her honor. We still have time. Christmas isn't for another two days." She gingerly hung the figurine.

"Where would we put them?" His voice quivered slightly.

"Good point. We'll put up three trees when I'm rich and have a mansion like Aunt Sally's. Hand me that red one, please."

"How are you planning on getting rich?" He handed her the clear glass bulb with a snow scene painted on it.

"I'm going to win the lottery... Just kidding. I plan on working hard and owning my own veterinary clinic."

"Now, that sounds like a plan." He shakily placed another ornament on the tree, inhaling and rubbing his hand over his face to keep his emotions in check. He picked up another homemade ornament, one of Jamie's mother holding Jamie during her first Christmas, and gazed at it.

"Dad, it's time you look at *Singlematch* again. You haven't been on a date for a while, and plenty of ladies are pinging you."

"I know what you're trying to do. I'm not interested in dating. I'm practicing what I preach; finish school and concentrate on that!"

"How are classes going?"

"All A's so far. I'm so proud of you for following my advice, even though it meant going to the dance by yourself. Maybe you'll be asked to attend a Mardi Gras ball by some young man at your school."

"I'll cross that bridge when I get to it. Let's get through Christmas. Do you have plans for New Year's Eve?"

"Other than watching the ball drop on television, nothing. What about you? You going to some wild party?"

"Nope, I think we have a date. Ball drop, old movie, and popcorn, here we come."

CHAPTER FIFTEEN

The Kiss That Shouldn't Have Happened

R ing! Ring! The students scattered in the hall as they disappeared into the classrooms before the tardy bell. Melissa and Jamie slammed their lockers in unison as Melissa sighed.

"Don't you think the halls look bare without all the Christmas decorations?" Melissa twisted her lips.

"Right? So does my house. Depressing. I guess that's what January does. Nothing to celebrate."

"At least Mardi Gras starts soon. We'll have plenty to do between marching in the parades and attending balls."

"I've never attended a Mardi Gras ball before. I've always wanted to go to the Endymion or the Rex Ball."

"You're kidding, right? This is *Nawlins*. Going to a ball is a rite of passage."

"Not when you don't have connections and are flat broke."

"Well, you do now. Preston's family is positioned high in the ranks of Endymion. Maybe you ought to make up with him."

"Never, ever in a million years."

"Speaking of Endymion. Have you heard who the Grand Marshall is?"

"Not that I can recall."

"You won't believe it."

"Try me."

"A real prince."

"Sounds intriguing, but I don't believe you."

"Okay, I'll prove it." Melissa typed something into her phone and showed Jamie the article.

Jamie's eyes bulged to the size of billiard balls. "Wait! What! How? Why? That's... that's... that's..." She swallowed hard, trying not to choke on her words.

"...Spit it out, girl. That's what?"

"Prince Karl. You know, the prince my Aunt Sally introduced me to?"

Melissa shook her head in disbelief. "Oh, my god, you have to call him. I have to meet him. This is so exciting. I get to meet a real-life prince and then marry him. I'll be known as Princess Melissa."

"Hold your pumpkins, Cinderella. I doubt he even remembers me."

"Don't look now, Jamie. Here comes Preston."

"He doesn't give up." She bit down on her lower lip, dreading the upcoming interaction.

Preston tapped Jamie on her shoulder. "I need a field trip buddy for the War World II Museum."

"Then you better ask Conrad. I'm not going. My dad forgot to sign my permission slip."

"Since when has that stopped you?"

"Grow up, Preston." Her venomous expression could be seen from a mile away. "I'm not going, especially with you."

Melissa smirked. "Besides, she's dating a prince."

"In your dreams."

"That's enough, Melissa. We'd better get to class."

James briskly walked into Angela's office as she focused on proofing the Legions Airlines' final campaign and smiled. "I think you missed your calling."

"Excuse me. I know I haven't finished my design degree, but give me time."

"Not that." She held up the ad poster. "You look like a pilot. Amazing job!"

"I'll never do that again. Too draining!"

She opened her desk drawer, pulled out an envelope, and handed it to him. "This might change your mind."

"What's this?"

"Open it and see."

James ripped open the envelope and retrieved a check. His eyes bulged. "This has to be a joke. I don't make this kind of money in an entire year."

"No joke! That's what professional models make for an international campaign shoot. Congratulations, you're officially the face of Legions Airlines."

"If John were dead, he'd be rolling over in his grave."

"No, not really. He's not concerned with you or me. He and Monique eloped on New Year's Eve. All he cares about is his campaign."

"So, did you pay me this, or did he?"

"Technically, I did, but with his money. That was the budget for the original model. You earned it."

"This money will pay off my house, my daughter's entire college education, and buy me a new truck."

"No need for a new truck." She opened her second drawer and handed him a set of keys. "It's technically not yours. It's a company car; well-deserved, by the way. I can't have my ad liaison and top model driving around in a beat-up pickup truck, now can I?"

"It's a Lincoln."

"I hope you like the color."

"As long as it's not black."

"It's silver."

"I'm not sure what to say."

"Try, thank you, followed by, I love you, Angela. You're the best boss ever."

Four Weeks Later

With their knees to their chests, Jamie and Melissa sat on the middle of Jamie's bed, applying nail polish to their toes, both in animal onesies, Jamie a pink unicorn and Melissa in a sloth. Melissa dipped her brush into the bottle before applying another layer. "There's nothing like a mani, then a pedi to fix our marching feet."

"If that's what you call it. It seems like I'm making more of a mess than giving myself a manicure, and marching all those parades gave me blisters. Not cool."

"By the way, where's your dad? I didn't see him on the parade route last night. He usually marches with us."

"Can you believe his overbearing, matronly boss made him work last night and tonight? I warned him she'd use him. And just like that, pow! She's using him and during Mardi Gras! Simply shameful."

"That seems a bit odd. Working at ten at night."

"I know, right?"

"Have you contacted Prince Karl yet?"

"No! I told you I'm not going to, and I mean it."

"Seriously! You can't pass this up. This is your chance. He's a prince."

"And I'm a commoner, according to his mother. After Preston's parents rejected me for being from the wrong side of the tracks, do you honestly think a king and a queen will accept me? I can never let my dad know, but her words stung."

"Can't say I know that answer."

"Exactly." Jamie's phone rang; she glanced at the caller's I.D. "It's him."

"The prince?"

"No, silly, Lance." She picked up the phone. "Hey, what's cookin' chicken?"

Lance reclined on his bed with his guitar lying beside him. "I have a surprise for you."

"I love surprises. What is it?"

"My mom has three extra tickets to the Rex Ball. She said I could invite whoever I wanted. So, you want to go?"

"How would we pull that off? No one knows we're dating."

Melissa tried to catch Jamie's attention. "I do!"

Jamie used her index finger and thumb, miming for her to zip her lips.

"My plan is to give you the tickets; then you can invite Melissa and your dad."

"I'm not so sure about this."

"I have it all planned out. You arrive with Melissa and your dad, not with me. Then we can accidentally bump into each other, and no one will be the wiser. We slip away and enjoy Carnival. What ya say? Will you go?"

"Let me talk it over with Melissa, and I'll get back to you."

"Just say yes."

"Okay, yes, it's a date." She hung up the phone.

Melissa lifted her brow. "What's a date?"

"Apparently, you, me, and my dad are going to the Rex ball."

Melissa leaped from the bed, jumping up and down. "I'm going to the Rex Ball!"

"Correction. We're going to the Rex Ball."

"Wait! What will we wear? I have absolutely nothing."

"Aunt Sally to the rescue."

"I don't get it."

"Let my nails dry, and we'll play dress-up. I have a couple of dresses. You'll see."

"Is it me, or is it getting hot in here?" Melissa sneezed.

"Not sure; I think I'm coming down with a cold. I'm not feeling so good. Feel my forehead; do I have a fever?"

The Mona Lisa Restaurant provided the perfect backdrop for an intimate dinner after a parade. The artsy style, with red and white checkered tablecloths and the myriad abstract art of the famous painting of its namesake, provided a fun-filled environment filled with other parade-goers. The waitstaff bustled about carrying large trays with orders as chatter filled the room. One waiter bumped into another, sending one tray crashing to the floor. Nestled at a corner table, Angela and James couldn't take their eyes off each other, layers of Mardi Gras beads hung from their necks. James lifted his champagne glass, "To us."

"I'll drink to that."

"That was some parade. I'm exhausted."

"I can't remember when I went to a parade and had so much fun. I'm usually stuck in the grandstands and not fighting over beads."

"Welcome to my world."

Angela stirred her food on her plate. "Have you thought about attending the Rex Ball with me?"

"I have. I'm just not sure how we'll pull it off. Don't you think people will know we're dating if we show up together?"

"That's why I want to give you two tickets. One for you and one for your daughter. She'll get to meet me, and no one will be the wiser."

"I'm sure she'd love to go. She's always dreamed about it. It's a date."

James sat on the edge of Jamie's bed, feeling her forehead with the back of his hand. Several empty glasses occupied her nightstand. "Honey, you're still burning up with fever."

"Now, what?"

"Drink lots of fluids, eat plenty of soup, and stay in bed."

"Not that, Dad. What do I do about the Rex Ball tonight?"

"You can't go. You have a high temperature."

"Check it again. It's wrong. I feel fine." She gagged, almost vomiting. "Please, just check it."

He shook the thermometer and then placed it under her tongue. "I know this is disappointing, but there will be other balls."

"Not this year." Her words, muffled by the bobbing thermometer in her mouth, made her seem more pitiful than ill.

"Shh. Don't talk. You can't get everyone else sick." He pulled the thermometer from her mouth and looked at the results -- 101.9. "Nope, still high. You're going to the emergency room if your fever doesn't break soon. You've been sick for a couple of days now."

"Like this is my fault. Just give me more aspirin." A tear dripped.

"Honey, don't cry. This too shall pass."

"I really, really want to go."

He felt her heartache, going soft inside from just looking at her. "I know. I'll tell you what. I won't go either. I'll stay home and watch movies with you."

She glumly nodded. "No, Dad. That's not fair to you. Go ahead without me. I'll be fine, really." Her lips pouted as if she was a spoiled two-year-old.

"What about Melissa?" He looked at her quizzically.

"I talked to her earlier. She's still sick too. The entire cheerleading squad got whatever this is." Several uncontrollable sneezes erupted. "Remind me never to march in a parade when it's cold and raining."

For one night, the Sheraton and Marriott Hotels transformed their ballrooms into majestic venues for the Rex and Comus Courts, Carnival, the pageantry, procession, and dancing. Unlike any other the city offered, this event provided a moment of surrealism, including decorations from previous floats provided by Mardi Gras World. The glittering conclusion to Carnival required all to dress to impress in purple, green, or gold, or in their most magnificent beaded and sequined Court attire to represent royalty. Angela was no exception, dressed in a Pamella Roland purple floral sequin-embellished ombre illusion gown; her diamond chandelier earrings accentuated her elegant face. Lance stood at her side in his tuxedo with a purple bow tie and cumberbund, his hair the only indication he might prefer Goth attire. They made small talk with several other revelers, not paying attention as she constantly glanced at her diamond-encrusted watch -- 9:48 p.m.

"Mom, you late for something?"

"Not at all."

"That's about the hundredth time you've looked at your watch. What gives?"

"Nothing. Just wondering when the procession will begin."

Gaile Koch, an overweight diamond heiress in her early forties, dressed in a gold and black Monique Lhullier, embroidered tulle V-neck ballgown complete with tulle sleeves, and her eighteen-year-old, five-foot-eight, modelesque, blonde debutante daughter, dressed in a shimmering green Rono Ruiz strapless, sequin-embroidered bustier ballgown approached.

Gaile encroached, pointing her nose to the sky with an air of arrogance. "Angela, my darling. You look radiant. Have you lost weight?"

"You look stunning as well." Angela gave the once-over to the debutante. "Please don't tell me this is Bentley."

"Yes, ma'am. I'm all grown up."

"She's a supermodel and has walked fashion week for the top designers. She's been on the cover of *Vogue* wearing nothing but our diamonds. She's become quite famous and has a starring role in an upcoming movie starring Mr. Top Gun himself. She's available for your magazine for a price."

Angela diverted her gaze toward Bentley, she held back her urge to brag about Lance taking the higher road. "I haven't seen you since I was in New York about ten years ago. My, my, you grew up to be gorgeous." She adjusted her focus to Gaile. "Where's George?"

"He's part of the Rex Court. He's a duke. Our first time here for Mardi Gras. I must say, New Orleans knows how to throw a party."

"Pardon my manners. Let me introduce you to my son, Lance."

Lance smiled and nodded. "Welcome to Carnival; it's a pleasure to meet you both."

In his tuxedo, James caught Angela's attention out of the corner of her eye as he gestured for her to head for the bar. "Excuse me, I have to say hello to one of my associates before the procession begins. Gaile, we have to have lunch before you head back to New York." She left, leaving Lance with Gaile and Bentley, creating an awkward moment.

Bentley smiled and batted her long lashes. "Lance, this ball is amazing. I'm not sure what is going on, though."

"I'll try to explain it. Tonight, is the meeting of the Courts."

"Courts?"

"Yes, King Rex and his Queen go to the Comus Ball and greet the Comus King and Queen. Once there, the pageantry begins. The Rex Court includes Rex, his Queen, eight maids, and eight dukes. Culminating the festivities, a grand procession from the Marriott follows from the Comus Ball to here. You'll see Rex and his Queen toast with Comus and his Queen. It's a spectacle but a must for Carnival. The tradition has been going on for over a hundred years."

"Are they real kings and queens?"

"Not really; they're chosen by the Carnival crew they belong to. Some wait for years to become a member of the Court. It's quite an honor to be chosen, but the icing on the cake is to be King or Queen."

"Why all the masks?"

"No one is supposed to know their identity until it is revealed."

"Sounds so secret."

"That it is."

"Where can I get something to drink?"

"This way, I'll be glad to show you."

Bentley tapped her mother's shoulder. "Mother, I'll return soon. I'm going to get something to drink. Would you like something?"

"No, thank you, dear. Enjoy yourself."

Across the ballroom, Angela met James, barely containing herself from hugging and kissing him. "Hello, Mr. Seamore. Glad you could make it."

"Why so formal? We can talk with no one suspecting us being in a relationship."

"Lance is here. He'll be watching my every move."

"Where is he? I'd like to meet him."

She pointed across the room at the refreshment table, which contained several punch bowls, finger sandwiches, chips and dips, and fruit and vegetable plates. "He's with that gorgeous debutante in green."

James turned his head, nodded, and smiled. "Wow, he's got great taste in women. She's gorgeous."

"I have my fingers crossed. Nothing would please me more than for those two to date. She's from a refined New York family. They're into diamonds. As for her mother, she's a bit overbearing and snobbish, but she wants what's best for her daughter."

"I wouldn't want to have to buy her an engagement ring."

"The mother or the daughter?"

They shared a laugh as the band played a New Orleans traditional song, *If I Ever Cease to Love*.

James did a two-step. "You know what this song means?"

"You're not from Nawlins if you don't."

"I take it you know it's the official song of Mardi Gras, then?"

"No, it's not. *When the Saints Go Marching In* is."

"Well, Ms. Abadie. Let me educate you. This silly song has been considered the official song of Mardi Gras since the late eighteen hundreds. It is still the official anthem of Rex."

"I never knew. Why?"

"Rumor has it that a king from who knows where was in love with a showgirl who sang this song. Neither were from here but ended up in Nawlins during Carnival. Newspaper reports went crazy, and everyone started playing the song. The rest is history, and we're stuck listening to it now."

"James Seamore, sometimes you surprise the heck out of me."

"I've only just begun. Look, the procession is starting." James took a few steps back, allowing Angela a better view.

"This is my favorite part of Carnival. The pageantry. The costumes. The toast. I don't want it to end."

"I don't want it to end for a different reason." He winked at her.

"What's that?"

"It's the last party to self-indulge before lent. Now, I have to give up my sins and eat fish on Fridays."

"You're Catholic? Good to know."

"I'm not Catholic; I'm a Methodist."

"We share that in common. I'm Wesleyan Methodist. But, I didn't know Methodists gave up meats too."

"When your father is Catholic, you do."

"Are you close with your parents?" *I don't need another fiasco.*

"I'm close to them. They live in Pittsburg, so I don't get to visit them much. It's been years since I've seen them. They run a family-owned animal shelter; and it's difficult for them to travel. I guess I should call them. Jamie probably could use a set of grandparents."

Angela felt a tap on her shoulder. She turned around, and John and Monique, dressed for the occasion, stood in front of her. "I didn't expect to see you both."

James extended his hand to John. "No hard feelings, I hope. Congratulations to you both."

"Thank you, that means a lot to Monique and me."

"Monique. I owe you an apology." Angela apologetically smiled at her former employee.

"Not in the least, Ms. Abadie."

"I think it's time you called me Angela. I'm sorry for firing you. I overreacted. You can have your job back if you want it."

"Apology accepted, Angela. And, as for the job, I've decided to concentrate on my marriage and travel the world with John. He doesn't want me working, and really, there's no need."

"Congratulations to you both on your wedding." Angela sighed in relief.

John smiled and nodded. "Thank you. I've never been happier in my life, and I owe it to *Elite Magazine*. So, you'll need to assign another person to take care of my campaign. I'm not going anywhere else."

"Thank you, John. By the way, does your mother know you're married?" Angela tilted her head toward him.

"Not yet; I'm saving that until I see her in person."

"She'll be very happy, I'm sure. Oh, look; the Kings and Queens have arrived."

The Comus Court was first to enter, followed by the pageantry of the Rex Court. The music continued to play as the revelers watched the procession.

Bentley gazed into Lance's eyes. "This is an experience I'll never forget."

"Glad you're enjoying it." His words were nonchalant to make casual conversation he wasn't interested in engaging.

Conrad skidded toward them, stopping before crashing into Lance. "Hey, my man, who's the babe?" He staggered, grasping for Lance's shoulder to keep himself steady.

"Whoa! You smell like a brewery. Seriously!"

After pulling out a silver-engraved flask, Conrad took another swig. "The best bourbon in the world; Blanton's. You want a swig?" The slur in his words made it difficult to understand him.

"No, thank you."

"I do!" Bentley snatched the flask and gulped it.

"Whoa! Take it easy; it's going to be a long night." Lance gently took the flask away from her.

"I got another." Conrad retrieved another flask, took a swig, and handed it to Bentley. "Don't listen to him; he's a party pooper. Drink up!"

"Happily." She downed as much as she could as quickly as possible.

"Great, now you both smell like a brewery. Disgusting."

Bentley grabbed Lance's cheeks, palms on each, and drew him closer, planting a wet kiss on his lips. Flash! Flash! Flash! Paparazzi swarmed. Flash! Flash! "Ms. Koch, who's your date?"

"Bentley, do we hear wedding bells in your future?"

"How long have you been dating?" Flash! Flash!

"Who's your fiancée?"

Lance grabbed Bentley's hand, pulling her away. "Come on. Let's get out of here."

Across the room, Angela noticed the paparazzi. "I wonder what's going on over there. Must be someone famous."

"Can't tell from here." James strained to get a glimpse.

CHAPTER SIXTEEN

Misery Doesn't Love Company

T he clock to the side of Jamie's bed read 10:38 a.m. She pulled the thermometer from her mouth and studied it. The numbers on them both should not have been so similar. "No! No!" Although her temperature had lowered, it was still 100.3. "Why? Why? Why?" A deep scowl twisted her forehead as her cell phone rang, and puzzled, she glanced at the caller's I.D. – Melissa and answered it. *Misery loves company.* "Hey girl, how ya feeling?"

"Probably better than you."

Jamie pulled her blanket up to her chin. "Yeah, I feel miserable… can't breathe, no appetite, chills. You name it, I've got it."

"You haven't checked Facebook, have you?"

"Nope, and don't intend to."

"You better."

"Not interested. It's just a bunch of misguided, ugly Karens."

"Okay, but don't blame me when you find out your boyfriend is engaged to a diamond heiress supermodel."

"What?! I'm seriously not in the mood for your dumb jokes."

"No, seriously, look. He… her… I mean, they're making headlines."

"Melissa, you're not making any sense."

"Look for yourself."

"Okay, hold on." Jamie opened her Facebook page, and the picture of Lance kissing Bentley hit her in the face. "I don't believe this." Her throat tightened as she fumed on the inside, ready to erupt like a volcano.

"Well, you better believe it. Pictures don't lie. He's a two-timing, no-good cheater! I warned you to stay away from him."

Jamie studied the picture again, then read the headline, "Diamond Heiress in Love with New Orleans Local." She shivered as she threw the phone across the room.

"Jamie? Jamie, you there?"

Jamie bolted from the bed and retrieved the phone. "Sorry, I... I just can't believe this is happening. That's it. I should've listened to you and called Prince Karl. That two-timing no good..."

"...I'm sorry I was the one who had to break this to you. But look at the bright side."

"There is no bright side."

"*Au contraire, mon cheri*! Nobody knows you two were engaged."

"Is that supposed to make me feel better? If so, it sucks! Just let me go. I need time to think."

"Jamie, call the prince before he leaves town."

"Bye, Melissa." She hung up as tears pelted her cheeks like a tropical storm. Sobbing violently, she could barely catch her breath, burying her face in her pillow.

Her phone rang again, but after seeing it was Lance, she slammed her fists against the bed. "I hate you!"

A text notification chimed in from Lance.

> Jamie, please answer. I had nothing to do with that girl. Please call me back. We need to talk before this gets out of hand. Meet me at the skatepark.

She fumed at his invitation. After pondering her response for several minutes, she texted back.

> Not in a million years. It's over!
> I don't want to speak to you ever
> again! Leave me alone.

James, dressed in a two-piece ISAIA black wool suit with a plaid Armani shirt and a blue silk tie that brought out his blue eyes, stood in front of Angela's desk. "You look amazing."

"You suggested I needed to dress the part, so I went shopping. Lots of spring sales right now. I'll eventually get more suits."

"I have a surprise for you."

"Another one? I haven't gotten over the truck yet."

"It's not another vehicle. Follow me."

Angela led the way out of the office, through the journalist bullpen area, and down a narrow hall to the left corner office. "It's all yours."

"I have a private office?"

"Yes, go in."

"It used to be for our Vice President, but it's been empty for about a year since his passing. It's all yours. Francis has already ordered a nameplate for it."

They stepped into the elegant office decorated in burgundy; the Cherrywood desk, cabinets, and credenza made a statement, as did the oversized leather chair. "You can redecorate however you want and make it your own. Just charge anything to your account."

"Are you serious? It's great as it is. I don't want to change a thing." He rubbed his hand across the desk.

"Sit. Take your chair for a spin."

James eased behind the desk and spun the chair several times before sitting. "This will take some time for me to get used to. I've never had a private office before. I'm going to miss my cubicle."

"First order of business. Don't you think you should resign from Blue Bayou?"

"My boss won't be happy about it, but I'll call him and forward my resignation letter."

"Speaking of a letter. You need to meet with Mr. Eagleton and review the resumes he's gathered to hire you a secretary."

"That's not necessary. I don't need a secretary."

"You will as your responsibilities grow. And she can write that letter and call your former boss. You know, things like that."

"Angela, really, you don't have to do this."

"I know that. You deserve it. Besides, I need someone I can count on in this office, and you've proven yourself over the last couple of months."

Francis, carrying what looked like a framed painting, knocked on the door. "Can I come in?"

James quickly stood. "Absolutely."

"Ms. Abadie, I have it ready. You want to give it to him now?"

"Excellent. Turn it around for him to see."

"What is it?"

"Consider it an office-warming gift."

After Francis turned the frame around, James' mouth dropped, still in shock by everything happening. "You shouldn't have."

"I take it you like it. Francis, hang it up for him."

"Yes, ma'am. Mr. Seamore, where would you like it hung?"

"You choose."

Francis walked to the north wall, removed an old portrait of the former occupant, and hung the new one of James' first cover shoot for Legions Airlines.

"I appreciate the gesture, but do I need that for everyone to see?"

Angela patted him on the back. "Of course, our clients must see we promote our own, and you are the face of Legions Airlines. Francis, I need a moment with James. Please check to see if Mr. Vanderhorn has arrived."

"Yes, ma'am." Francis quickly left, closing the door behind her.

"Now, where were we, Mr. Seamore?" She flashed a flirtatious grin and inched her way toward him. "I believe you wanted to show me gratitude."

They kissed, only to be interrupted by James' cell phone buzzing. He glanced at the caller's I.D. "It's my daughter. She's been moping about since Mardi Gras; for over a month. It's times like this that she needs her mother. Any advice?"

"Yes, just listen to her. Maybe it's time for a movie night at home with her. You do that tonight, and I'll take Lance out to eat. He's not been himself since Mardi Gras, either. Kids!"

With nothing but kernels left in a bowl of popcorn between them, James and Jamie watched the ending of *Casablanca*. The credits rolled as he flipped the television off.

Jamie huffed, wiping away a tear. "Well, that's not your typical Hollywood ending. Even they don't end up together."

"Not sure what you mean."

"You know, boy meets girl. Boy and girl fall in love, and live happily ever after."

"You got a point."

"Love is useless. I'm never falling in love again."

"What do you mean, again?"

Jamie's eyes filled with tears. "Daddy, I have a confession. I didn't mean to lie to you."

"What on Earth are you rambling about?"

"I've been hiding my boyfriend from you; I didn't want to disappoint you since you said I needed to concentrate on school. I met a boy at school after I broke it off with Preston. I love him, but I caught him cheating on me."

"Then it's a good thing you broke it off."

"Well, he didn't exactly cheat on me; he got caught up in a situation, and a girl kissed him, and I found out, but he hasn't seen her since, and I miss him. It's hard going to school and seeing him every day. He keeps trying to get back together with me."

"Do you trust him?"

"I think so."

"Do you still love him?"

"Yes, he's the best, really, he is. I'm just so confused and don't know what to do."

"Well, if your mother were here, she'd probably tell you to follow your heart. True love only comes around once."

"Is that why you don't want to date? You know you won't find true love again because of Mom?"

"It's complicated."

Jamie pouted, slumping her shoulders.

"Honey, if you really love this guy, give him a second chance. It doesn't mean you have to marry him. You have the rest of your life for that. Take baby steps."

"Thanks, Dad. I feel better. I'll call him tomorrow."

"Call him tonight; if he's half the man you say he is, he'll want to hear from you."

After taking a long, deep breath, she kissed her dad on the cheek and headed for the door, dialing her phone.

"So, when do I get to meet this boyfriend of yours?"

"Not until he's my boyfriend again, and I'm sure it'll work out." She left for her room, holding the phone to her ear.

Ring. Ring. Ring. "This is Lance. I'm either sleeping or skating. You know what to do. If you don't, don't call me again."

Please answer the freakin phone. She dialed again, to no avail, as her heart sank in sadness. Frustrated and heartbroken, Jamie retrieved her floral stationery from her second drawer and composed a letter. She pondered for several minutes, tapping her pen against the paper with one hand and rubbing her chin with the other.

Dear Prince Karl,

You may not remember me, but we briefly met at my Aunt Sally's house over the Thanksgiving holidays. I'm the girl whose dad embarrassed and made me leave before dinner. I'm hoping you'd be interested in attending my senior prom with me. Unfortunately, I don't have a date. The school's name is George Sidwell Preparatory Senior High School. Oh, the dance will be at the Roosevelt Hotel on May 15th this year in New Orleans.

Sincerely,

Jamie Seamore

She folded the letter and placed it in the envelope, sealing it with a kiss. *Someday my prince will come because it certainly isn't Lance, the cheater.* She hummed the familiar tune from *Snow White* as she sprayed her gardenia perfume on the envelope.

Jacques-Imo's, a two-story shotgun house turned restaurant in Uptown, provided the perfect backdrop for Angela and Lance's mother-son time. The beige paint peeled in several areas, and the bright blue trim reflected the New Orleans architecture. Inside were wooden plank floors, a ceiling with lots of eclectic local art, wooden chairs, and a different colorful plastic tablecloth on each occupied table. One first had to walk through the bar and kitchen to get to the seating area. Angela and Lance sat at a corner table, eating their main dishes.

"Mom, I know this isn't your kind of place, but thanks for bringing me. It's the only place that serves mushroom-stuffed salmon."

"Honey, whatever do you mean? This isn't exactly a fast-food chain. You act like I only go to five-star restaurants. Besides, this blackened redfish is to die for." She gestured imperiously.

"Thanks again; I needed this distraction."

"Now, tell me again about the space shuttle connection."

"A chef's coat and menu flew on the space shuttle. There's a plaque somewhere telling the details. Pretty cool, huh?" Lance's heart clearly wasn't in his words.

"Pretty cool? I think that's incredible. What's wrong? You've been sulking for weeks. Do you want to talk about it?"

"Nope."

"Lance, I'm willing to listen to whatever is bothering you."

"Girl troubles. My girlfriend broke up with me."

"I didn't even know you had one. Tell me about her."

"No need; it's over between us." He pursed his lips, stamping down the emotion.

"You really like her, don't you?"

"I'd say. She's very special."

"If she means that much to you, make up with her; do whatever it takes."

"She won't even answer my calls or text me back. To top it off, she avoids me at school. How am I supposed to talk to her?"

"Write her a letter."

"That's old-fashioned."

"Then send her an email and flowers. Tell her how beautiful she is, and that you were wrong. We love it when a man admits it."

"It won't work. I'm doomed."

"I'll tell you what; call her now and offer to meet up with her tomorrow."

"I'm not so sure about that."

"Just do it."

He nodded as he frowned, reaching for his phone. "Oh, no!"

"What is it?"

"I left my phone in the car."

The following morning, Jamie heard a knock on the door, which woke her up. Wiping sleep from her eyes, she squinted at her clock -- 8:45 a.m. *Really? It's early.* Knock! Knock!

"Okay, I'm coming!" She bolted from her room and swung the front door open. A colossal spring bouquet in a clear vase covered a DoorDasher's face. Puzzled, Jamie took a deep breath and sighed. "Can I help you?"

"I have a delivery for Ms. Jamie Seamore."

"I'm Jamie."

"Great." He handed her the flowers as an envelope floated to the ground. Sniffing them, she carried the flowers into the house, and placed them on the side table. When she returned to close the door, she noticed the envelope and picked it up, carefully opening it.

Jamie,

I miss you so much. I'm really sorry about what happened, but honestly, it wasn't my fault. No! It was my fault! I was wrong in so many ways. I shouldn't have gone to the ball without you knowing you were sick. That's on me. I was wrong. I should've ignored her, but I was trying to be nice. My fault. Conrad brought a flask, and they swigged it. I was wrong not to have taken it away from them. I was wrong on all accounts. Please forgive me if you can. I really want to make it up to you and will if you give this wrong guy half a chance. I love you so much. I can't take not being with you. Please meet me at the skatepark today at 4:15. I love you.

Forever XOXO, Lance.

She flopped down on the sofa, not knowing how to respond to his admission of wrongdoing. *Should I go?* An internal battle erupted like a volcano, but his words contributed much toward her decision.

CHAPTER SEVENTEEN

The Games They Play

A Black elderly school janitor in a gray shirt and pants stood on a ladder, changing the school's front billboard sign to read, "Cheerleader tryouts – May 4th. Sign up now!"

Inside, Jamie and Melissa strolled down the hall carrying homemade cheerleading announcement posters. Every couple of feet, they stopped and hung another.

"Melissa, hand me another piece of tape. Longer this time." She pressed the poster up against the wall.

After ripping a piece of tape from the roll, Melissa plastered it onto the poster to attach it to the wall. "I can't believe we're not trying out this year."

"Duh, we're seniors. It's sad, though."

"Sad, I'll really miss this. Won't you?"

"Probably, but I'm hoping to cheer in college."

"I thought you haven't been accepted."

"I haven't, but it's only a matter of time."

"Don't look now; guess who's coming your way?"

"Preston?"

"Nope, Mr. Cheater."

Jamie glanced over her shoulder. "Great. Just great."

Lance stopped a couple of feet away. "Jamie, I really need to speak with you. Please meet me after school at the park."

212

"Fine, just leave me alone."

He nodded and proceeded down the hall, disappearing into a classroom.

Melissa cleared her throat. "I thought you weren't going to see him again. Like never!"

"You know what they say about the word never. I think I need to hear his side of the story."

"You've got to be kidding. He's a cheater. Once a cheater, always a cheater. A tiger's stripes don't change."

"That kiss wasn't his fault. Conrad tried to explain to me what had happened. According to him, Lance was a victim."

"Some victim! Poor baby, I had to kiss a diamond heiress." Melissa pretended to play an invisible violin.

"She was drunk and grabbed him."

"Since when do you defend a no-good, two-timing cheater? Oh, the games we play for love."

"I'll put it to you this way; he admitted he was wrong. I admire that. Besides, I really miss him, and I love him. I owe it to myself to at least listen to what he has to say."

"The way I see it, this story has three sides; his, hers, and Conrad's."

"Add a fourth one; the truth."

"Fine, don't say I didn't warn you when he breaks your heart. That's what cheaters do."

James sat behind his desk as Francis handed him another resume. "Here, maybe you'll like this one. This candidate has plenty of experience and references. A top graduate too."

He glanced at the stack of resumes on his desk. "This will be the thirteenth interview. I'm over it, but send her in."

With a smirk on her lips, Francis left James to review Casey Cochran's resume.

He rubbed his chin, scanning the credentials. *Definitely qualified.*

Knock! Knock! James looked up and saw a flamboyant young man, dressed in a bright pink leather jumpsuit, smelling like a perfume shop standing at the doorway. "Mr. Seamore."

"Yes, may I help you?"

"I'm here for my interview."

"Excuse me, you're Casey Cochran?"

"Absolutely, there's no missing me."

"You got that right. Please come in and take a seat."

Casey sashayed to the chair across from James' desk and, with dignified poise, lowered himself with a straight, stiff back, clasping his hands onto his lap. "I'm all yours, darling."

"First, cut the darling. I'm Mr. Seamore."

"I didn't mean anything by it. I call everyone darling."

"You're hired!"

"But, wait. You haven't asked me any questions."

"No need. You're hired. When can you start?"

"As soon as you give me the word."

"I'll call human resources and get the ball rolling… darling."

Casey puckered his lips. "Can't wait to get started." He glanced up at the Legions Airlines' poster. "Nice pic! Mmm. Fabulicious!"

James sighed. *What have I gotten myself into?*

Casey pranced to the door, smashing into Angela. "Excuse me; I'm so very sorry."

Angela's eyes widened with a questioning expression. She slipped to the side simultaneously with Casey as if a well-choreographed waltz had commenced. Angela put her right hand up. "Stop! You go. I insist."

"Thank you, darling." And off Casey went strutting down the hall.

"Angela, guess you just met my new secretary."

"Looks promising, I think."

"Considering I didn't want one, he'll be great. His resume is impeccable, and I like how he didn't give in to me. A bit cocky, but he'll do just fine around Posey and Javier. They'll be like three peas in a pod."

"I'll leave that one right where it is. The games we play."

"What brings you to my office?"

"We're invited to a journalist awards banquet. I'm presenting and need a date."

"I thought no one could know we're dating."

"They won't. After all, you're employed here as my ad liaison. I have a table for ten, so others from the company will be joining us."

"Sounds so romantic; how can I turn that down?"

"Put it on your calendar."

Lance sat on the hilltop on a small blue fleece blanket, his skateboard and gear beside him. He glanced at his watch -- 4:30 p.m. *She's not coming.* His heart sank as he sighed, falling onto his back, and gazing at the sky. A shadow covered his face.

"Hi, Lance."

He bolted upward as if he were a ninja. "Jamie! I'm so happy you came." He grabbed her into a bear hug, holding her tight. "I've missed you so much."

She pushed back, distancing herself. "We've got to talk."

"I told you, I'm really, really sorry. I don't even like Bentley."

"Please don't ever say her name around me, again."

"What can I do to convince you I'm in love with you and not Bent...?" He stopped himself from finishing the heiress' name.

"I believe you."

"I'll do anything to get you back. I'll marry you. I'll go to prom with you. List your demands. Please, I'm begging you to believe me."

"I said, I believe you."

"You do?" His voice was uncharacteristically unsure and shaky told Jamie everything she needed to know about his sincerity. "That's a relief."

"Not so fast, lover boy. I love you; it made a difference that you admitted you were wrong. So, my first demand is for you to ask me to prom, and then we'll take it from there. But this doesn't mean we're back together. Got it?"

He nodded his head, sitting straight up as his eyes met hers. "Will you go to prom with me?"

"That really means a lot to me. Of course, I'll go with you. I already know the dress I'll wear."

"So, does this mean we can tell everyone we're together?"

"We don't need rumors."

"Oh, rumors will fly regardless, when we show up at prom."

Mardi Gras World's main ballroom provided the perfect backdrop for the *17th Annual Southern Journalist Awards* ceremony. Tables of ten throughout the area were draped in royal blue linen tablecloths with fresh flower centerpieces, each table with a reserve table card. Several Mardi Gras floats surrounded the area's outskirts, creating a festive ambiance. At *Elite Magazine*'s table were Angela, James, Francis, Posey, Javier, Casey, and a couple of other journalists, including Katie, who worked with them. Everyone was dressed to impress as they ate, drank, and enjoyed the ceremony.

Casey gently wiped his lips. "This food is the best. Thank you, Ms. Abadie, for allowing me to attend."

"No need to thank me. You're part of this team."

James held up his champagne glass. "To *Elite Magazine*."

"To *Elite*!" The toast sounded more like a football cheer than a toast.

On stage, the Master of Ceremony held up a beautiful glass trophy. "Now, without further ado, it is time to present the Journalist of the Year Award."

James winked at Angela as if he knew something she didn't.

Without warning, Angela's father and mother approached. Mr. Abadie tapped Angela on the shoulder, and she quickly jerked her head around. "Dad! Mom! What are you doing here?"

"We wouldn't miss this for the world."

"In the last decade, you have never once attended this ceremony. Why the sudden change now?"

The Master of Ceremony tapped on the microphone. "May I please have the founder and CEO of *Elite Magazine*, Mr. Arthur Abadie, to the podium?"

Angela's father smiled. "I'm here by special request. We wanted to surprise you. You have your answer now." He strolled to the front.

James quickly stood. "Mrs. Abadie, please, have a seat."

"Why, thank you, young man. And what do you do for the magazine?"

"Mom, this is James Seamore. He's our ad liaison."

"I didn't know such a title existed."

"A pleasure to meet you, Mrs. Abadie." James grabbed an empty chair from a nearby table, and eased it next to Angela's mom, and sat.

With self-importance written all over his expression, Mr. Abadie shuffled to the podium in a gentlemanly manner, all eyes on him as he cleared his throat, straightening his shoulders. "It's always a pleasure to be surrounded by journalist royalty. The brightest and best are in this room tonight, and many have received well-deserved awards. However, nothing can compare to the pride her mother and I have for our daughter, Angela Abadie. I have groomed my daughter since the day she was born to run *Elite Magazine*. When I retired, she took over the reins, leading our company to even further greatness. I am honored to present the Journalist of the Year award to her."

The crowd erupted into cheers and a standing ovation. Taken aback, Angela's jaw dropped; in a daze, she stood and hugged her mother and then, overly excited, hugged James, planting a kiss on his lips. Her father watched from the stage with an expression of poorly hidden fury, and as she made her way to the front, he glared at her.

When she reached him, he heaved the trophy into her hands. "What was that?"

"Dad, what are you talking about?"

"Don't pretend that I didn't see that." He stormed off the stage, nostrils flaring like a mad bull ready to attack a matador in a red cape, advancing straight toward James; his shuffle quickly dissipated the closer he came to confronting him, stomping his feet.

Angela took a deep breath, keeping a sharp eye on her father, feeling as if butterflies fluttered inside her stomach. "I can't thank all of you enough for this outstanding award. It doesn't belong to me, but to everyone at *Elite Magazine,* as we're a team, a family of journalists."

Mr. Abadie stood bullnose-to-nose with James. "What game are you playing?"

"Thank you, everyone." Angela swiftly left the stage carrying her trophy and raged toward her father, who seemed ready to throw the first punch.

"Angela, explain yourself." Mr. Abadie's face turned crimson as he puffed his cheeks, not taking his gaze off James.

"Dad, I don't know what you think is going on, but what is your problem?"

Feeling the full impact of her laser stare, he pointed his finger an inch away from James' nose. "Him! I saw you kiss him. Who the hell is he?"

His hesitation was momentary as James extended his hand. "Sir, I'm James Seamore. I work for the magazine."

"I didn't ask you; I asked my daughter." He spun to face her. "Angela!"

"Dad, not now, not here."

"Explain your behavior."

"Well, if you must know, James and I are dating."

Everyone at the table gasped; Javier bobbed his head. "I knew it."

"I didn't." Posey rolled his eyes as if he'd been purposefully left out of a secret.

Angela grabbed James' hand. "Stop it, everyone. Yes, James and I are an item. Now, get over it."

"Angela, as your father, I don't approve. I don't know what game you're playing, but it will not happen under my watch. Break it off. Make a choice. It's him or the magazine. You can't have both."

James stormed from the table. "I quit! We should've never been together. Angela, take your magazine."

"James! Wait! Dad, how could you?" Angela shoved the trophy into her father's chest and bolted after James, leaving everyone stunned.

Mr. Abadie took one step to follow Angela, only to be stopped by his wife's firm grip on his forearm. "Leave them be. You've done enough damage, don't you think?"

Jamie was sitting on the sofa watching an old movie when James scarpered through the door. "Dad, you're just in time. *How to Marry a Millionaire* just started."

He plopped down next to her, clenching his jaw, both actions were uncharacteristic of him.

"Whoa! Dad, what's up?"

"You wouldn't understand."

"Try me."

"Let me put it to you this way. I had a bad date."

"Date! I didn't even know you had one. Did you meet her on *Singlematch*?"

"You could say that. I really like her."

"What happened?"

"Let's say it's a Preston situation. I'm from the wrong side of the tracks."

"Oh! That!"

"Yea, that."

"Then you don't need her, anyway. There are plenty of others on *Singlematch*."

"You don't get it. I think I'm in love with her. I didn't want to tell you because of your mother."

"Now, who's lying? So, you've been dating all along and didn't tell me."

"Like father, like daughter."

"Then, follow Mom's advice. Go after her. Follow your heart."

"How did that work out for you?"

"We're back together, but taking it easy to see how things go."

"I don't stand a chance of getting her back."

"The answer is no until you try."

"I guess. I'll make the popcorn. Let's watch this movie."

"Yea, maybe we'll learn how to marry a millionaire."

"Cute, Jamie. Real cute."

Jamie stood in front of her closet, pulling out the four dresses Aunt Sally gave her during Thanksgiving, tossing them onto the bed. She dug through the closet, looking for each dress's matching pair of heels. She found the red and purple pair, but only one pink stiletto. "Oh, no!" She continued tossing all shoes from the closet. "I know you're in here." Her cell phone rang, and after looking at the caller's I.D., she quickly answered it.

"Hey, Melissa. What's up!"

"Happy birthday! You're legally an adult now. How does it feel to be eighteen?"

"No different from seventeen."

"Good to know. What are your plans?"

"Don't have any. Usually, my dad takes care of that."

"Well, let me know. I have a present for you, and I'm kinda throwing you a surprise birthday party."

"It's not a surprise if you tell me about it."

"You know me, I'm not good at keeping secrets."

"You can say that again."

"I'm not good at keeping secrets."

"I didn't mean literally."

"Oh, have you decided what dress you'll wear for prom? It's this weekend."

"I'm pretty sure; I just need to find the shoes. I have no idea where the oink pair are."

"Well, I'm wearing my rhinestone tennis shoes so I can dance without my feet killing me all night. I suggest you do the same."

"What are you wearing?"

"I just told you, my rhinestone tennis shoes."

"Melissa, your dress?"

"Can I borrow your royal blue one? I love that dress."

"Sure, it looks better on you, anyway."

James approached the door, interrupting her search. "Happy birthday!"

"Thanks, Dad. Give me a minute; I'm on the phone."

He nodded his head and left.

"Gotta go. Dad wants me. I bet he has my birthday present."

"Love you, girl. Bye."

"Dad! I'm off the phone." Just as she decided to leave her room, he reappeared, and they bumped chest to chest. "Oops!"

"Honey, I have to go for a bit. I haven't forgotten your birthday, but there's something I have to do."

"It's about her, isn't it?"

"Her?"

"Your date from last night."

"As a matter of fact, it is. I'm going to try to make things right and follow my heart."

"Dad, I don't want to disappoint you, but do you mind if I hang out with Melissa tonight? She wants to throw me a small surprise party for my birthday, considering tomorrow night is prom. Then it's Sunday, then Monday…"

"…I get it. Go be with your friends. You only turn eighteen once."

She hugged him. "Thanks, Dad. You're the best."

"Honey, wait. I have your birthday present. You ready to see it?"

"Of course."

"Okay, first, I have to blindfold you. Then I'll take you to the living room."

"I'm in."

He gently placed a makeshift, ripped T-shirt blindfold he removed from his back pocket over her eyes, tying it caringly in the back. "Can you see anything?" He waved his hands across her face to test if she could.

"Nope."

"Good." Grasping her by the shoulders, he guided her to the living room and opened the front door.

"We're going outside?"

"Yep, watch your step." He assisted her down the stairs. "Ready?"

"More than ready."

He tenderly removed her blindfold, and sitting in the driveway was a new red SUV with a big red bow across the hood.

A blood-curdling scream erupted from Jamie as if Freddie Krueger had pounced on her. "Is this really mine?"

"Yes, I thought the SUV would help you more when you move to college. I hope you like it."

"I love it, Dad."

"Happy birthday!" Melissa, holding something rolled up in her hand and a Sharpie pen, jumped from behind the vehicle. The rest of the cheerleading squad bolted out from the side of the house. "Surprise!"

"Seriously, Melissa! I was just on the phone with you. This is my surprise party?"

"Yep! Gotch ya. Happy birthday!"

The cheerleading squad sang their unique version of *Happy Birthday*, cheerleader style, bouncing on their toes and clapping. "Happy, happy birthday, happy birthday to you; happy, happy birthday, from all of us to you. Hey! Goooo, Jamie!"

Jamie shook with excitement, hugging her father. "We can't afford this. I can't take it."

"Honey, since working for *Elite Magazine* and doing the cover ad for Legions Airlines, we can afford this. You deserve it. Enjoy!"

Melissa approached James. "Can I have your autograph?" She handed him a copy of *Elite Magazine* with him on the cover and the Sharpie. "You look so hot!"

"Melissa, leave my dad alone."

Sullen, James, glanced around his office with glum despair. He set one file box on the floor and picked up an empty one, tossing it onto his desk. He shook his head and heaved a sigh. Slowly, he emptied each drawer's contents into the box. *It was great while it lasted.*

Angela tapped on the door before entering. "You don't have to quit."

He glanced up at her, narrowing his eyes, and threw his stapler into the box.

"Please, stop packing. I need you here, and I'm in love with you. What about us?"

"It won't work, Angela. The fiasco at the banquet proved that. Your dad is furious."

"My dad can't dictate who I date or, for that matter, who I will or will not marry."

"I can't let you lose the magazine over me. I'm not worth that. Nobody's worth that. "

"I'll start another one. Hell, I'm the Journalist of the Year. I'll strike while the iron is hot."

"That won't fix anything. Your dad hates me and will never approve of me."

"That doesn't matter."

"It does matter. I'm not good enough for you by his standards and never will be. I won't let you give up the magazine for me. So, we're finished. Which means I'm finished here at *Elite*. I'll go back to being your window washer. That's the only way!"

"Stop being ridiculous. I'm a grown woman and won't let my dad bully me into not seeing you or threatening to take the magazine away. He'll eventually come around and see things my way."

He placed the lid on the top of the box and then stood. "I'm sorry things ended this way because I really love you. I want to marry you. But we're different, you and me. To quote my daughter, we're from the wrong side of the tracks. Be honest, isn't that why you never introduced me to your son? Deep down, you knew I wasn't good enough."

"Nonsense. I haven't introduced you to my son because he doesn't think I should be dating, at all. Not even John, a billionaire, was good enough, and he gave me problems about dating him, so this has nothing to do with who you are or what kind of family you came from. He has dreams of his dad and me getting back together, which, for the record, will never happen."

"Maybe you should consider it. Then everyone will be happy."

"Absolutely not! I'm in love with you. I, Angela Abadie, am in love with you and want to spend the rest of my life with you. Please, James, unpack and stay. I need you. The magazine needs you."

"I can't, Angela. As much as I love you... it hurts for me to leave. I'm doing this because I love you. Hell, I've even fantasized about marrying you and growing old together. Maybe if it was another time and another place, we could've worked things out." He latched onto the boxes, stormed out of the office, and for good measure, slammed the door behind him.

"James, wait!" She kicked the corner of the desk, thinking of what her father had done. Pain shot up her foot as she cried out, jumped up and down, and then clutched her toes, rubbing them to ease the pain.

CHAPTER EIGHTEEN

Under the Stars

Jamie, wearing her pink plaid pajama pants and a solid pink T-shirt, stumbled from her room into the living room, where her dad sat in his recliner. The brewed coffee gave off a pleasurable aroma as she sniffed the air. "Good morning, Dad. Glad you made coffee." She kissed him on the top of his head, then yawned and stretched.

"Nothing good about today." James sighed and then sipped his morning cup of Joe.

"I take it you didn't make up with that woman?"

"I sure didn't. It's over, and that's final." Sadness enveloped him.

"That explains your long face."

"I plan on getting a couple of steaks and grilling them tonight. After that, we can watch a movie. That's the only thing that will make me feel better. What ya say?"

"It's prom night, Dad."

"Already? I guess you and the girls will be dancing the night away."

"I actually have a date."

"Whoa! I wasn't expecting that. Sounds promising. This means you made up with your boyfriend."

"Not exactly. Let's say he's on trial."

"Trial? Sounds like you think he's guilty."

"In a way, I'm just being super cautious. I don't want my heart to get broken again."

"Sounds reasonable. So, do I finally get to meet him? What time is he picking you up?"

"Sorry, Dad. I'm meeting him there; I'm driving my new SUV. That way, I'm not stuck at prom with him if things don't work out."

"Sounds like a plan."

"Can we talk about my curfew?"

"You're eighteen. I think your curfew days are over. Just be careful and don't be out too late. Okay?"

"I won't; I promise. Dad, why don't you ask that lady out tonight? I know you want to."

"I'll think about it."

"Stop thinking and do it."

James took the last sip of his coffee. "Honey, you mind getting me another cup?"

"My pleasure. I need one too. It's going to be a long day."

Dressed in his black jeans and T-shirt, Lance bounced into the kitchen. Angela sat at the counter reading the newspaper as Miriam busied herself with the dishes. "Good morning, Mom!"

"My, aren't we happy today? What gives?"

"It's a new day."

"Something's up. You've spent over a month moping about, and now this. What's got you so happy? I could use some of that."

"Why, what's wrong?"

Miriam dried her hands on her apron. "She's down in the dumps."

"Mom, what's got you down?"

"I have a lot on my mind, is all."

"It's Grandpa, isn't it?"

"Why on Earth would you say that?"

"Because this is exactly the way you behave when he interferes. The writing is on the wall."

"It'll blow over, I'm sure."

"Whatever Grandpa is up to, do what you want. It's your life, so live it. You always said don't worry about what you can't control.

Concentrate on the controllable and make things happen. Take charge of your life. So, why don't you practice what you preach?"

"Lance, sometimes you're so wise. Great advice."

"I know. By the way, I'll be out late tonight."

"Whatever for?"

"It's prom night."

"Since when do you go to a school dance?"

"I lost a bet."

"Who's the lucky girl? Bentley?"

"Never in a million years."

"Too bad. I have high hopes for you two. So, then who?"

"Nobody you know, but she's great, beautiful, smart, and spunky."

"Sounds like puppy love."

"Maybe a little bit more than that."

"Well, have fun!"

"What's your plan, Mom?"

"Honestly, I was thinking of driving to Orange Beach and spending a few days there to clear my mind. Any objections?"

"I think you should."

Miriam nodded in agreement. "I'll hold down the fort and keep Master Lance in line."

James, carrying a handful of mail, strolled from his mailbox to the front porch when he received a text from Angela.

> Please, let's talk about this. I really miss you.

He frowned and sat on the porch step. A couple holding hands passed in front of his house, and when he looked up, she flashed her engagement ring. "We're getting married!"

"Congratulations." His thoughts were on Angela. *To think I wanted to marry her*. He texted Angela.

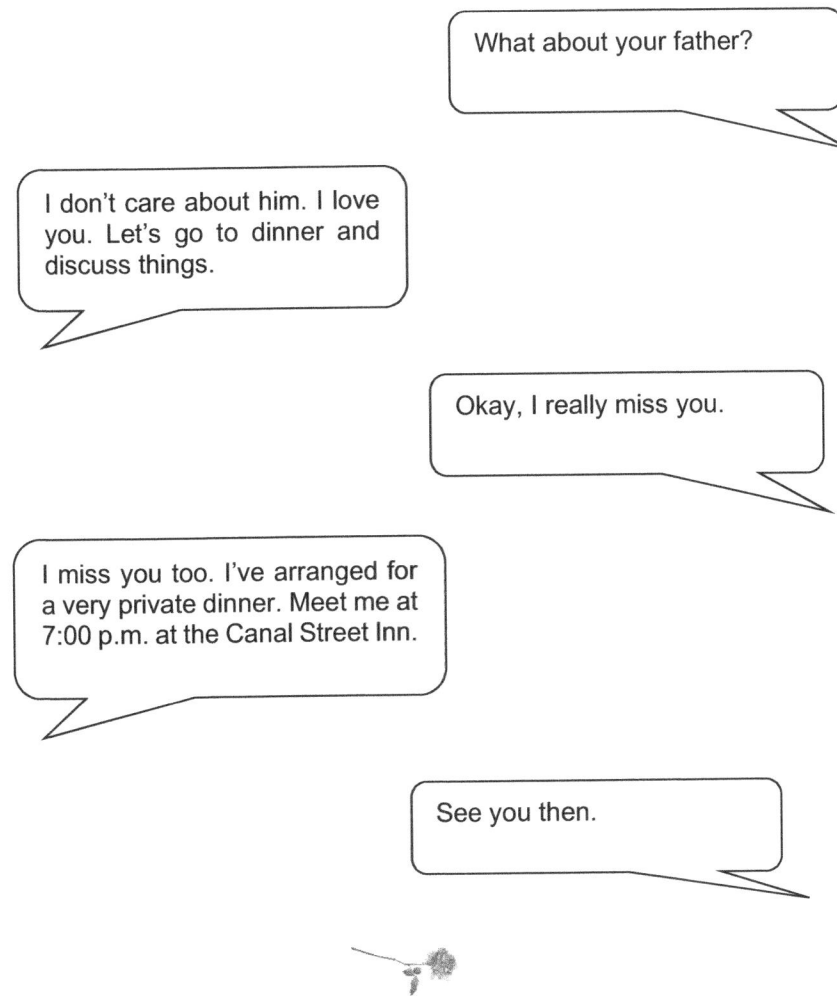

What about your father?

I don't care about him. I love you. Let's go to dinner and discuss things.

Okay, I really miss you.

I miss you too. I've arranged for a very private dinner. Meet me at 7:00 p.m. at the Canal Street Inn.

See you then.

Jamie, wearing the pink dress from Aunt Sally and her rhinestone tennis shoes, walked into the Blue Room at the Roosevelt Hotel. She saw the prom theme banner across the stage that read, "Under the Stars," first. Decorated like a fairytale beneath a starry night, the atmosphere was vibrant. A selfie booth with a night sky filled with sparkling stars was in one area. Across the way were the food and beverage area and the front near the stage. Ten couples stood in line at the photographer's station for prom night portraits. The DJ played dance songs as the dance floor was filled with celebrating teenagers.

Jamie glanced around, hoping to find Lance. Suddenly, she felt a tap on her shoulder, followed by a kiss on the cheek.

"Looking for someone special?"

She twirled around and gave Lance a huge hug. "You came!" Gobsmacked, she studied Lance's new haircut. His long hair was now short and stylish; and he no longer looked like a Goth punk star.

"Of course, I did. A promise is a promise."

"Whoa! I've never seen you dressed up like this." She gave a once-over glance at his tuxedo. "You clean up nicely, and your hair. My, you really look fantastic."

"I must say, you look beautiful. Beautiful enough to marry."

"Why, Lance, is that another proposal?"

A slow song played. "Let's dance." He grabbed her hand and led her to the dance floor.

She wrapped her arms around his neck and lay her head on his shoulder.

A loud commotion at the front entrance caught both of their attention. Jamie frowned, jerking her head toward the commotion. "I wonder what's going on."

Out of nowhere and without fanfare, Prince Karl dressed in his official royal attire, including the royal sash across his chest with the official Family Crest, military emblems, lapel pins, and his entourage entered. Jamie's missing pink stiletto was in his hand, which she had left on Aunt Sally's stairs that dreadfully embarrassing night.

"Oh, no!" Jamie swallowed hard.

Lance shook his head. "Look at that idiot; he thinks he's Prince Charming."

"He is a prince, you dork. That's Prince Karl."

The girls ran toward Prince Karl. Melissa was the first to arrive, curtsying. "I'm Melissa Sidwell, Your Royal Highness."

"A pleasure to meet you, Ms. Sidwell. You wouldn't happen to know a Ms. Jamie Seamore, would you?" He put the shoe behind his back to hide it.

"I do. I'm her best friend, and that must be the shoe she can't find."

He held up the shoe. "Silly of me." He tossed it in the trash can.

"She was right over there." Melissa pointed to a crowd across the room. "Wait, I don't see her now."

"You know that idiot?" Lance raised his eyebrow.

"It's a long story, but I think he's looking for me. Let's get out of here." She grabbed Lance's hand, and they headed for the exit, bumping into Preston and his goons.

"Well, well, look who the cat dragged in."

"Zip it, Preston!" Jamie glared at him, almost as if daring him to say another word.

Conrad staggered toward them, taking a swig from his flask. "This all seems interesting."

Lance pulled Jamie toward the door. "Let's go!" They slipped out the exit and headed through the hotel's front revolving door.

James strolled up the sidewalk to the main entrance of the Canal Street Inn, a place of such grandeur and sophistication it took your breath away. The magnificent mansion stood elegantly under the starry sky. As if the mansion and grounds weren't glorious enough as a standalone, the dazzling privacy it offered couldn't be resisted. Angela peeped out the window and waved, then immediately opened the door, and bolted to James, giving him a huge kiss. "It's so good to see you. I thought I lost you forever." She felt like a ray of sunshine had kissed her back, immediately brightening up from being in James' arms.

"This has been the hardest couple of days of my life without you." James squeezed her hand.

"I feel the same way. Are you ready for one of the best meals in your life?"

"Can't wait. I didn't know this place served dinner."

"Not exactly. I rented the entire mansion and hired a private chef just for us."

"Impressive, but you shouldn't have."

"Let me put it to you this way, only the best, since I'm getting married tonight."

"Wait! What? Married? I'm confused."

Angela gazed deep into his eyes. "James Seamore. I don't want to live another day without you in my life. Will you marry me tonight?"

Stunned, he gulped. "I think we need a marriage license to do that."

"I have that covered." She gestured her hand, and within moments, a female Justice of the Peace approached carrying a piece of paper.

"This must be the groom?" She stuck out her hand toward James. "I'm Caroline Hardy. I have your marriage license; you only need to sign it after the nuptials."

"Angela, are you sure about this?"

"I've never been more sure of anything in my life. Marry me!"

"What about the kids? Shouldn't they be here?"

"We can have a different ceremony after we marry, just like Ben and J-Lo. Besides, it's better this way; no one can stop the wedding. What do you say?"

"Yes! Let's get married." James' face broke into a disbelieving smile.

"Follow me." She grasped his hand, led him through the front door, and stopped in front of the foyer's massive, obscene antique credenza. On it was a lavender boutonniere rose and a matching bridal bouquet. Angela carefully secured the boutonniere on James' lapel and took in a long sigh of relief.

"You thought of everything. Even a lavender rose meant for our first date."

"Most brides do. I planned this for a couple of days before we broke up. Did you know that a lavender rose symbolizes love at first sight?"

"You're kidding?"

"No, red for romantic or passionate love, yellow for friends, white for healing or purity, and a lavender rose, love at first sight. Just like us."

"Is that why you chose that for our blind date?"

"No, I think that was Francis' idea of setting the tone. Looks like she was right."

"Angela, are you really sure about this?"

"I've never been more sure of anything in my life."

Caroline strode through the foyer. "This way, we have a wedding to begin."

Flurried with excitement, they headed to the backyard, decorated for a wedding under the stars, including the large arbor entwined in lavender roses, baby's breath, and sparkling lights in the trees illuminating the area representative of a starry night. A violinist played Santana's song, *Europa*, and Mr. and Mrs. Gladstone, an elderly couple, stood by as witnesses.

Mrs. Gladstone smiled as if she was the proud mother of the bride. "You're such a lovely bride."

"Thank you. Any advice for us?"

"Thomas and I have been married for fifty-three years. The secret is to love your spouse more than you love yourself."

Angela nodded as she smiled.

Caroline stood in front of the couple. "You two ready?"

Both nodded, holding hands and gazing into each other's eyes.

"Wait, we don't have rings." James rubbed his chin.

Angela giggled and handed Caroline an heirloom diamond wedding ring and a man's gold wedding ring. "These were my grandparents. I always knew one day, when I found true love, I would use them."

"I don't know what to say." He smiled.

"Are you both ready to be united in Holy matrimony?" Caroline steadied her *Bible* in both hands.

The couple looked into each other's eyes as they smiled. They both nodded in agreement.

"Do you, Angela Katherine Abadie, take James Edward Seamore to be your lawfully wedded husband?"

"I do!" She fluttered her long lashes, attempting to hold back her joyful tears.

Caroline handed him Angela's wedding ring. "James, place the ring on her finger."

James slipped the ring onto Angela's finger.

"Angela, repeat after me. With this ring, I devote my life to you as your wife."

"With this ring, I devote my life to you as your wife." Her voice nervously cracked as her eyes flushed.

"James Edward Seamore, do you take Angela Katherine Abadie as your lawfully wedded wife?"

"I most certainly do!"

"Angela, place the ring on his finger."

"James, repeat after me. I, James Edward Seamore, take Angela Katherine Abadie to be my lawfully wedded wife."

Angela slipped the ring on his finger.

"I, James Edward Seamore, take Angela Katherine Abadie as my lawfully wedded wife."

"I now pronounce you husband and wife. You may kiss your bride."

The newlyweds embraced and kissed as the violinist played.

Lance and Jamie leaned against the wall just outside the Roosevelt Hotel. The iconic bar with the six-foot parrot statue next to the hotel brimmed with patrons. A solo saxophone player stood on the corner as the song drifted toward them. She looked up at the sky. "The stars are beautiful tonight."

"Yes, but they're not as beautiful as you."

"You can say the most romantic things. Can you believe Tuesday is our last day of school?"

"Officially, yesterday was. Remember, we're exempt from our finals and don't have to return until our graduation ceremony."

"You going to miss it?"

"Graduation. Not at all. I'm ready to get on with my life."

"No, silly goose. High school."

"I only have two things on my mind."

"Two? I give."

"Marrying you and winning at nationals. We're still engaged, right?"

Jamie's cell phone repeatedly buzzed from her dad, calling her. "That's weird. I better answer this. Hello, is everything okay?"

"Better than okay. I took your advice and met up with the woman from *Singlematch*."

"You called to tell me that?"

"No, I called to let you know we took a ride, and I won't be home until late tonight or tomorrow, depending on how things go. I didn't want you to worry about me."

"Okay, Dad. No worries. You must really like this woman."

"I do. She's the last one you set me up with on *Singlematch*. But that's not important. How is prom?"

"The best dance ever. I'm having a great time. Don't worry."

"That's good to hear. Okay, I'll see you tomorrow. Have fun!"

"I will, Dad." She hung up the phone. "That was really weird. My dad has a date with some lady he met on *Singlematch*."

"I can't believe you encouraged that. I still think women who try to find their husbands on that creepy site are not worth having. Most are sluts or discards."

"I'll hold my judgment until I meet her. It's not like they're eloping and getting married."

"Why don't we?"

"Why don't we what?"

"Get out of here and get married. Let's elope. What do you say?"

Jamie was silent for a moment. "How would we pull that off?"

"They won't even miss us with the parental units out of the way."

"What about your mom? She tracks you like a hawk."

"She went to the beach for a couple of days to clear her head. She won't even know what's happened until she gets back."

"Okay, let's get married." Jamie let out a giddy laugh. "Now what?"

"I researched a place while you were on the phone with your dad; there's a little chapel open twenty-four-seven in the French Quarter that will marry us on the spot. They give you the license and everything. Look at us. We're already dressed. Jamie, marry me tonight." He got down on one knee. "Jamie Seamore, I love you more than anyone or anything, including my skateboard. I promise to never lie to you and always treat you like a princess. Will you marry me?"

Her eyes gazed at his face; her heart pounded. She pulled him up to his feet and jumped into his arms. "Yes, let's get married. Wait, don't we need a witness?"

Lance pointed across the way. "I think we found them."

Jamie turned and saw Melissa and Prince Karl heading toward them. "This ought to go over well."

Lance, confused, darted his eyes toward them.

The prince and Melissa stopped in front of them.

"Your Royal Highness. A pleasure to see you again." Jamie immediately curtsied.

Lance's stunned expression said it all. "I thought you were joking. He's a real prince?"

"Indeed. I'm the Reigning Prince of Maldovichia." He lowered his head in a quick bow. "A pleasure to meet you, sir."

"How do you know Jamie?" His stance became defensive and formidable.

"Prince Karl, this is my fiancée, Lance." Jamie nervously cleared her throat, staring at the prince as she shook her head as if to tell him to keep quiet. Her throat thickened, and her palms sweated, anticipating his response as if she was caught with her hand in the cookie jar.

"My parents are acquaintances of Ms. Seamore's auntie. We've had an occasion for our paths to cross."

"What brings you to our prom? Seems weird for a prince."

Melissa promptly stepped forward. "I invited him. It was a long shot, but I knew he was in town. You know, one day my prince will come, that whole thing. Didn't I, Prince Karl?" She elbowed him.

He nodded, maintaining his composure. "I believe you did."

Relieved, Jamie blew air from her lips. "Melissa. Prince Karl. We have a favor to ask. We're eloping tonight and need two witnesses. You in?"

"Your dad is so going to kill you."

"He won't know until after graduation, so you're sworn to secrecy."

"I'm in." Melissa held up her pinky; and the girls instantly locked their fingers, rotating them in their secret move.

"Great, the wedding chapel is only five minutes away. We can walk." Lance grabbed Jamie's hand, and the four headed out. He looked over his shoulder at Melissa and Prince Karl. "Follow us."

"Lance, we don't have rings." Jamie twisted her lips.

"I do. I'm way ahead of you."

"Wait! How?"

Lance stopped and turned her around. "I've wanted to marry you for quite some time. Although we have discussed getting married, I have never given you an engagement ring. I planned on asking you to officially marry me tonight and brought your engagement ring with me so I could propose the right way." He pulled out a small velvet ring box. He revealed the wedding ring set -- the bridal band featured a marquis two-carat diamond set in platinum with a solid platinum band that matched the groom's ring. "These were my parents. After they split up, my mom gave them to me for this reason. They've been in my dad's family for two generations."

Jamie shivered, wide-eyed. "They're stunning. I don't know what to say."

Lance flashed his famous, white-toothed grin. "How about, where's the wedding chapel?"

The four briskly strode through the French Quarter until they came to the small venue -- The French Quarter Wedding Chapel on Burgundy Street. When they entered, Jamie, gobsmacked, stopped in her tracks, gawking at the massive white arch with two small pedestals on each side and white flower sprays. A long oriental runner about two feet wide and twenty-six feet long made the path to the altar between several rows of wooden antique church pews. Just behind the altar to the left and right were two sizeable floor-standing crystal chandeliers with eighteen-lit globes. Floor-to-ceiling white drapery served as the backdrop. The beamed ceiling held hundreds of dollar bills stapled to it, along with hundreds of Mardi Gras beads. The ceiling, with a massive crystal chandelier, highlighted the brick walls as the light gently kissed them.

Jamie put her hands over her mouth and then hugged Lance. "This place is amazing. So cute. Better than I could have imagined. It's perfect; a church, but not a church."

Prince Karl cleared his throat. "I don't understand you, Americans. Why is there money attached to the ceiling?"

A man dressed in a suit with black-rimmed glasses approached the foursome from the side entry private office. "Which of you are the bride and groom?"

Jamie and Lance raised their hands as if in a classroom, ready to answer a teacher's question. "We are!"

Melissa stepped forward. "The Prince and I are the witnesses."

"Very well. We can get the ceremony underway as soon as we clear up some paperwork. Now, which package do you want?"

"Package?"

"Wedding package. We have several, which include a violinist, flowers, cake, and a thirty-minute carriage ride."

Jamie shrugged. "I don't know. We just want to get married."

"I suggest the elopement package, then."

Melissa raised her hand. "Does this mean we don't get a carriage ride?"

"Melissa, stop it. I'm the one getting married, carriage ride or not."

The man tilted his head, looking over his black-rimmed glasses. "Let me get your names and proof of identification. You both are of age, right?"

CHAPTER NINETEEN

Mr. and Mrs.

The French Quarter Wedding Chapel's door flew open as Lance and Jamie, both giddy, bolted through them, followed by Melissa and Prince Karl. Jamie tossed her pink daisy and white carnation bouquet over her shoulder, straight into Melissa's hands. "It looks like you're next!"

Melissa smiled. "In my dreams."

"I can't believe it. I'm now Mrs. Lance Billiot."

Lance squeezed her hand. "Mrs. Lance Billiot has a ring to it."

Jamie flashed her left-hand ring finger. "No, you put a ring on it."

"That I did. Now, we have a lot to figure out."

"Like what?"

"Breaking the news to the parental units, for one. Figuring out where to live. Graduation. College. Nationals. Children."

"Children! Hold it, Mr. Billiot. Mrs. Billiot doesn't want children until we finish college."

Melissa sighed. "That's a relief. I thought maybe since the rush wedding, you were, you know, expecting."

"Seriously, Melissa? You know I'm saving myself for my wedding night."

"Trust me; she waited." Lance grinned. "Now, let's figure out how to break the news to the parentals."

"After graduation, for sure."

"Agreed. Until then, nothing changes."

"Except that we're married."

The Abadie beachfront penthouse, decorated in soft blues and greens with oversized leather furniture in Orange Beach, Alabama, on the fifteenth floor, provided a spectacular view of the Gulf of Mexico. The morning sun radiated through the blinds, revealing a golden sunrise like no other; even the puffy clouds brought a welcome hello, with one shaped like a white dove swooping toward the skyscraping condo building. Gentle waves foamed as they kissed the white sugar sand beach line, scattering several seagulls searching for their morning meal. A hundred yards out, a pod of dolphins played as if to celebrate Angela's and James' nuptials.

Angela, feeling like the entire world was now reduced to the 2,500 square foot condo, felt like a queen as she and James cradled in each other's arms in the master suite with a picture-perfect floor-to-ceiling view of the beach. The white down comforter and pillows offered pure, relaxed pleasure. A pallet of sensations succumbed to them as they opened their eyes for the first time as Mr. and Mrs. Their ravening desire seemed unquenchable and punctuated their matrimony.

James beamed as he caressed Angela, gently stroking her long, silky hair. "You're even more beautiful when you first wake up. I love you this way."

"What way?" The corner of her mouth teasingly tilted.

"The natural look; no makeup. Just you."

"I finally get what Miriam told me months ago."

"What's that?"

"When love bites you in the ass, there's no stopping it. It's a forbidden thirst for love." She blinked her eyes, yawning in sleep satisfaction.

"I'd say more of a love-crazed mind. What did I ever do to deserve you?"

"Let me see. You didn't sue me after I shot you, for starters." A tinge of righteous justification held tight in her voice.

"No need. I wouldn't be married to you if you hadn't. From the moment I first saw you, I felt something. It didn't take me long to realize I was in love with you."

"You mean when you woke up after I shot you?"

"Not then, but when we bumped into each other on the street that morning. I felt it when we looked into each other's eyes."

"This means you fell in love with me for the right reasons."

"The right reason is that you are you."

"No, silly. Love at first sight."

"That too."

"You being perfect was just a bonus. Even if you weren't perfect, I would've still fallen in love with you."

"But will you still love me when I'm sixty-four?" She sang her words, mimicking the famous Beatles' tune.

"I'll love you until my last breath." He tenderly scooted her closer and passionately kissed her. "I love you. I honestly love you."

"When are we going to tell the kids?" A chagrinned smile came and went.

"Let's call them now and break the news."

"Not over the phone. Thank goodness Lance thinks I'm at the beach."

"Well, you are."

"That's not what I meant. He's not expecting me home for a few days, so I guess this is our unofficial, official honeymoon."

"That leaves me telling Jamie. She probably expects me home today. I really don't have an excuse to be gone."

"Now you do. Tell her your boss asked you to go out of town to take care of an ad campaign."

"She'll probably go for that, but then I'd be lying."

"Then tell her we got married."

"I can't do that either. Remember, she thinks you're the bad lady and doesn't like you?"

"What a fine mess we've gotten ourselves into."

"I'd rather think of it as a lifelong partnership. We're in it for the long haul." He blew air through his lips. "Frankly, there isn't going to be an easy way to tell her."

"This might help. I'm still your boss. So, I demand you take time off to take care of a situation for me. I need you to… let me see." She pondered a minute. "Yes, you're the ad liaison for the Vanderhorn campaign. The good news is this won't require you to lie to your daughter. He and his wife are here in Orange Beach this week. That's one reason I took time off to come here. I have plans… make that, we now have plans to meet them for dinner tonight. So, I need you here with me. Tell her that. You won't be lying, and then we can have a couple of days for our first honeymoon."

"That sounds promising. But, when the time comes, how will we tell the kids?" James thought intensely, as his brow furrowed. "We could take them to dinner, sit at adjacent tables, and then break the news that way. Like, we accidentally bumped into each other kind of thing."

"I don't like that. I could tell Lance that I got married and then tell him you're meeting him. Then you could tell Jamie during one of your movie nights."

"They'll hate us for that. We could invite them both to a party, where they're the only guests, and break the news then."

"No, but that gives me an idea. I've got it."

"Okay, Mrs. Seamore, what's the plan?"

"First, I'm not going to change my last name. I didn't with my first marriage and won't now."

"Good to know. I guess I could change mine to Mr. Abadie."

"Nonsense. We'll keep our last names."

"I was kidding. But on a serious note, what's your idea?"

"After graduation. We'll figure it out from there. Call your daughter and tell her you won't be home for a few days."

"That settles that. You're a genius." He kissed her again. "But before I call her, I do have something else on my mind."

"Oh, what's that?" She gasped, curiosity tingling inside.

"I'll have to show you." His warm breath fanned her skin. James extended his arm, wrapped it around her waist, and tenderly stroked her cheeks. "You're the love of my life." Their bodies melted into one as they made love; the passion was undeniable as they erupted together.

James rolled onto his back and gazed at the ceiling. "Just think; we get to do this the rest of our lives."

"Yes, I believe it's called 'until death do we part.'"

She rolled over and put her head on his chest, her long blonde hair falling gently across his impeccable torso. She ran her fingers up and down it, sending chills down his spine.

"You hungry?" James ran his fingers through her hair.

"Beginning to get that way." Her stomach growled, as if to prove her point.

"Sounds like there's no getting to it. If my memory serves me correctly, across the street is the Ruby Slipper. If it's like the one in Nawlins, it's gotta be good."

"It's the same. And, they make the best Bloody Mary you'll ever have on the gulf."

"I'm in."

"First, call Jamie."

He exhaled as he reached for his phone. "I guess I ought to."

She nodded, winking at him. "Do you want me to give you some privacy?"

"Not necessary. You're my wife." He dialed the phone.

In a hotel room at the Roosevelt Hotel, Jamie snuggled with Lance before answering her cell phone on the second ring. "Hello, Dad."

"Honey, how was prom?"

"Uneventful." She looked over at Lance, wiggling her ring finger in the air. "But, it'll be one I'll never forget."

"That's great, honey. Memories are important to make."

"You home?"

"That means you're not."

"True. I hope you're not mad. After the prom, Melissa had a room at the Roosevelt, and we all decided to pack in instead of driving." She paused. "Wait, this means you're not home either."

"No, I'm not. In fact, I won't be home for a couple of days."

Jamie's brow furrowed. "Why? Is everything okay?"

"My boss requested I travel to Alabama. It seems we have an important client I have to meet up with to smooth things over; their ad is in the developmental stage, and they're unhappy."

"I told you she was a mean woman. You see, just like I warned you about her using you. Now she's monopolizing all your time, dictating where you go and what you do. Next, who knows? I don't like her."

"Jamie, you will when you meet her."

"Not interested."

"What do you mean, not interested?"

"Exactly what I said. I don't care to meet her."

"Well, you will, because she's an important part of our lives."

"Just because she signs her name on your paycheck doesn't mean I have to get to know her. She lost that chance. I don't bow down to rich snobs who think they're better than the rest of us."

"We'll discuss this later. For now, please take care of the house. I'll be home in time for your graduation. I promise."

"Don't you need to ask your wicked-witch boss if you can have time off?"

"That's enough, Jamie. I have a job to do. Take care of the house, and don't have a party or bring your boyfriend over. You know how I feel about guys in the house, especially if I'm not there."

"I know the rules. The only guy I can have at the house when you're not there is my husband. Got it. I promise Dad I will definitely follow that rule."

The graduation ceremony held at the school's gymnasium began. The janitorial team had erected a small platform stage at one end. The shiny floor held thirty rows of chairs for the graduates who wore red caps and gowns, waiting until their row was called to the front by the teacher on duty. The school's band provided the background music before the ceremony began. Angela sat in the front row in one section of the grandstand, and James sat more toward the back in another. They secretly shot longing glances back and forth, wishing they could be next to each other. One teacher motioned for the first three rows of graduates to make their way to stage right. Having a last name early in the alphabet, Lance was third in line, as Jamie sat in the next to the last row. The music stopped as Mr. Hayes took to the podium.

"Thank you, band for that wonderful performance. Without further ado, I'll present the diplomas to our graduating class. Conrad Alexander." Mr. Hayes readied the diploma as Conrad stepped onto the stage and strutted to him.

"I did it, Mom!" Conrad beamed with pride as Mr. Hayes handed him his diploma, a gentle applause ensued as Conrad exited the stage.

"Dexter Baytown." Dexter rolled his wheelchair from the back of the stage, received his diploma, fist-pumped, and then returned.

"Preston Billiford." Preston snaked onto the stage, making a spectacle of himself, as usual, by twerking before he reached Mr. Hayes.

"Lance Billiot."

Jamie cheered and then quickly sunk into her chair, not wanting to draw attention to herself.

Student after student received their diploma to a myriad of applauses, some louder than others. As students received their diplomas, other graduates from the waiting rows lined up. Finally, it was Melissa's and Jamie's turn as they stood impatiently in line at the bottom of the stairs to the raised platform.

"How's married life?" Melissa leaned in closer to Jamie's ear.

"So far, so good."

"Today is the day."

"I know; we finally graduate."

"Not that, Mrs. Billiot. You finally get to tell your dad you're married."

A pit formed in Jamie's stomach at the thought.

"Jamie Seamore." Mr. Hayes glanced over at Jamie and Melissa, who were still whispering. "Jamie Seamore. Do you want to graduate or not?"

"Oh, so sorry, Mr. Hayes." She tripped up the stairs and gracefully regained her composure to accept her diploma. "Thank you, Mr. Hayes, for everything."

"Melissa Sidwell." Melissa took her time getting to Mr. Hayes to receive her diploma, soaking in the moment. After he handed her the diploma, she waved princess-style high in the air to the crowd.

"That's enough, Ms. Sidwell."

She left the stage, giggling all the way.

"Last but not least, Zachariah Zachery."

Zachery ran to Mr. Hayes and received his diploma.

Mr. Hayes nodded with the most unusual smile. "And that concludes the ceremony. Graduates, please stand for the processional."

All graduates stood, tossing their caps into the air.

Outside the gym near the student parking lot, the assembled graduates were greeted by their celebratory families. When Jamie saw her dad, she bolted straight for him, throwing her arms around his neck.

"Congratulations! You did it, young lady. This calls for a special celebration! Your mother would've been so proud of you."

"I'm pretty proud of myself." She glanced at her wedding ring, hiding her hand quickly behind her back. "What kind of celebration do you have in mind?"

"What makes you think I have something planned?"

"You've been acting strange since you got back from Alabama. I can tell when you're keeping a secret. So, what gives?"

"Okay, you busted me. I have something in mind." James looked across the way at Angela, who was embracing Lance.

"Do tell. I can't wait. Oh, it's another car." Her tone, teasing in nature, delighted her dad.

"Hate to disappoint you; it's not a car."

"I really didn't think so, but I can't imagine what you've been keeping from me. Just tell me already."

"Nope, that would ruin the surprise."

"How about a little hint?"

"Nope. This is something so special; you have to see it to believe it. I'll tell you this, though. You'll have to wear a blindfold while I drive you there, and you can't take it off under any circumstances until I say so. Got it?"

"You're so silly. When it involves a blindfold, the surprise is pretty amazing. I'm in. Let's go. I don't want to wait any longer."

"Now, listen up. I'm taking you somewhere very special. When we get there, don't say a word no matter what you hear. It'll ruin the surprise. Got it?"

"Got it."

"You promise?"

"Dad, I got it; I'm not to say a word."

"That's my girl. And don't remove the blindfold. When the time is right, I'll do it for you."

"Oh, boy, I can't imagine what this surprise will be."

No, you can't.

Angela and Lance entered their home through the front door, greeted by Miriam, who wiped her hands on her starch, crisp white apron. "Congratulations, Master Lance. We finally got you out of high school."

"Thanks, Miriam. It seems like it took me all of my life."

Angela laughed as she handed Miriam her purse to put it away. "Son, it did! Now, onto college."

"Not now, Mom. I have Nationals, and that's where all my energy will go. I'm not even thinking about college. I have months before that happens."

"Regardless, I'm so proud of you, son."

"I wish dad would've been here."

"You know him; he's across the world. I don't know why you set yourself up for disappointment like that."

"Because he's my dad. Can we just celebrate and forget about this for a while?"

"Yes, and I have a surprise for you."

"Can't wait!"

"You'll have to."

"What for?"

"You'll see." Her cell phone vibrated, and she looked at the text that chimed through from James.

> We're on our way. Be there in less than five minutes. Put the blindfold on him.

A smile crossed her face as her heart raced, knowing the moment of truth was near.

"Mom, everything okay?"

"Absolutely. Your surprise will be here in a few minutes. I don't want to ruin it for you, so I'll have to blindfold you."

Miriam nodded as she handed Angela a black sleeping mask.

"Here, put this on. Make sure you can't see anything."

"Mom, sometimes you're so dramatic."

"Just appease me and put it on."

"Fine. Can I sit first?"

"Absolutely."

Lance plopped onto the sofa and quickly put the mask over his eyes. "You happy now?"

"Son, you have no idea." She gestured toward Miriam to get the champagne ready as the doorbell rang. "I'll get it, Miriam." Angela headed for the door.

"Mom, we're having company?"

"It's your surprise. Don't say a word until I give you the go-ahead, or it'll ruin it. Promise."

"I promise."

Angela opened the front door and nodded at James as she put her finger to her mouth, indicating for him not to say anything. He winked at her and blew her a silent kiss, and guided Jamie by her shoulders into the living room. Angela stood over Lance, ready to remove the blindfold. She held three fingers up and slowly counted down. Simultaneously, Angela and James removed the blindfolds from their children.

Jamie thought her heart might stop as Lance stood. "What is this?" He shook his head, baffled.

"Son, this is James and Jamie Seamore."

Lance's eyes widened, feeling his throat tightening. "I know Jamie from school, but why are they here?"

Jamie gazed at her dad. "Yea, Dad. Why are we here?"

Angela reached out her hand to shake Jamie's, who immediately stepped backward.

"Wait, I know who you are. You're the lady who shot him and his boss. Dad, I can't believe you are doing this to me."

"Honey, she's more than my boss."

"Wait!" She looked at Lance. "This is your mother?"

"Yes, unfortunately. So, your dad works for my mom, and this is the woman you hate?"

"I had no idea she was your mother."

"I had no idea the window washer she shot was your dad. You never said anything. You said he was injured at work."

"I was embarrassed to tell you he was shot. I don't get it. That's Ms. Abadie. Your last name is Billiot. I'm so confused."

"She goes by her maiden name. I have my father's last name."

"That doesn't explain why we're here. Dad, what's up?"

"Yea, Mom. What's up?"

"I think everyone should sit." Angela gracefully eased into a chair.

Jamie took a defensive posture, her stomach apprehensively filling with butterflies. "I'll stand."

"This is so awkward." Lance scratched his head.

The room fell silent as James collected his courage to break the wedding news. He looked at Jamie and smiled.

"Dad, what is it? I know that look. That means something serious is about to go down."

"Jamie... There's no simple way to say this. Angela and I are married."

Stunned, Jamie choked. "This is a joke. Right?"

"Afraid not."

Lance shivered. "Mom, please tell me this is a joke or a bad nightmare."

"No, son. We've been married; we just didn't want to tell you until after you kids graduated."

"Well, *touché*, Mom. Jamie and I are married, too."

James and Angela laughed until Lance doubled down.

"Mom, I'm serious. Jamie and I got married on prom night."

"Jamie Seamore, explain this!" James sternly glared at his daughter as if she'd stolen all his money from his wallet.

She lifted her left hand, presenting her ring finger. "We're married. There's nothing more to explain."

Angela's mouth fell open in astonishment as she felt her blood rip through her veins. "If there's any truth to this, there will have to be an annulment."

"I agree with Angela. You're both way too young to get married. This marriage will be annulled."

"Dad, I'm eighteen; I'm legal, and I won't let you destroy my marriage."

James felt his blood boil. "I forbid this."

"I'm a grown woman and a married one at that. I'm Mrs. Lance Billiot."

Angela tightened her jaw, feeling sick to her stomach. "This can't be happening."

"But, Mom, it is, and there's nothing either of you can do to separate us." Lance glowered at his mother.

Jamie's heart raced. "I think I'm going to be sick. This means that my husband is my stepbrother. Dad, how could you do this to me?" Alligator tears shredded her cheeks. "You've ruined everything."

Lance immediately went to console her, hugging and compassionately drying her tears with his fingers. "Jamie, everything will be okay. Trust me."

"No, everything won't be okay! You two can't be married." James stepped toward Jamie.

"Stop it, Dad! Don't come near me. I hate you right now."

"Jamie, please."

"Don't Jamie me. You lied to me. This whole time you said you were dating a woman you found on *Singlematch*. You lied!"

"I never lied. We had our first date through *Singlematch*. We were paired. You arranged it. You know the woman you said to bring a lavender rose for."

"That's not her!"

"Yes, it is, Jamie. She used a different picture."

"Mom, you've got to be kidding. Didn't I warn you about those dating sites?"

"Lance, please. I didn't want a man to fall for me because of who I was, but for the person he met."

"See, I told you she's deceiving." Jamie threw her hands up in the air.

Miriam entered carrying a tray of appetizers, including crab dip, Tabasco sauce, and four glasses of champagne. "A celebration toast is in order for the newlyweds."

All heads turned toward her.

"Not now, Miriam!" Angela pursed her lips.

Lance retrieved the dip. "My bride is allergic to crab; please take it back to the kitchen."

"Yes, Master Lance. Right away." She sat the tray down, took the crab dip, and immediately retreated to the kitchen.

"Master Lance!" Jamie gave him a whatever glance.

"She's called me that since I was a baby."

"Lance Garrett Billiot, this marriage, or whatever you want to call it, will be annulled." Angela glared at him.

"No, Mom. If anyone's marriage is getting annulled, it will be yours."

Everyone started talking at once; each became louder than the others in their accusations and backhanded compliments, so much so that nobody noticed the front door opening.

Lance's face turned crimson. "Mom, how dare you? No respectable woman finds a respectable man on those sites. You've got to be kidding."

"How dare you talk to me like that?"

Grandpa pressed his thumb and index finger to his lips with his wife at his side and whistled, bringing silence to the room again. "What in hell is going on here?"

Angela took a deep breath, gaping at her parents. "What are you two doing here?"

"We received the graduation invitation and thought we'd attend. We ran into some setbacks, our flight was delayed, and we missed it."

Anna looked at her daughter. "Angela, what's going on?"

"This isn't how I wanted things to go."

After a stare-down, Grandpa glanced over at James. "What's he doing here?"

"Dad, unlike you, he belongs here. James is my husband."

Lance took a deep breath. "Grandpa and Nana; this is my wife Jamie, and James is her father."

Aghast, Grandpa shook his head, hardening his expression, eyeing both couples. "Let me wrap my head around this. How can something like this even happen?"

Nana patted her husband on the back. "Now that's a question I want to hear the answer to."

All the newlyweds talked at once.

"We met in school and fell in love. We kept it a secret because we didn't want problems." Lance pulled Jamie closer to him.

"Son, how did that work out?" Angela moved closer to James. "You should've told me."

"Well, Mom, why didn't you tell me you were dating?"

"You were insistent that I didn't, so I thought it was best to keep it a secret."

James looked at his daughter. "Jamie, this is the guy you went to prom with?" His mental picture gave way to his resolute expression.

"Yes, and we eloped that night."

"So, you were keeping this a secret that long?"

"Dad, when did you and Angela get married?"

"Prom night."

"So, you've been keeping this a secret, too?"

Anna put her hands on her hips. "This is what you call secret romances. One thing is for certain, none of you look happy right about now."

Miriam cleared her throat entering the living room. "I know this isn't my business, but may I say something?"

"What is it, Miriam?" Angela twisted her lips short-tempered.

"Since prom, I've never seen you or Master Lance so happy. Now I know why. Your forbidden thirst for love bit you in the asses."

"Oh, the tangled web we weave." Nana smiled. "Now what?"

Grandpa quizzically looked at his daughter. "Do you love him?"

"With all of my heart. I've never been happier." She gazed into James' eyes. No one could deny Angela's new contentment.

"Lance, do you love her?"

"With all of my heart, Grandpa."

Nana squeezed Grandpa's forearm so tight he winced. She meant business, and he had better respond appropriately.

"Then it's settled. No more secrets! Or should I say, no more secret romances? I'll make everyone a deal. James, I was wrong about you, and I apologize for the other night." He flitted his eyes at his wife. "Trust me, I got the 'what for' many times since that night."

Nana winked at Angela. "Honey, trust me, I raked him over the coals. He'd forgotten I came from the wrong side of the tracks, and we didn't have his parent's approval."

Grandpa nudged Nana. "Yes, somehow, I got lost, so we came this way so I could apologize to you both in person. I needed to make things right." He swallowed hard, hesitating his words as if it were impossible to say them. "Angela... I should have never threatened to take the magazine away from you. Please accept my apologies."

"Only if you accept James as my husband." The stony detachment of her expression was clear as she leered at him.

Grandpa reached over and firmly shook James' hand. "Congratulations, son. I see you doing great things for the magazine. Welcome to the Abadie family."

"Thank you, sir. But my love is for your daughter and Jamie. The magazine takes third place in my life."

"Call me Arthur."

"Thank you, Arthur."

Grandpa patted Jamie on her shoulder. "As for you, young lady, you're now an Abadie."

"Actually, I'm a Billiot according to our marriage license." She giddily smiled.

"Although I think you and Lance are too young to marry, I'll also support this marriage." He darted his eyes between James and Angela. "As should both of you."

"That means a lot to me. Thank you." Jamie grasped Lance's hand.

"Not so fast. I have my demands. Jamie, since you're an Abadie, you'll attend Harvard just like all Abadie's.

"Sir, I can't even afford a junior college, much less an Ivy League one."

"Nonsense! I'll cover all your expenses just like I planned on covering Lance's. We have a family scholarship fund set up for this. That's part of the perks of being an Abadie."

"Miriam, bring two more glasses of champagne. We have a lot of celebrating to do." Angela smiled and squeezed James' hand.

Miriam quickly went to the kitchen.

Angela took Jamie's hand. "Welcome to the family. I know we've gotten off to a bad start, but I'll do my best to make it up to you."

"Thank you, Ms. Abadie."

"Call me, Mom! If you're not comfortable with that, Angela will be just fine."

Jamie nodded toward Lance and then looked at her father. "Dad?"

"Okay, you win." James hugged Lance hard, manly patting his back. "Take care of her. She's special."

"I promise you, sir, I will."

"Call me..." He gulped and shivered. "...Dad." He chuckled uneasily.

Miriam returned and passed out the champagne glasses. "I still want all the salacious details. How does something like this happen?"

Grandpa held his glass up. "To the newlyweds! All four of you."

The toasts continued, and James leaned over and kissed his bride after each one.

Lance squeezed Jamie's hand. "Excuse us, parental units. I want to talk with Jamie. We have lots to discuss now that the cat's out of the bag."

Angela nodded. "As do we. First on our agenda is our living arrangements."

James shook his head. "This should get interesting since we haven't discussed it before."

"I've got everything figured out. Well, for all of us, now." Angela winked at her husband. "You'll move in here."

"Wait, Dad, does this mean you'll be moving out of our house?"

"That seems to be the case."

"Then that means Lance and I can live in ours until we get our own place near campus."

Nana chuckled. "See, everything is going to work out. I love a romantic, happy ending."

CHAPTER TWENTY

To Nationals or Bust

Moving day for the newlyweds seemed effortless as James packed his room to move into the Abadie mansion. Several boxes lined his walls. Jamie entered and plopped down on his bed. "I'm going to miss you."

"Miss me! I'm not moving out of state. I'll be less than twenty minutes away."

"I know. But no more movie nights and popcorn for us."

"Who says? We can still have those; it'll just be a little different. I'll have Angela, and you'll have Lance. It gives a whole new meaning to father-daughter date night. So, don't you worry about that."

"Since you're moving out, I get to move into this room, right?"

"It's all yours. I mean, yours and Lance's. I can't believe you're married. I didn't even get to walk you down the aisle."

"I can't believe you're married. I didn't even get to be there. What do you think Mom would say?"

"Honestly, I think she'd be happy for us. She was a true romantic at heart."

"Do you miss her?"

"Of course I do. That'll never go away. Angela completely understands. By the way, she has no intention of replacing your mother."

"I didn't think she did. Dad. I owe you an apology."

"Whatever for?"

"I was headstrong against Angela; you told me I would like her if I ever met her, and I do. I feel really bad about it."

"You have every right to your opinions. I apologize too. I should've been upfront from the beginning about dating her. But, you were so adamantly against her."

"Sorry about that."

"Apology accepted... I still can't believe you're married."

"Ditto! We all have a wonderful future ahead of us."

"I'll say. I love you, Dad."

"I love you too, sweetheart."

Her eyes flushed uncontrollably.

"Don't cry!"

"They're happy tears."

Angela entered Lance's room while he packed his belongings. All skateboards had been removed from the walls and placed in open boxes by the door. "I can't believe you're moving out."

"Believe it, Mom. You knew this day would come."

"Yes, but I always thought it would be because you went off to college, and not because you got married." A lump formed in the back of his throat.

"I get that. But I'm really happy."

"You know you and Jamie can live here with us, don't you?"

"That's a great offer, but we want to start our marriage in our own place without the parental units."

"Things won't be the same."

"Is that a bad thing?"

"No, a sad thing."

"You'll be fine, Mom. You and James seem happy. You deserve it."

"You mean that?"

"Absolutely."

"You've never approved of anyone for me before."

"I'm sorry about that. I was being pretty immature. But I've grown up since then. You deserve all the happiness in the world."

Tears filled her eyes. "You don't know how much that means to me to hear you say that."

"I think I do. Have you told Dad yet?"

"No, and I don't plan to. I'm sure he'll know when it hits the society papers and will have to deal with it on his own. Like I said, it's his loss, not mine."

"Yikes, you still hold a grudge?"

"Absolutely. He's the one that left us."

"When was the last time you spoke to him?"

"Don't really remember. Can we change the subject?"

"Sure; what do you want to talk about now?"

"Nationals; it's just around the corner."

"I'm ready. I can't wait."

"About that."

A frown enveloped Lance's brow. "What now?"

"Oh, don't worry; it's nothing bad."

"Whew! You had me worried for a second. You're planning to go, right?"

"I wouldn't miss it for the world. I just wanted to make sure it was okay to invite James."

"I don't think Jamie would forgive me if he didn't come."

"Oh, Grandpa and Nana want to come too."

"Perfect."

"And John and his new wife."

"Wait! John got married? Y'all are still friends? I mean, after your split."

"I'll put it to you this way; we were never meant to be. I know that, and he knows that. Besides, he's a huge supporter of yours. And, he plans on bringing Tony Lark too."

"The more, the merrier, I guess."

The sound of the front door opening echoed through the house. "Honey, I'm home."

Angela hugged Lance. "I'll leave you to your packing."

"Mom, that's the biggest excuse I've ever heard. I know you're excited he's moving in. Jamie and I feel the same way."

"Remember, you always have a home here. You and Jamie. And, when you have babies, them too."

"Don't get too excited about a grandbaby. We may be young, but we're not stupid. We've decided to wait until after college. Now, go and greet your husband."

"That has a nice ring to it."

Lance entered the Seamore's shotgun house. Where the painting of the rustic cabin and the Mardi Gras posters once hung, the sun-faded silhouette outlines looked dingy on the sage walls. Her father's manly items were gone, as well as his brown-tattered leather recliner. The flower loveseat had a hunter-green slipcover with almond piping, one black throw pillow at each armrest, and two hot pink throw pillows centered on it. In the corner, a ladder and at the feet of it, a can of white linen paint, a rusty paint pan, complete with a plastic liner, a drop cloth, and a roller brush. "Honey, I'm home! Jamie!" he waited for a response.

"Surprise!" Jamie, Melissa, and Prince Karl bolted from the other room.

"Well, this isn't what I expected."

Jamie hugged him and kissed him on the cheek. "They insisted."

Melissa smiled, excited. "We brought you a wedding gift."

"That's so thoughtful."

"I'll be right back." She entered the other room, brought out a beautifully wrapped white gift with a matching giant lavender bow, and handed it to Jamie. "Open it."

"This is so exciting. I can't imagine what it is."

"Be careful; it's breakable."

Slowly, Jamie unwrapped the present. "I don't want to open it because it's so beautiful."

"Just open it already." Melissa impatiently ripped the wrapping paper from the box. "See how easy that was?"

After removing the last piece of paper that secured the lid to the box, Jamie lifted it to reveal an engraved silver frame with the date of her wedding showcasing her and Lance leaving the French Quarter Wedding Chapel. "It's beautiful. Thank you, Melissa."

"It was actually Prince Karl's idea."

"Yes, in our country, it is the traditional gift our attendants give."

"Attendants?" Lance's brow furrowed.

"I believe in America, you call them bridesmaids."

"Oh, that. Thank you. We'll cherish it forever." Lance carefully took it from Jamie and sat it on the side table.

Melissa admired the picture once again. "Oh, one more surprise."

"Now, I'm even more intrigued." Jamie twisted her finger in a strand of hair, curling it.

"I'll be right back." Melissa returned to the kitchen and quickly returned with a small wedding cake. "We thought since you didn't have a reception, we'd give you this."

Prince Karl bowed his head. "Melissa insisted it was an American tradition. I must get used to these strange American customs."

Puzzled, Jamie's nose wrinkled. "Prince Karl, whatever for?"

"Well, there's been a change in my plans. I'm going to stay here in New Orleans and attend Tulane University. I'm growing rather fond of this city."

"Not to mention me!" Melissa grinned mischievously.

Jamie sniffed the cake. "Smells delicious. It must be chocolate."

Lance smiled, nodding. "It looks fantastic. Must come from a great bakery."

"It's from your family's bakery, Lance."

"That explains things." Jamie grabbed the cake knife. "Let's cut this thing."

"Wait! Wait! Let me take a video of it." Melissa grabbed her cell phone. "Ready!"

Excitement filled the air at the 34th Annual US National Skateboard Championship. Standing in the grandstands in the front row behind the railing, wearing matching T-shirts featuring Lance riding his skateboard, were James, Jamie, Angela, Grandpa, Nana, Melissa, Prince Karl, Conrad, John Legions, and his new bride, Monique. The crowd packed the small area. The competition was electrifying as, one at a time, each skater completed their runs to the cheering crowd. Jamie applauded, bouncing on her toes. "This is so exciting. I can't believe we're all here."

"Believe it." James wrapped his arm around Jamie. "I'm a nervous wreck."

"Try being his mother." Goosebumps ricocheted down Angela's arms.

Grandpa cleared his throat. "This is very exciting. I'm glad we made it."

John kissed Monique. "Hey, I'm going after a beer. Does anyone want anything?"

James looked around at everyone waiting for their responses. "Nope, I think we're all good."

"I'll be back in a jiffy. Lance will be up shortly." He brushed Angela as he made his way down the aisle. "By the way, you were right. My mom loves Monique."

"I knew she would. Does this mean you'll being seeing more of her?"

"Looks that way. It's time to put hard feelings aside. Besides, she's going to be a grandmother."

"That was quick. Congrats."

"We're very excited. Are you sure you don't want a beer?"

Angela shook her head no. John continued his path toward the concession stand.

Aunt Sally made her way up the steps toward the group. "Toodledo!"

"Oh, for Pete's sake. What's she doing here?" James rolled his eyes.

"Sorry, Dad. She called to check up on me, and I accidentally slipped and told her about nationals."

"Oh, my sweet peach." Aunt Sally inched her way through the row to get to Jamie. "How's the bride?" She pinched Jamie's cheeks. "I'm still mad you eloped, but I'll live as long as you allow me to host a wedding reception."

Jamie giggled. "You better make that two receptions at once. My dad got married too."

"Holy peaches! What is in the water here? Married, to who?"

"Aunt Sally, these are my new in-laws. My mother-in-law is also my new stepmom, Angela."

"Did I hear you correctly? Your new mother-in-law is also your new stepmom?"

"As weird as it may seem, yes." James, with a don't-go-there scowl, glared at Aunt Sally.

Jamie pointed to Grandpa and Nana. "This is Arthur and Anna, Lance's grandparents. I believe you know Prince Karl, and this is my best friend, Melissa."

"My, my. I don't know what to say. How does something like this even happen?"

In unison, everyone spoke. "Don't ask!"

"A pleasure to meet you all. Prince Karl, I didn't expect to see you here. I thought you returned to your country." Aunt Sally twisted her peachy lips.

"I chose to remain and obtain my education stateside."

"I hope with the King's approval."

"Indeed, ma'am. I would never go against the Crown."

"Aunt Sally, Lance is about to make his run!" Jamie inhaled with excitement, pointing to him, fidgeting on the sidelines, and talking with Tony Lark.

Aunt Sally stood next to Monique as John returned to the row. Everyone inched over to allow him to be next to Monique, isolating Aunt Sally at the end.

Tony stood before Lance, safety gear on, clenching his skateboard. "Not that you need my advice, but to win this race, remember it takes speed, degree of difficulty, originality, and perfect execution. Doing that new trick you've been working on wouldn't hurt your score. Judges love to see new things, and you'll be champion if you complete that maneuver."

"Got it. Thanks for the pep talk."

"Go make us proud. This is the final run, and it's all yours."

Lance took a deep breath, looked up at the grandstands, and flashed a thumbs up to Jamie, who was all smiles.

Lance's turn to execute his first run arrived to thunderous applause. He had dreamed of this moment since first stepping onto his skateboard at age seven. He took in a long, deep breath. *Let's fly.*

"This is the moment we all have been waiting for." The announcer's adventurously engaging voice echoed through the grandstands. "Lance Billiot is preparing for his final run and teased earlier that he has a new trick up his sleeve. If he pulls this off, he'll win, as Becker McDaniel has given him a real run for his money and could bring an upset. The defining moment is here!"

Lance took off, ramping his speed and momentum down the slope.

"Incredible, Lance's first trick is a hardflip. Seriously, that's the second hardest trick any skateboarder can do, and he begins his run with it. He'll have to pop hard so the board can get vertical enough, allowing him to maneuver into a flick and follow up with a kickflip. Look at this guy. Incredible! He's giving a master class with this run. Now, look at him."

Lance scooped the board with his back foot and pushed it forward, completing a 360-spin.

"Are you kidding me? Billiot just completed a trick called the Impossible. It's called that because you have to be better than great to master this maneuver. Can you believe the vertical height? This kid is one of the best I've seen."

Without giving anything a rest, Lance executed a perfect nine hundred to a cheering crowd.

"Unbelievable! Wait for it; the best is coming up. When Billiot makes his final pass, he'll attempt a three-sixty laser flip followed by a two-forty. To accomplish this, he'll have to flick his back foot down and back to make the board spin three hundred and sixty degrees in the air with no other flips. He'll then have to rely on a varial heelflip combined with a front shuv. This has never been attempted here at Nationals."

Jamie grasped her dad's hand. "This is his final trick. I'm so nervous."

"He's got this, Jamie."

Angela could barely watch as she hid her face in her hands as if watching a scary movie.

"Lance Billiot has done it! He's our new National Champion. The world of skateboarding will never be the same!" The crowd erupted into ear-piercing congratulatory screams as if in the Superdome and the Saints won the Super Bowl.

"He won! He won!" Jamie busted into tears, jumping up and down.

Angela finally exhaled. "To Nationals or bust is his motto."

Grandpa, with a proud expression, puffed his chest. "I taught him everything he knows, but I didn't teach him everything I know."

"In just a moment, we'll be presenting the trophy. Lance is making his way to the winner's platform. There will be plenty more coming from Lance Billiot in his future. I predict right now, he'll win gold at the Olympics."

Lance walked his victory path down the sidelines, fist-bumping everyone as they congratulated him. When he reached Jamie, he leaped to hug and kiss her. Her lips parted as she stood on the tip of her toes, straining to reach him. Their kiss was tender as the crowd cheered his victory.

"I'm so proud of you. You did it. You're the National Champion." Jamie's smile stretched from ear to ear.

"We did it, and this is only the beginning for us."

Tony Lark approached Lance, carrying a skateboard. "This is for you. I understand you collect them."

"Thank you so much. I have a spot in my room for this."

Jamie cleared her throat. "You had a spot; you're living with me now, hubby."

Their laughter seemed to drown out the crowd.

To be continued.

AN EXCERPT FROM THE KEYSTSROKE KILLER

Absolute Author
Publishing House

New Orleans – 2058 - MATTHEW RAYMOND, a private investigator, locked into a maze of deceit and deception, uncovers Project Transcendence's truth.

For Matthew Raymond, his job as a private investigator is personal. Extremely personal. After the disturbing 2053 murder of his sister Livia, Matthew left in a rage searches for her killer and answers to the mysterious questions that lurked around her death. Now years later, Matthew realizes his problems just went from bad to worse as he discovers himself immersed in a city where the wealthy and corrupt politicians rule. With his sister's murder still his focus, he finds himself in a cunning game of cat-and-mouse when he stumbles across The Keystroke Killer and uncovers a secret device capable of sending people to the fourth dimension without a trace. Project Transcendence becomes Matthew's new fixation. Searching the Deep South for answers, he uncovers family secrets, lies, corruption and a world on the brink of destruction. Can Matthew survive and save the world from the threat? Will he untangle the mystery of Livia's death? Find out in this powerful story, *The Keystroke Killer*.

THE KEYSTROKE KILLER: TRANSCENDENCE

Excerpt from Chapter 3

There's No Place Like Home

Matthew rose and kicked the chair beside him. "Damn it." *Why didn't I listen to her?*

The desk clerk slid open the frosted window divider. "Detective Raymond." She waited for a response. "Detective Raymond."

Matthew's eyes flushed. *If I'd only gotten there in time.*

"Detective Raymond!"

"I'm not a detective. I'm a private investigator." He approached the door that led to a hall.

"Good luck in there."

A loud hum released the locked door. He stepped through the uninviting invitation.

In the middle of the hall stood two additional armed guards. The area consisted of several recessed secured eight by ten-inch lockers, a checkpoint station, and an ironclad entry door that included an eye recognition keypad developed by Dimension Global. The door, dark gray metal six inches thick and eight feet tall, and how it sounded as it locked behind him, made the biggest impression on Matthew over the last four years.

A loud buzzer, a clang, and a big bang echoed throughout the hall. Going out didn't sound as menacing. As he approached the guarded area, his heart raced, his temperature rose, and the tension throughout his entire body increased. He soon would sit across from the monster who killed his sister.

"Mr. Raymond, check your weapon here." The husky guard remained alert as Matthew gently removed his gun from the holster.

"I know the drill." He handed it to him. "I don't like being unarmed."

The second guard pierced his eyes. "You don't have a choice if you want to visit Milo. Or, you could stop your yearly visitations."

"Not a chance. That shithead knows what happened to my sister. If it's the last thing I do, I'll beat the truth out of him."

"Don't you mean get the truth out of him?"

"Yea, that's what I meant. The bastard murdered my sister."

"Your sister was a victim of the Co-Ed serial killer? I thought you were the U.S. Marshall who captured him?"

"I should have killed him on the spot."

"Meaning, you could have?"

"Can I get on with this or am I the one being interrogated?"

The guard stepped to the retinal scan. The red light zipped across his eye and turned green. Click. The locker opened, and the guard secured Matthew's weapon.

Clang. The door slid into the recess of the wall, giving way to the rancid urine smell, and smeared, dried fecal matter on the walls. The guards led Matthew down the unwelcoming hall. A faint whisper of burned flesh permeated from the left, the odor of carbolic soap from the staff restroom on the right and the stench of unwashed clothes from the air vents filled the air.

Matthew looked at the visitor's restroom door. "I need to go in."

"Make it quick. Visiting hours are almost over."

***

The restroom door creaked as it shut behind him. Someone took a dump in the toilet and left it unflushed.

In the far corner by the janitor's closet, a rusty tin bucket served as the final resting place to an enormous and decomposed rat which reeked of rotting decay stifling Matthew.

"Disgusting people." *Did they leave their manners and dignity outside the gate*? He shuffled to the sink and scrutinized his reflection wrinkled by torment. A tear fell from his left bloodshot eye as he thought of the exact moment Milo slaughtered his sister.

***

Milo clutched Livia's hair as he dragged her into the Army green public restroom at Kenner City Park. The pervasive odor of urine filled the air.

Matthew, in hot pursuit, retrieved his magnum and sprinted toward them. He raced into the bathroom high on angered emotion, out of breath.

Milo held a machete against Livia's throat as he grinned sinisterly. "You made it in time to watch your sister die."

"Let go of her."

"If I let her go, you will kill me." Milo taunted him as he pressed the knife harder against Livia's throat. "And, if I don't let go, you will kill me. Either way, you lose."

"Let go now!" Matthew's muscles contracted, knowing the monster before him would take her life.

"What will big brother do? Save baby sis, or capture a serial killer?" His ice-cold stare of gunmetal gray prevailed.

265

"Both. I'll do both. Put the fucking knife down and we all can walk away."

"Giving up your vow to serve and protect?" Milo taunted to get a rise out of Matthew. "You'd let me walk if I let her go? I think not. I must protest."

"I'll kill you. Put down the knife and let her go."

"Too bad." Milo slit Livia's throat and shoved her to the ground. "You're too late, hesitation kills."

Matthew lunged to save Livia. He kneeled over her and tried to stop the sprouting blood from her neck with his hands pressed hard against the wound. "Livia." Her eyes rolled back; she took her last breath.

Milo snickered as he watched the loving embrace between a brother and a very bloody sister.

"You're a butcher. You'll pay for this!" Matthew lunged toward Milo and struck the cumbersome machete from his grip. He heaved him against the cracked roach infested sink. Milo's cheek connected to it and split open. Blood smeared onto the sink and dripped down Milo's face. Matthew grabbed Milo by the shoulders and heaved his head against the mirror, which shattered into several pieces and crashed into the pool of Livia's blood.

Milo snatched a sharp mirror fragment, charged Matthew, stabbed him, and sliced his left shoulder.

Matthew glowered at him, bent to deliver a reverse round kick, but slipped on Livia's blood, falling backward onto his butt.

Milo laughed as he held back his mental powers to provoke Matthew. "I'm just getting started."

Matthew bolted up quick onto his feet and delivered a round kick. His foot connected solidly into Milo's ribcage, cracking several ribs.

Airborne, Milo slammed against the wall. He grunted, took a deep breath, and charged Matthew.

Matthew outmaneuvered the serial killer. He dodged him, clutched Milo's shoulders, and used the momentum to propel him headfirst, slamming him against the wall.

Bloody, Milo zigzagged toward Matthew.

Matthew rushed him, grabbed his shoulders, and butted his head against his forehead.

The room spun as Milo staggered toward his opponent. His eyes rolled into the back of his head, collapsing next to Livia.

Matthew kicked Milo's ribs. He yanked his handcuffs from the pouch so hard it busted his lip.

Milo groaned and barely opened one eye, more of a wink.

A drop of blood fell from Matthew's nose onto the back of Milo's bald tattooed head. Matthew dropped to his knees and handcuffed him. "I have you now, you son of a bitch. You will rot in Hell for what you have done."

Matthew knelt by his sister, checked her pulse, and closed her eyes brushing his fingers across them. He stood and kicked Milo's face.

Police sirens blared as seconds ticked away.

Matthew glimpsed his bloody reflection in the mirror. He ambled to the sink and washed his face.

A light blue electrical power surge, originating at the overhead light fixture, radiated downwards onto the mirror, which captured his attention. The blue light pulsated, zipped through the running water, across the metal pipes, and onto the floor to Livia's blood. Livia shimmered a faint blue as the surge entombed her. She became transparent and vanished along with her crimson blood.

Matthew became faint as he felt Livia's life leave her body. "No!"

S.W.A.T. burst into the restroom, pointing their rifles toward Matthew. Matthew raised his hands above his head. A red laser dot centered on his forehead. Without lowering his hands, he pointed at the unconscious and bloody Milo. "That's the Co-Ed serial killer. Notify my father, Squad Commander of the New Orleans Police Intelligence Unit, Matthew Raymond."

***

Matthew exited the bathroom. The guard escorted him to the interview room at the end of the dreary hall. "You have ten minutes. Anything before that, knock on the door and I'll let you out."

The nine by nine-foot room had a two-way mirror on the north wall. By mandate, Warden Stronghold and several guards watched the conversation between the rugged investigator and the ice-cold serial killer. The camera mounted high in the corner of the room reflected onto a bare bulb hung from the fourteen-foot ceiling.

Milo, shackled at his feet and chained at his wrists, sat on a metal stool behind a metal table. Both secured to the floor by bolts. A single wooden chair on the opposite side of the table near the door entrance awaited the interrogator.

When Matthew entered, Milo's hands pulled tight against the round metal restraint. He jerked the chains sneering at Matthew. "These necessary? I thought by now you and I understood each other."

Matthew didn't fall for the bait unaffected by Milo's threatening gesture or posturing and calmly sat. "Had, is the operative word. Why should I trust you without them?"

"You're not dead, are you?" *I could kill you with one thought.*

"The chains stay."

"Then, I don't talk." *He's an idiot.*

A standoff ensued, as neither the interrogator nor the killer wanted to retreat. Matthew maintained the upper hand confronting Milo. He sat stiffly. Milo followed suit. Neither man wanted to blink first as they glowered into each other's eyes. The silence roared until Matthew made the first move as he tussled his fingers through his scruffy, uncombed hair. "Let me remind you the position you're in. I put you here. I can keep you here."

The table vibrated as Milo scowled back, unnerved. He responded to Matthew's emphatic statements by sneering, more amused than intimidated. "That's supposed to make me talk?" Milo jerked toward the resolute Matthew. Only the chains that bound Milo prevented him from reaching his visitor.

Matthew didn't flinch. Not one recoil gave Milo the result he hoped.

"Oooo! I'm really scared now. Big brother needs protection by the chains that bind me. You're afraid to unchain me. Rightly so."

Matthew reached into his back pocket, grabbed a folded envelope, and pretended to hand it to the chained prisoner.

Milo gritted his teeth, grunted, and growled.

Matthew pretended not to notice as he dangled the envelope back and forth in front of Milo one inch out of his reach. "Open it."

"Not today." Milo desired to keep the upper hand.

"You scared of what you'll see?"

"Nothing in your show and tell game scares me." Milo extended his left middle finger and wiggled it.

A sneer crossed Matthew's lips; he didn't take the jeering bait as he placed the envelope onto the table out of Milo's reach. He flexed his fingers, folded his hands, and slowly placed them on the table. Matthew sat upright. "What I can show you should scare the piss out of you. It's from Nathan Hammer."

"You piqued my curiosity." Milo tried to slam his bound hands onto the table.

A lump formed in Matthew's throat as he secured the envelope between his thumb and index finger and lowered it one inch from Milo's shackled hands. "I'm not interested in what does or doesn't pique your interest." Matthew provoked Milo by fanning the envelope.

Unnerved, Milo deepened his cold stone stare, remained motionless fighting the urge to use his telepathic ability to suck air from Matthew's lungs.

The chair scraped across the floor as Matthew rose. "Maybe next time you'll show me respect and play my show and tell game, as you emphatically called it." He strode to the door.

Milo sneered as he chomped his teeth to taunt him.

Matthew used his knuckles and tapped on the door protruding his middle finger. "Up yours."

Tap. Tap. Tap.

Unamused and unaffected by Matthew's blatant gesture, Milo leered at Matthew. "Watch your back. That's if you can."

"Meaning?"

"You couldn't watch your sister's. Now, could you?"

Matthew turned toward Milo as his eyes trickled the calculated insolence of his stare. "You're not allowed to talk about my sister." He spewed spit with each angered word.

"You should have seen her face when I slit her throat." Milo gloated him further. "Oh, excuse me. You did." His tone in Joker fashion more befitting a character in *Batman* seemed to bounce in the room against the walls. "Such a thing of beauty to feel as her body jerked, going limp before her last breath. Big brother couldn't save little sister." Milo smirked and tilted his head to the side. "I remember her sweet perfume and the silkiness of her hair." A grin of wry amusement dashed across his lips.

Matthew bolted toward Milo, grabbed the villain's head, and slammed it against the table. Blood oozed from Milo's nose. He pressed Milo's bloody face relentlessly on the table as if he had the strength of a Western lowland gorilla from the jungles of Africa. "You son of a bitch!"

Milo strained to avert Matthew's glare. His yellow stained teeth bloody.

"Where did my sister go?"

Milo's blank stare enraged an already violent Matthew.

"How did you make her vanish?" Matthew slammed Milo's head against the table over and over.

"Lost control big brother? I think so."

"You son of a bitch."

"That's the only name you have left in your arsenal? Low on vocabulary for a Tulane graduate."

Matthew slammed Milo's head three more times against the already bloody surface. "How's this for vocabulary? You're demonic."

Three guards rushed into the room and restrained Matthew. To break free, Matthew thrashed in their arms to escape from the three-man hold.

Milo licked the blood from his lips and sat up. "Tastes like your sister's."

A.D.A.M.

By Dr. Melissa Caudle

A scientist. An alien lifeform. A secret base.
Consequences for mankind.

Meet Dr. Sandra Eve Bradford, an astrobiological researcher in charge of the A.D.A.M. Extraction Team who discovered a microbe which thrives off arsenic on the bottom of Mono Lake in California. General Anbar, Chief in Charge of the U.S. National Defense, orders his team to confiscate the samples and her research.

Dr. Bradford enlists her fellow researchers, Dr. Gregory Peterson, and her undergraduate assistant, Jessica Parker, to retrieve a new sample setting off a series of events and consequences.

In a government research facility, the microbe transformed into something alien. Once it becomes apparent to General Anbar the life form presents a national security risk, he orders his men to kidnap Dr. Bradford and holds her captive in an underground facility to continue her research.

The life form over a seven-day-stretch, morphs into a humanlike lifeform aging every moment toward death. His journey makes him question - What is life? What is love? What is hate? And, is there a God? This a story of possibilities and raises the questions - Are we alone in the universe? What else could be out there?

A.D.A.M.
Excerpt

CHAPTER TWO – TRUTH

Dr. Bradford drove her hunter-green Fiat on Interstate 10 from New Orleans towards Slidell.

Jessica twisted her long brunette hair into a bun and secured it with a pink scrunchy. "I'm hungry. I'm not waiting any longer to eat." She dug through a white fast-food paper sack that rested in her lap, retrieved a breakfast sandwich, and unwrapped it. The odor permeated through the car. Jessica curled her nose. "The eggs smell rotten."

"Get over it. Nothing has smelled good to you since you took in that mouthful of salty water at Mono Lake."

Jessica gagged, crumpled her breakfast sandwich back into the wrapper, and threw it back into the paper bag. "You can eat yours if you want, I'll wait for lunch."

Dr. Bradford darted her eyes over at Jessica. "Give me mine."

Jessica dug through the bag and retrieved another wrapped breakfast sandwich and handed it over.

Dr. Bradford unwrapped it, took one bite and spit it immediately back into the wrapper.

"Told you, but, no! You didn't believe me."

"Please be quiet, let me think."

Silence between them ensued as they crossed the bridge over Lake Pontchartrain.

Jessica leaned toward the dash to stretch her back. "Are you sure it's safe to go to the lab?"

"They can't kill me in public; so, I believe it's safe."

"It makes me nervous. Let's listen to Stephen Stone Diamond. He's talking about extraterrestrials today."

"That's what we need, an alien conspiracy."

"I thought that's what we're in now." Jessica pressed the radio's knob. "It's not working."

"That's the best news I've had all day."

Jessica grabbed her phone and opened her blog radio app.

". . . Not just life here on earth, but also extraterrestrial life." Stephen Stone Diamond's deep and golden voice enhanced the mysterious topic. "It is unknown whether there is any connection to the mysterious deaths of Dr. Gregory Peterson and the late husband of Dr. Sandra Bradford, Dr. Jeffrey Peck, who were both members of N.A.E.T. For those of you who don't know what N.A.E.T. is, I will gladly inform my listeners. It is a branch of NASA and stands for National Astrobiological Extraction Team. Coincidently, the research team led by Dr. Sandra Bradford. Phone lines are open."

Dr. Bradford slammed her fist onto the dashboard. "Damn! It's out on Blog radio."

"I'm Stephen Stone Diamond. I'll be right back to take your calls."

Dr. Bradford clenched her jaw. "Turn it off. I don't care to listen."

Jessica grabbed her earbuds. "That's exciting. E. T. phone home. I got to call in."

"Like hell, you will."

Jessica secured her earbuds, dialed the blog radio number, and waited. "I'm on hold."

"Jessica. Hang up. You can't bring attention to yourself or to me. Now hang up."

"So, why are you doing a press conference?"

"The public needs to know the truth about my research. If the public gets wind of what I've discovered, they'll demand the truth."

"Well, in my opinion that is exactly what Stephen Stone Diamond will do."

"Jessica!"

NASA Astrobiology Institute between the Louisiana and Mississippi border not only provided jobs but also fundamental research. From the spacecraft and booster shuttle rocket, the entry to the multi-functional compound reflected the nation's attitude about space exploration. Everyone wore either an official NASA or N.A.E.T. employee badge representing they worked either as an independent scientist on the National Astrobiological Extraction Team or a part of NASA. Visitors must sign in and wear visitor badges on their lapels too.

Dr. Bradford rushed toward the three story "Carl Sagan Astrobiology Lab" which housed the N.A.E.T. lab. Behind her, Jessica, Rebecca Newcombe and George, a cameraman, quickly followed.

Without provocation, Dr. Bradford collided into Dr. Phyllis Gordon, a forty-four American scientist, and Dr. Edward Stolz, a fifty-two German scientist. Rebecca motioned for George to roll the camera.

Dr. Gordon's eyes pierced toward Dr. Bradford's. "You've gathered quite a following since our discovery."

"I'd have to agree."

"Too bad our samples were confiscated."

"This isn't the time nor the place to discuss this." Dr. Bradford strode briskly toward the N.A.E.T. research building.

The entourage followed as Rebecca motioned for George to continue to roll the camera. "What was all that about?" She caught up to Dr. Bradford.

"Common professional jealousy. That's all there is to it."

Jessica frowned. "I think not. It's about…"

"…Loose lips sink ships." Dr. Bradford motioned using her fingers as if locking a key for Jessica to close her mouth.

Jessica confirmed when she moved her fingers across her lips as if zipping a zip-lock baggy.

Rebecca glowered at George. "Cut the camera. Damn it!"

The entourage barged into the N.A.E.T. building.

The morning sun reflected off the five test tubes of murky water which rested on one of the lab's counters. A microscopic particle floated inside one test tube and, for a nanosecond, glowed neon yellow.

Moments later, the entourage entered Dr. Bradford's lab. Jessica flipped on the lights as she wrinkled her nose and smelled the faint musky and sulfur smell. "I'll never forget this smell."

The well-equipped lab included beakers, flasks, a Liebig condenser, and graduated cylinders showed the lab's importance. Most prominent, a silver and white 60X-2599X-2 binocular turret professional biological microscope proved essential in isolating micro-organisms. In the corner, an assortment of lab experiments and three twenty-five-gallon tanks filled from the murky waters retrieved from several lakes labeled Lake Pontchartrain, Grand Isle and Honey Island Swamp filled the area. On the wall above the door, a twelve-inch round battery-operated clock and a sign - "A.D.A.M. Extraction Team" marked the entrance to the lab. Each white cabinet had stainless steel handles which enhanced the sterile environment.

Rebecca tapped George on his shoulder. "Be sure to capture everything in the lab. I want lots of B-Roll."

Dr. Bradford and Jessica dressed in their white lab coats, proceeded to the sink, and washed their hands.

Jessica prepped a microscope and a sterile slide. "I'll make sure everything is ready, Dr. B."

"Perfect Jessica. Just follow protocol. We have to get this correct." Dr. Bradford stepped to a locked cabinet, retrieved a bottle of arsenic and an eyedropper, and placed the items next to the microscope onto the lab counter. "Rebecca, it won't take much longer to set up."

"That's good to know. I don't have much longer."

Dr. Bradford retrieved the test tube which contained the particle. She extracted a sample as Jessica handed her the glass microscope slide. Dr. Bradford placed three drops of the murky liquid onto the sterile slide.

Jessica lifted her brow with excitement. "Isn't this amazing?"

Rebecca's frown deepened. "That's it, a test tube full of murky water and three drops on a slide."

Dr. Bradford defended her actions. "It's evidence that challenges the way we think and view life as we know it."

Jessica handed another test tube to Dr. Bradford. She filled the tube using the water sample and handed the vial back to her. "Jessica, mark this sample A."

"Yes, Ma'am." Jessica looked at Rebecca. "It's in there. I've seen it."

Again, Dr. Bradford's posture became defensive. "You can't see it without the aid of a microscope." She filled the second vial and handed it to Jessica.

"Sample B." Jessica nodded with pride.

Dr. Bradford confirmed with a nod. "Remember, at its current state, it is a microbe." She placed the prepared slide beneath the microscope as everyone observed and focused the microscope.

"I'll prepare the boiling water." Jessica predicted what Dr. Bradford would want, as it had become standard procedure in the lab. She briskly strode across the room, filled a teakettle, and set it onto the single electrical coil burner. She walked away, but quickly returned to turn the knob to the on position.

As Dr. Bradford viewed the microbe under the powerful microscope, it vibrated and morphed into Dr. Bradford's eye. She lifted from the microscope, blinked, and rubbed her eyes.

Jessica noticed. "Something wrong Dr. B?"

"Nothing, an eyelash was in my eye." Dr. Bradford peered through the microscope and adjusted the focus again.

Rebecca's patience grew thin. "How did you obtain these samples? I thought the government confiscated them."

Dr. Bradford exhaled. "A few more seconds… There you are, look." Dr. Bradford stepped to the side as Rebecca stepped to the microscope. She glanced at Dr. Bradford before she lowered to view the microbe.

Dr. Bradford rubbed her neck. "Jessica, hand me my notebook, please."

Jessica strode to Dr. Bradford's desk, retrieved a brown leather journal and strutted to Dr. Bradford and handed it over.

The tea kettle whistled. Jessica at once prepped a beaker of hot boiling water and brought it to Dr. Bradford.

Dr. Bradford handed her journal back to Jessica and then placed five drops of arsenic into the beaker.

Rebecca peered through the microscope. "Honestly, I see nothing."

Dr. Bradford exhaled in disappointment. "My best hypothesis is the microbe transitions as fast as I isolate it. I'll isolate it again for you."

The two women exchanged places. Dr. Bradford once again adjusted the microscope settings.

"You never answered my question. How did you obtain these samples?"

"Let's suffice it to say I was on the extraction team and managed to keep a sample for further study."

"You stole it?"

Jessica came to Dr. Bradford's defense. "We didn't steal it. We went…"

Dr. Bradford lifted from the microscope long enough to glare toward Jessica and twisted her fingers as if locking a door.

Jessica put her hand over her mouth as she lifted her brows.

Rebecca annoyed at the silent gesture, huffed. "You agreed you would tell me everything." She gazed harshly at Dr. Bradford.

"I promised you an exclusive interview for a no question asked policy. When the time is right, we'll reveal our evidence and our source as to how we obtained another sample."

"I'll get another Emmy."

"I'll surely get my doctorate."

Dr. Bradford gave Jessica another cold glance.

"Well, I will. Won't I?"

The lab became uncomfortably silent as Dr. Bradford continued to isolate the microbe.

Rebecca tapped her foot. "Anytime would be ideal. I have a deadline for tonight's news."

"Patience, I almost have the microbe isolated."

"Yes, Dr. B always tells me that patience is a virtue."

"We go live at six. After the murder of your husband and Dr. Peterson, the world is waiting with bated-breath to hear from the now infamous Dr. Sandra Bradford."

A reflective sadness came over Dr. Bradford; but she regained her professional composure. "You sound skeptical, Rebecca."

"Wouldn't you be? You claim to have evidence of an alien life form."

"Don't forget about me. I've seen it. Be sure to add that to your story. You know how to spell my name, right?"

Rebecca rolled her eyes. "This sounds ripe for a sci-fi murder mystery for *The Twilight Zone* and not the headline news story I wanted to break."

"I've isolated it, be quick this time." Dr. Bradford backed away from the microscope.

Rebecca quickly assumed her position and peered it as she squinted her left eye. "Like before, nothing."

"Maybe you don't know what you're looking for."

"Insults I don't need and won't tolerate."

"I didn't mean it to demean you. I apologize if I came across that way."

"Let's talk about the murders of your associates."

"I can't speak to the murders. I can only comment about the great men who were taken from this world. I was shocked to learn my husband was involved in a head on collision and it was an accident. The investigators ruled there was no foul play involved. Frankly, I'm horrified Dr. Peterson was gunned down while on a boating vacation on the same lake where we made our discovery."

Jessica bit her lower lip and paced. *I don't like the way this is going.*

"Doesn't this frighten you?" Rebecca swallowed and leered toward Dr. Bradford with unashamed confidence.

"Of course, I am as anyone in my situation would be. You never know who your enemy is even if they stood in front of you as a friend. It's a cut-throat industry when claiming a scientific discovery."

"Especially one that's as big as this." Jessica beamed with delight.

A quiet knock on the lab's door caught everyone's attention.

Dr. Bradford looked at the samples and over toward the door as Jessica jumped and dropped Dr. Bradford's journal as a wallet size photograph of an infant tumbled from it and onto the floor.

FBI Agent Morrison, a handsome African American male, late forties, and Agent Turner, an African American female in her late thirties, brashly entered.

Jessica's eyes widened as her trembling hands went straight toward the ceiling. "Whoa, gun!"

276

Agent Morrison flashed his shield. "Miss, you can put your hands down. We're here to speak to Dr. Bradford. I'm FBI Special Agent Morrison and this is my partner Special Agent Turner."

Jessica slowly placed her hands to her thighs as she glanced at the journal and the photograph. She retrieved the journal and placed the photograph back inside the journal.

Dr. Bradford stepped forward. "I'm Dr. Bradford. How may I be of assistance?"

Agent Turner stepped forward. "Not in the presence of others. What we have to say is confidential. Everyone needs to leave, but Dr. Bradford."

Agent Morrison put his hand in front of his face and grabbed George's camera with the other. "Stop filming. You're in that directive, too."

George jerked his camera out of Agent's Morrison's hands and stepped backward to put distance between them.

Jessica stomped her foot. "You're telling me you barge into our lab and ask us to leave."

"We're not asking." His stare, as cold as ice, seemed menacing.

"But, I'm her graduate assistant."

"I have Freedom of the Press on my side." Rebecca stood steadfast.

Dr. Bradford raised her hand chest high. "Wait, anything I have to say, they can hear."

Agent Turner stepped closer toward Dr. Bradford. "In that case, you leave us no choice but to take you to FBI headquarters. Please, Dr. Bradford, retrieve your belongings and come with us. It will be easier for all involved."

A silent standoff prevailed.

"I'll consent, but I want it documented that I am cooperating." Dr. Bradford gathered her belongings and headed for the door.

Rebecca motioned for the George to follow. He pursued the agents and Dr. Bradford as they exited from the lab.

"Wait! Dr. Bradford, your journal." Jessica handed over the journal.

Dr. Bradford hesitated. "You keep it. Jessica, lock down the lab. Use protocol FRIC."

"FRIC?" Agent Turner's brow creased. "And, that is code for what?"

"Factual Research Investigative Control."

Jessica smirked in agreement. "Lock up the science experiment to avoid contamination. FRIC that!"

Agent Morrison looked at Dr. Bradford. "Come with us, please."

The two agents escorted Dr. Bradford from the lab as Rebecca, George, and Jessica chased after them. The door shut behind them.

In a few seconds, Jessica re-entered the lab and secured the samples. The murky water in one of the five tubes glowed neon yellow as the water vibrated around it. She retrieved her cell phone and dialed.

⟡ NEVER STOP ⟡
RUNNING

A modern visionary and one of the newest authors to come from America, Dr. Melissa Caudle combines a suspenseful thriller and the search for truth in regard to past lives and reincarnation in this mind-bending novel in the tradition of "This Body: A Novel of Reincarnation" by Laurel Doud, "Journey of Souls," by Michael Newton, and Past Lives, "Many Masters" by Brian L. Weiss. The result is a masterful original fiction novel as profound as it is awe-inspiring. "Never Stop Running" is a page-turning thriller that begs to be read in a single sitting as this mental time travel spanning centuries and numerous past lives through regression hypnotherapy unfolds .Based on a true story of one woman's struggle to recover her memories after a devastating accident left her with retrograde amnesia. This is an astonishing novel from an unforgettable author and is a must read. What happens when the unthinkable occurs? What would you do if your loved one all of sudden woke up and didn't know who you were or for that matter who your family was either? For David and Jackie Hennessey they had the perfect white picket fence life, marriage, family and careers until the unthinkable happened - an accident that left Jackie with no memory. The couple struggled to find the balance between what they once shared and their new life. After David discovered Dr. Grayson, a well-known regression hypnotherapist, he convinced Jackie to seek his services in order to retrieve her subconscious memories. During her sessions, her memories surfaced only to uncover her past lives which crisscross centuries in her mental time travel. Faced with a moral dilemma of believing the dreams were once a reality and twisting her religious convictions on reincarnation, Jackie questioned her sanity and feared for her life after seeing her deaths in her previous lives. She believed she could never stop running as her marriage degrades and falls apart. Based on real events of regression hypnotic sessions of one brave woman, this is a tale of destiny and soul mates not to be missed. The most intriguing book you'll read all year. You don't have to believe in reincarnation to enjoy this tale, but it will get you to thinking about the possibility.

1. OPEN THE DOOR

D r. Grayson sat in a Victorian chair; his eyes focused on Jackie who lay in a deep hypnotic state on a worn royal blue velvet chaise. The scar, which ridged from her scalp to below her cheek, covered by make-up, embarrassed Jackie as she leaned her face against the pillow to hide it.

"From this point on, when I say sleep and snap my fingers, you will remember this state and go to it. Now breathe in and out." Dr. Grayson drew a deep breath.

Jackie responded to his suggestion with a huge-heaved sigh of relief.

"Jackie, I'm going to ask you a series of questions. You will not awaken, but stay in this peaceful state. You will remain aware of your surroundings. Noises won't bother you. You will only respond to my voice. Do you understand?"

"Yes."

"Jackie, search through your past and find a door and enter." Dr. Grayson observed Jackie's body language and eye movement beneath her eyelids, giving her time to select a door. "Do you see the door?"

"I don't know which one to enter."

"The choice is yours. Think of a time in your past and open the door."

Her eyelids fluttered, her facial muscles flattened, and she looked more mannequin than human. Her right index finger lifted. "That one."

Dr. Grayson shook his head in approval. "That's great Jackie, open the door and step through. Where are you?"

"I'm in a scary place. I feel cold. It's really cold… dark… It's misty."

"Nothing can harm you, Jackie, you're safe. What are you doing in this place?"

"I'm in a dark alley."

"Are you alone?"

She barely shook her head. "Someone else is here… He's calling a woman's name."

In his hypnotherapist mind, Dr. Grayson analyzed her statement. "What name?"

"Gertrude."

"What is Gertrude doing?"

∞

Gertrude, age twenty-three, dressed in an 1880s overcoat with a silver-fox fur collar and an 1880s hat ran down a dark alley lit only by the orange glow of the oil street lamps and the blood moon. Fog graced the area as a light mist sprinkled. She tried to catch her breath. Smoke from the heat of her breath clashed with the cold, misty night air.

A large man who wore a black Gothic cape chased her. "Gertrude! Stop! You'll never get away with this."

Gertrude ran to escape him. She tripped and fell, scrapping both knees; the ground ripped her silk stockings. With the man in close pursuit, she pushed herself up and ran. She lengthened her stride as she looked over her shoulder.

Within an arm's-length of her, the man gained ground; he swiftly closed in. He lifted a butcher knife, lunged at her, and pierced her through her back.

Her body lurched forward as she fell in slow motion and landed in a mud puddle face down. The clammy chill of death gripped her.

He kneeled, rolled her over and jerked her brass crystal domed watch pendant from around her neck. She heaved as she took her last breath.

∞

Jackie raised her hips, wiggled her shoulders, and exhaled.

"Relax Jackie, he can't harm you, you're safe."

Jackie jolted. "He killed Gertrude, I saw him kill her." Jackie heavily breathed as her heart pounded against her ribcage.

"Jackie, what year did Gertrude die?"

"October eleventh, eighteen seventy-nine."

He pondered the date. "All right, Jackie, let's move somewhere else. I want you to think of a calm, peaceful place, a beautiful place."

Jackie bolted up with her eyes wide opened. She put her hand on her forehead and heaved. "I don't want to do this."

"Please know you made extreme progress."

"I'm finished for today; I want to go home."

"Jackie, remember your subconscious has a way to deal with your fears if you allow it."

Jackie's voice cracked as emotions flowed. "It's just overwhelming." Jackie cleared her throat and held back her tears.

"I understand. Sometimes when we witness past events, we can become confused and scared. This is a normal process."

"I don't understand what just happened." A tear rolled down her mascara-smeared-scared face. "Who did I see die?"

2. WHITE PICKET FENCE

One Year Earlier

The digital alarm clock's repetitive buzz blared in the otherwise silent master bedroom.

David groaned as he rolled over and swatted, bleary-eyed, at the obnoxious intrusion. The silver-framed photograph of him and Jackie kissing on their honeymoon in front of the Golden Gate Bridge wobbled dangerously close to the nightstand's edge. He slapped the alarm clock again and accidentally collided his fingertips against the picture frame, sending it crashing onto the floor. When it smashed against the hardwood floor, the glass across the frame cracked down the middle, which divided the couple and flipped over onto a pair of fuzzy brown moose slippers.

Exasperated, David bashed the alarm clock, and at last silenced the annoying abrupt alert. "Just five more minutes." He buried his head into his pillow, groaned, and pounded his fist onto the mattress. "Five forty-five is too early!"

Jackie pulled the taupe thick goose down comforter over her face with her right hand and nestled deeper into the rack-monster pillow top bed complete with sage green thick bamboo luxurious sheets. "Did you hit the snooze button?" Her words, muffled by the comforter, barely caught David's attention.

"Do you really need to ask?"

"Considering you forgot last week, I thought I should. I can't be late for work again."

"Go back to sleep while you can, unless you want a morning quickie."

"Five more minutes of sleep sounds good. I was up with the baby most of the night, he's cutting his back teeth. He was miserable."

He snuggled against her warm slim body as he gently pulled her waist closer to him; his eyes remained opened. *She must be exhausted.* "I'll take the shift tonight if he's still in pain. Now close your eyes and get five more minutes of shut-eye while you can."

"They're already closed, silly. Do you mind giving me a little space?" She scooched away from him and rolled over onto her stomach.

David rotated onto his other side, accommodating her fatigued request. He found it challenging not to stare wide-eyed at the digital alarm clock which now blinked "5:47 a.m." *What good is a snooze button if I can't snooze?* He gazed at the intermittent red numbers as the intrusive seven changed into an invasive eight. His green eyes seemed to absorb the color. Even after he closed them, the obtrusive numbers seemed as if possessed by a neon emergency flashing light as they brightened through his eyelids, and in his mind, the time clock's ticking annoyingly amplified. He tossed one way, then flipped to another. *Seriously! I just want five more minutes of sleep.*

Click. Click. Click.

"Can that clock get any more annoying?" As he sat up, he yawned, and then he wiped the crusted-sleep from his eye. After he stretched, he gently stroked Jackie's long thick brown wavy hair, gave her a gentle kiss on the back of her neck, and then eased out of bed almost stepping onto the favored honeymoon photograph conveniently cradled between one moose horn and the other moose slipper.

As he retrieved the silver-framed photograph, the cracked glass caught the morning sun. *She's going to kill me.* He rubbed his finger along the fracture that divided he and Jackie, and then shuddered as if a cool chill filled the air. *I'll buy her a new frame for our anniversary, she'll love that.* Gently, he returned the photograph to its rightful place onto the middle of the nightstand.

After David reset the snooze button for ten more minutes, he grabbed his brown terry cotton mid-calf robe from the valet to the right of the nightstand. As he wrapped his robe around his torso, he gazed at Jackie. A broad, white-toothed smile beamed as he drew a deep breath. His feet slipped into his moose house shoes.

He tiptoed out of the room, eased toward the bedroom to the right at the end of the hall and checked on his oldest son, Tyler, age four, who snuggly slept beneath his *Paw Patrol* fleece blanket. A grin crossed David's sleepy face. After he closed Tyler's door, he tiptoed to Sebastian's nursery and peeked inside. Sebastian's twelve-month-old foot protruded between the crib's slots as he slept cuddled on his stomach, clutching his blue fleece *Thomas the Train* blanket. *They are so cute when they sleep.* He gently closed the door.

The cold wooden floor creaked below David's feet as he headed down the stairs to the kitchen.

284

ABOUT THE AUTHOR

"When you meet the love of your life and marry them, you are blessed." **Dr. Melissa Caudle**

Dr. Melissa Caudle, AKA Dr. Mel, is an award-winning American author and screenwriter. She is best known for her novels *The Keystroke Killer: Transcendence, Never Stop Running, The Creek Dweller,* and *A.D.A.M.* She is also the founder and CEO of Absolute Author Publishing House, where she has helped hundreds of authors reach their publishing dreams. As an artist, Dr. Mel illustrated many adult and children's coloring books. She describes her style as a mixture of Picasso and Salvador Dali. She uses professional markers, acrylic paints, and watercolors. Take a look for yourself below. Dr. Mel also sells original art pieces on her website.

She lives in New Orleans, LA, with her husband and two cats. She is the mother of three daughters and has six grandsons and one granddaughter. When she is not writing or drawing, she loves to go to the

New Orleans Saints games, ballroom dance, swimming, camping, and spending time with her family. She is also a self-professed cruise addict, goes as often as she can and authored the bestselling book, *Cruising Tips & Hacks from a Professional Cruise Addict,* which debut as a bestseller and has maintained that title since publication. In fact, she finished this novel on the last voyage of the Carnival's *Ecstasy.* Her goal is to keep living life to the fullest and cherish every moment.

For more information, check out Dr. Caudle's website at www.drmelcaudle.com and subscribe to her blog at www.drmelcaudle.blogspot.com.

Also, follow her on her social media sites.

https://twitter.com/#! /DrMelcaudle
https://www.facebook.com/DrMelCaudle
https://www.facebook.com/The Keystroke Killer Fan Site
linkedin.com/in/dr-mel-caudle-650a4036

Absolute Author Publishing House

www.absoluteauthor.com

Cruising Tips & Hacks from a Professional Cruise Addict: A Complete Planning Guide with Cruise Planning Journal, Packing Checklist, Cruise Hacks, and Lots More for Your Perfect Cruise Vacation

If you love cruising and want to go on a cruise for a vacation of a lifetime, then this book is for you!

Don't get trapped into making mistakes and plan your trip like the professional addicts!

Learn from a self-proclaimed cruise addict the tips and hacks of cruising.

Whether you're a first-time cruiser or a veteran cruiser, this book is for cruise lovers.

In this book you will learn:

- **How to book a cruise and find the best deals**
- **Ways to pay for a cruise**
- **Cruise documentation you will Need**
- **Cabin categories**
- **What is not allowed in your stateroom**
- **Items to bring on a cruise**
- **Cruise hacks**
- **Must have cruise items for cruising during COVID**
- **Decorating your stateroom and door**
- **Packing hacks**
- **Traveling with children**
- **Excursions**
- **Beverage packages**
- **Specialty dining**
- **What to do if you get sick on a cruise**
- **Cruise planning guide for more than fifty cruises**
- **Packing checklists for more than fifty cruises**

Plan your cruise vacation and avoid the hassles of not knowing what to do, what to wear, and more.

ADULT COLORING BOOKS

BY DR. MELISSA CAUDLE

One of my hobbies, other than writing, is drawing abstract faces in a Picasso kind of way. I put together my favorites in a series of Adult Coloring Books. I also have many more that include animals, mazes, and mandalas. You can buy them on Amazon, Barnes and Noble, my website: www.drmelcaudle.com, and other online retailers. I also have my art for sale on my website and at The Family Tree Antiques & Treasures in Bay St. Louis, MS.

Children's Books by Dr. Melissa Caudle

And, many, many more!

Dear Readers:

First, I want to thank you for reading this book. It was a labor of love. As an author, I take pride in every book I write and I always value your feedback. If you would be so kind, please leave me an honest review on Amazon and Goodreads. I would greatly appreciate it.

Best regards,

Dr. Mel

www.ingramcontent.com/pod-product-compliance
Lightning Source LLC
Chambersburg PA
CBHW062127170626
46813CB00002B/596